LET ME OUT

AN ONI PRESS PUBLICATION

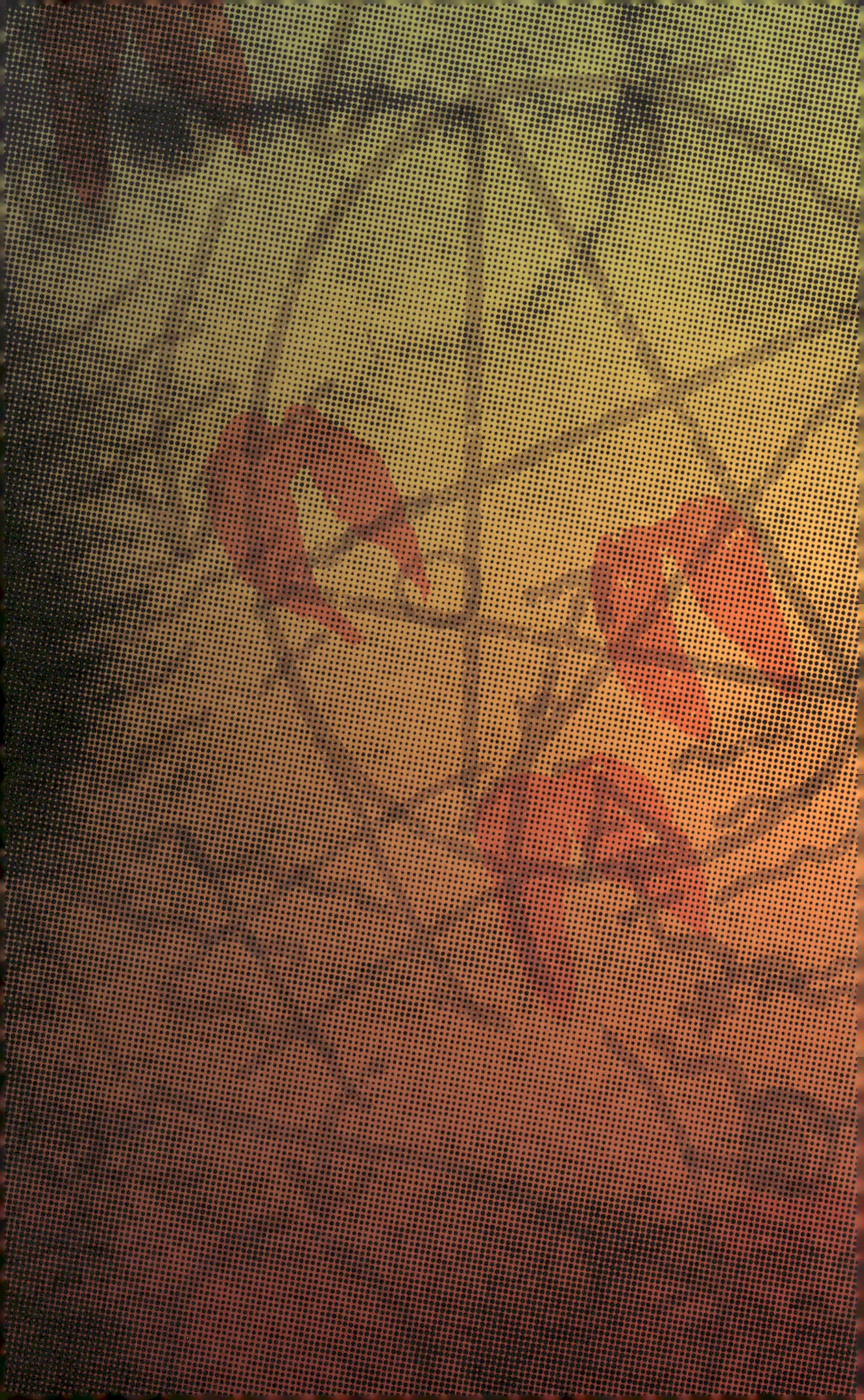

LET ME OUT

EMMETT NAHIL
GEORGE WILLIAMS

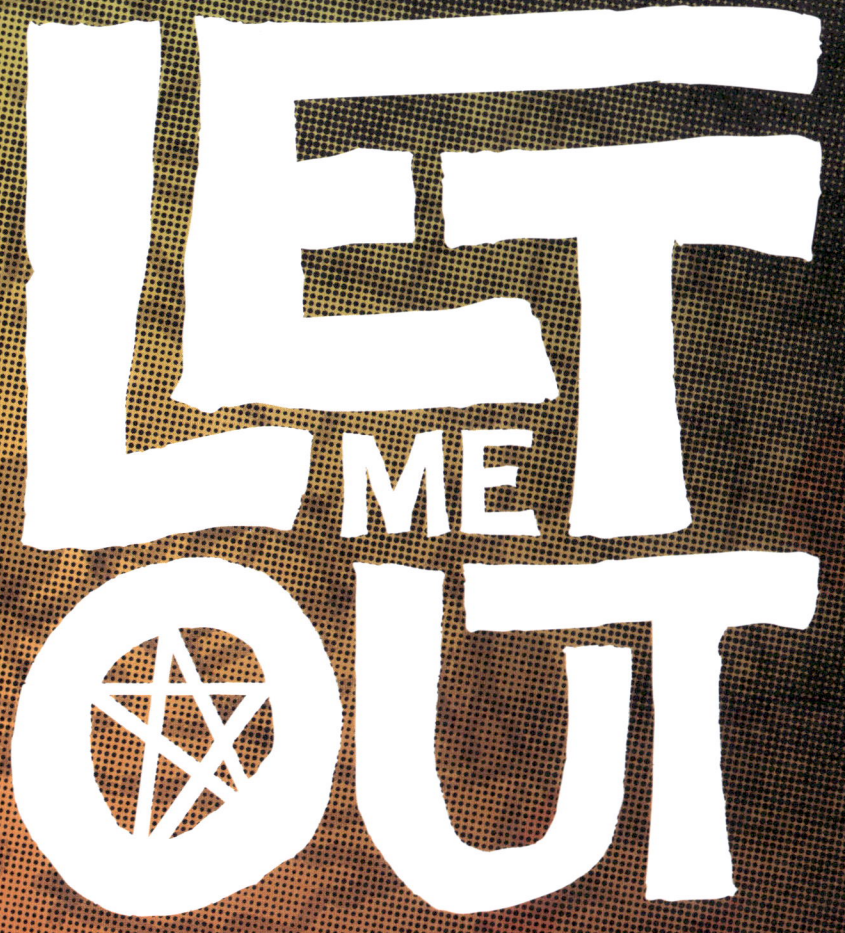

EDITED BY
DESIREE RODRIGUEZ & JUNG HU LEE
DESIGNED BY CAREY SOUCY

PUBLISHED BY ONI-LION FORGE PUBLISHING GROUP, LLC.
1319 SE Martin Luther King Jr. Blvd. Suite 240 Portland, OR 97214

Hunter Gorinson, president & publisher • Sierra Hahn, editor in chief • Troy Look, vp of publishing services • Angie Knowles, director of design & production • Katie Sainz, director of marketing • Chris Cerasi, managing editor • Bess Pallares, senior editor • Grace Scheipeter, senior editor • Gabriel Granillo, editor • Zack Soto, editor • Michael Torma, senior sales manager • Desiree Rodriguez, digital marketing manager • Sarah Rockwell, senior graphic designer • Carey Soucy, senior graphic designer • Winston Gambro, graphic designer • Matt Harding, digital prepress technician • Sara Harding, executive assistant • Jung Hu Lee, logistics coordinator & editorial assistant • Kuian Kellum, warehouse assistant

Joe Nozemack, publisher emeritus

ONIPRESS.COM • FACEBOOK.COM/ONIPRESS
TWITTER.COM/ONIPRESS • INSTAGRAM.COM/ONIPRESS

FIRST EDITION **OCTOBER 2023** • ISBN **978-1-63715-236-2** • EISBN **978-1-63715-252-2**
PRINTED IN **CHINA** • LIBRARY OF CONGRESS CONTROL NUMBER **2023932172**
1 2 3 4 5 6 7 8 9 10

LET ME OUT VOL. 1, October 2023. Published by Oni-Lion Forge Publishing Group, LLC., 1319 SE Martin Luther King Jr. Blvd., Suite 240, Portland, OR 97214. Let Me Out Vol. 1 is ™ & © 2023 Emmett Nahil & George Williams. All rights reserved. Oni Press logo and icon are ™ & © 2023 Oni-Lion Forge Publishing Group, LLC. All rights reserved. Oni Press logo and icon artwork created by Keith A. Wood. The events, institutions, and characters presented in this book are fictional. Any resemblance to actual persons, living or dead, is purely coincidental. No portion of this publication may be reproduced, by any means, without the express written permission of the copyright holders.

CONTENT WARNING

Let Me Out is an adult queer horror graphic novel, and some elements of the story might be triggering or distressing. *Let Me Out* contains discrimination against queer characters, transphobia including the use of deadnames, misgendering, gory violence, and strong language throughout. For readers, please take care when reading.

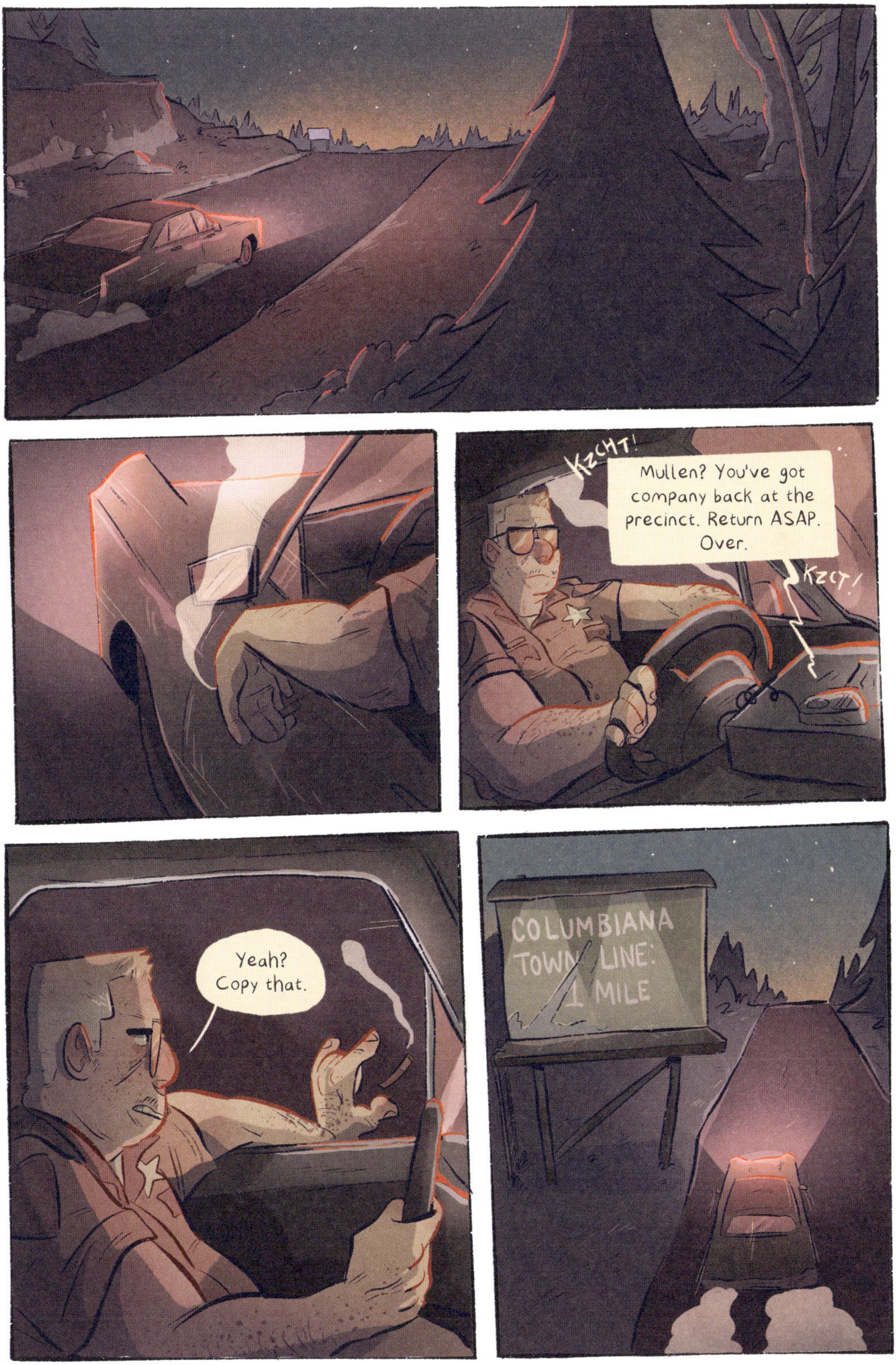
KZCHT!
Mullen? You've got company back at the precinct. Return ASAP. Over.
KZCT!
Yeah? Copy that.
COLUMBIANA TOWN LINE: 1 MILE

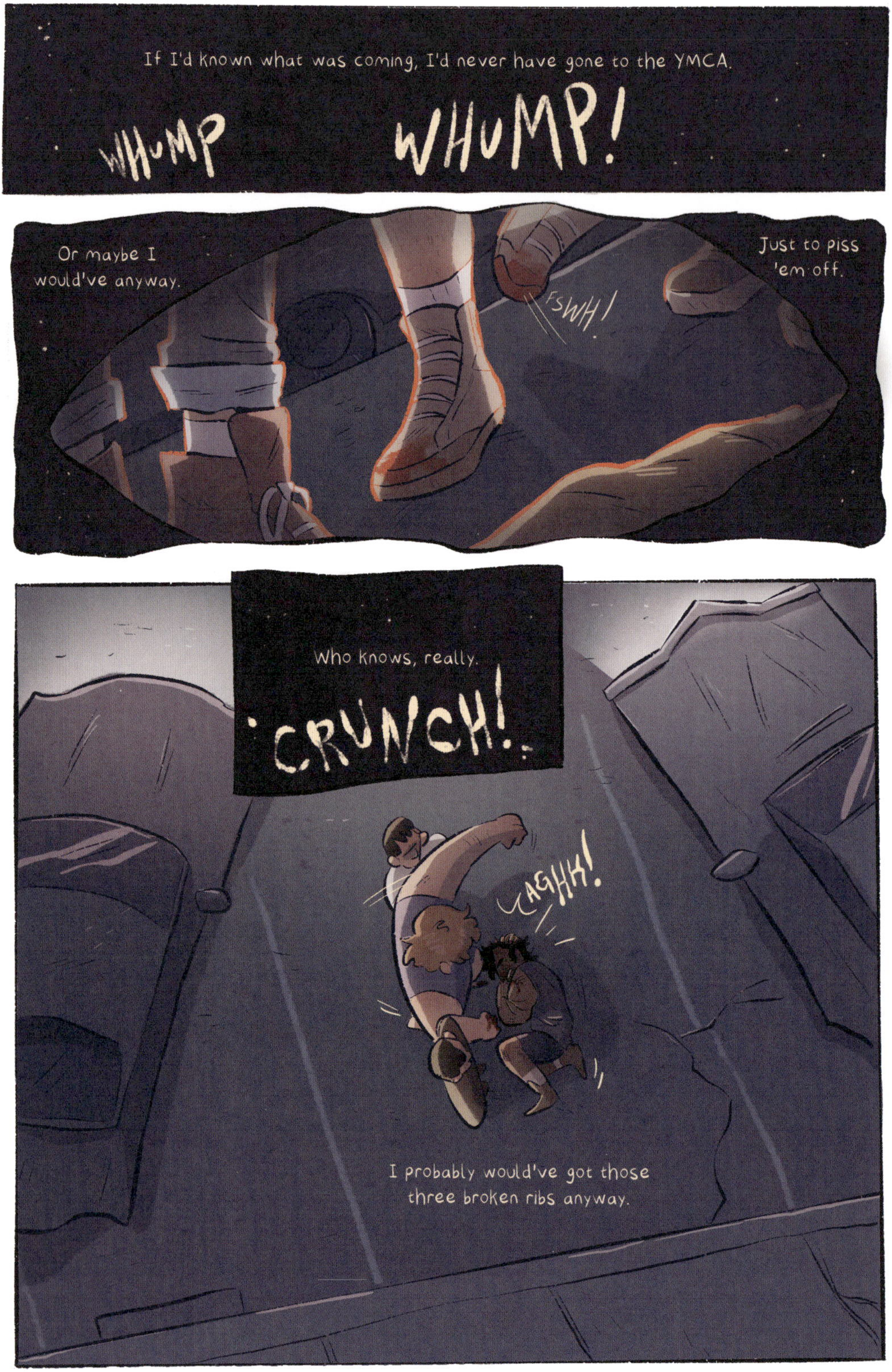

If I'd known what was coming, I'd never have gone to the YMCA.
WHUMP
WHUMP!
Or maybe I would've anyway.
FSWH!
Just to piss 'em off.
Who knows, really.
CRUNCH!
AGHH!
I probably would've got those three broken ribs anyway.

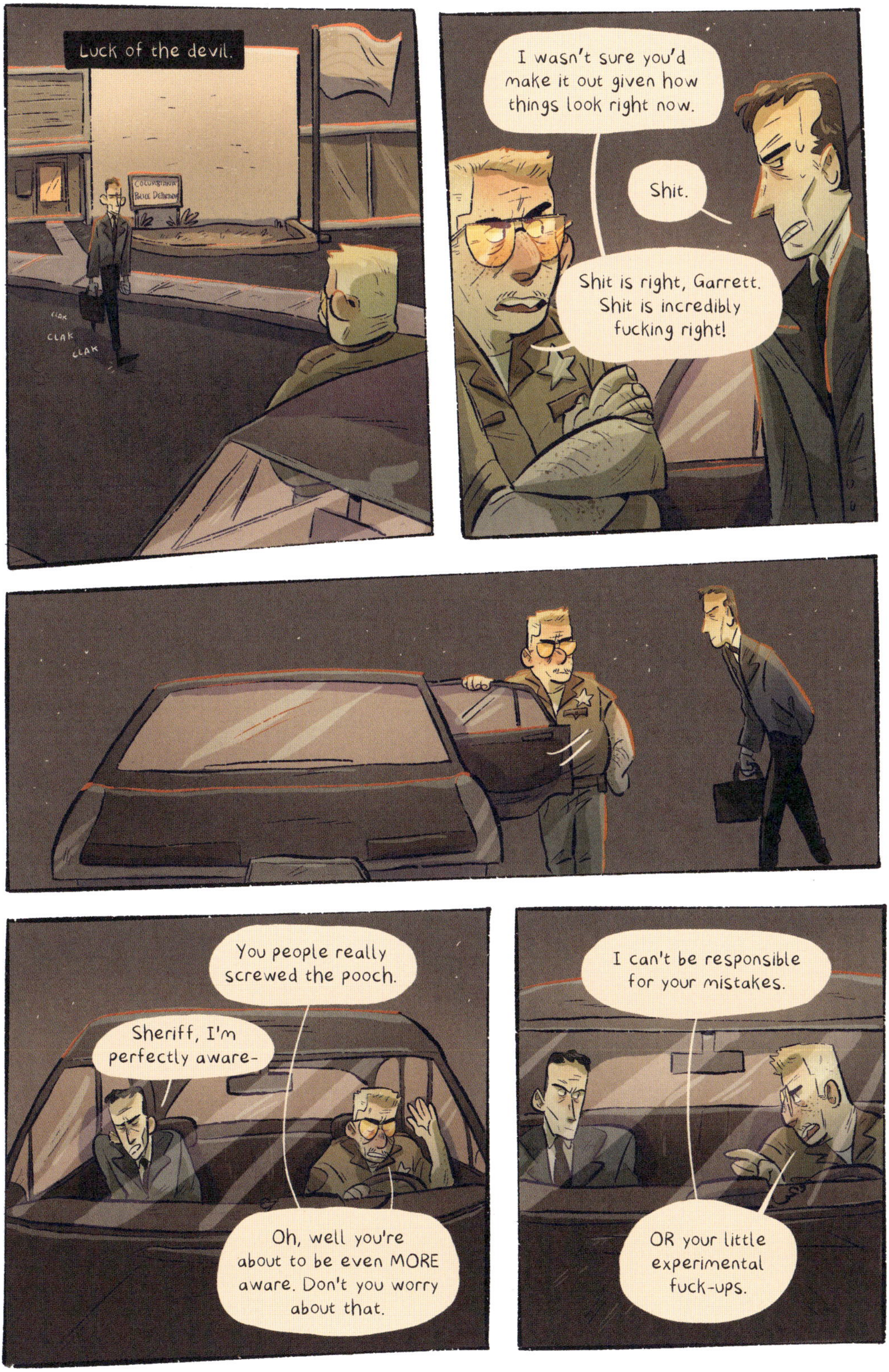
Luck of the devil.
CLAK
CLAK
CLAK
I wasn't sure you'd make it out given how things look right now.
Shit.
Shit is right, Garrett. Shit is incredibly fucking right!
You people really screwed the pooch.
Sheriff, I'm perfectly aware-
Oh, well you're about to be even MORE aware. Don't you worry about that.
I can't be responsible for your mistakes.
OR your little experimental fuck-ups.

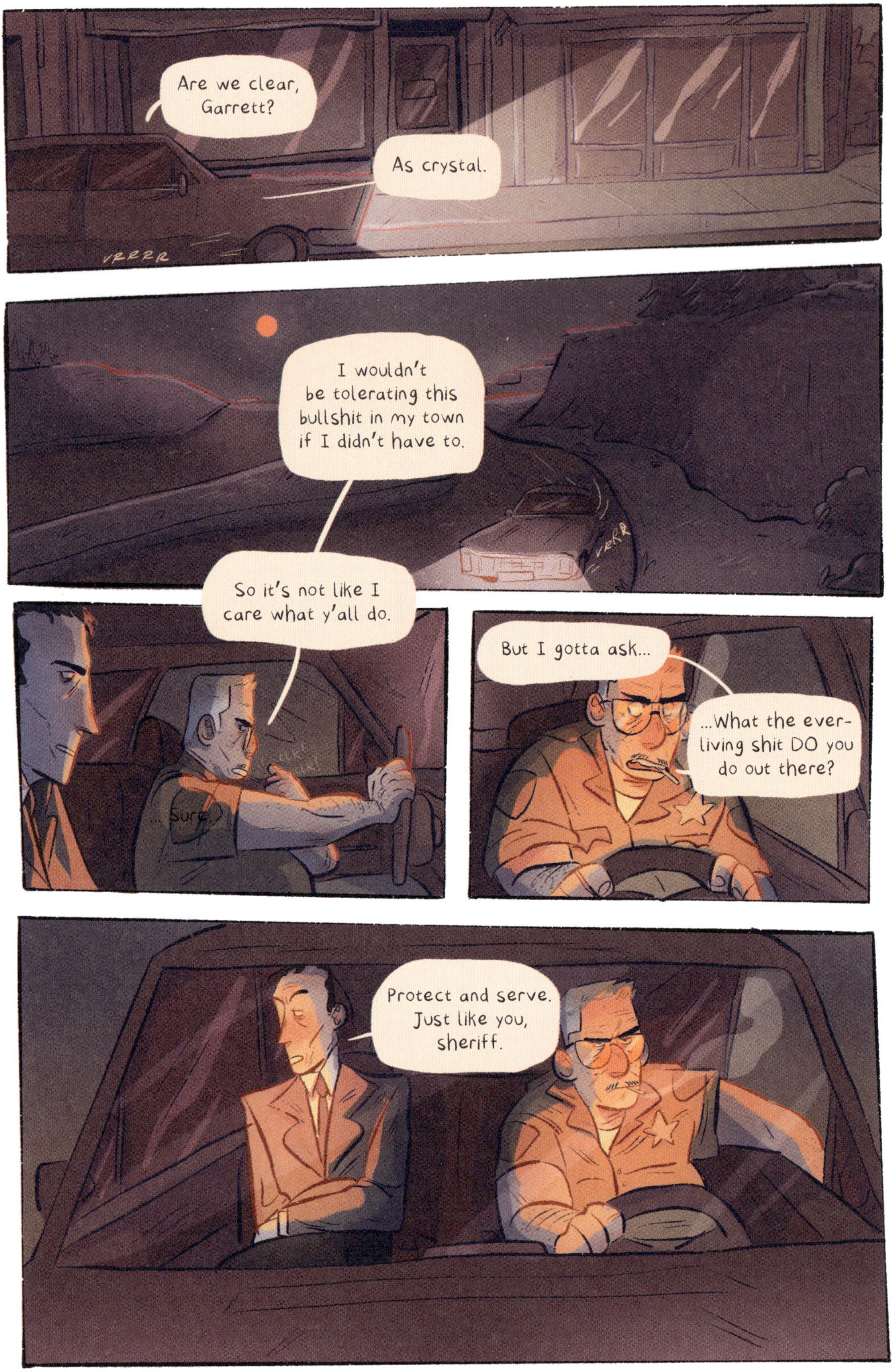

Are we clear, Garrett?
As crystal.
VRRRR
I wouldn't be tolerating this bullshit in my town if I didn't have to.
VRRR
So it's not like I care what y'all do.
...Sure.
But I gotta ask...
...What the ever-living shit DO you do out there?
Protect and serve. Just like you, sheriff.

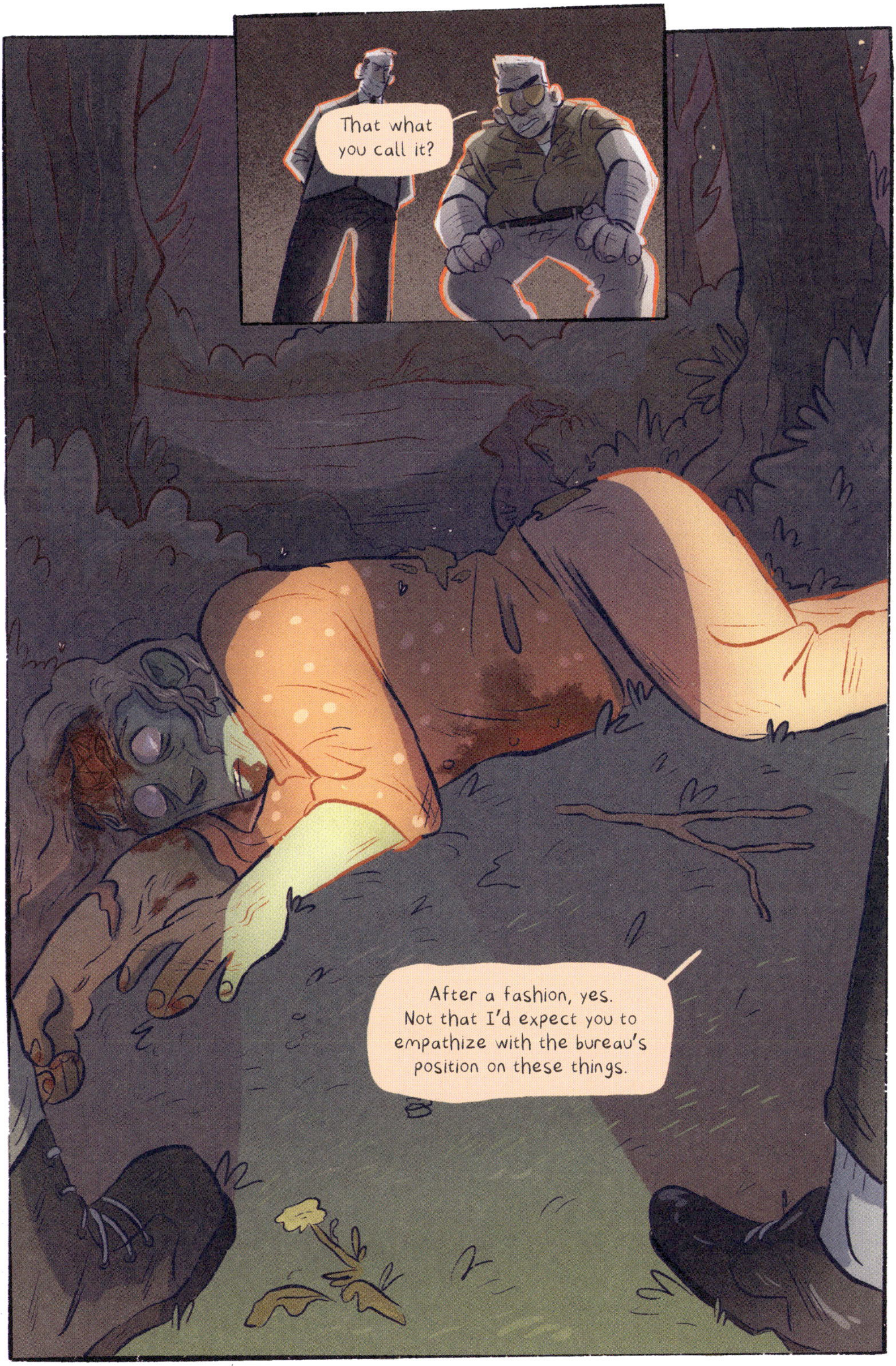
That what you call it?
After a fashion, yes. Not that I'd expect you to empathize with the bureau's position on these things.

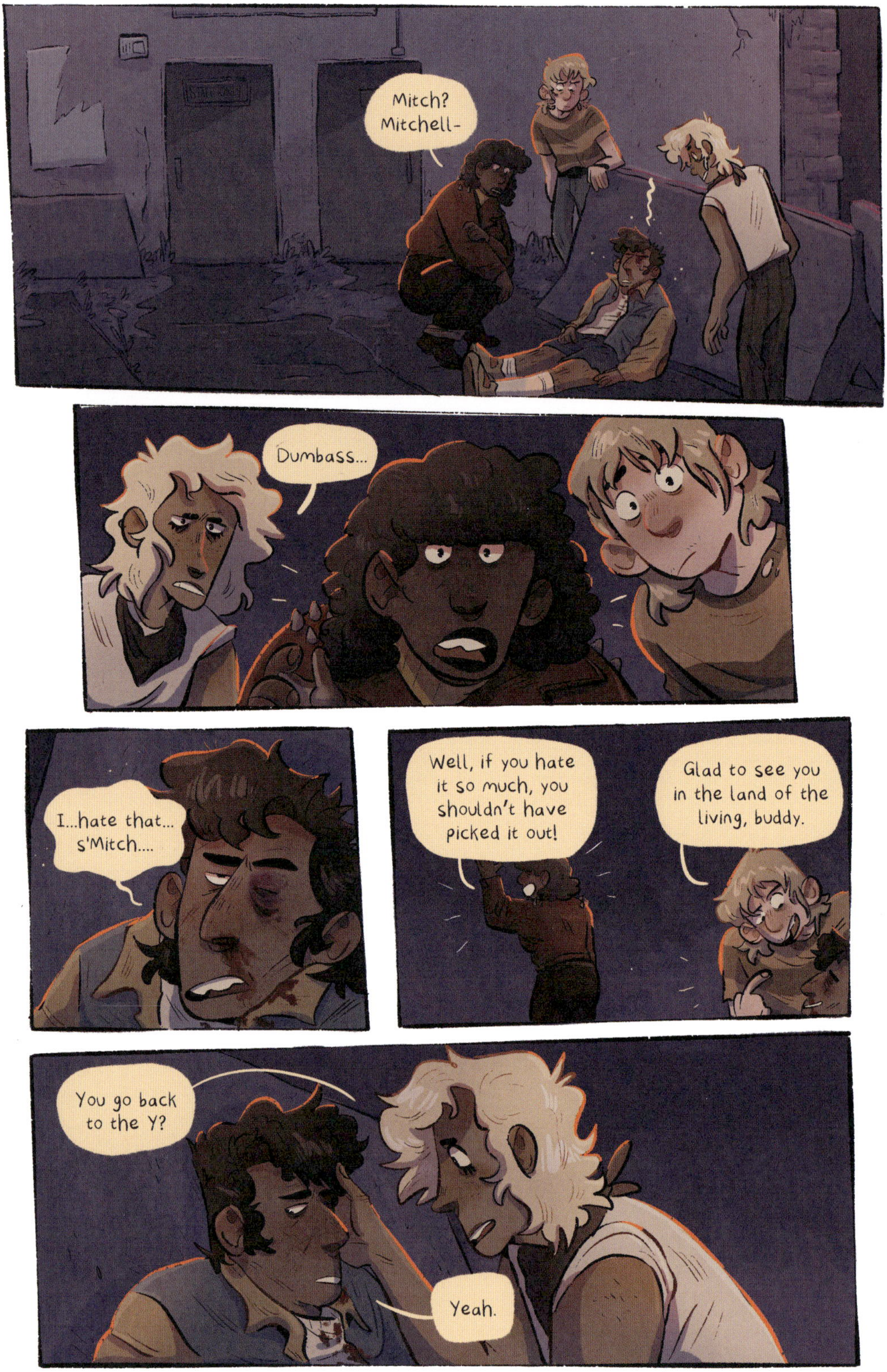
Mitch? Mitchell-
Dumbass...
I...hate that... s'Mitch....
Well, if you hate it so much, you shouldn't have picked it out!
Glad to see you in the land of the living, buddy.
You go back to the Y?
Yeah.

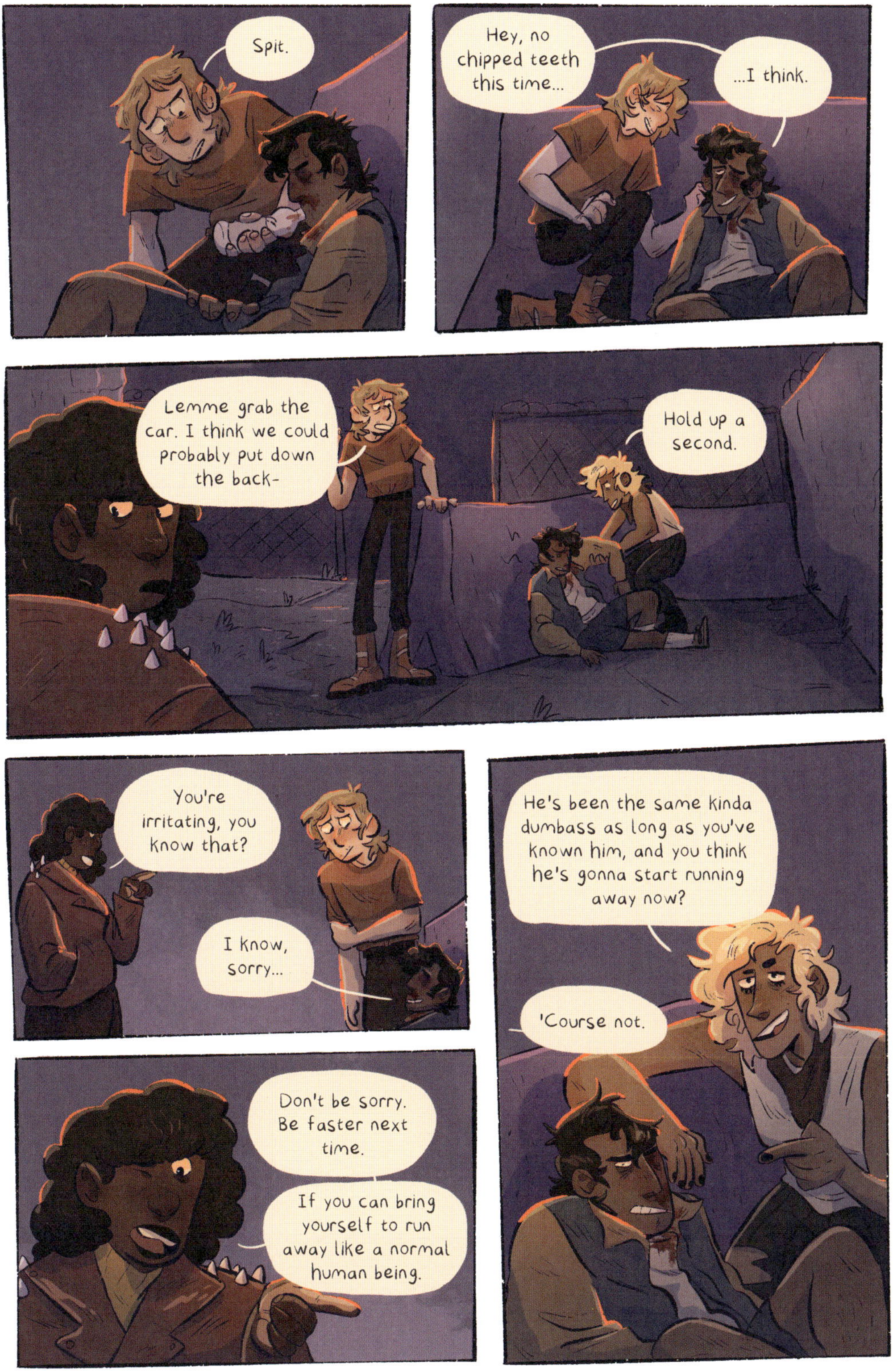
Spit.
Hey, no chipped teeth this time...
...I think.
Lemme grab the car. I think we could probably put down the back-
Hold up a second.
You're irritating, you know that?
I know, sorry...
He's been the same kinda dumbass as long as you've known him, and you think he's gonna start running away now?
'Course not.
Don't be sorry. Be faster next time.
If you can bring yourself to run away like a normal human being.

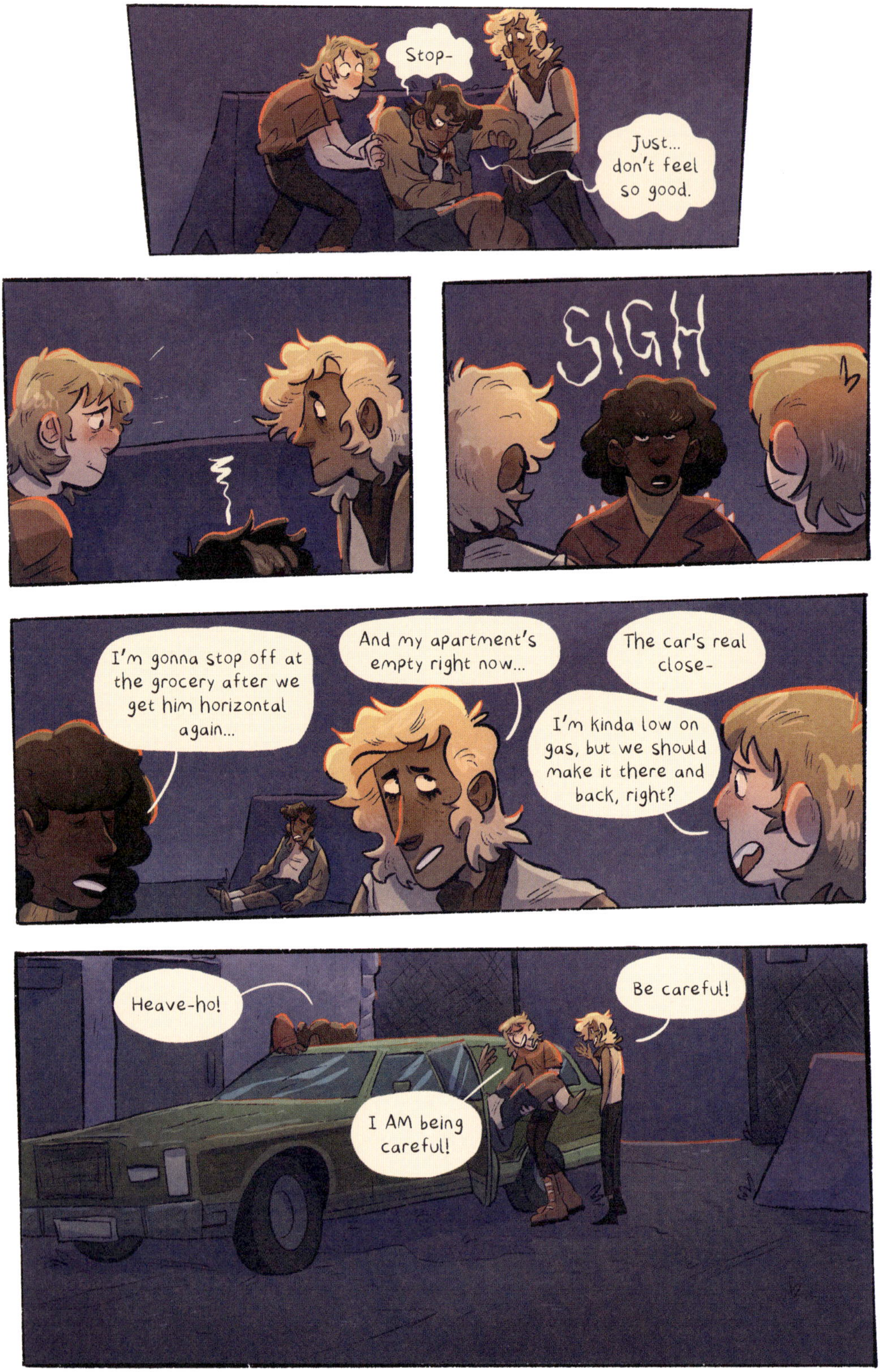
Stop-
Just... don't feel so good.
SIGH
I'm gonna stop off at the grocery after we get him horizontal again...
And my apartment's empty right now...
The car's real close-
I'm kinda low on gas, but we should make it there and back, right?
Heave-ho!
Be careful!
I AM being careful!

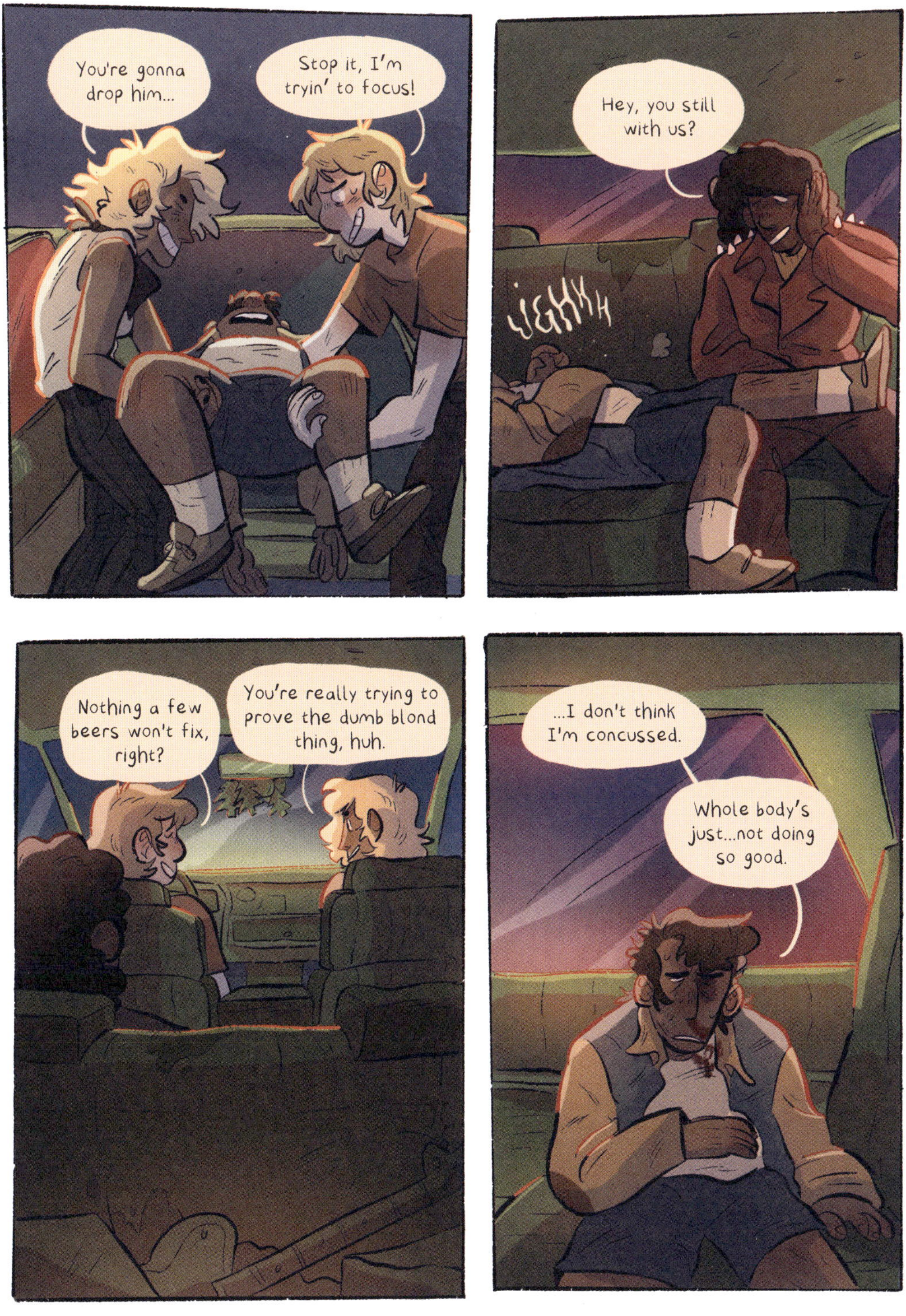
You're gonna drop him...
Stop it, I'm tryin' to focus!
UGHHH
Hey, you still with us?
Nothing a few beers won't fix, right?
You're really trying to prove the dumb blond thing, huh.
...I don't think I'm concussed.
Whole body's just...not doing so good.

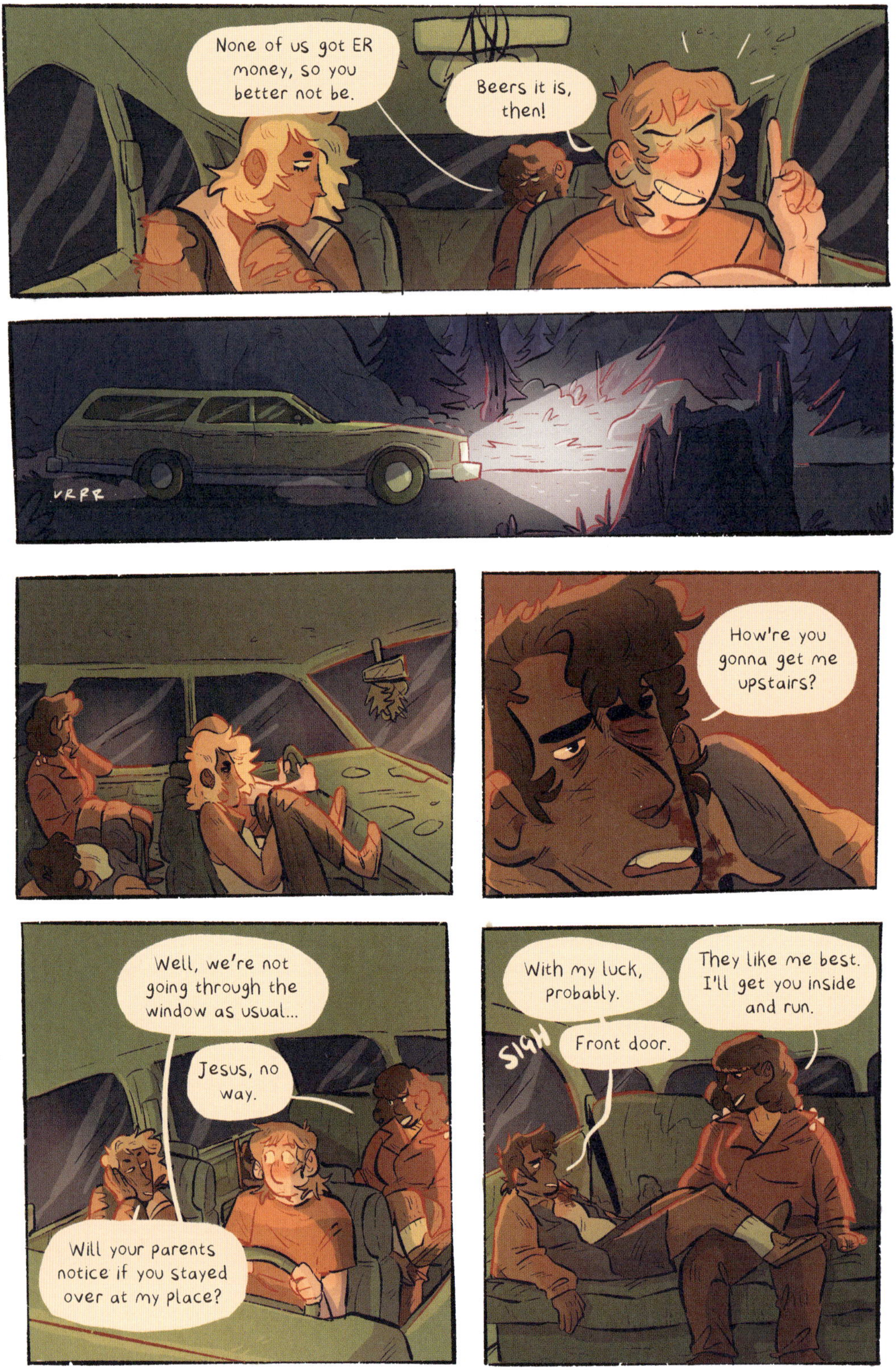
None of us got ER money, so you better not be.
Beers it is, then!
VRRR
How're you gonna get me upstairs?
Well, we're not going through the window as usual...
Jesus, no way.
Will your parents notice if you stayed over at my place?
With my luck, probably.
They like me best. I'll get you inside and run.
SIGH
Front door.

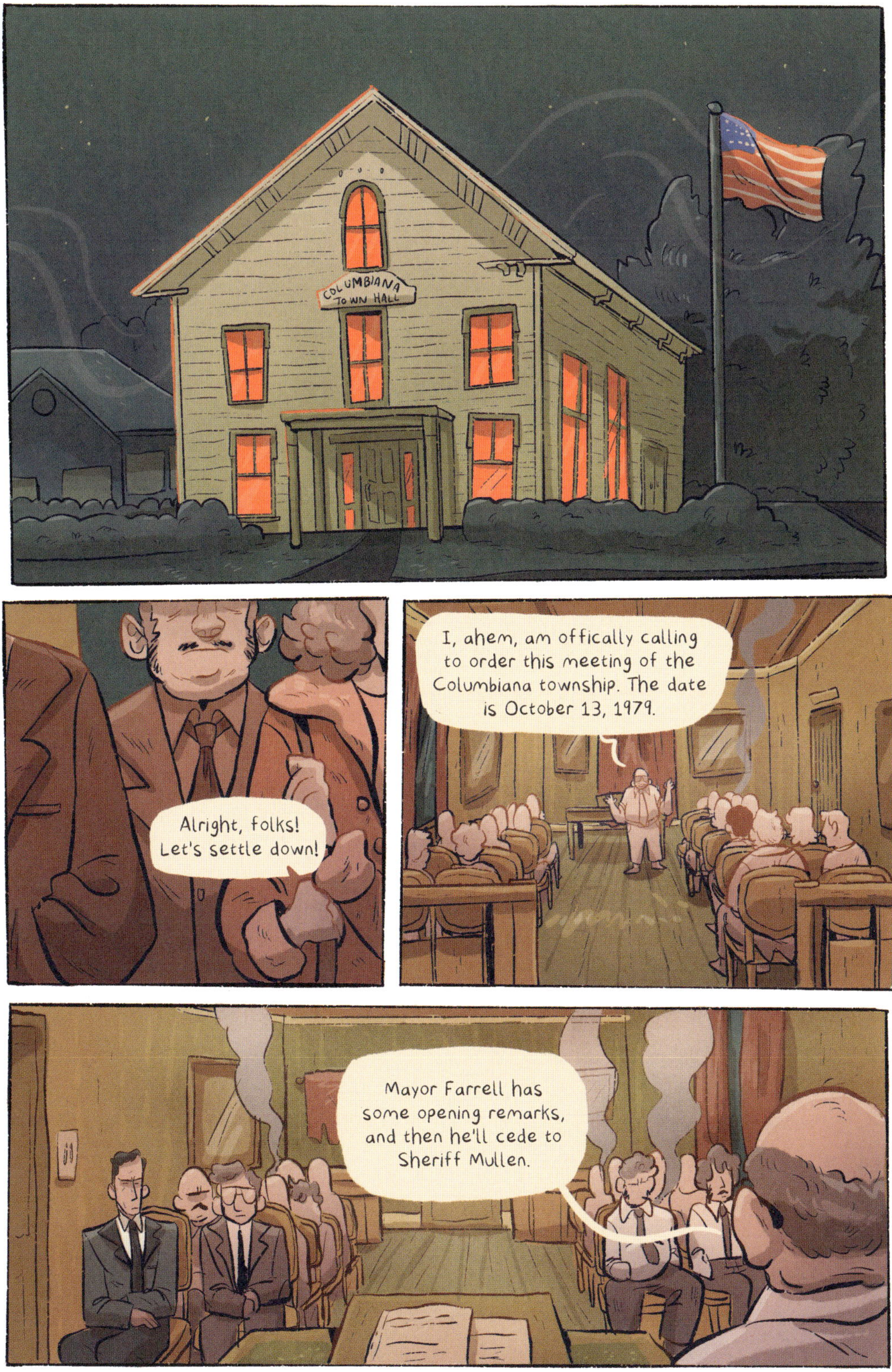
COLUMBIANA TOWN HALL
Alright, folks! Let's settle down!
I, ahem, am offically calling to order this meeting of the Columbiana township. The date is October 13, 1979.
Mayor Farrell has some opening remarks, and then he'll cede to Sheriff Mullen.

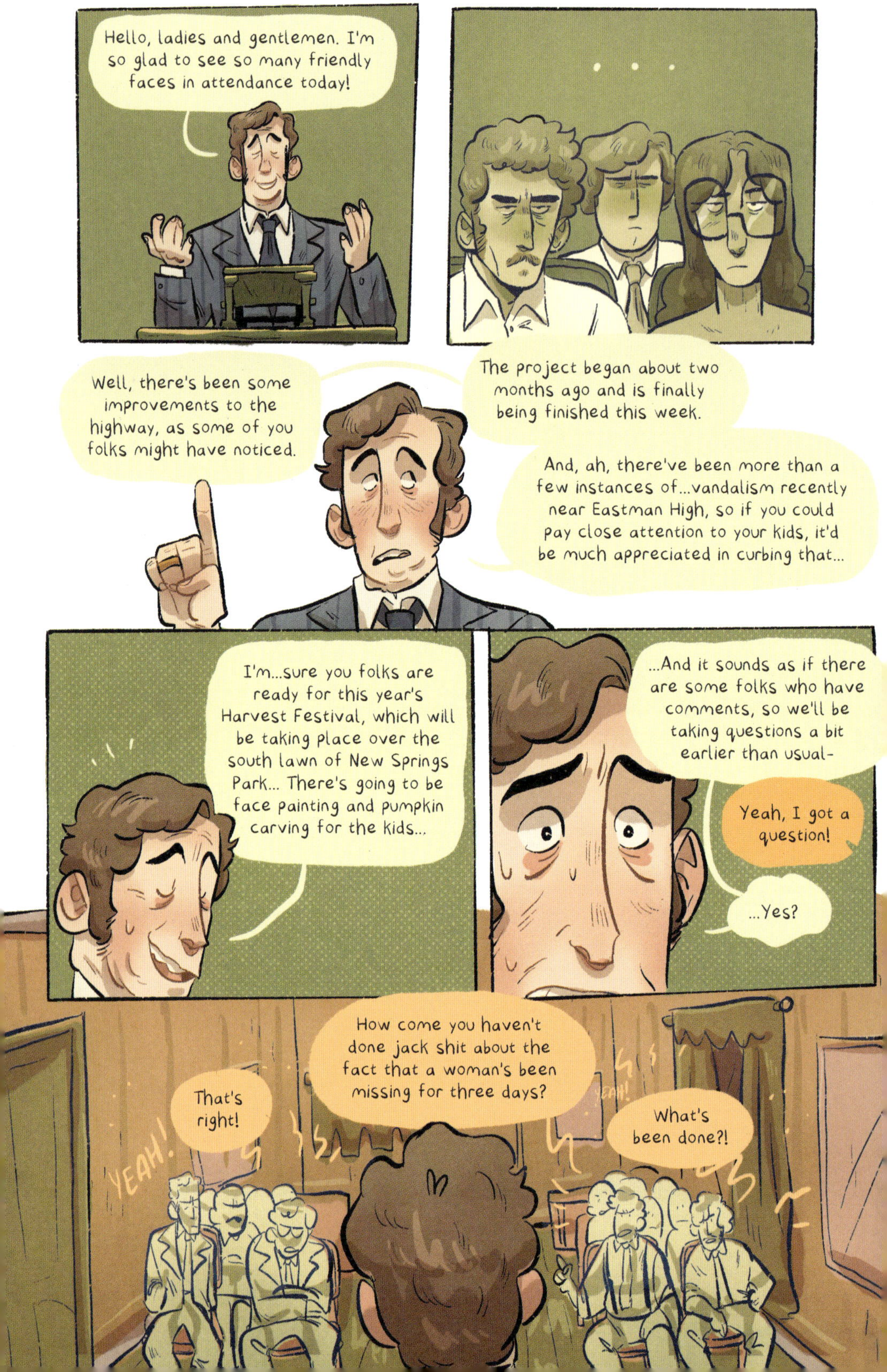
Hello, ladies and gentlemen. I'm so glad to see so many friendly faces in attendance today!
...
Well, there's been some improvements to the highway, as some of you folks might have noticed.
The project began about two months ago and is finally being finished this week.
And, ah, there've been more than a few instances of...vandalism recently near Eastman High, so if you could pay close attention to your kids, it'd be much appreciated in curbing that...
I'm...sure you folks are ready for this year's Harvest Festival, which will be taking place over the south lawn of New Springs Park... There's going to be face painting and pumpkin carving for the kids...
...And it sounds as if there are some folks who have comments, so we'll be taking questions a bit earlier than usual-
Yeah, I got a question!
...Yes?
How come you haven't done jack shit about the fact that a woman's been missing for three days?
That's right!
YEAH!
YEAH!
What's been done?!

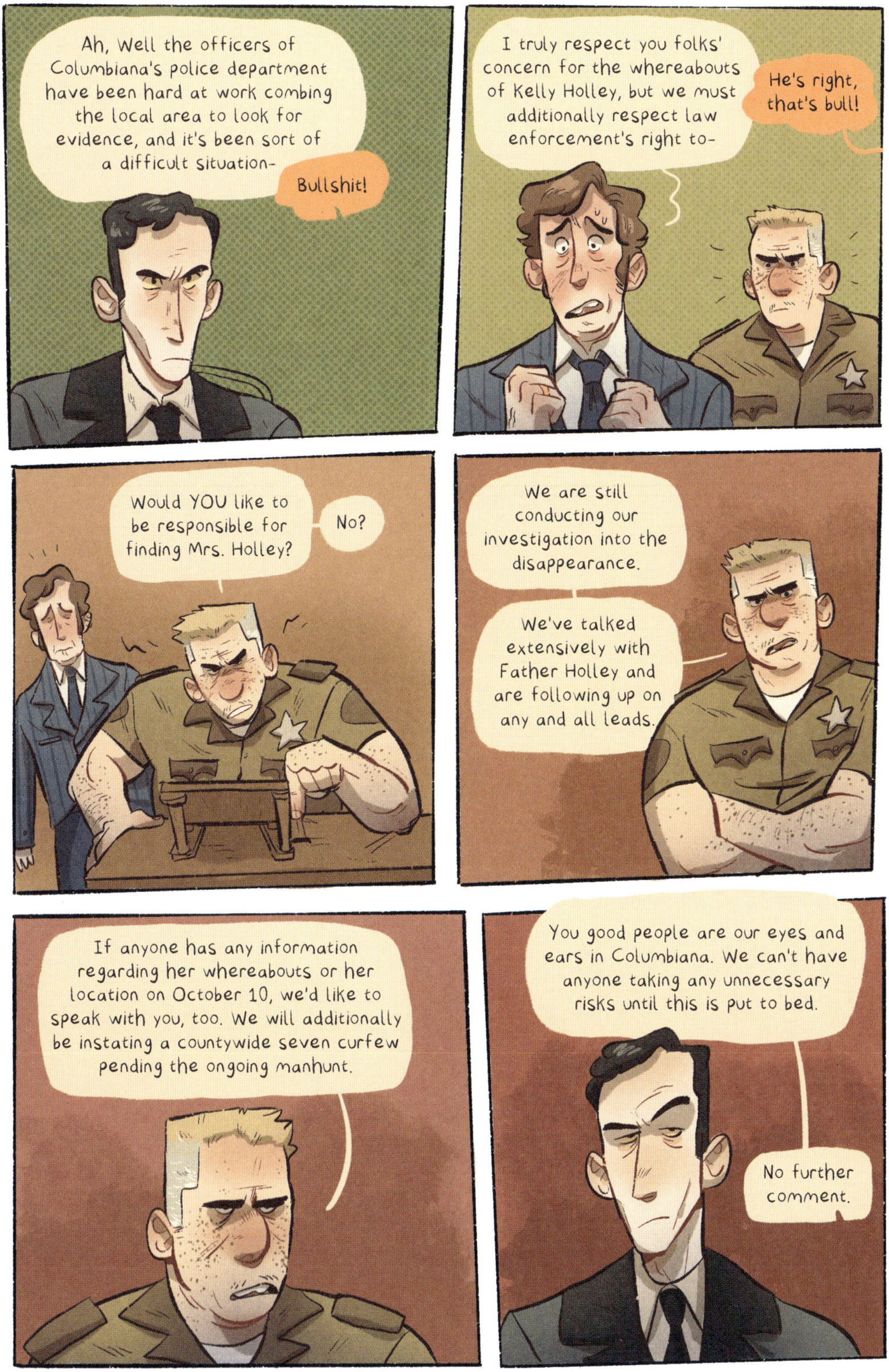

Ah, Well the officers of Columbiana's police department have been hard at work combing the local area to look for evidence, and it's been sort of a difficult situation-
Bullshit!
I truly respect you folks' concern for the whereabouts of Kelly Holley, but we must additionally respect law enforcement's right to-
He's right, that's bull!
Would YOU like to be responsible for finding Mrs. Holley?
No?
We are still conducting our investigation into the disappearance.
We've talked extensively with Father Holley and are following up on any and all leads.
If anyone has any information regarding her whereabouts or her location on October 10, we'd like to speak with you, too. We will additionally be instating a countywide seven curfew pending the ongoing manhunt.
You good people are our eyes and ears in Columbiana. We can't have anyone taking any unnecessary risks until this is put to bed.
No further comment.

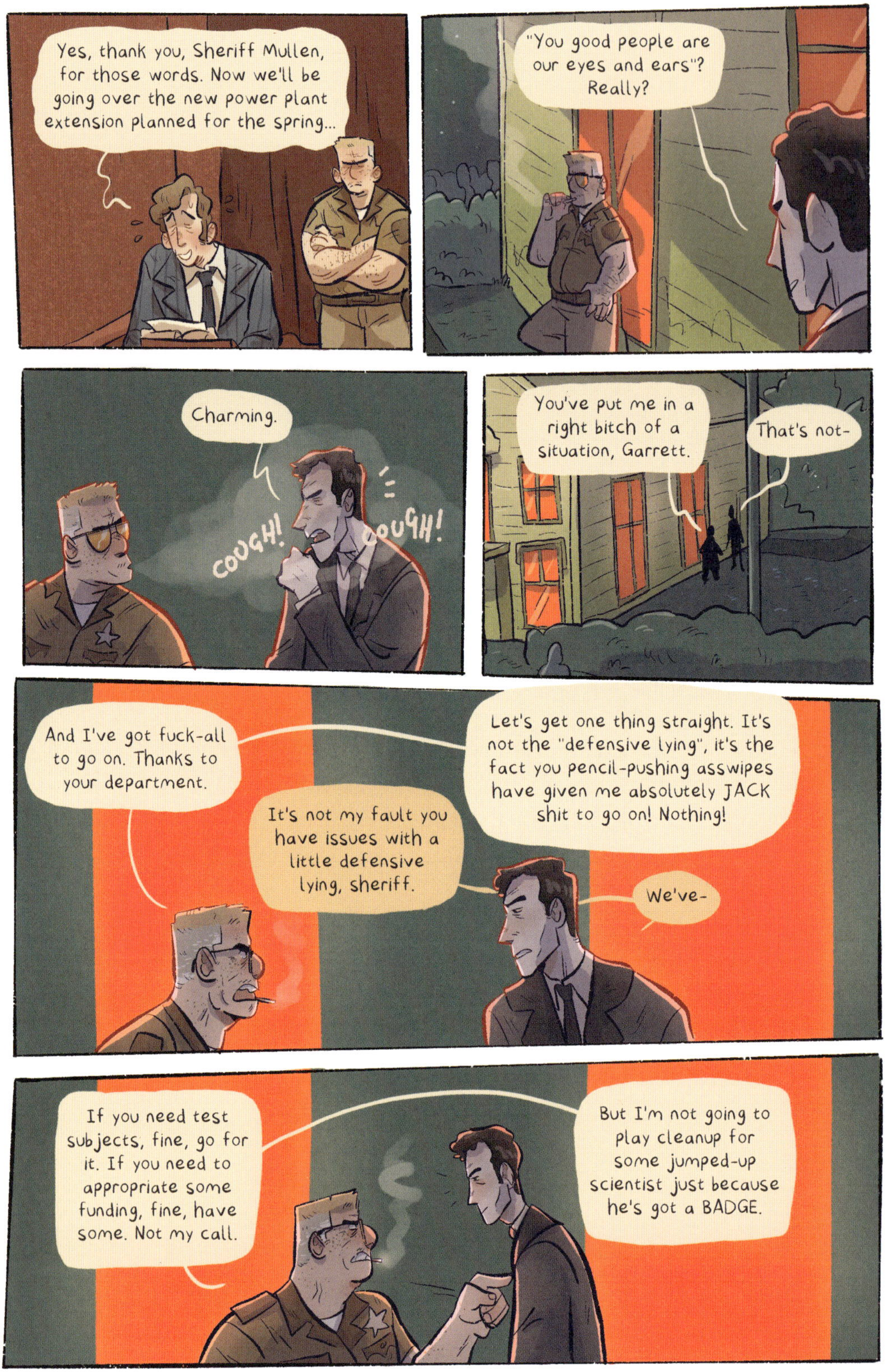
Yes, thank you, Sheriff Mullen, for those words. Now we'll be going over the new power plant extension planned for the spring...
"You good people are our eyes and ears"? Really?
Charming.
COUGH! COUGH!
You've put me in a right bitch of a situation, Garrett.
That's not-
And I've got fuck-all to go on. Thanks to your department.
It's not my fault you have issues with a little defensive lying, sheriff.
Let's get one thing straight. It's not the "defensive lying", it's the fact you pencil-pushing asswipes have given me absolutely JACK shit to go on! Nothing!
We've-
If you need test subjects, fine, go for it. If you need to appropriate some funding, fine, have some. Not my call.
But I'm not going to play cleanup for some jumped-up scientist just because he's got a BADGE.

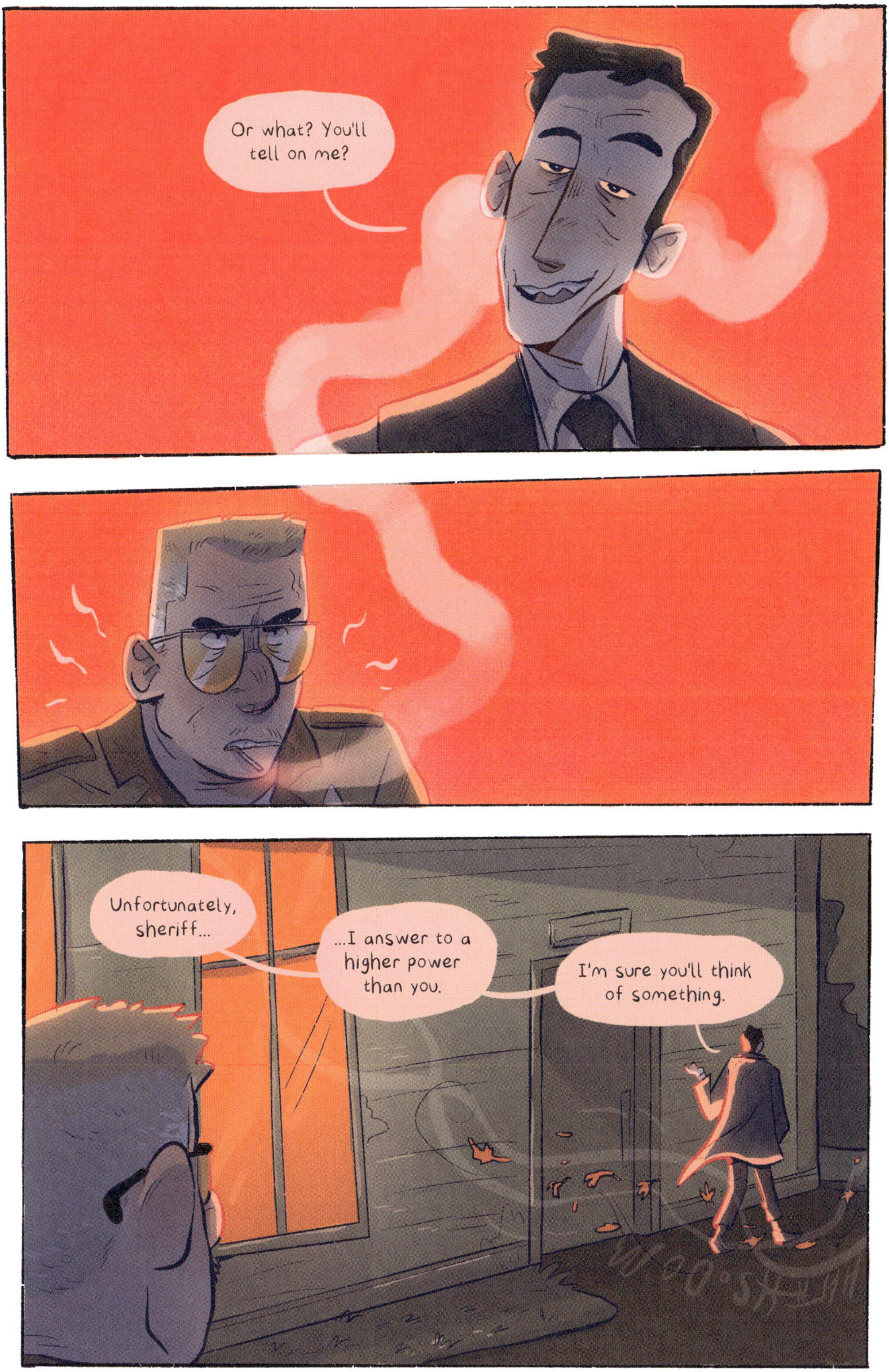
Or what? You'll tell on me?
Unfortunately, sheriff...
...I answer to a higher power than you.
I'm sure you'll think of something.

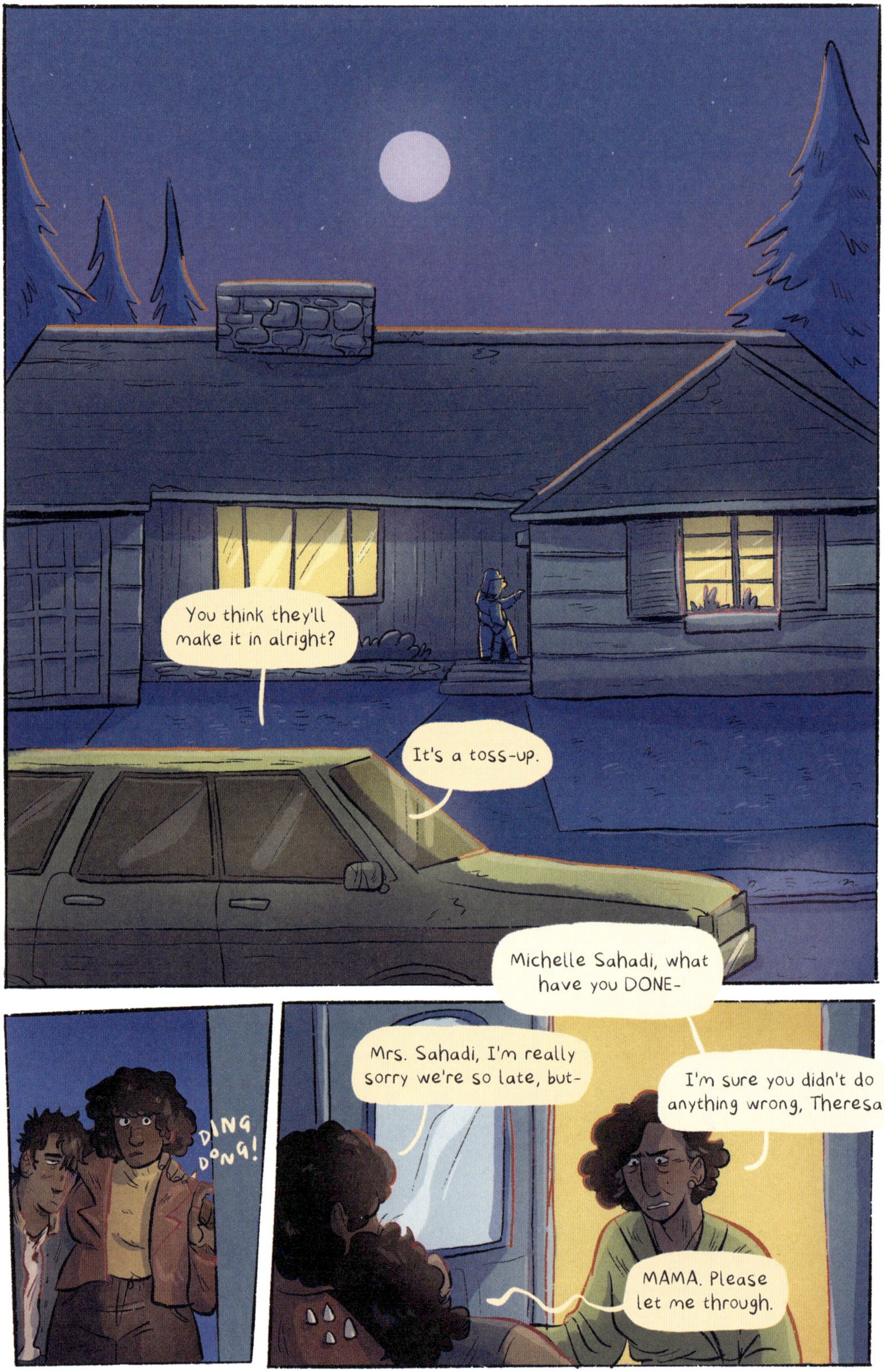
You think they'll make it in alright?
It's a toss-up.
DING DONG!
Michelle Sahadi, what have you DONE-
Mrs. Sahadi, I'm really sorry we're so late, but-
I'm sure you didn't do anything wrong, Theresa-
MAMA. Please let me through.

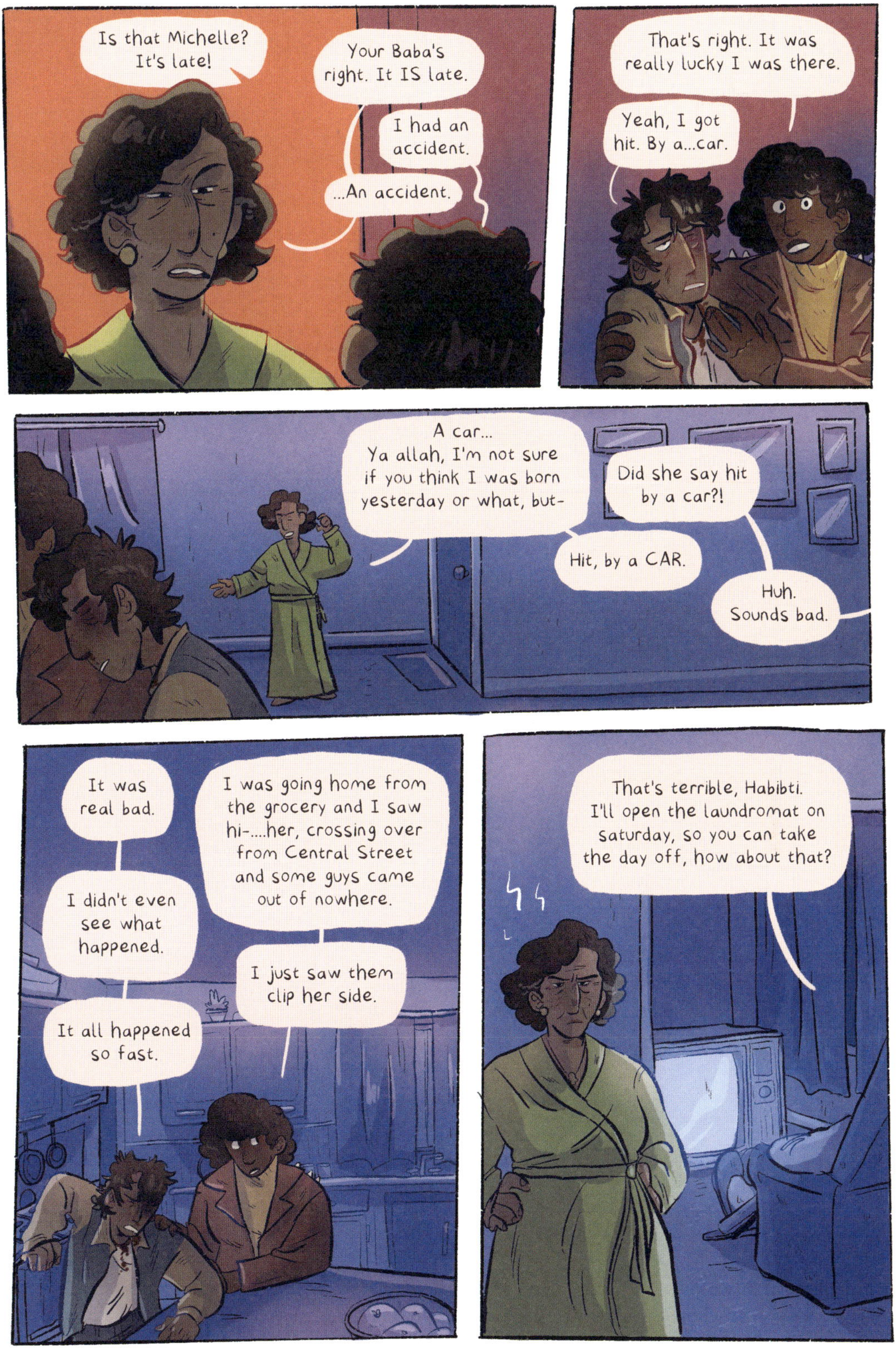
Is that Michelle? It's late!
Your Baba's right. It IS late.
I had an accident.
...An accident.
That's right. It was really lucky I was there.
Yeah, I got hit. By a...car.
A car... Ya allah, I'm not sure if you think I was born yesterday or what, but-
Did she say hit by a car?!
Hit, by a CAR.
Huh. Sounds bad.
It was real bad.
I didn't even see what happened.
It all happened so fast.
I was going home from the grocery and I saw hi-....her, crossing over from Central Street and some guys came out of nowhere.
I just saw them clip her side.
That's terrible, Habibti. I'll open the laundromat on saturday, so you can take the day off, how about that?

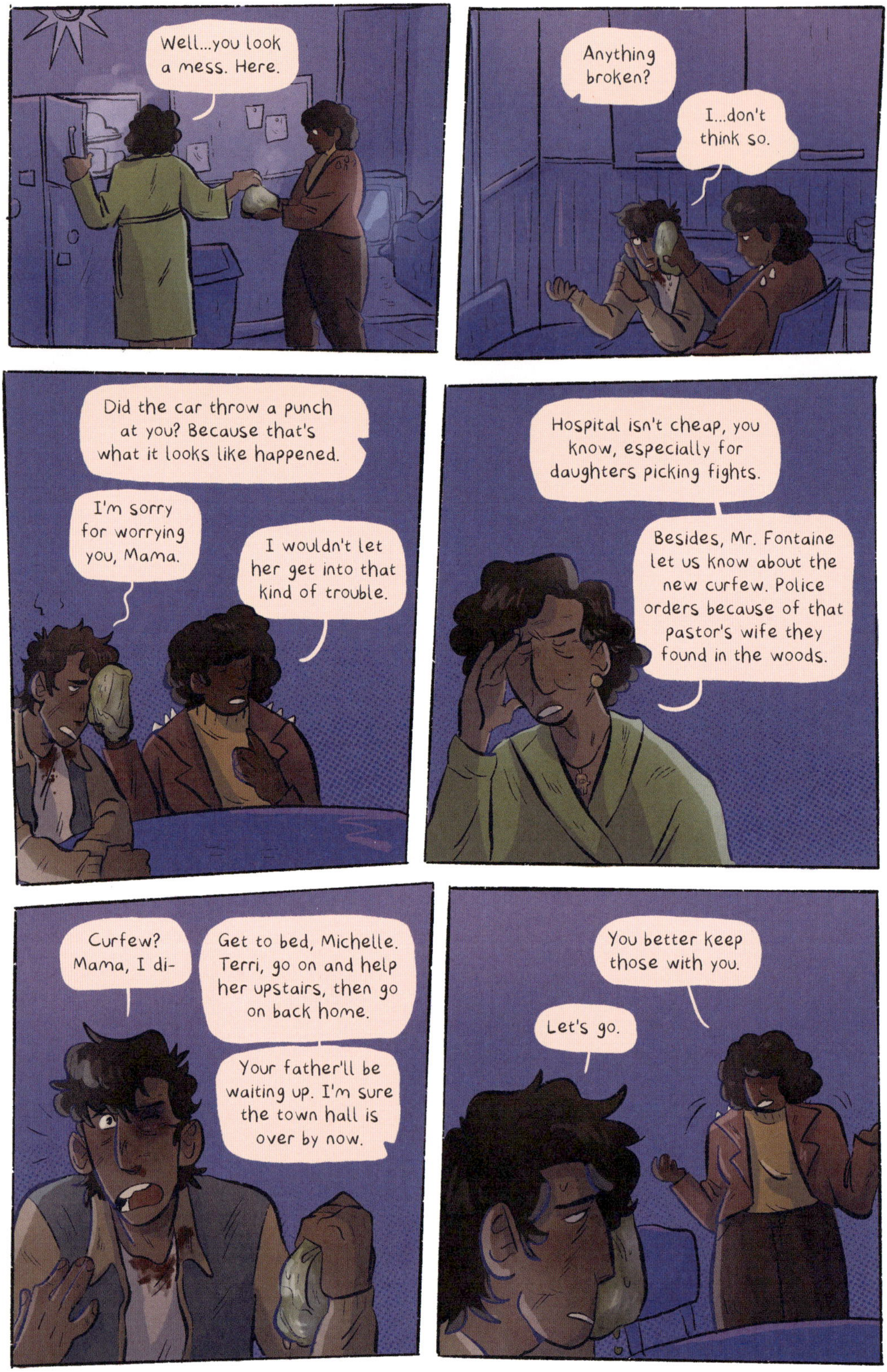
Well...you look a mess. Here.
Anything broken?
I...don't think so.
Did the car throw a punch at you? Because that's what it looks like happened.
I'm sorry for worrying you, Mama.
I wouldn't let her get into that kind of trouble.
Hospital isn't cheap, you know, especially for daughters picking fights.
Besides, Mr. Fontaine let us know about the new curfew. Police orders because of that pastor's wife they found in the woods.
Curfew? Mama, I di-
Get to bed, Michelle. Terri, go on and help her upstairs, then go on back home.
Your father'll be waiting up. I'm sure the town hall is over by now.
You better keep those with you.
Let's go.

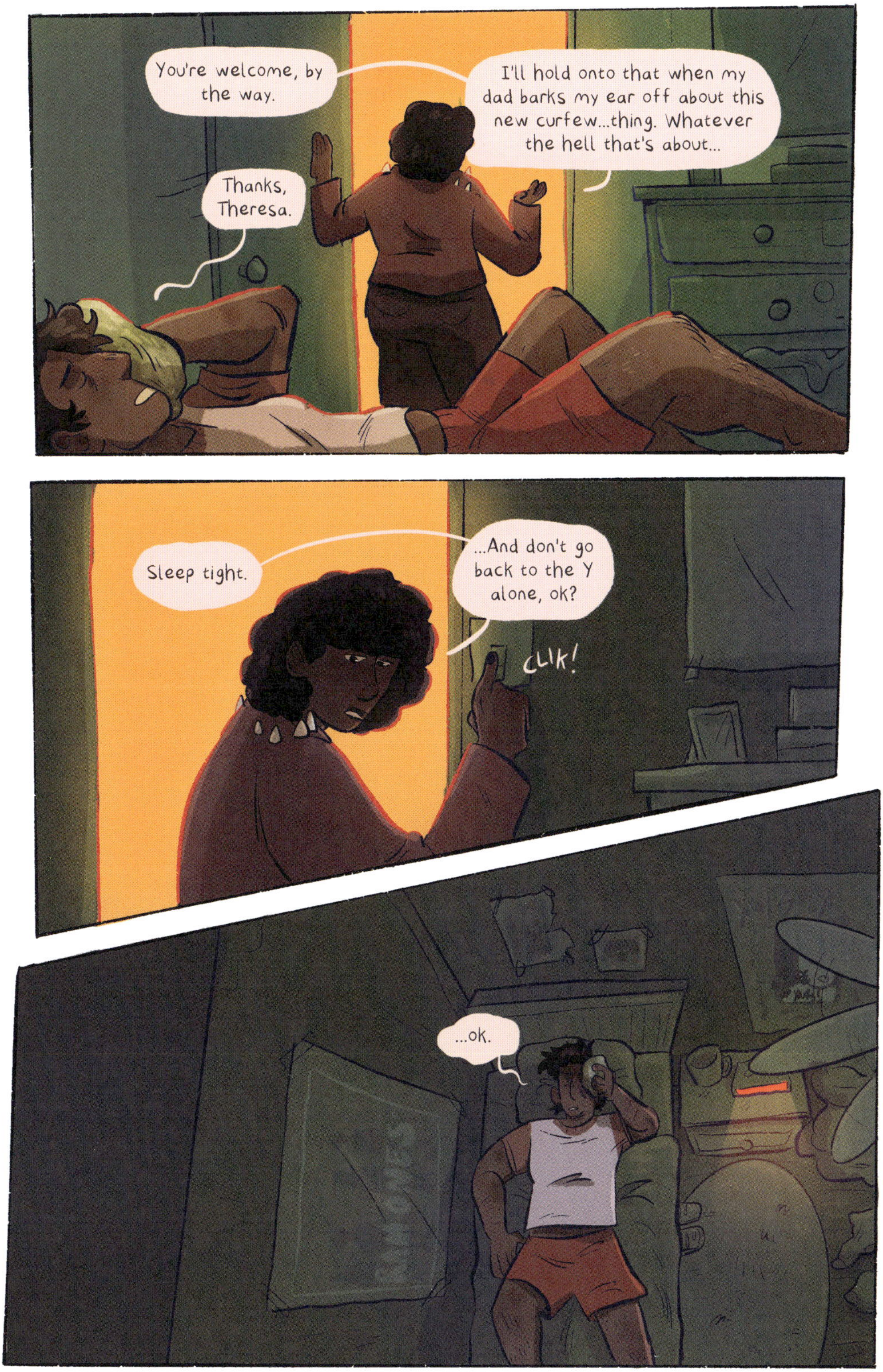
You're welcome, by the way.
I'll hold onto that when my dad barks my ear off about this new curfew...thing. Whatever the hell that's about...
Thanks, Theresa.
Sleep tight.
...And don't go back to the Y alone, ok?
CLIK!
...ok.
RAMONES

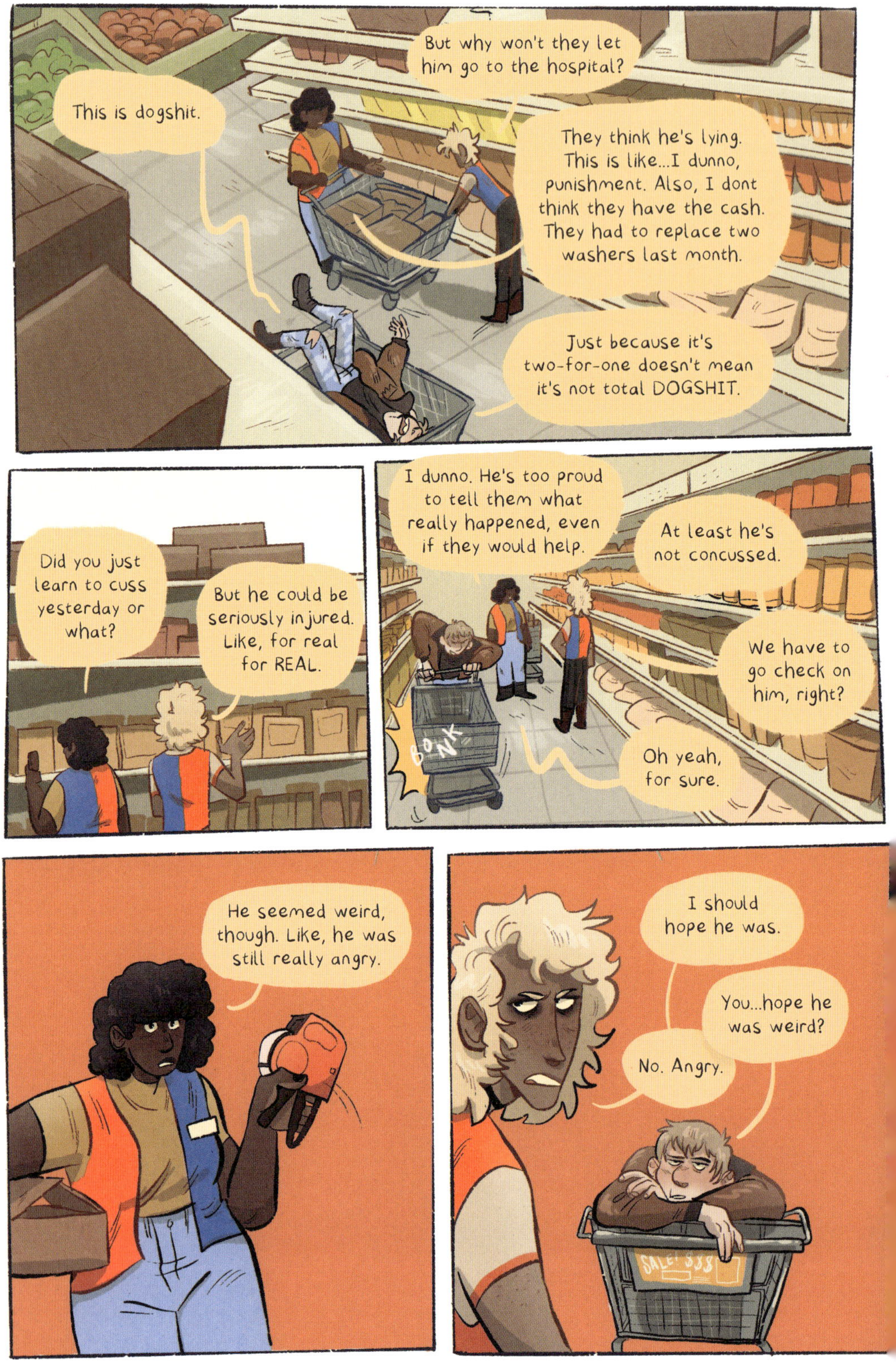
This is dogshit.
But why won't they let him go to the hospital?
They think he's lying. This is like...I dunno, punishment. Also, I dont think they have the cash. They had to replace two washers last month.
Just because it's two-for-one doesn't mean it's not total DOGSHIT.
Did you just learn to cuss yesterday or what?
But he could be seriously injured. Like, for real for REAL.
I dunno. He's too proud to tell them what really happened, even if they would help.
At least he's not concussed.
BONK
We have to go check on him, right?
Oh yeah, for sure.
He seemed weird, though. Like, he was still really angry.
I should hope he was.
You...hope he was weird?
No. Angry.
SALE! $$$

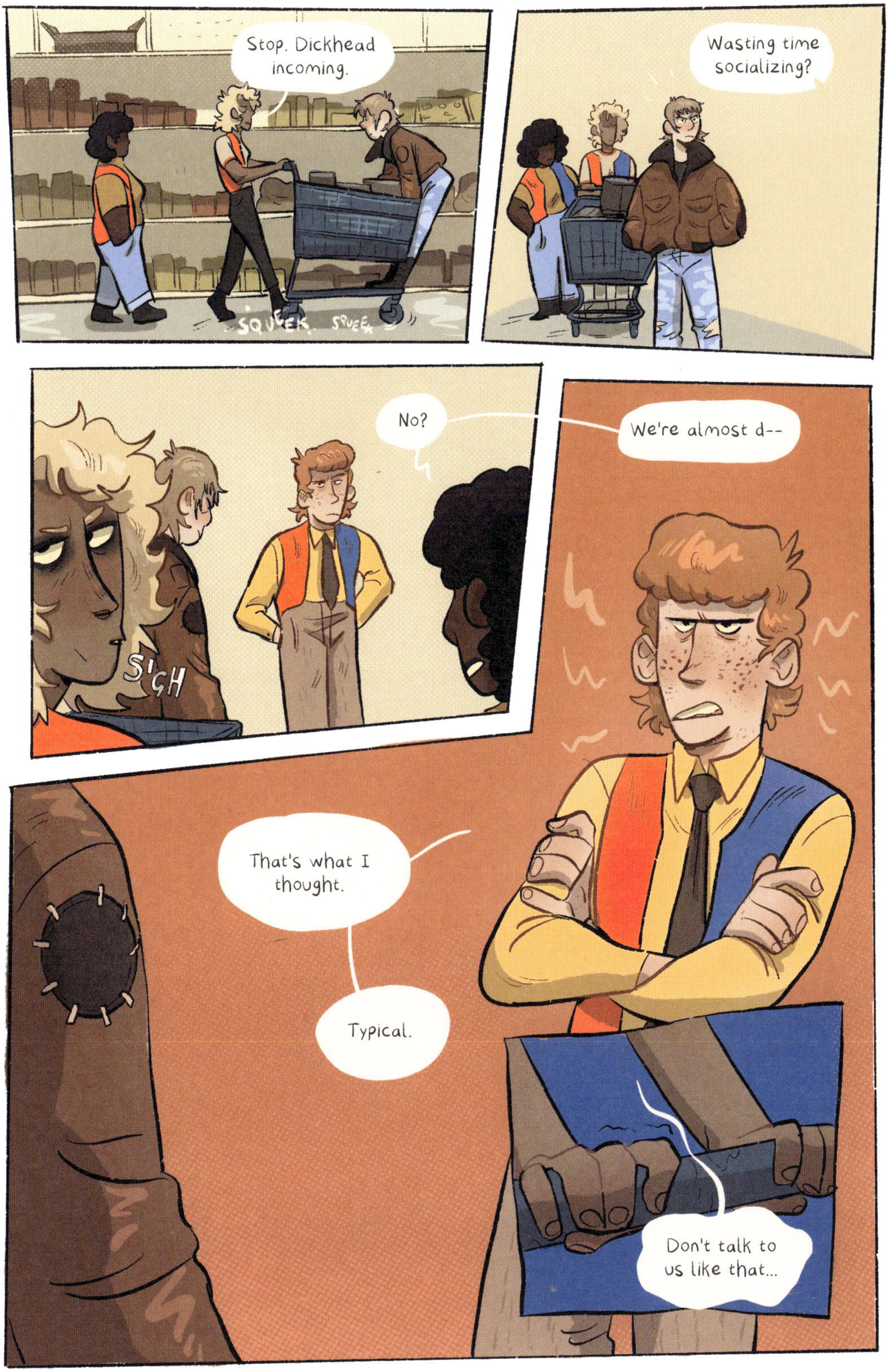
Stop. Dickhead incoming.
SQUEEK. SQUEEK
Wasting time socializing?
No?
We're almost d--
SIGH
That's what I thought.
Typical.
Don't talk to us like that...

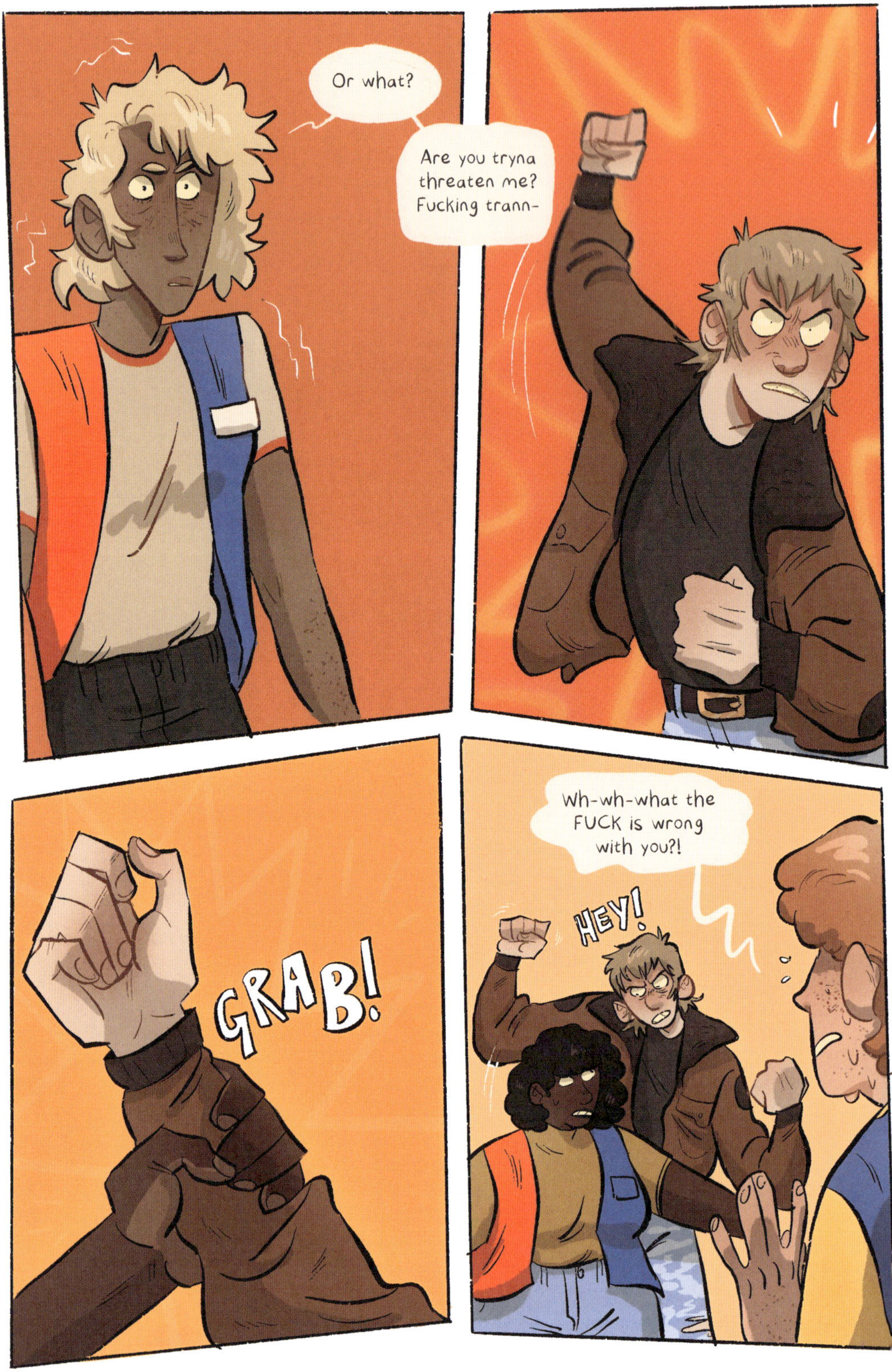
Or what?
Are you tryna threaten me? Fucking trann-
GRAB!
Wh-wh-what the FUCK is wrong with you?!
HEY!

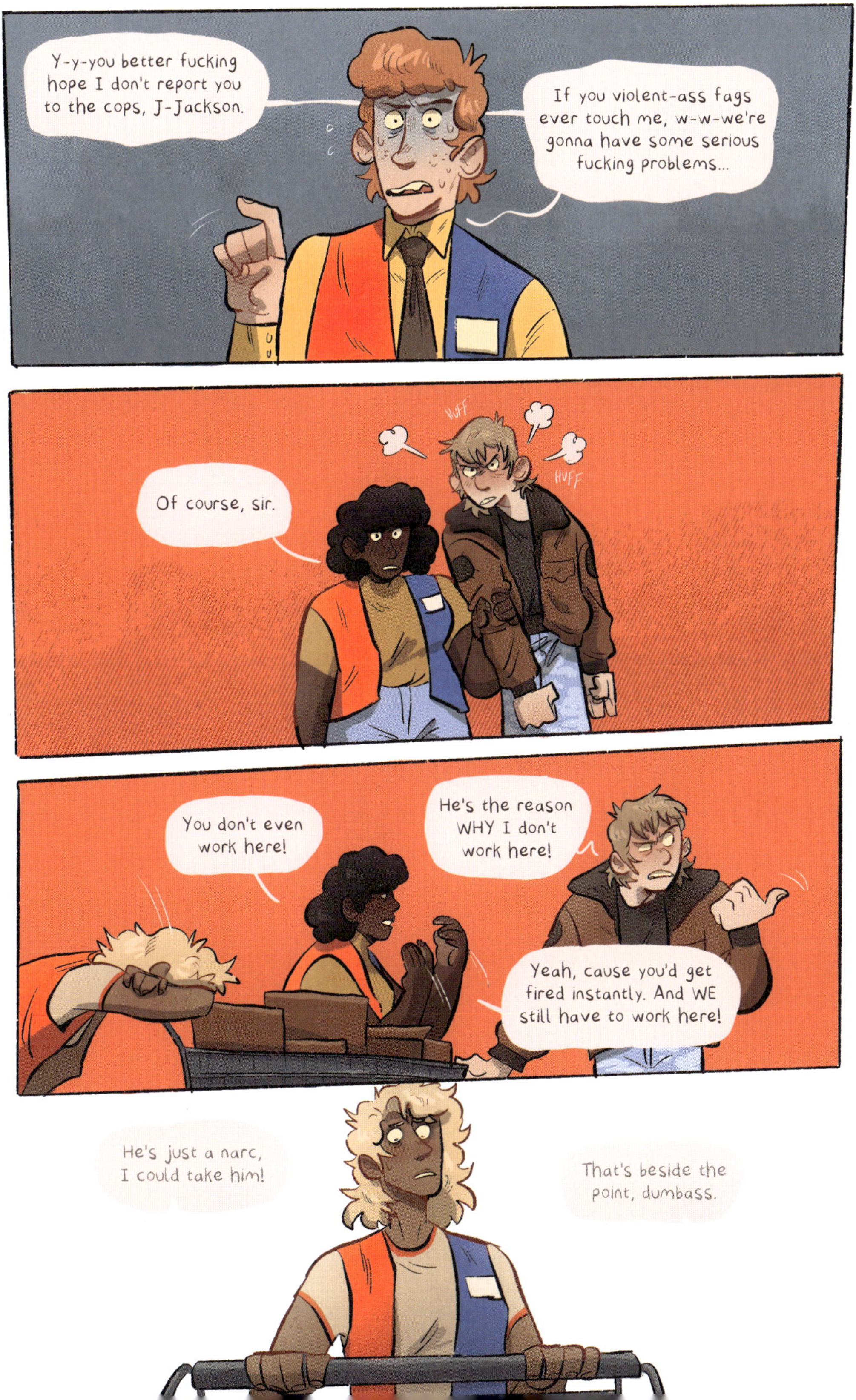
Y-y-you better fucking hope I don't report you to the cops, J-Jackson.
If you violent-ass fags ever touch me, w-w-we're gonna have some serious fucking problems...
HUFF
HUFF
Of course, sir.
You don't even work here!
He's the reason WHY I don't work here!
Yeah, cause you'd get fired instantly. And WE still have to work here!
He's just a narc, I could take him!
That's beside the point, dumbass.

Now we have to avoid him for the rest of the shift.
I mean, I don't have to...
Babysitting is above my pay grade. Hey, Lupe? You ok?
Yeah. I'm good...
Why would he call the cops on us if they're so damn busy looking for that murderer?
Don't know. Imbecile minds work in mysterious ways.
My dad was saying the sheriff was cracking down hard on it. He was pretty shook up...but I guess everyone's freaked about it.
I guess so...I mean, it's creepy as hell.
We've still gotta go check on him, curfew or not.
Well, I'll grab my first aid kit anyway, just in case.
We can all get up to his window, right?
Look, I know I'm the old lady here, but I can still scale a drainpipe.

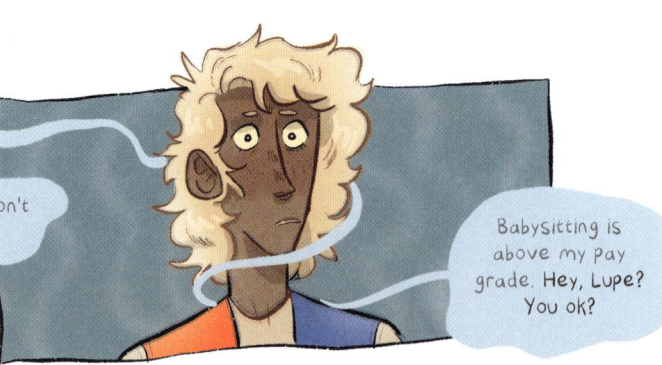

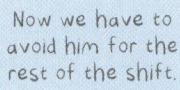

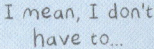

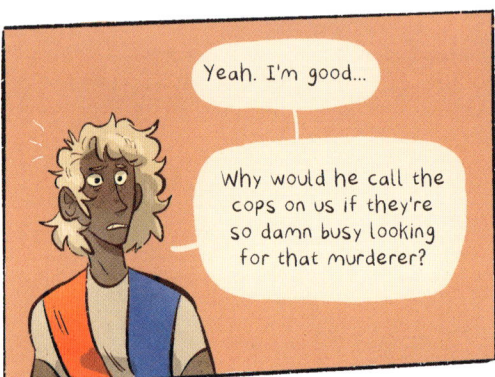

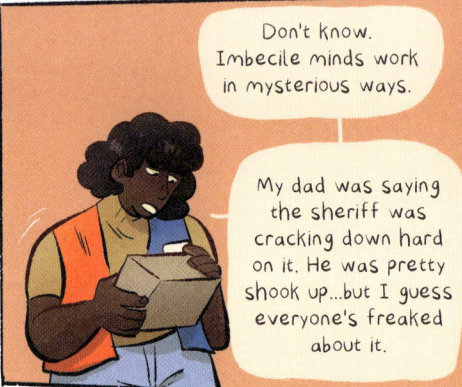

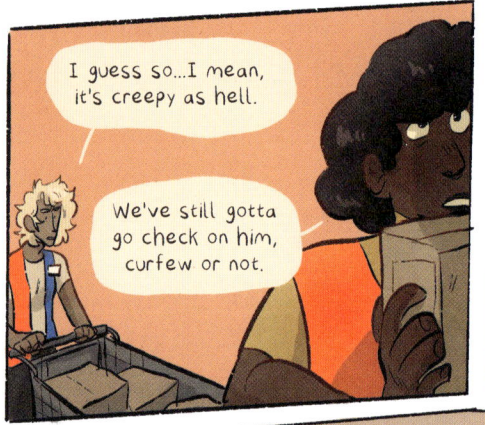

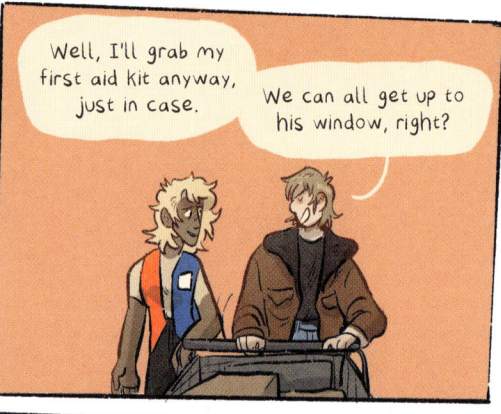

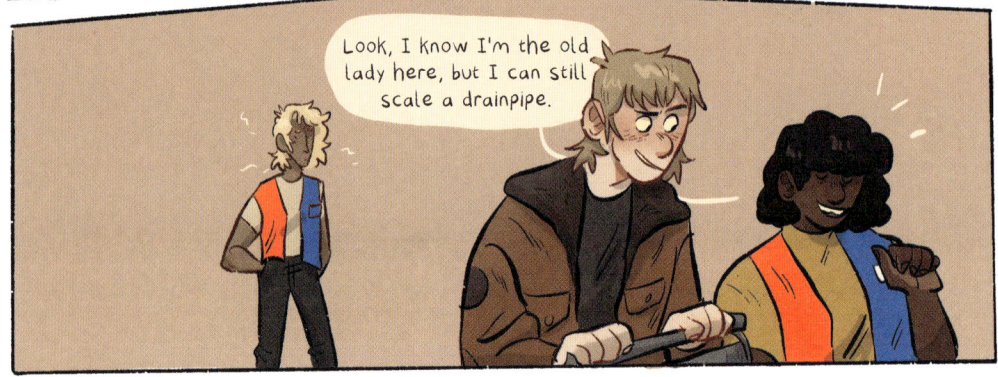

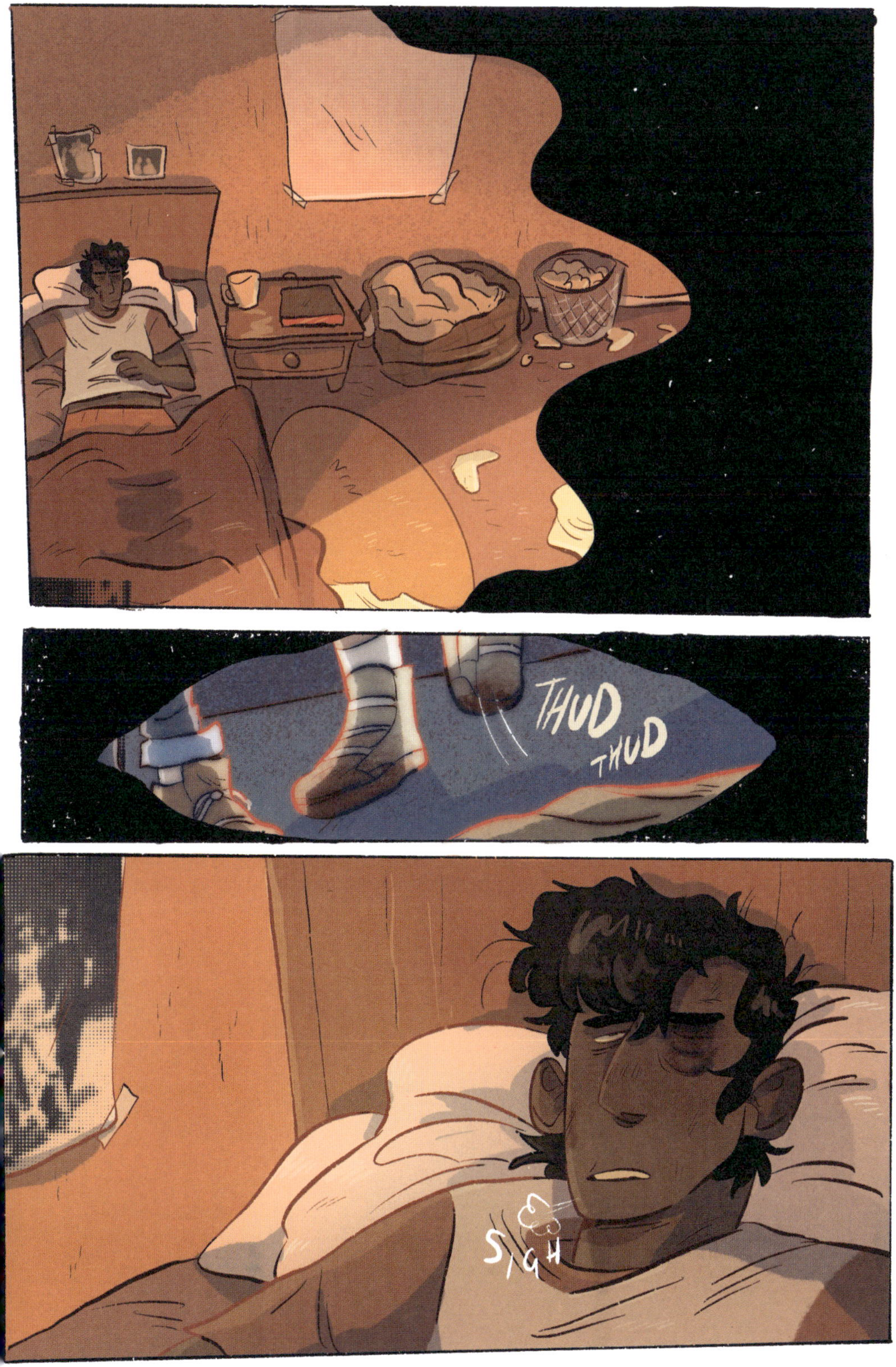
THUD
THUD
SIGH

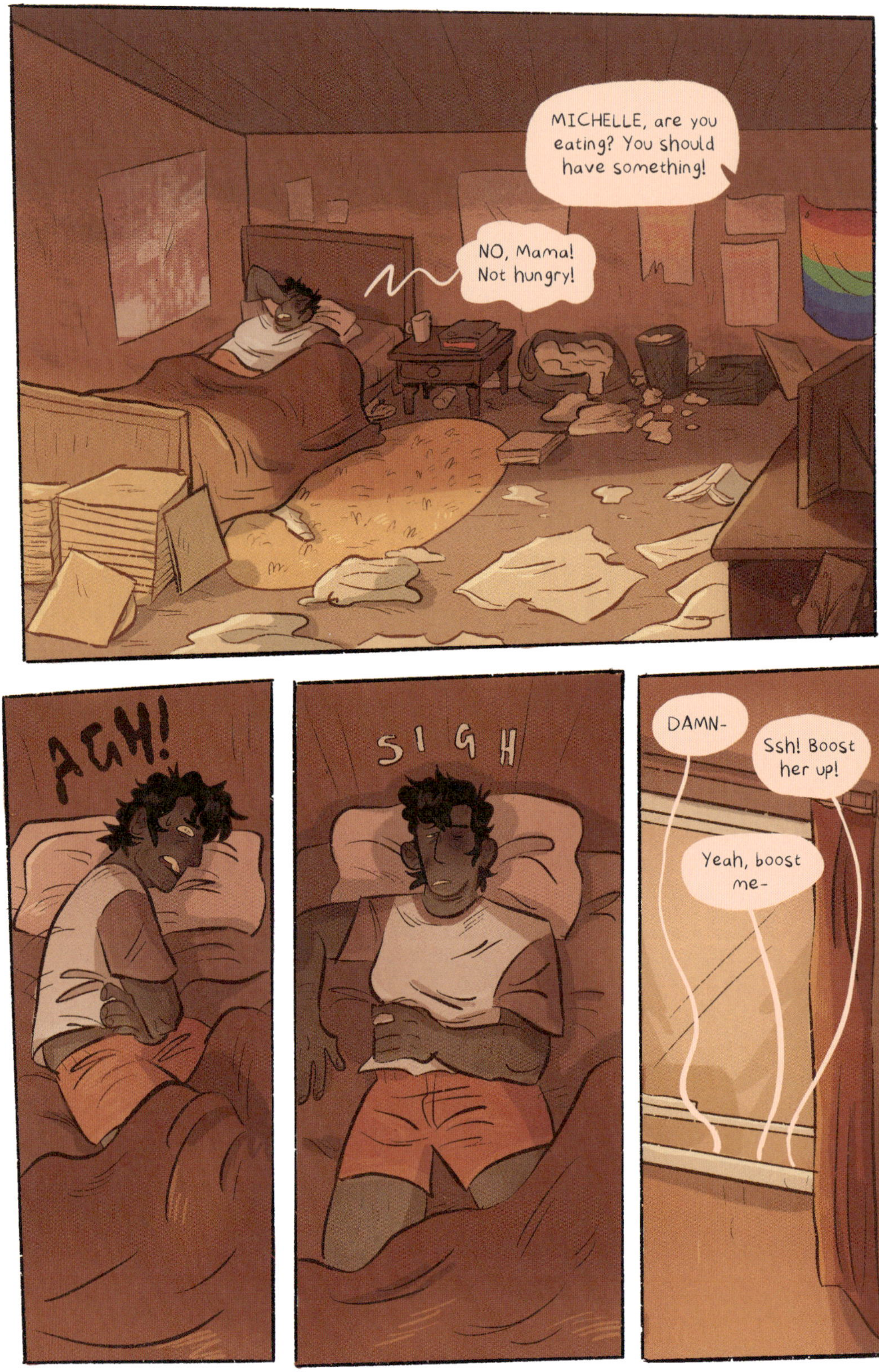
MICHELLE, are you eating? You should have something!
NO, Mama! Not hungry!
AGH!
SIGH
DAMN-
Ssh! Boost her up!
Yeah, boost me-

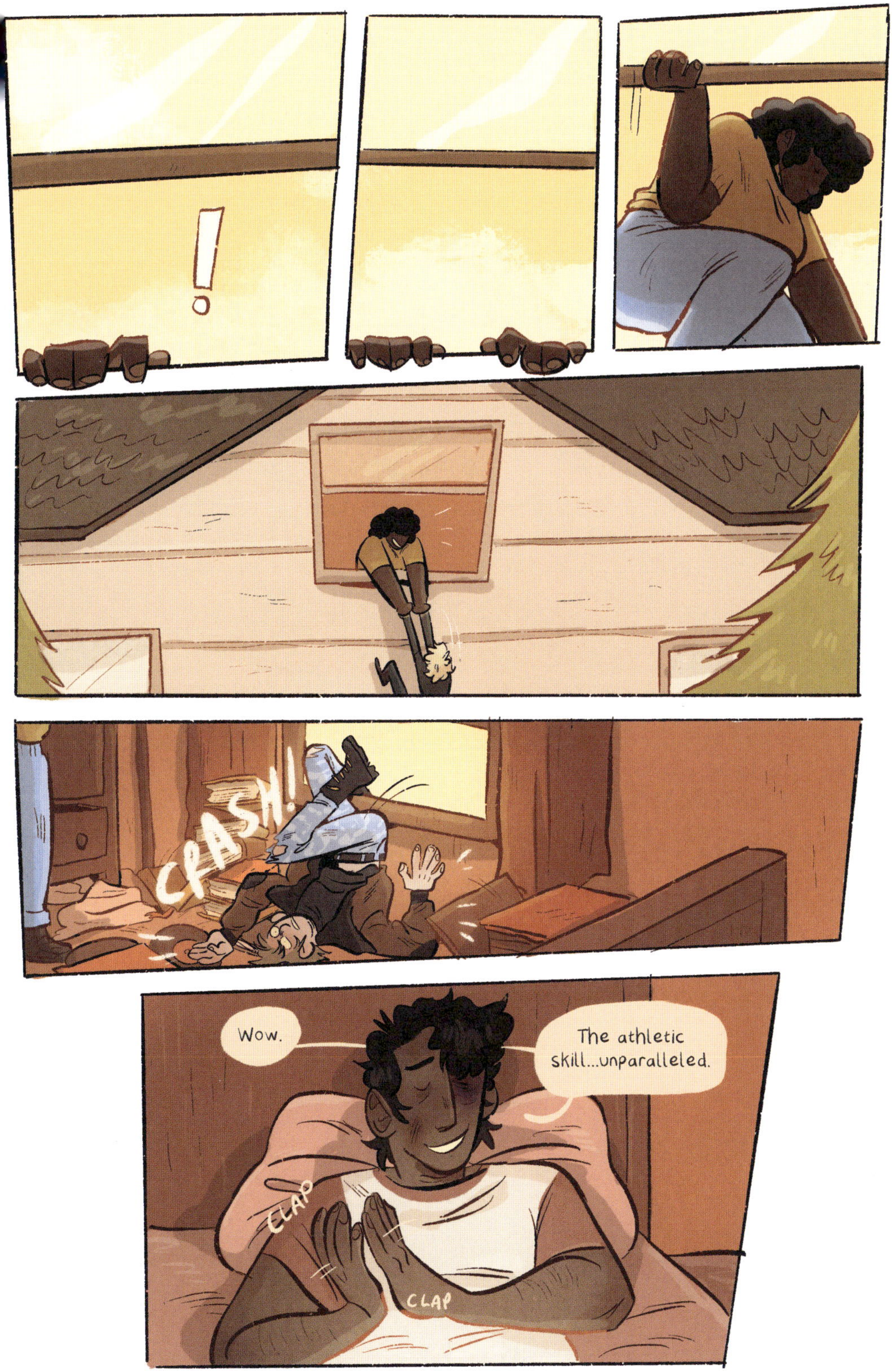
!
CRASH!
Wow.
The athletic skill...unparalleled.
CLAP
CLAP

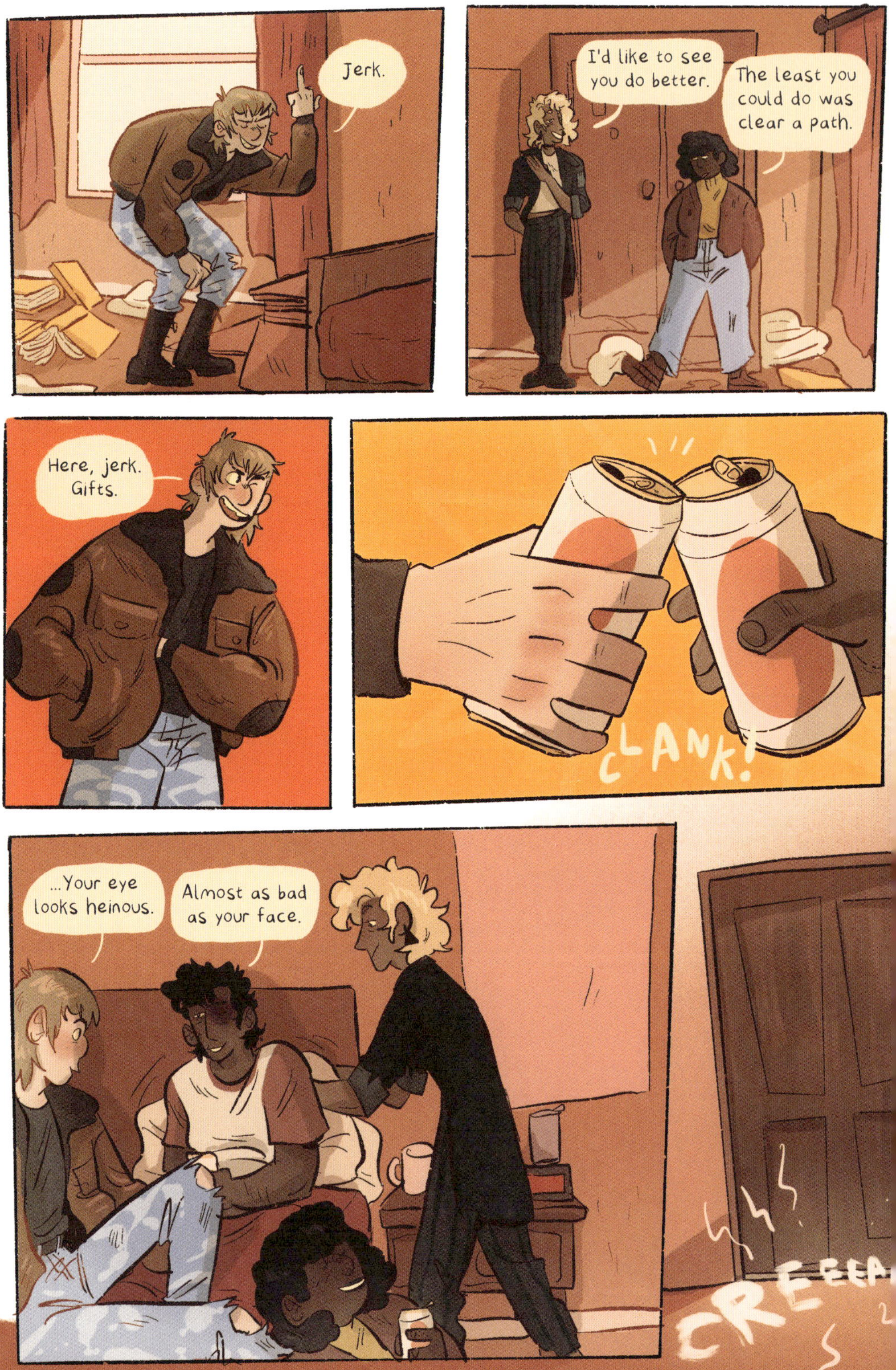
Jerk.
I'd like to see you do better.
The least you could do was clear a path.
Here, jerk. Gifts.
CLANK!
...Your eye looks heinous.
Almost as bad as your face.
CREEEEA

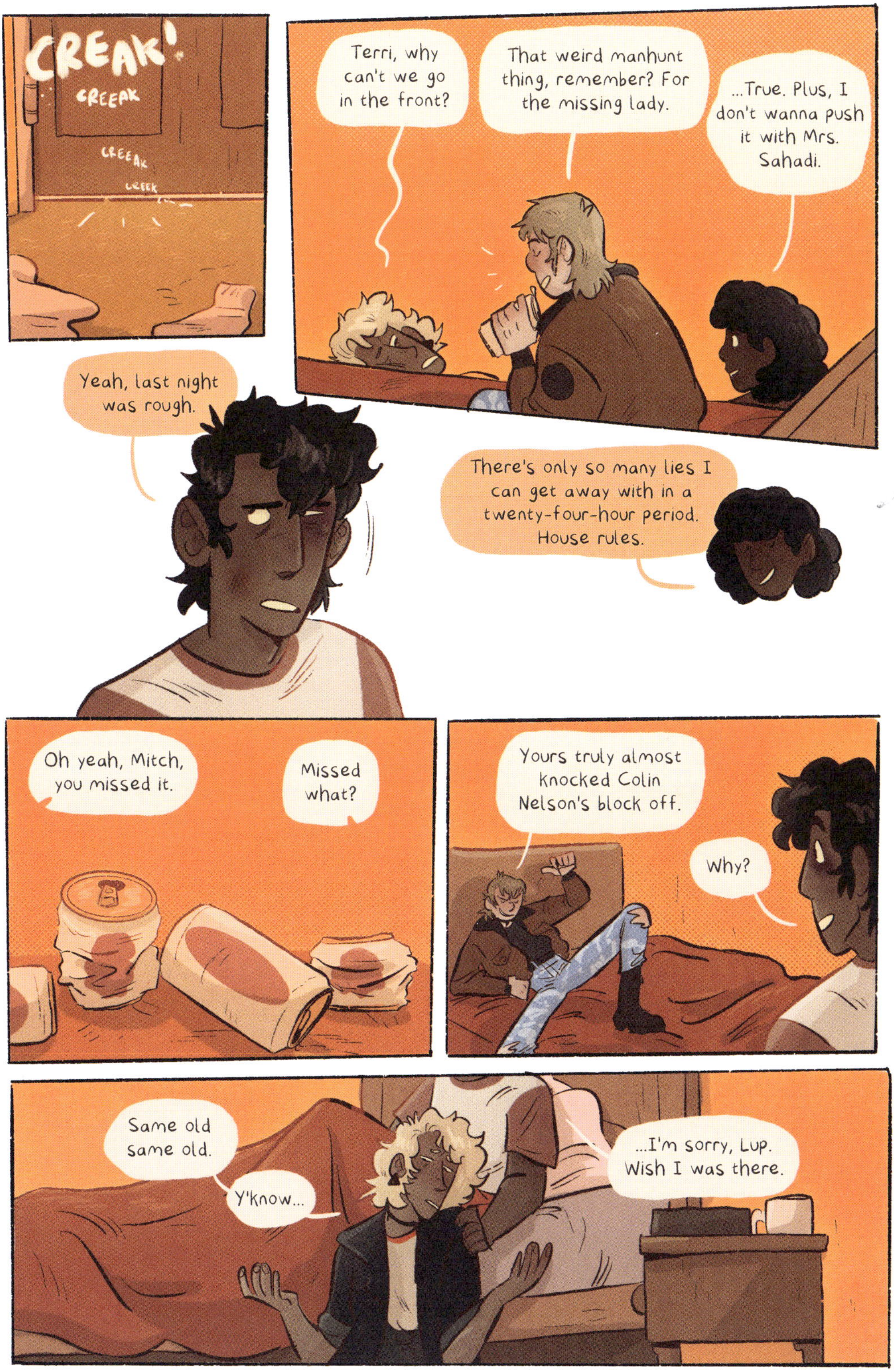
CREAK!
CREEAK
CREEAK
CREEK
Terri, why can't we go in the front?
That weird manhunt thing, remember? For the missing lady.
...True. Plus, I don't wanna push it with Mrs. Sahadi.
Yeah, last night was rough.
There's only so many lies I can get away with in a twenty-four-hour period. House rules.
Oh yeah, Mitch, you missed it.
Missed what?
Yours truly almost knocked Colin Nelson's block off.
Why?
Same old same old.
Y'know...
...I'm sorry, Lup. Wish I was there.

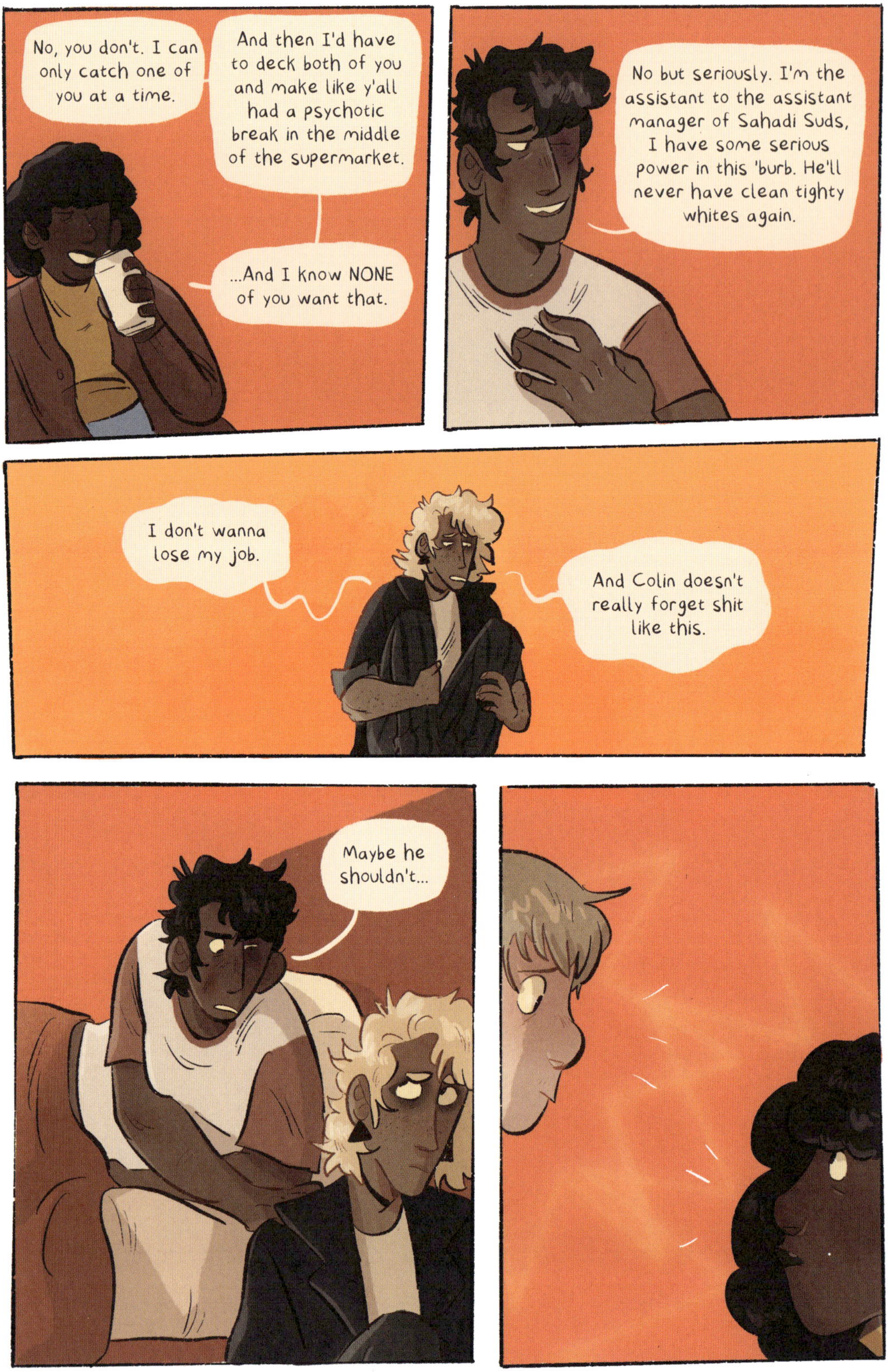
No, you don't. I can only catch one of you at a time.
And then I'd have to deck both of you and make like y'all had a psychotic break in the middle of the supermarket.
...And I know NONE of you want that.
No but seriously. I'm the assistant to the assistant manager of Sahadi Suds, I have some serious power in this 'burb. He'll never have clean tighty whites again.
I don't wanna lose my job.
And Colin doesn't really forget shit like this.
Maybe he shouldn't...

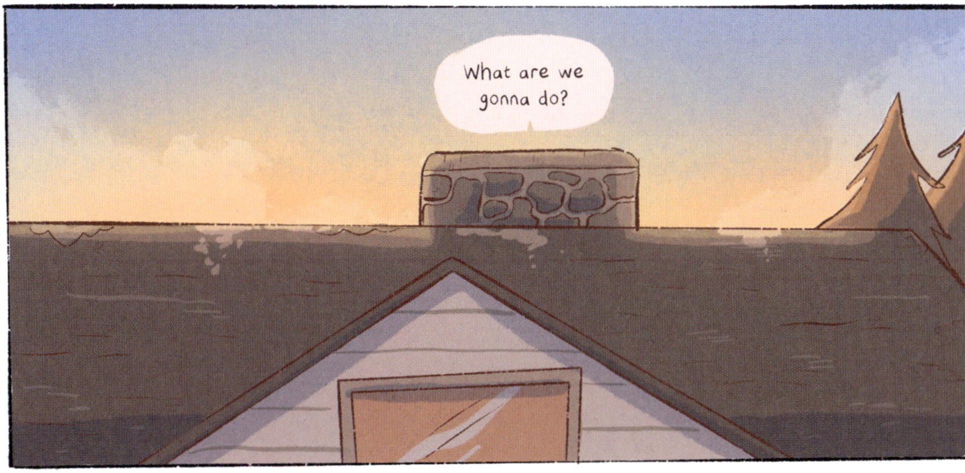
What are we gonna do?

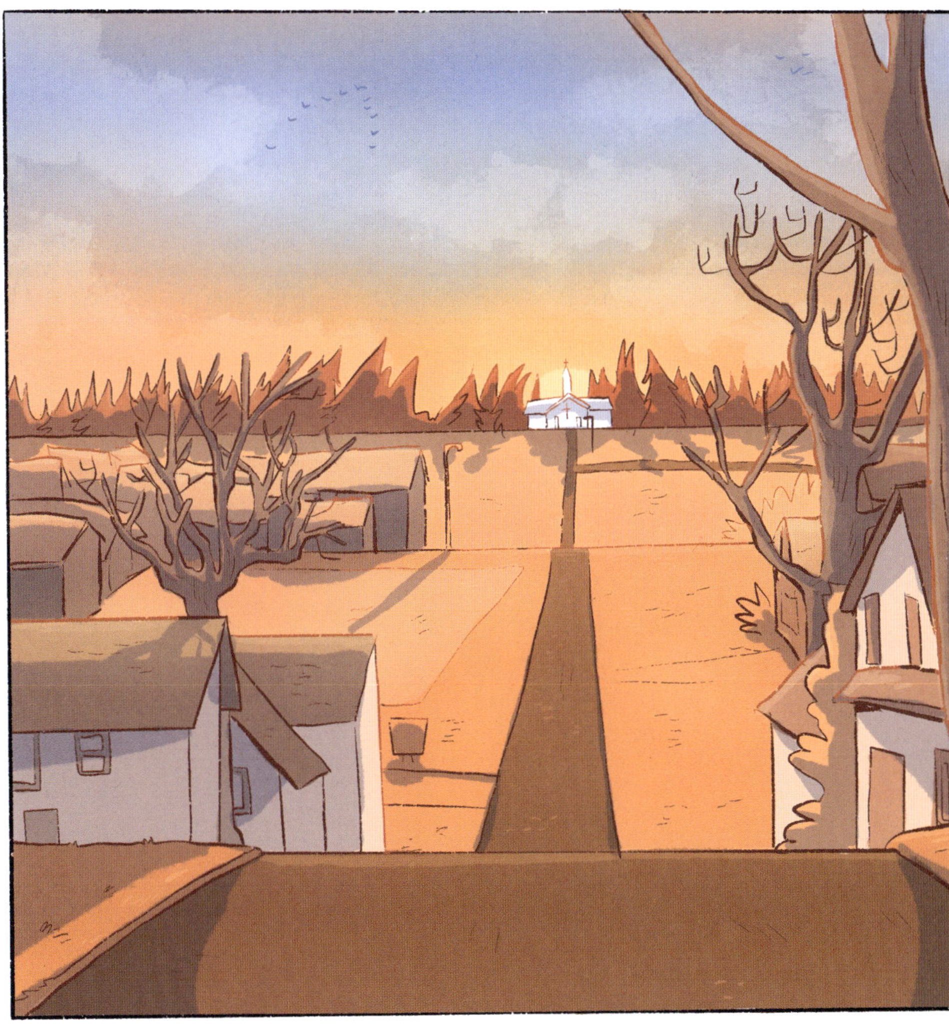

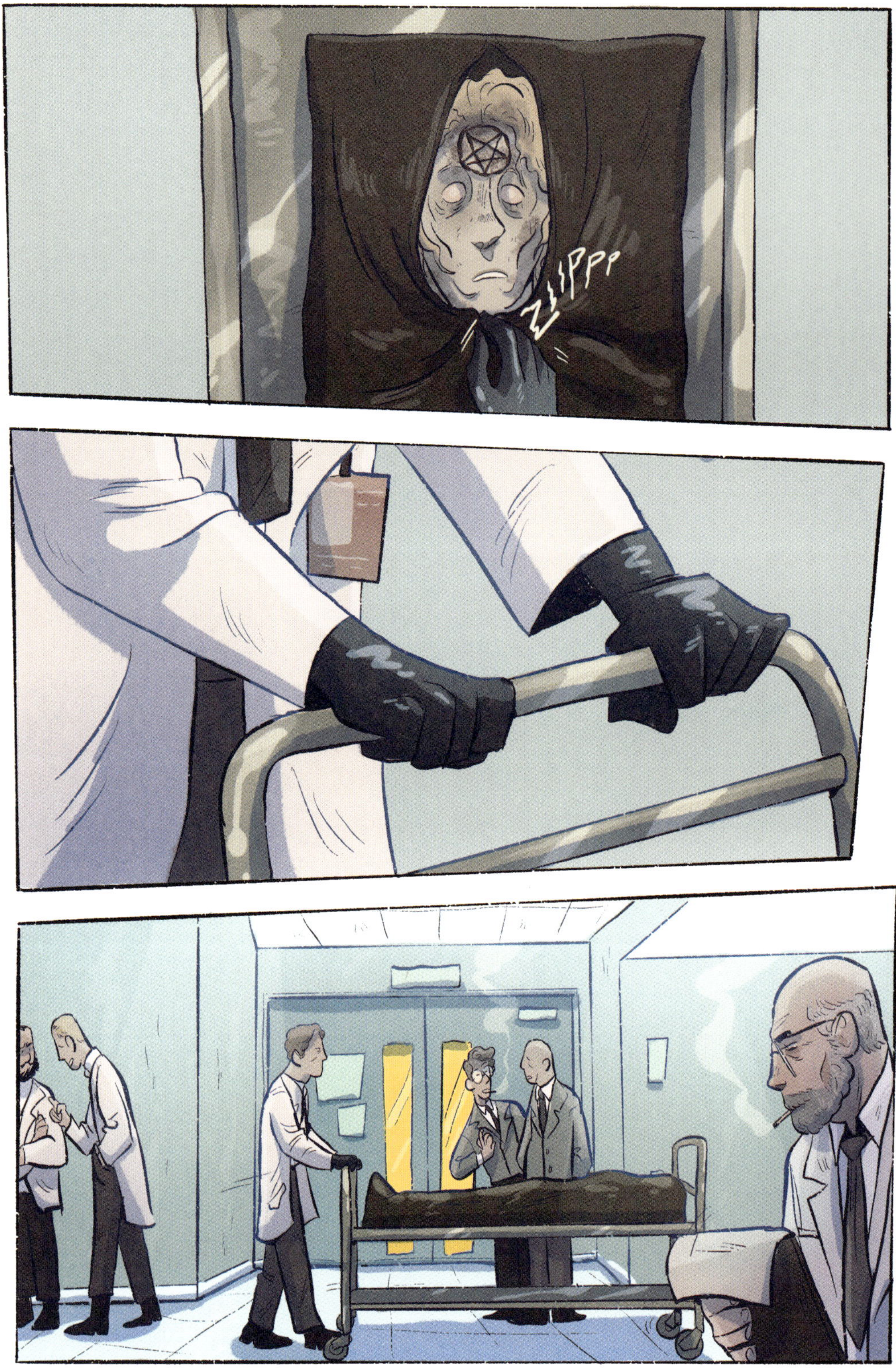
ZIIPPP

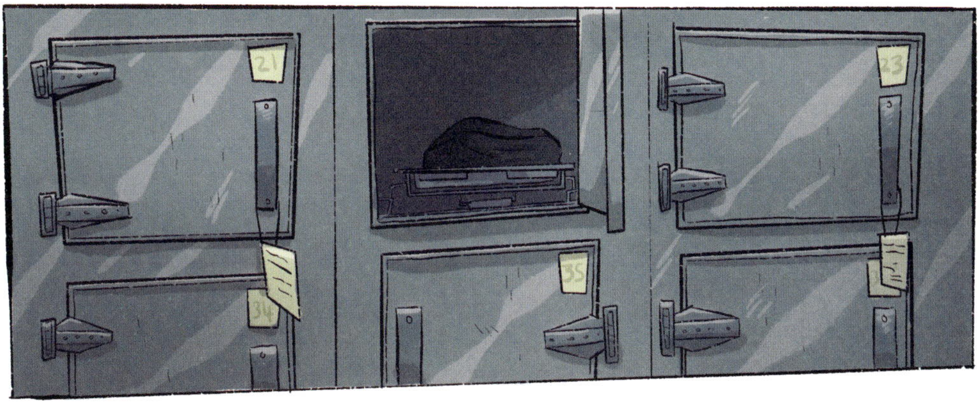

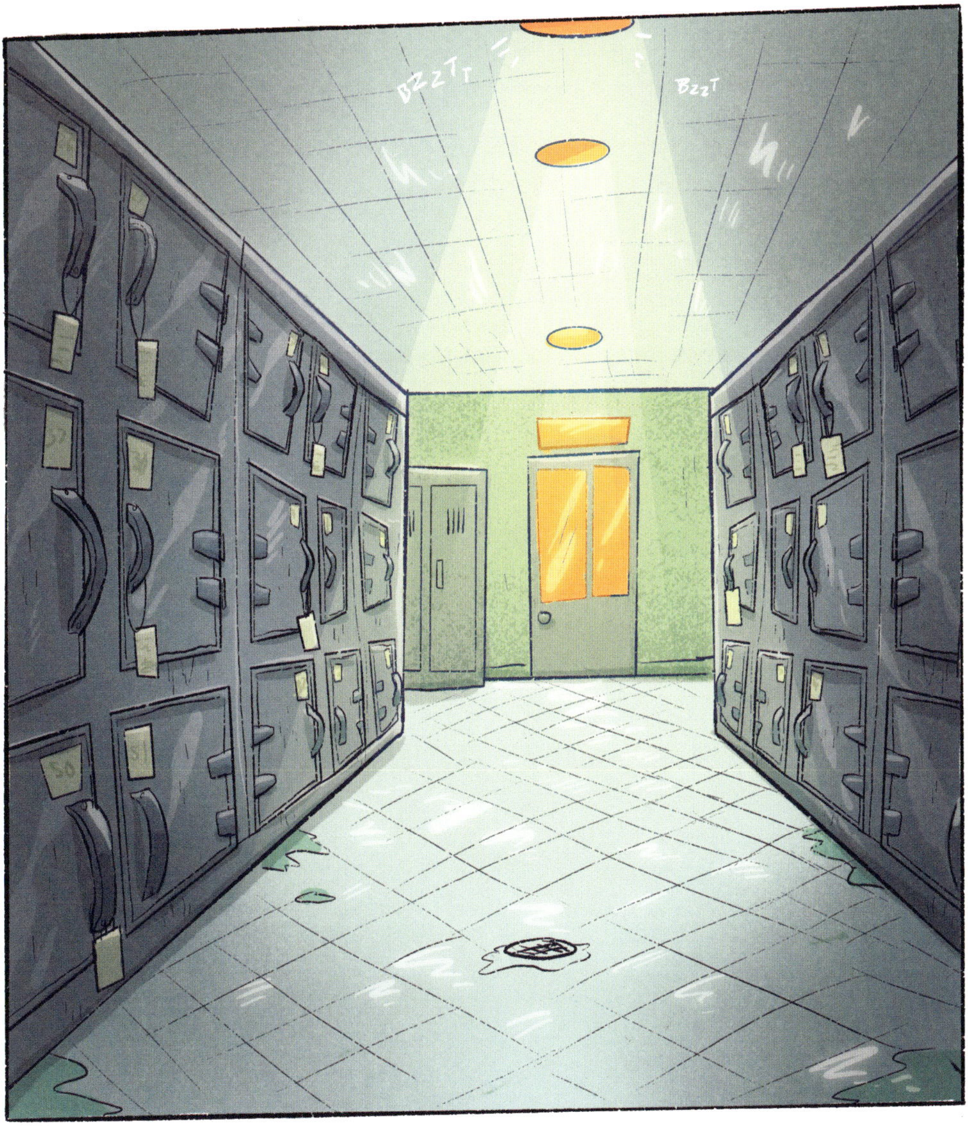
BZZTT
BZZT

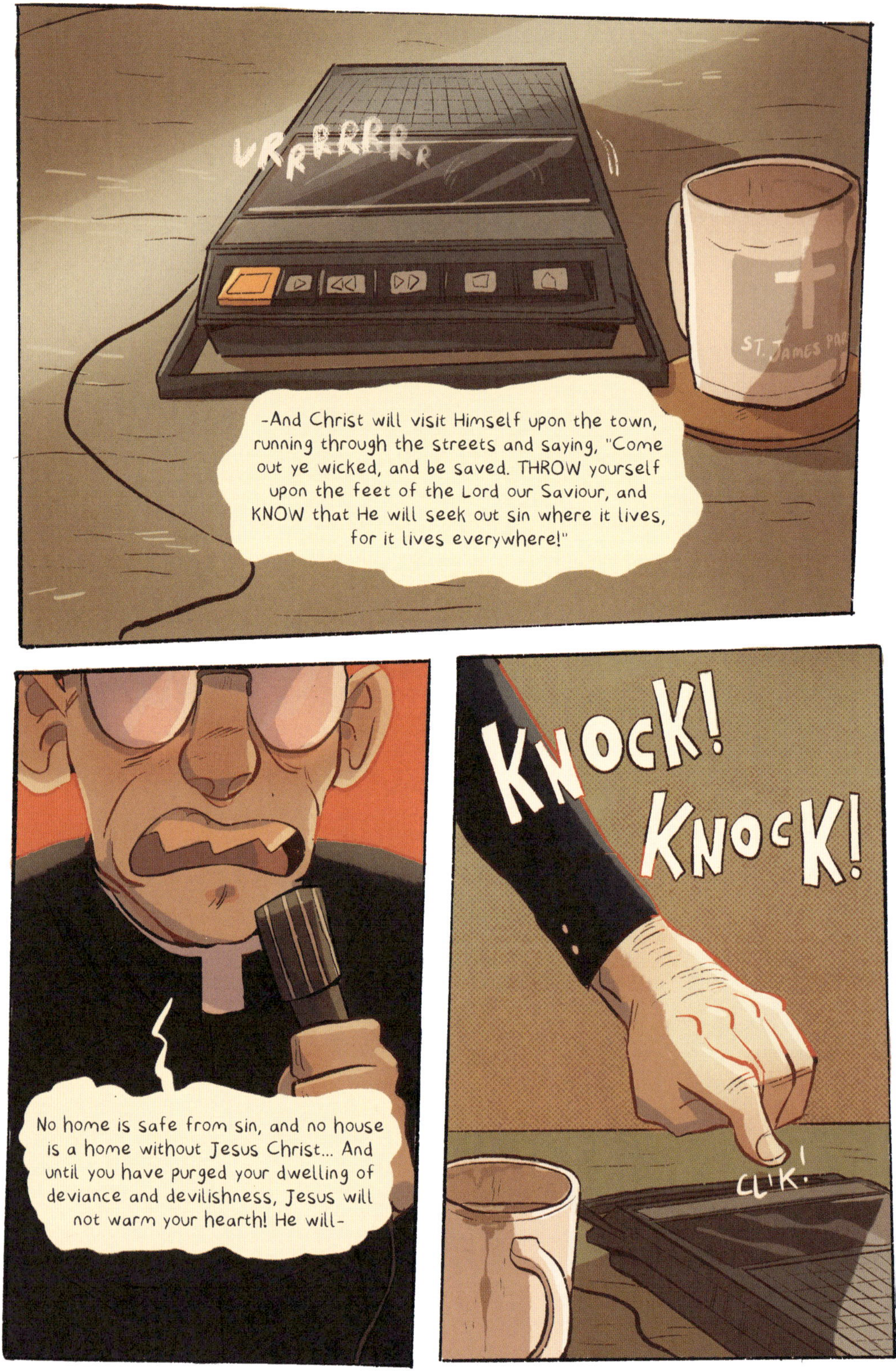
URRRRRRR
ST. JAMES PAR
-And Christ will visit Himself upon the town, running through the streets and saying, "Come out ye wicked, and be saved. THROW yourself upon the feet of the Lord our Saviour, and KNOW that He will seek out sin where it lives, for it lives everywhere!"
No home is safe from sin, and no house is a home without Jesus Christ... And until you have purged your dwelling of deviance and devilishness, Jesus will not warm your hearth! He will-
KNOCK! KNOCK!
CLIK!

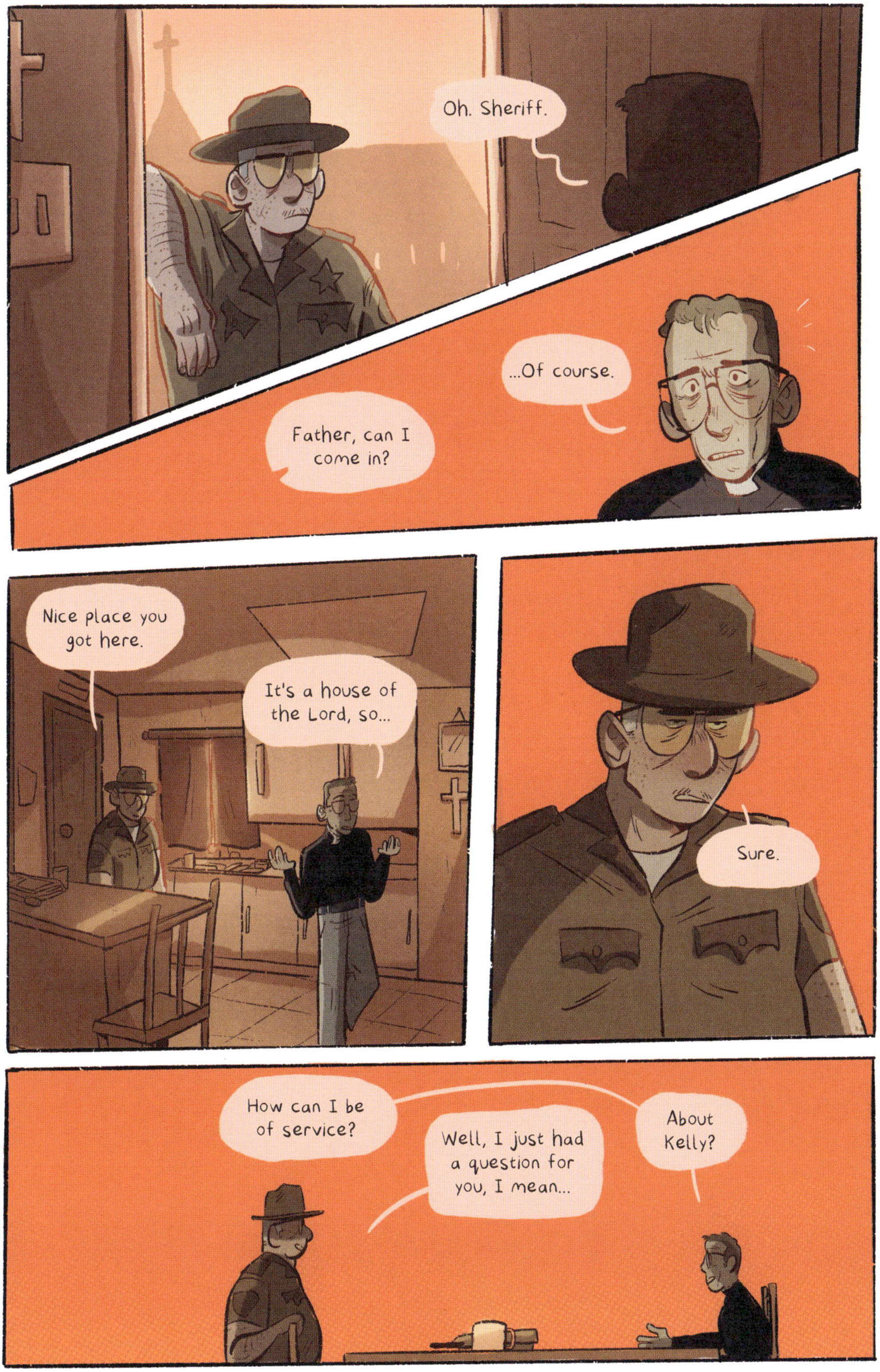
Oh. Sheriff.
Father, can I come in?
...Of course.
Nice place you got here.
It's a house of the Lord, so...
Sure.
How can I be of service?
Well, I just had a question for you, I mean...
About Kelly?

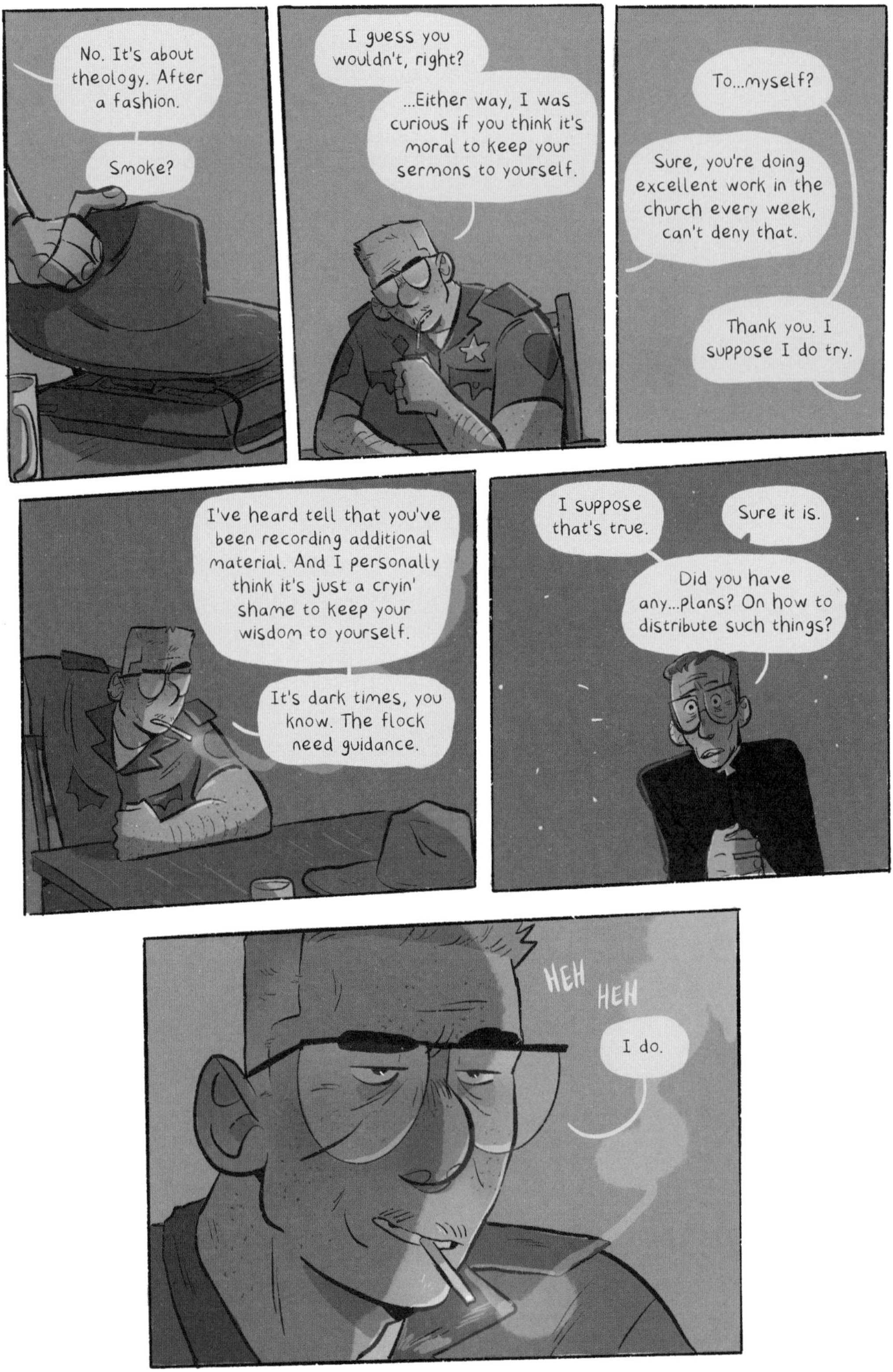
No. It's about theology. After a fashion.
Smoke?
I guess you wouldn't, right?
...Either way, I was curious if you think it's moral to keep your sermons to yourself.
To...myself?
Sure, you're doing excellent work in the church every week, can't deny that.
Thank you. I suppose I do try.
I've heard tell that you've been recording additional material. And I personally think it's just a cryin' shame to keep your wisdom to yourself.
It's dark times, you know. The flock need guidance.
I suppose that's true.
Sure it is.
Did you have any...plans? On how to distribute such things?
HEH
HEH
I do.

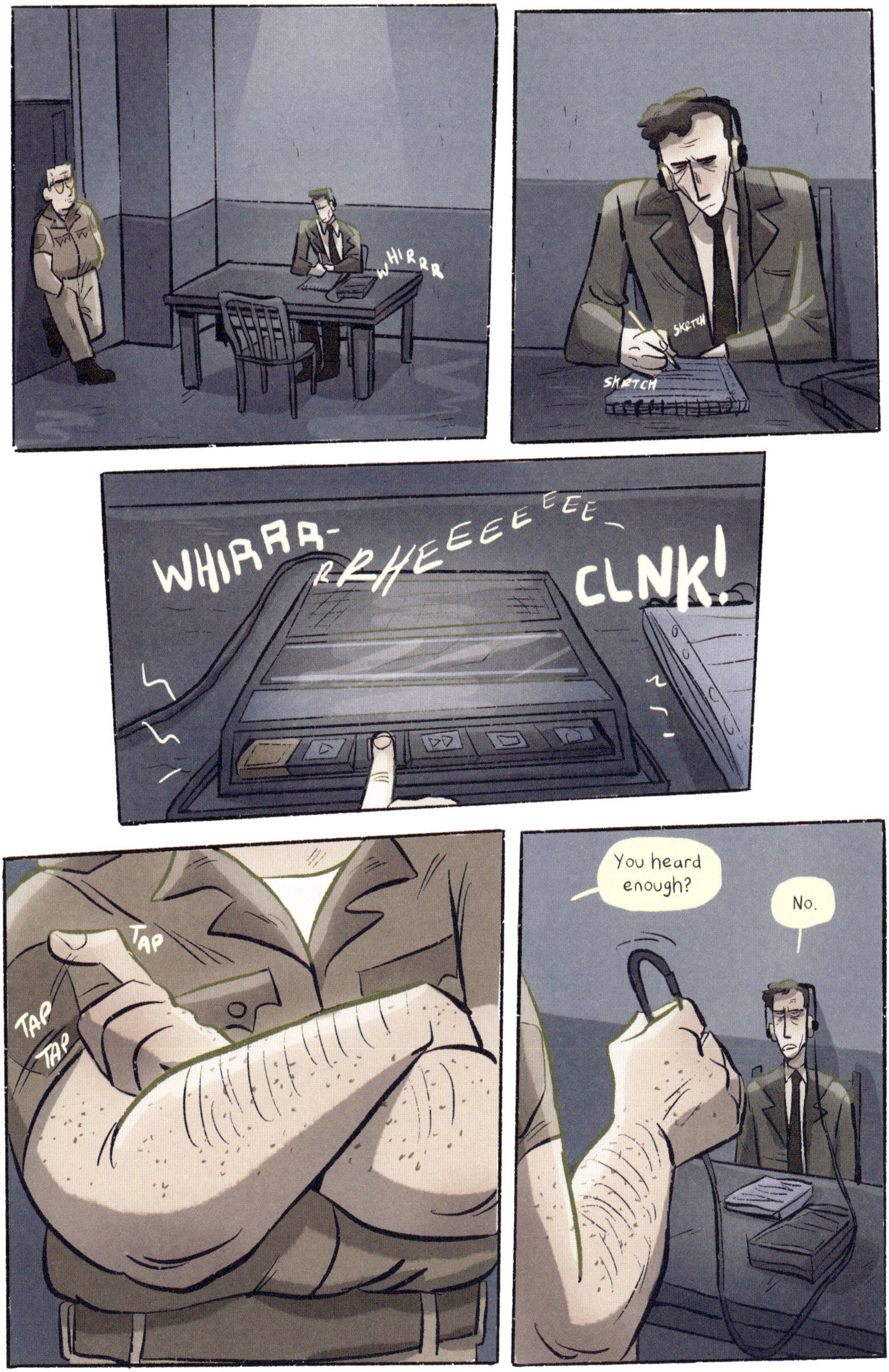
WHIRRR
SKETCH
SKRTCH
WHIRRR-RRHEEEEEEEE-
CLNK!
TAP
TAP
TAP
You heard enough?
No.

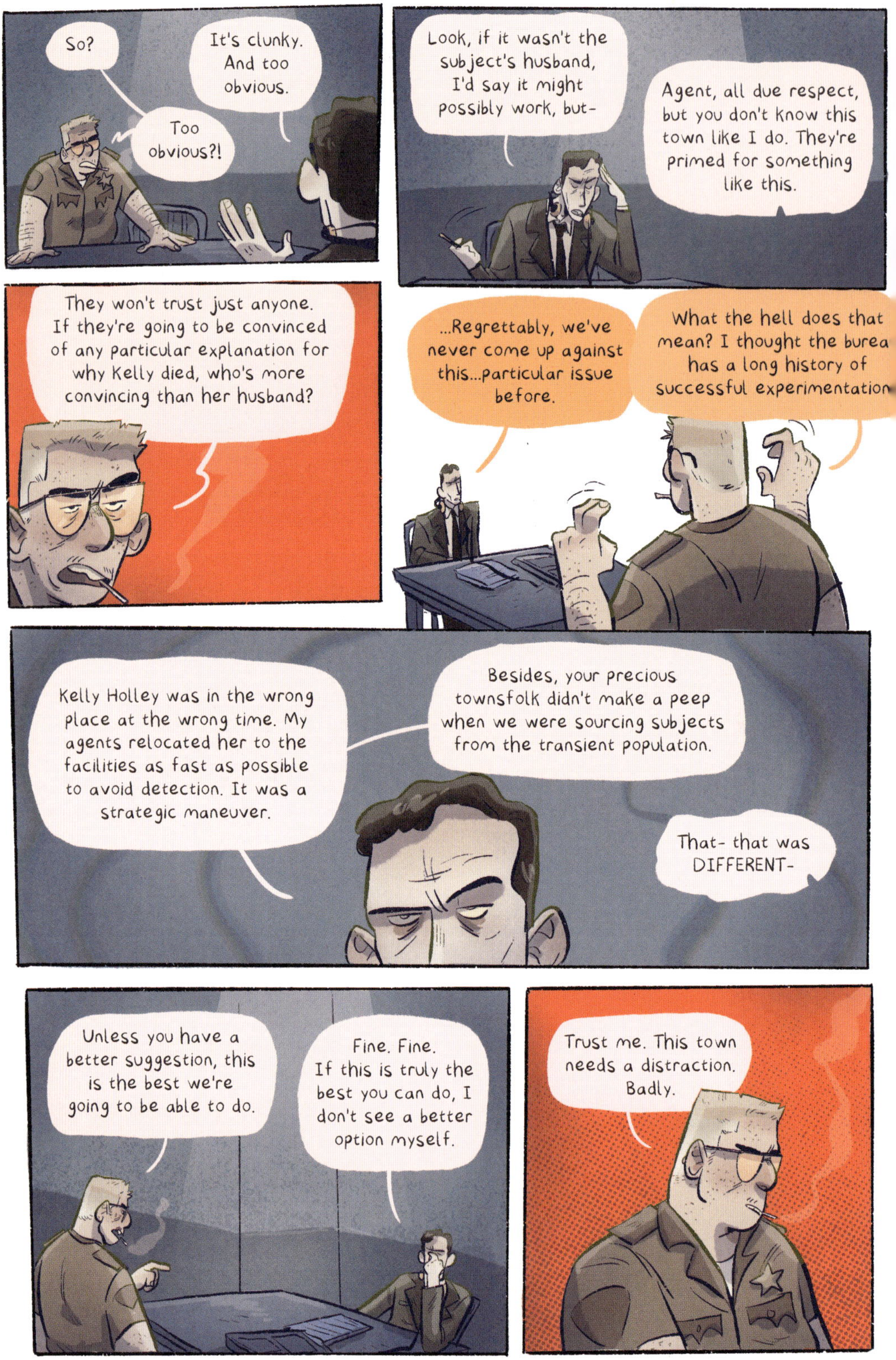
So?
It's clunky. And too obvious.
Too obvious?!
Look, if it wasn't the subject's husband, I'd say it might possibly work, but-
Agent, all due respect, but you don't know this town like I do. They're primed for something like this.
They won't trust just anyone. If they're going to be convinced of any particular explanation for why Kelly died, who's more convincing than her husband?
...Regrettably, we've never come up against this...particular issue before.
What the hell does that mean? I thought the burea has a long history of successful experimentation
Kelly Holley was in the wrong place at the wrong time. My agents relocated her to the facilities as fast as possible to avoid detection. It was a strategic maneuver.
Besides, your precious townsfolk didn't make a peep when we were sourcing subjects from the transient population.
That- that was DIFFERENT-
Unless you have a better suggestion, this is the best we're going to be able to do.
Fine. Fine. If this is truly the best you can do, I don't see a better option myself.
Trust me. This town needs a distraction. Badly.

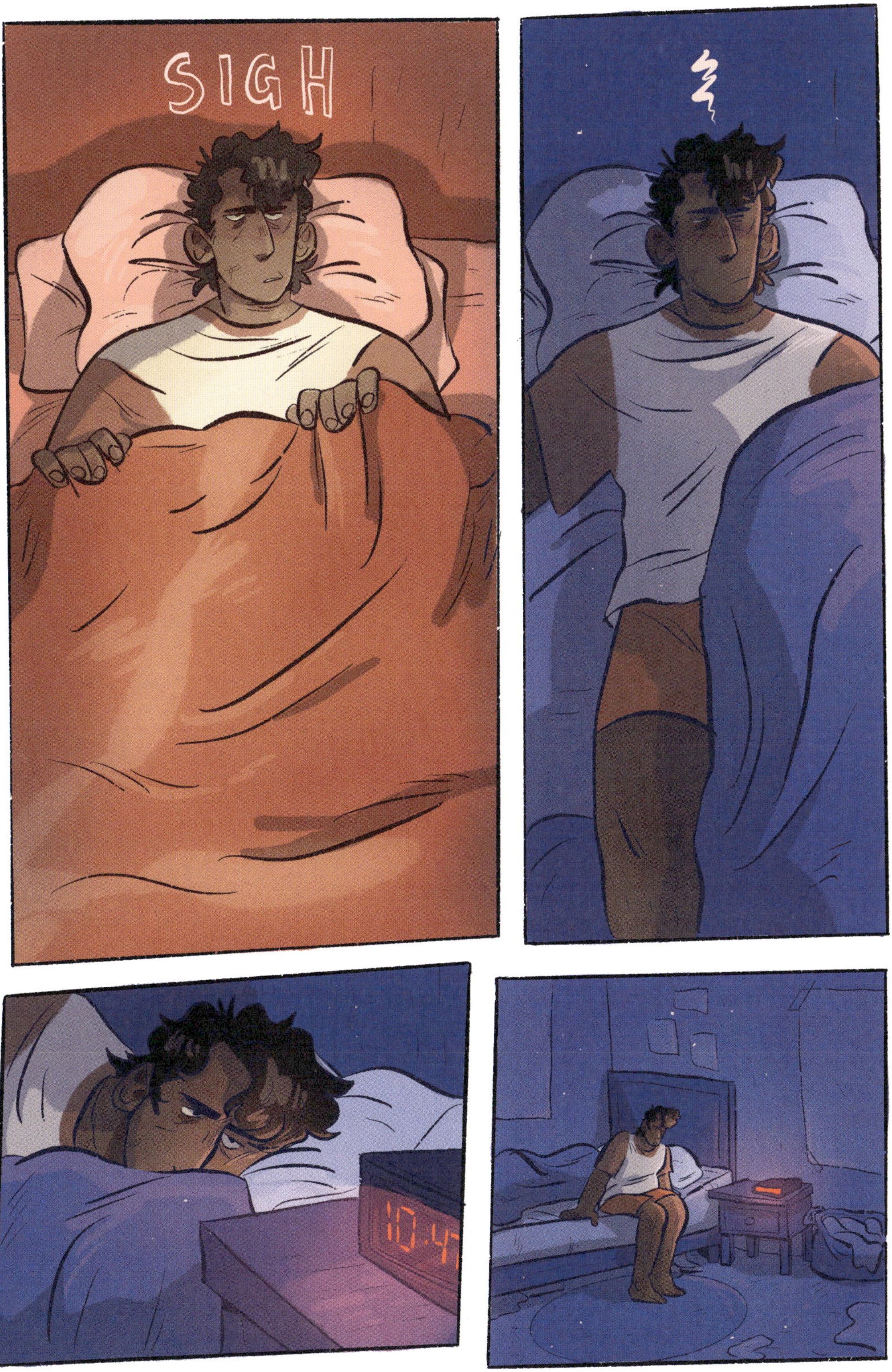
SIGH

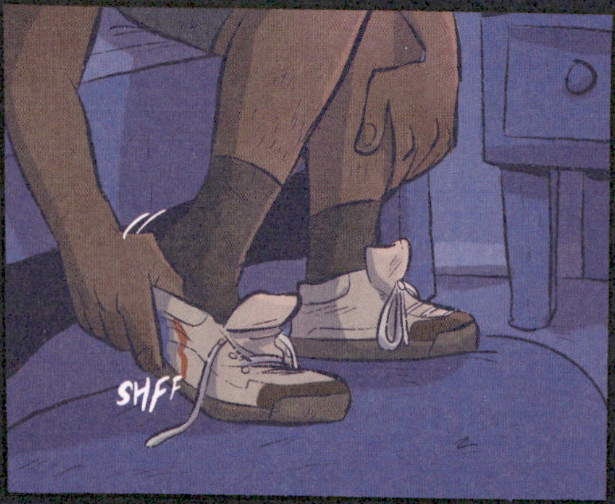
SHFF

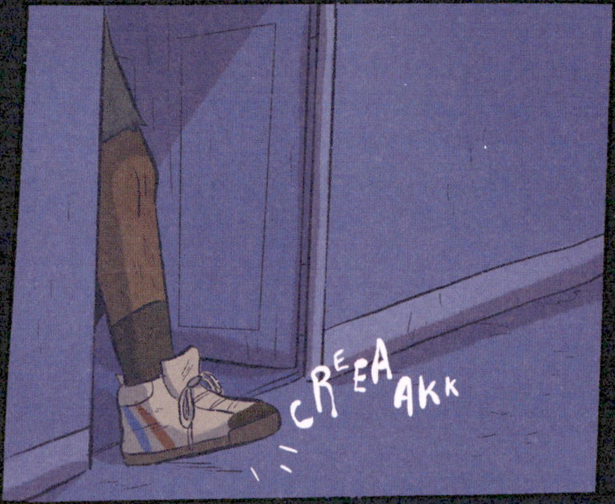
CREEAAKK

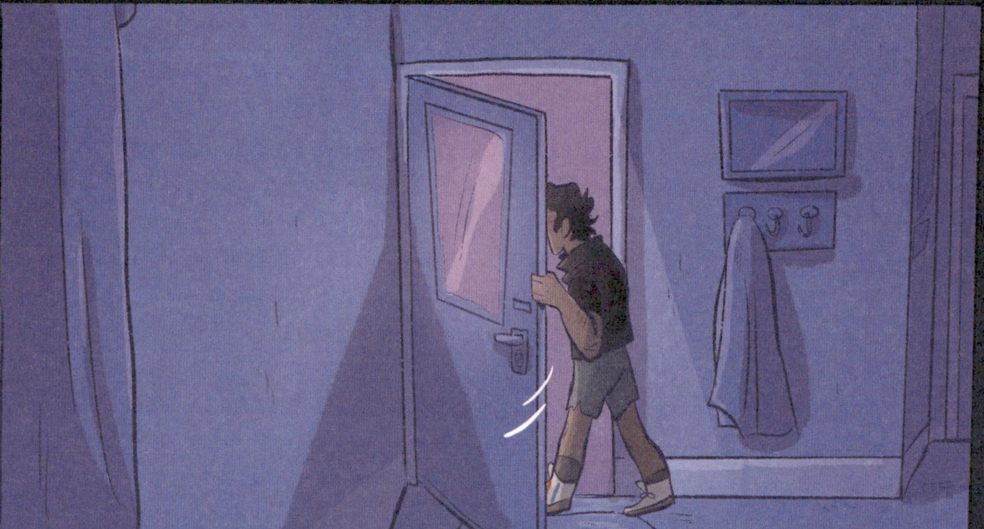

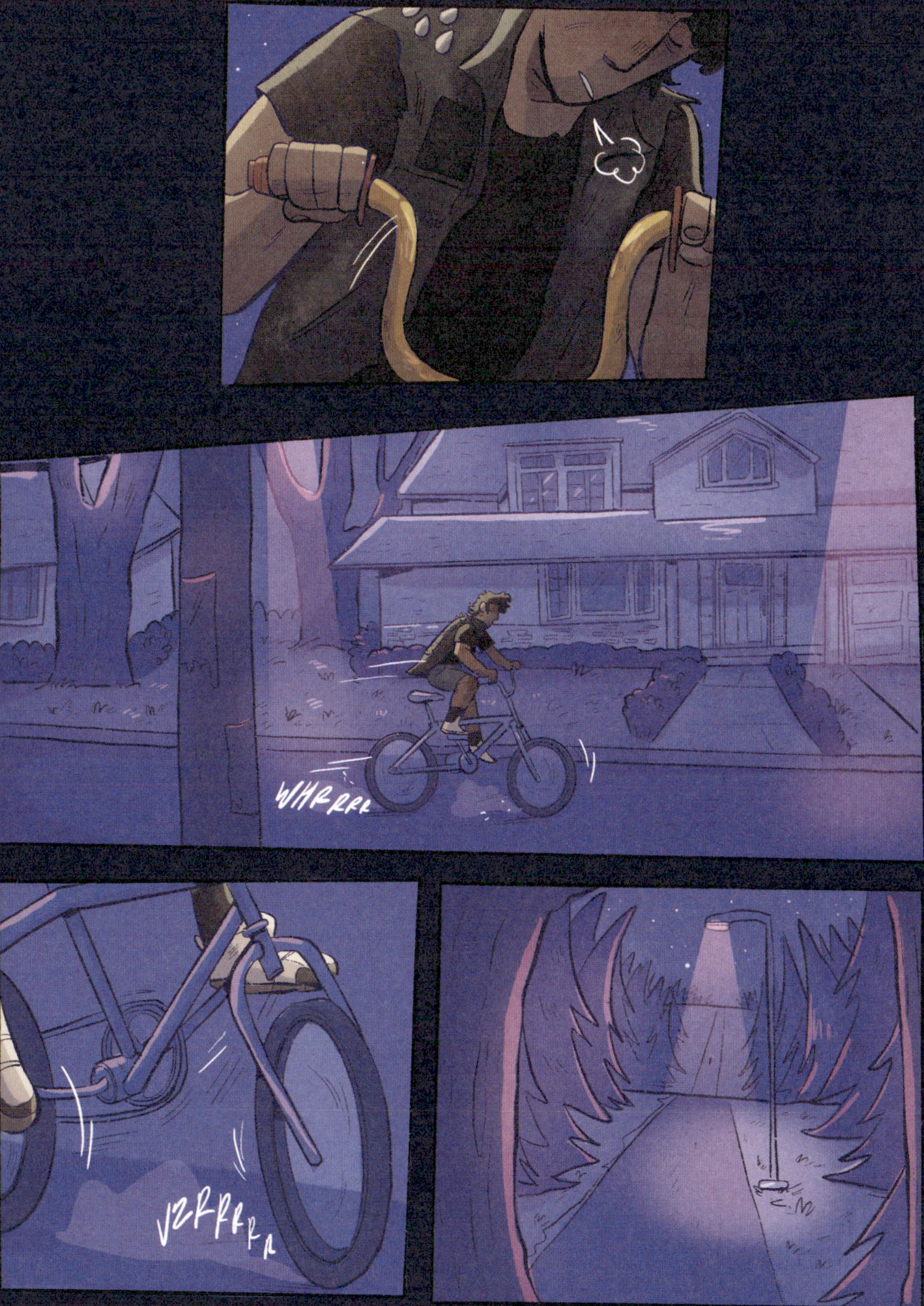
WHRrrr
VZRRRRrr

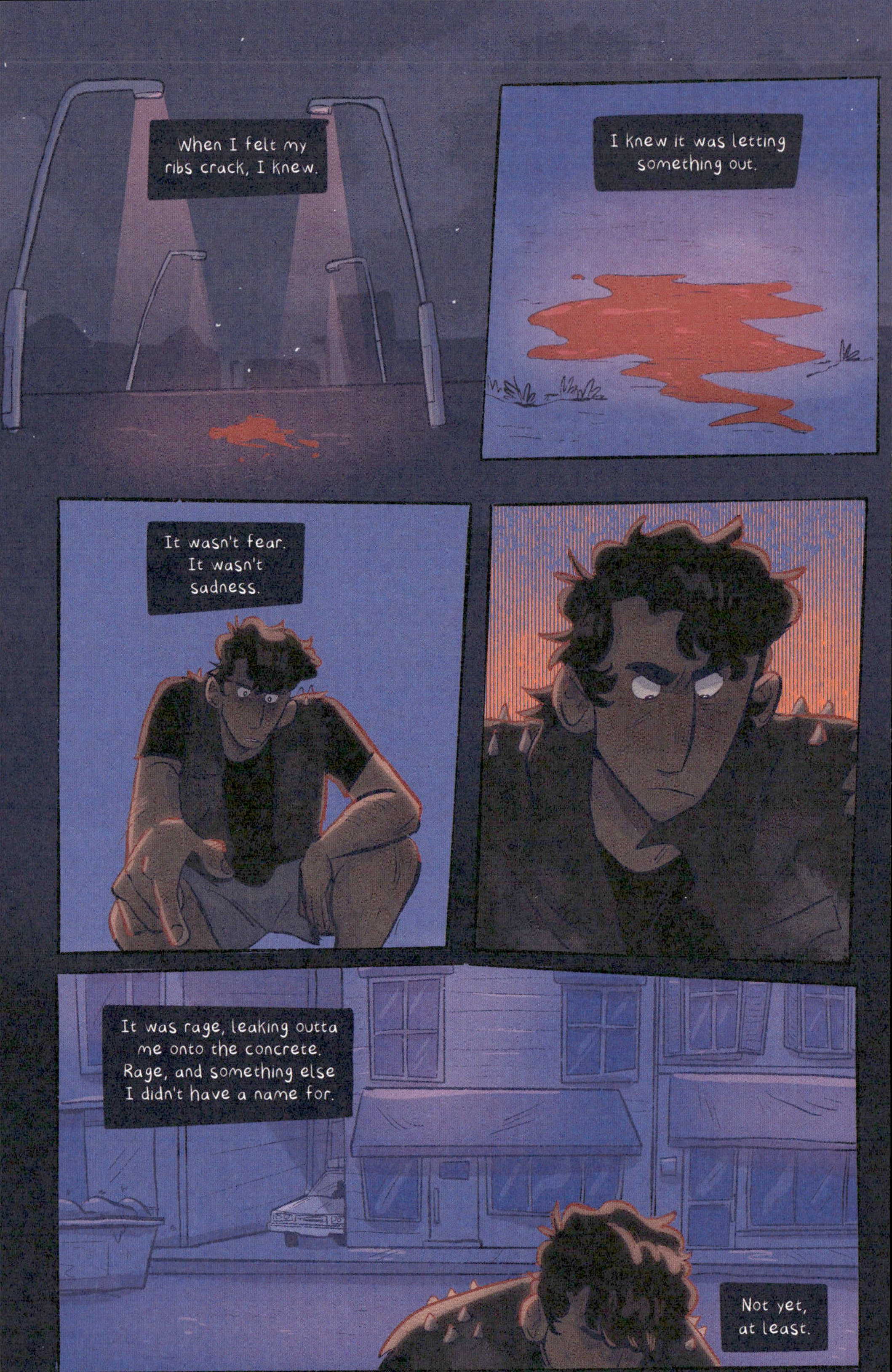
When I felt my ribs crack, I knew.
I knew it was letting something out.
It wasn't fear. It wasn't sadness.
It was rage, leaking outta me onto the concrete. Rage, and something else I didn't have a name for.
Not yet, at least.

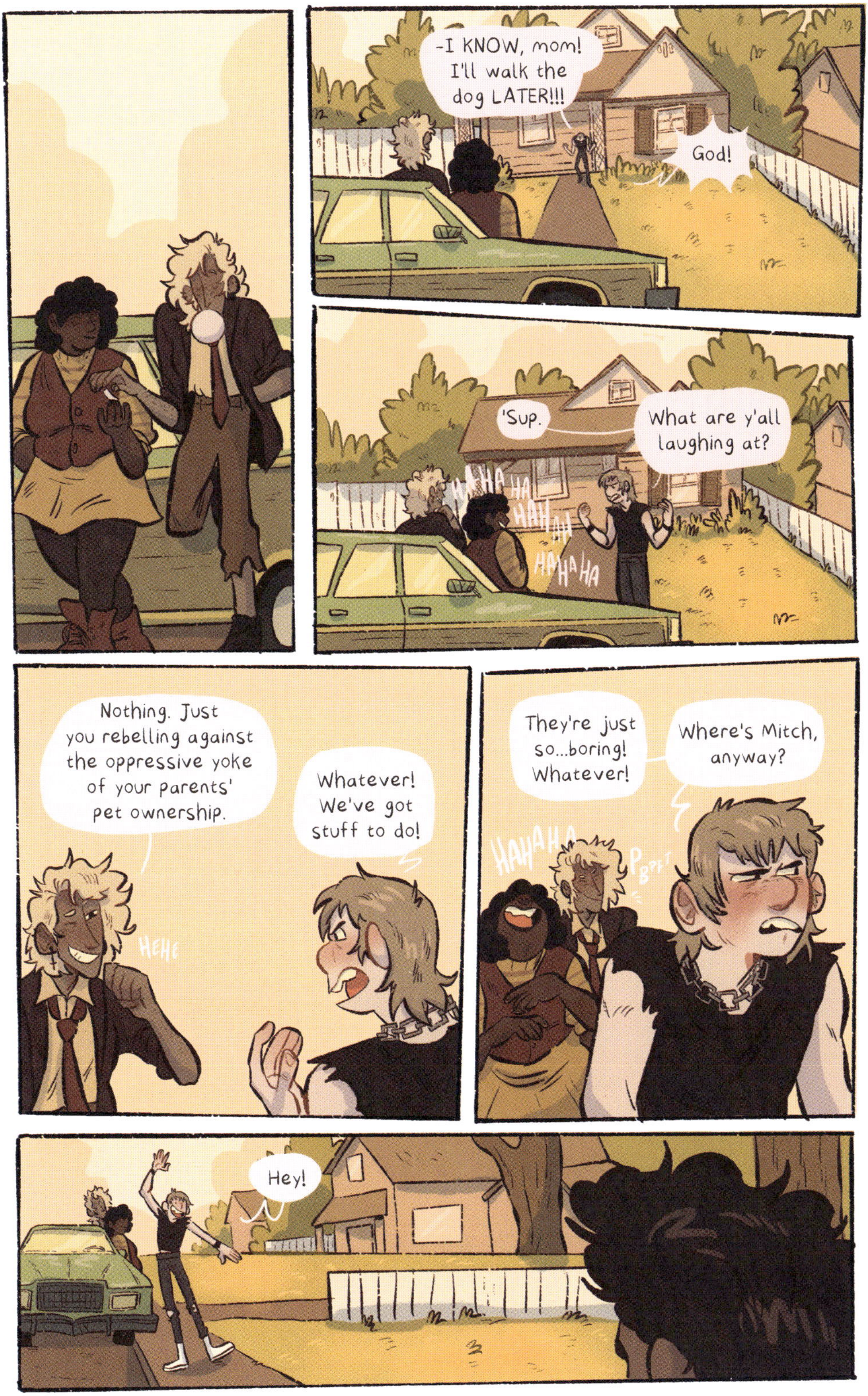
-I KNOW, mom! I'll walk the dog LATER!!!
God!
'Sup.
What are y'all laughing at?
HAHAHA HA HAHAHA HAHAHA
Nothing. Just you rebelling against the oppressive yoke of your parents' pet ownership.
HEHE
Whatever! We've got stuff to do!
They're just so...boring! Whatever!
Where's Mitch, anyway?
HAHAHA
PBPFT
Hey!

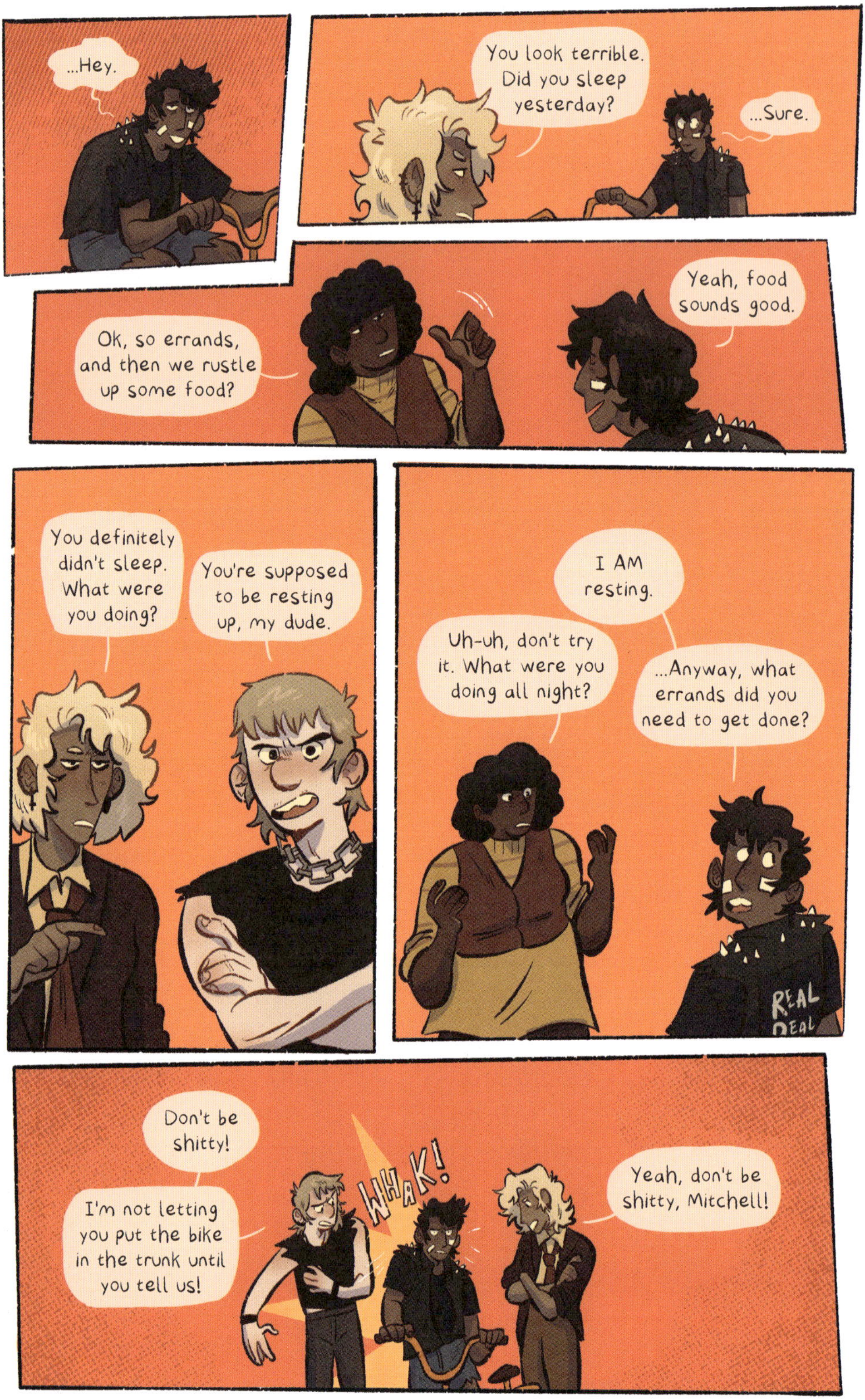
...Hey.
You look terrible. Did you sleep yesterday?
...Sure.
Ok, so errands, and then we rustle up some food?
Yeah, food sounds good.
You definitely didn't sleep. What were you doing?
You're supposed to be resting up, my dude.
I AM resting.
Uh-uh, don't try it. What were you doing all night?
...Anyway, what errands did you need to get done?
REAL DEAL
Don't be shitty!
I'm not letting you put the bike in the trunk until you tell us!
WHAK!
Yeah, don't be shitty, Mitchell!

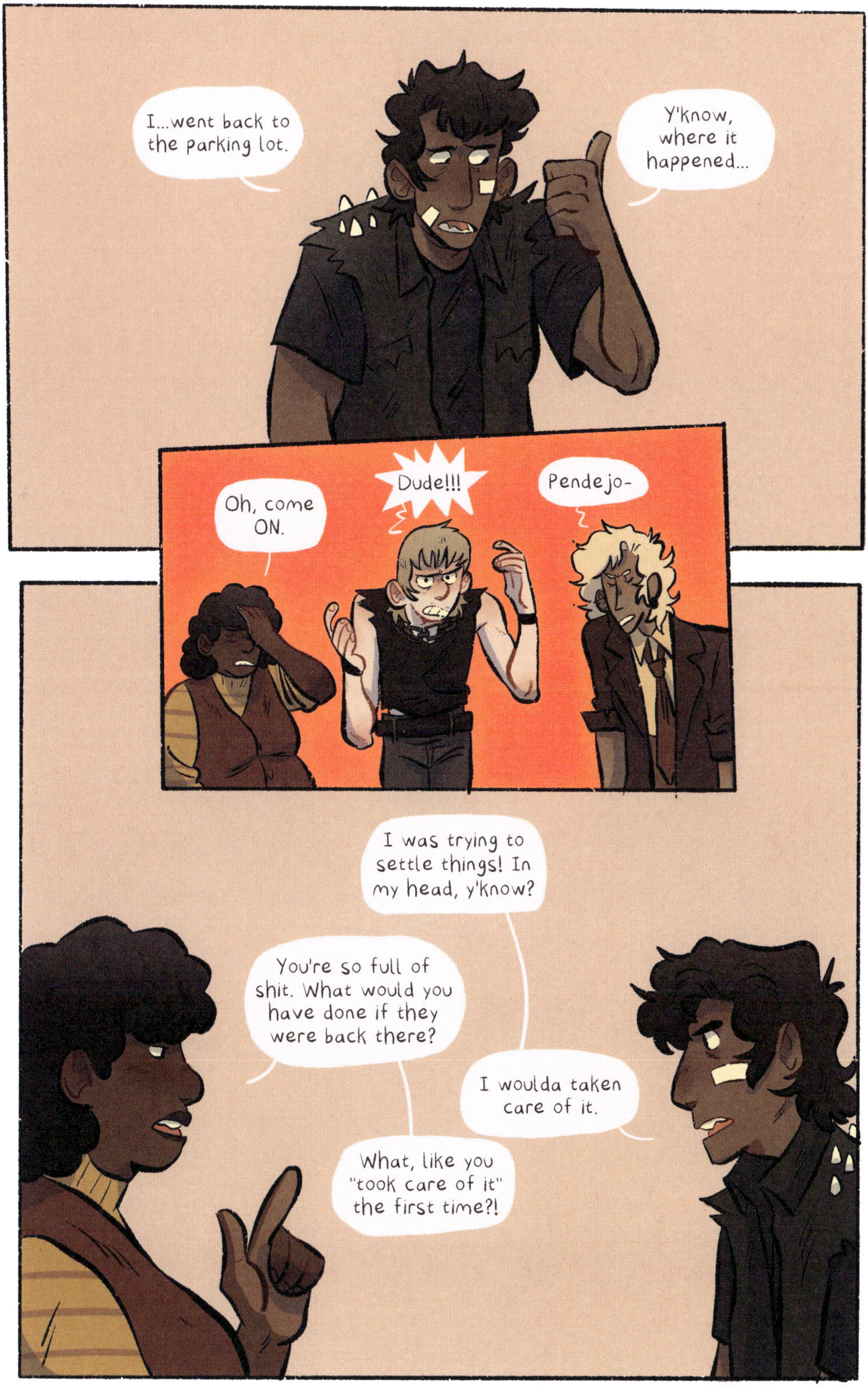
I...went back to the parking lot.
Y'know, where it happened...
Oh, come ON.
Dude!!!
Pendejo-
I was trying to settle things! In my head, y'know?
You're so full of shit. What would you have done if they were back there?
I woulda taken care of it.
What, like you "took care of it" the first time?!

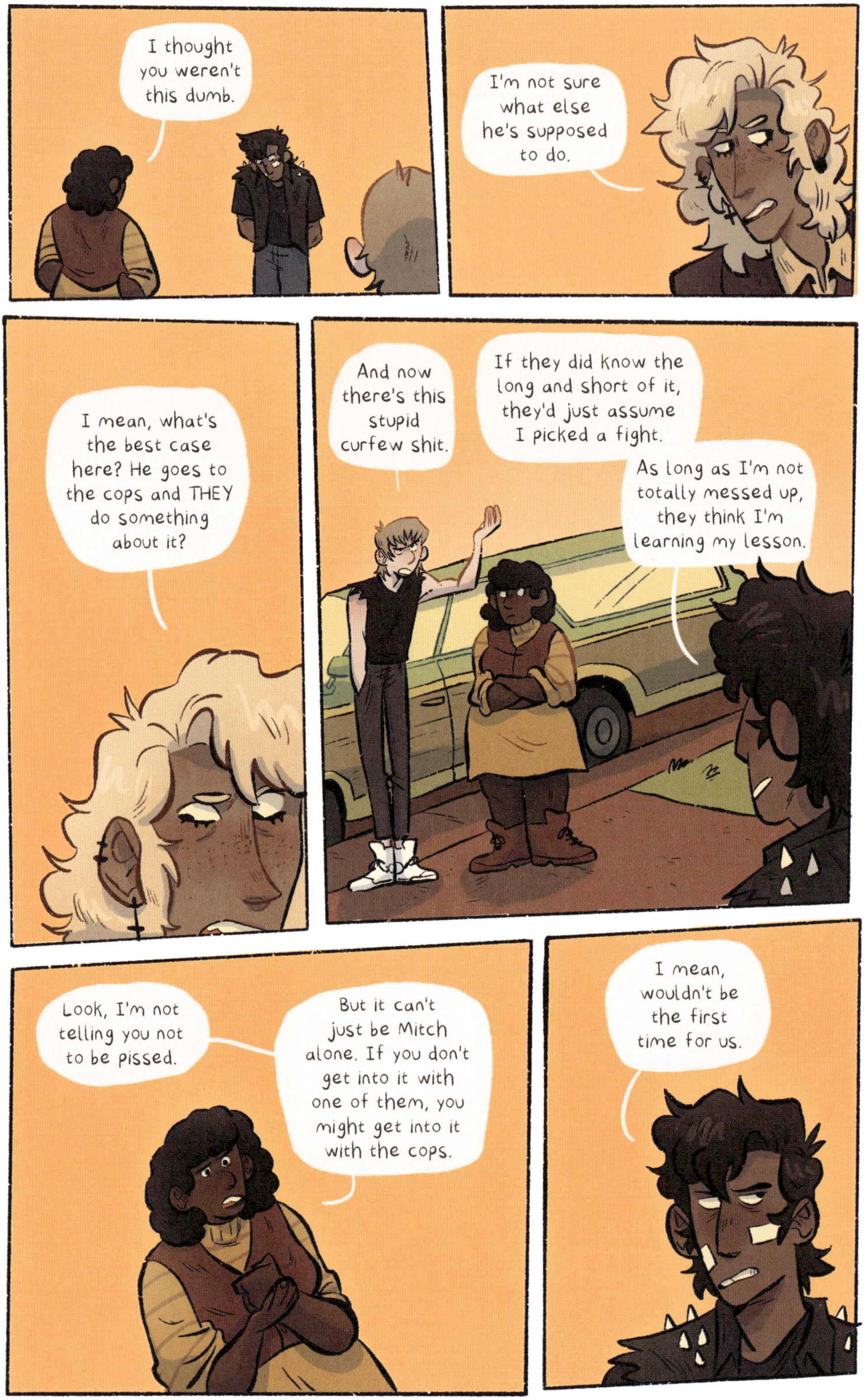
I thought you weren't this dumb.
I'm not sure what else he's supposed to do.
I mean, what's the best case here? He goes to the cops and THEY do something about it?
And now there's this stupid curfew shit.
If they did know the long and short of it, they'd just assume I picked a fight.
As long as I'm not totally messed up, they think I'm learning my lesson.
Look, I'm not telling you not to be pissed.
But it can't just be Mitch alone. If you don't get into it with one of them, you might get into it with the cops.
I mean, wouldn't be the first time for us.

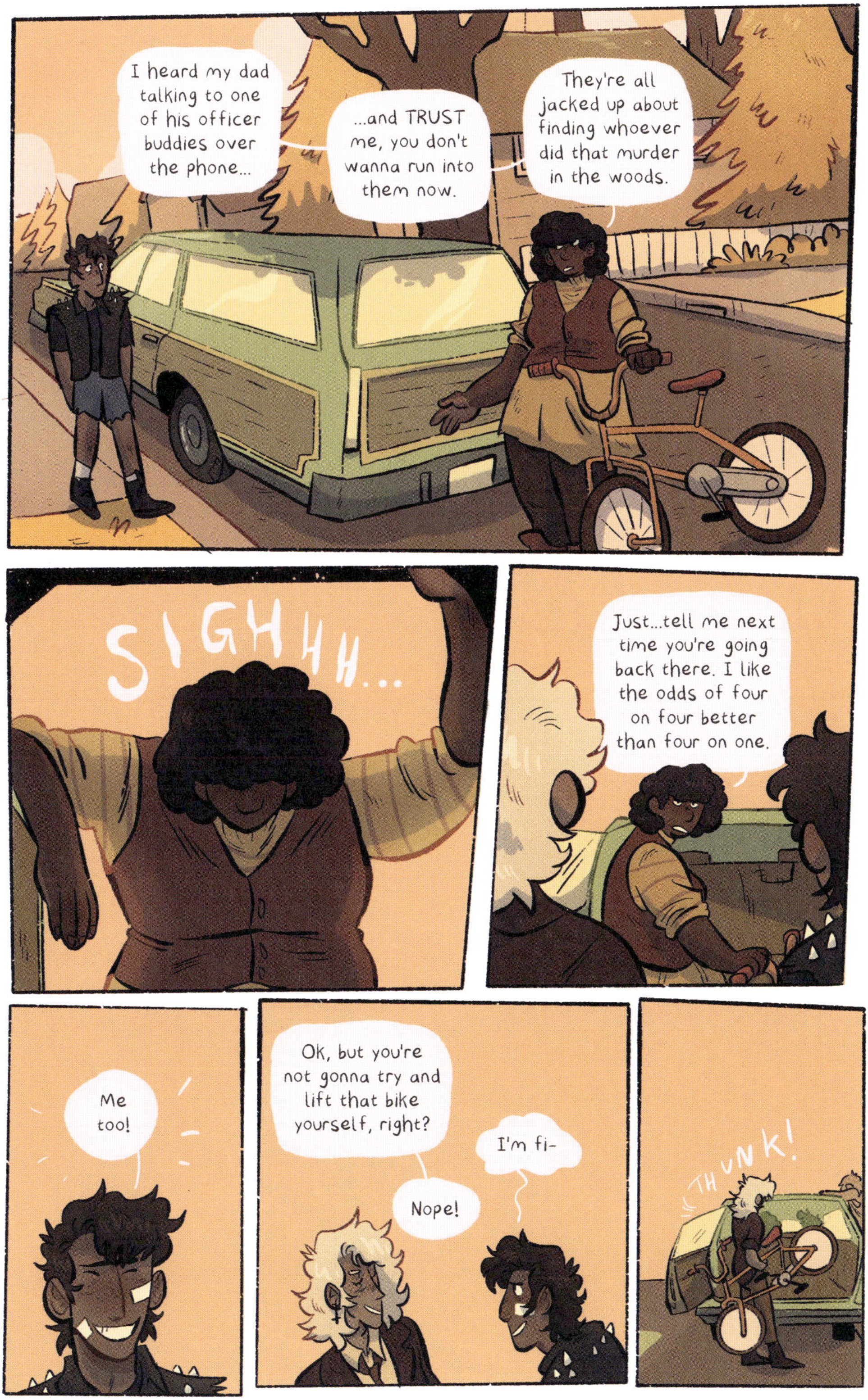
I heard my dad talking to one of his officer buddies over the phone...
...and TRUST me, you don't wanna run into them now.
They're all jacked up about finding whoever did that murder in the woods.
SIGHHH...
Just...tell me next time you're going back there. I like the odds of four on four better than four on one.
Me too!
Ok, but you're not gonna try and lift that bike yourself, right?
Nope!
I'm fi-
THUNK!

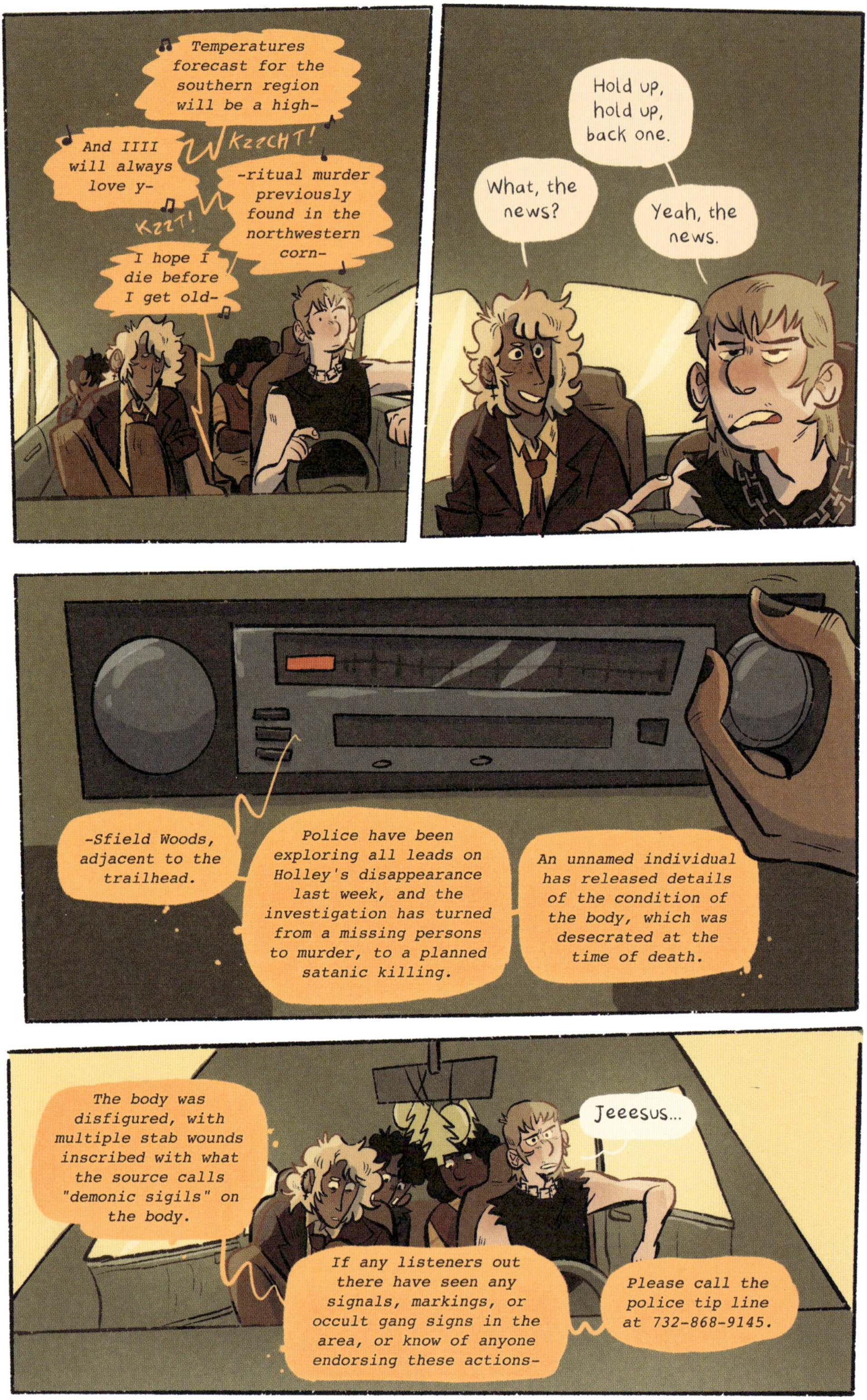
Temperatures forecast for the southern region will be a high-
KZZCHT!
And IIII will always love y-
-ritual murder previously found in the northwestern corn-
KZZT!
I hope I die before I get old-
Hold up, hold up, back one.
What, the news?
Yeah, the news.
-Sfield Woods, adjacent to the trailhead.
Police have been exploring all leads on Holley's disappearance last week, and the investigation has turned from a missing persons to murder, to a planned satanic killing.
An unnamed individual has released details of the condition of the body, which was desecrated at the time of death.
The body was disfigured, with multiple stab wounds inscribed with what the source calls "demonic sigils" on the body.
Jeeesus...
If any listeners out there have seen any signals, markings, or occult gang signs in the area, or know of anyone endorsing these actions-
Please call the police tip line at 732-868-9145.

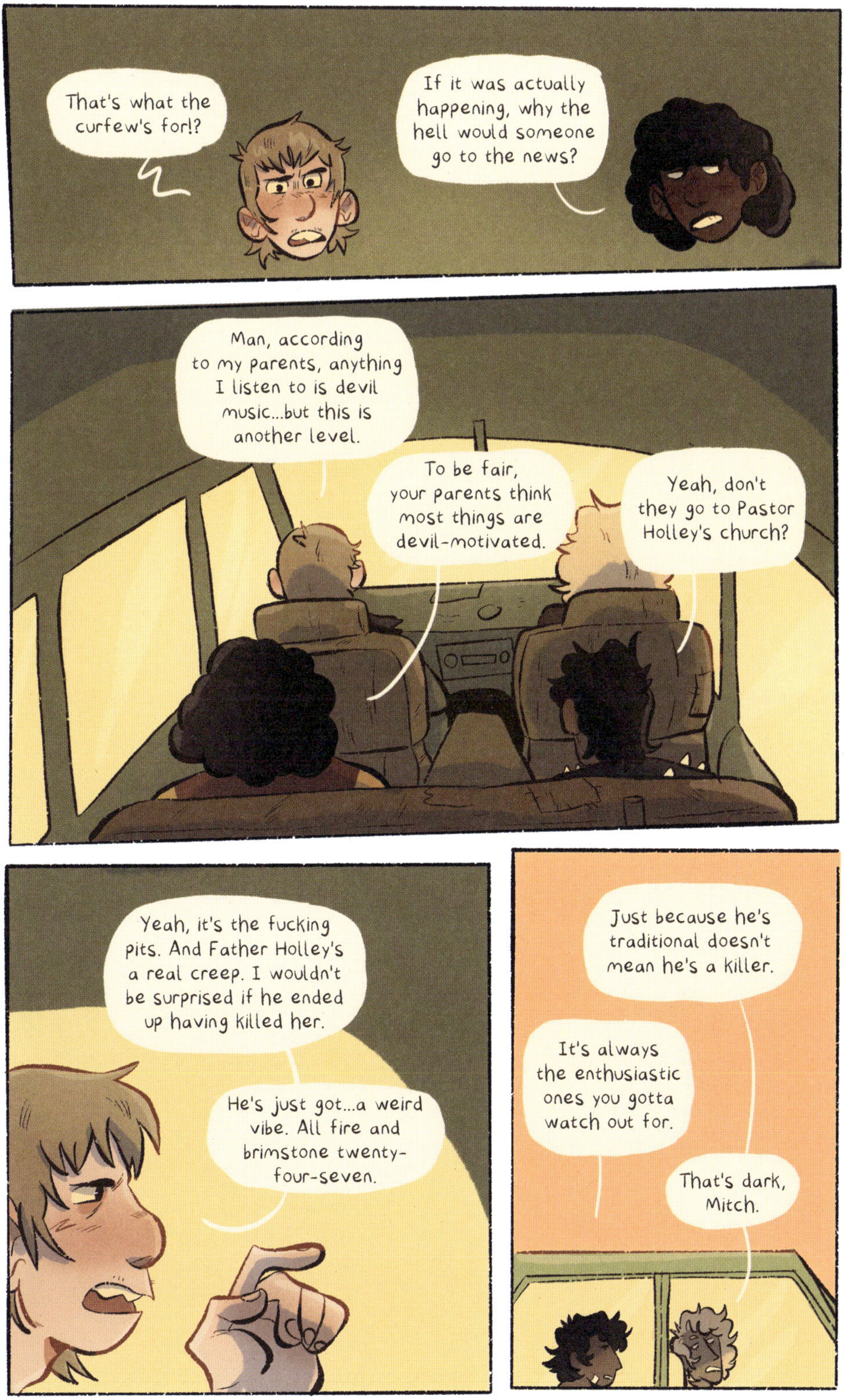
That's what the curfew's for!?
If it was actually happening, why the hell would someone go to the news?
Man, according to my parents, anything I listen to is devil music...but this is another level.
To be fair, your parents think most things are devil-motivated.
Yeah, don't they go to Pastor Holley's church?
Yeah, it's the fucking pits. And Father Holley's a real creep. I wouldn't be surprised if he ended up having killed her.
He's just got...a weird vibe. All fire and brimstone twenty-four-seven.
Just because he's traditional doesn't mean he's a killer.
It's always the enthusiastic ones you gotta watch out for.
That's dark, Mitch.

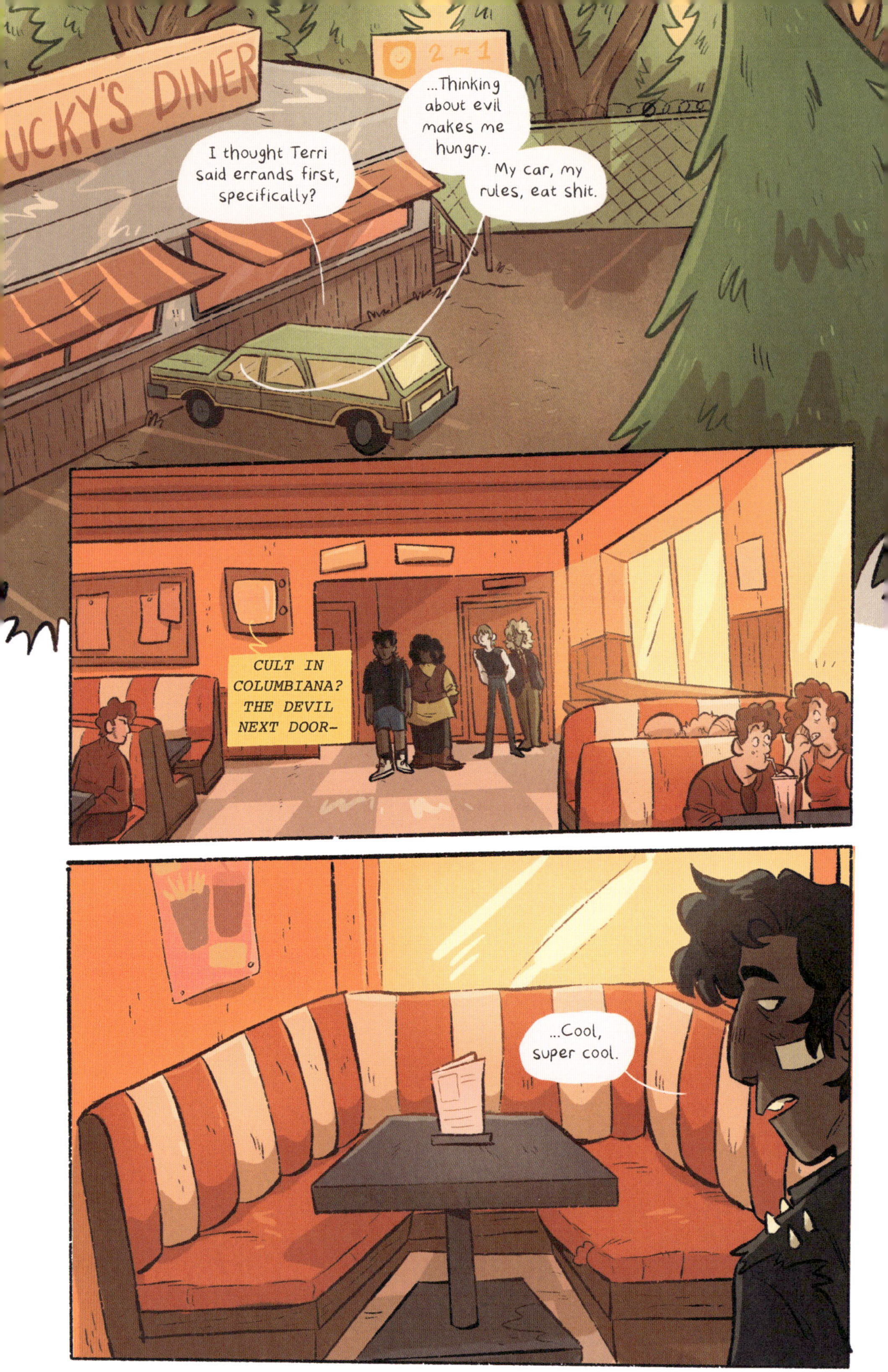
UCKY'S DINER
2 FOR 1
I thought Terri said errands first, specifically?
...Thinking about evil makes me hungry.
My car, my rules, eat shit.
CULT IN COLUMBIANA? THE DEVIL NEXT DOOR-
...Cool, super cool.

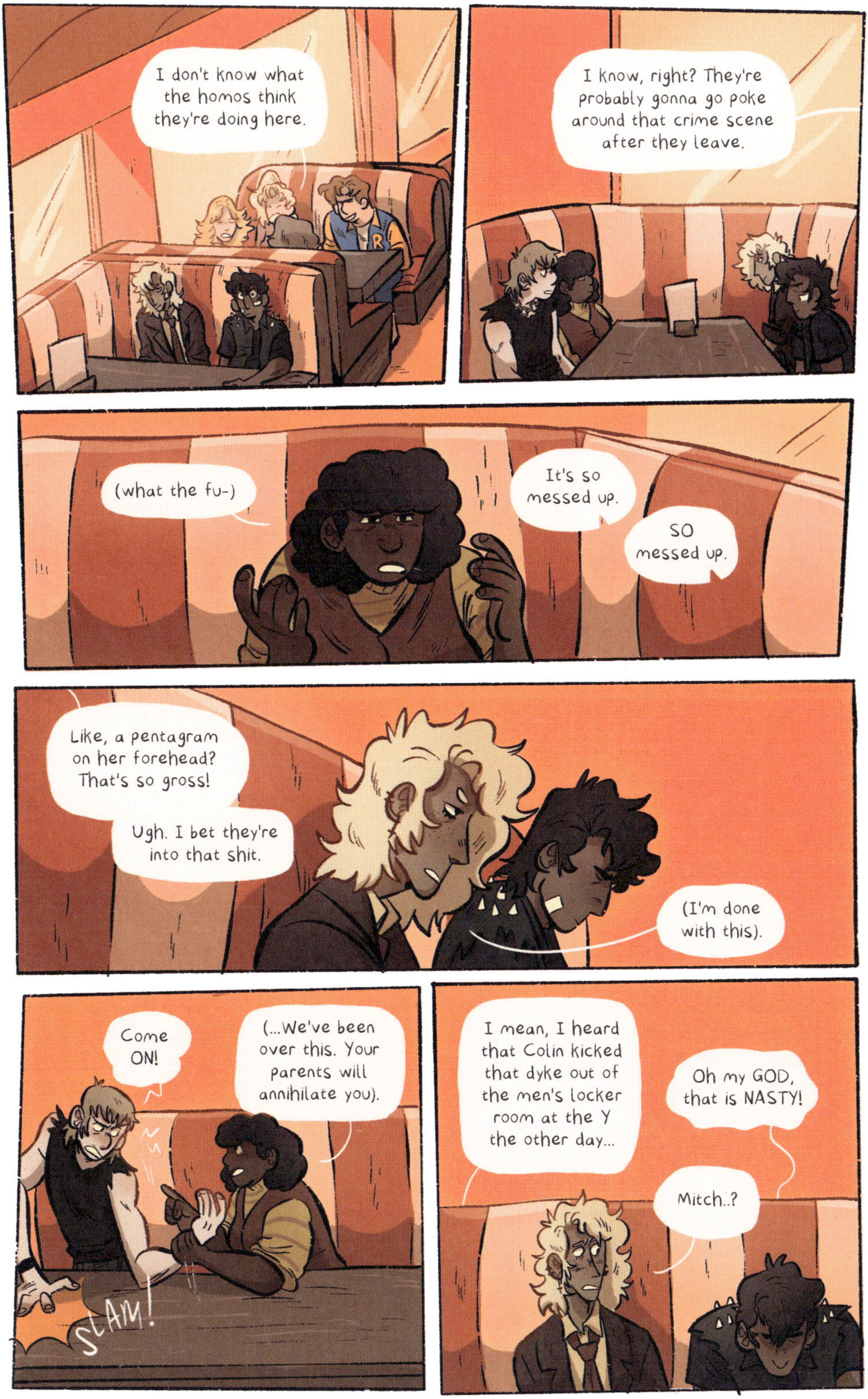
I don't know what the homos think they're doing here.
I know, right? They're probably gonna go poke around that crime scene after they leave.
(what the fu-)
It's so messed up.
SO messed up.
Like, a pentagram on her forehead? That's so gross!
Ugh. I bet they're into that shit.
(I'm done with this).
Come ON!
SLAM!
(...We've been over this. Your parents will annihilate you).
I mean, I heard that Colin kicked that dyke out of the men's locker room at the Y the other day...
Oh my GOD, that is NASTY!
Mitch..?

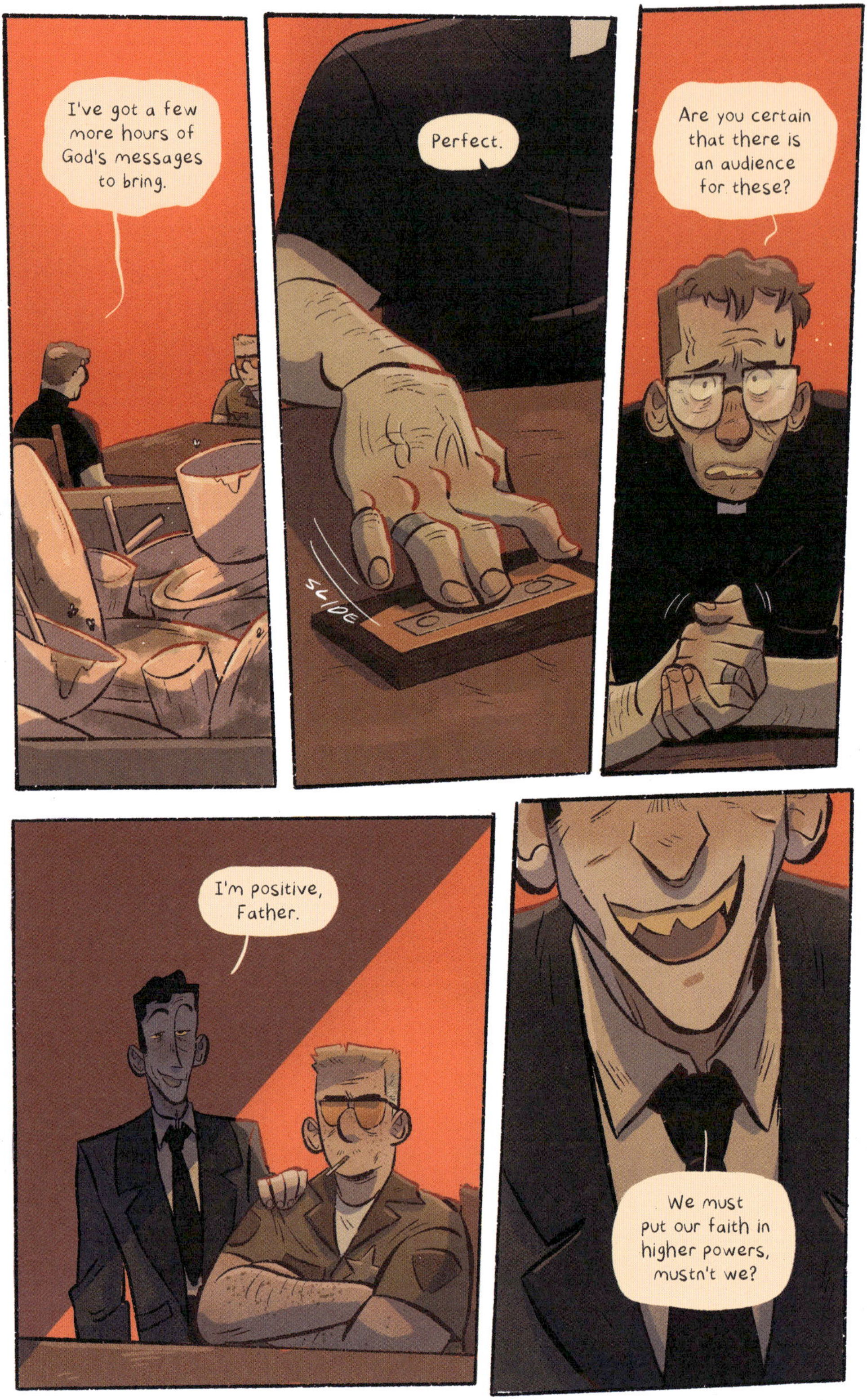
I've got a few more hours of God's messages to bring.
Perfect.
SLIDE
Are you certain that there is an audience for these?
I'm positive, Father.
We must put our faith in higher powers, mustn't we?

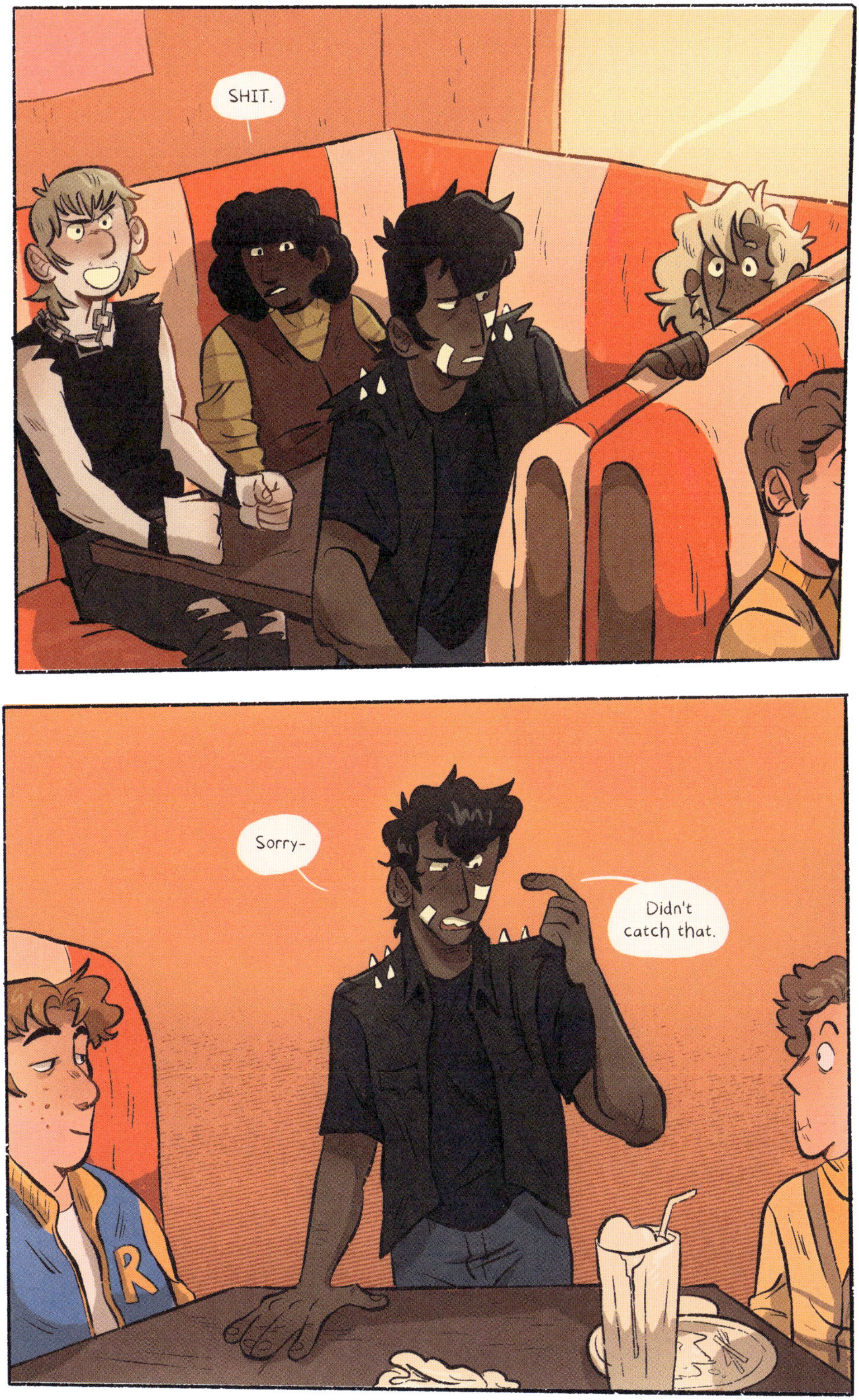
SHIT.
Sorry-
Didn't catch that.

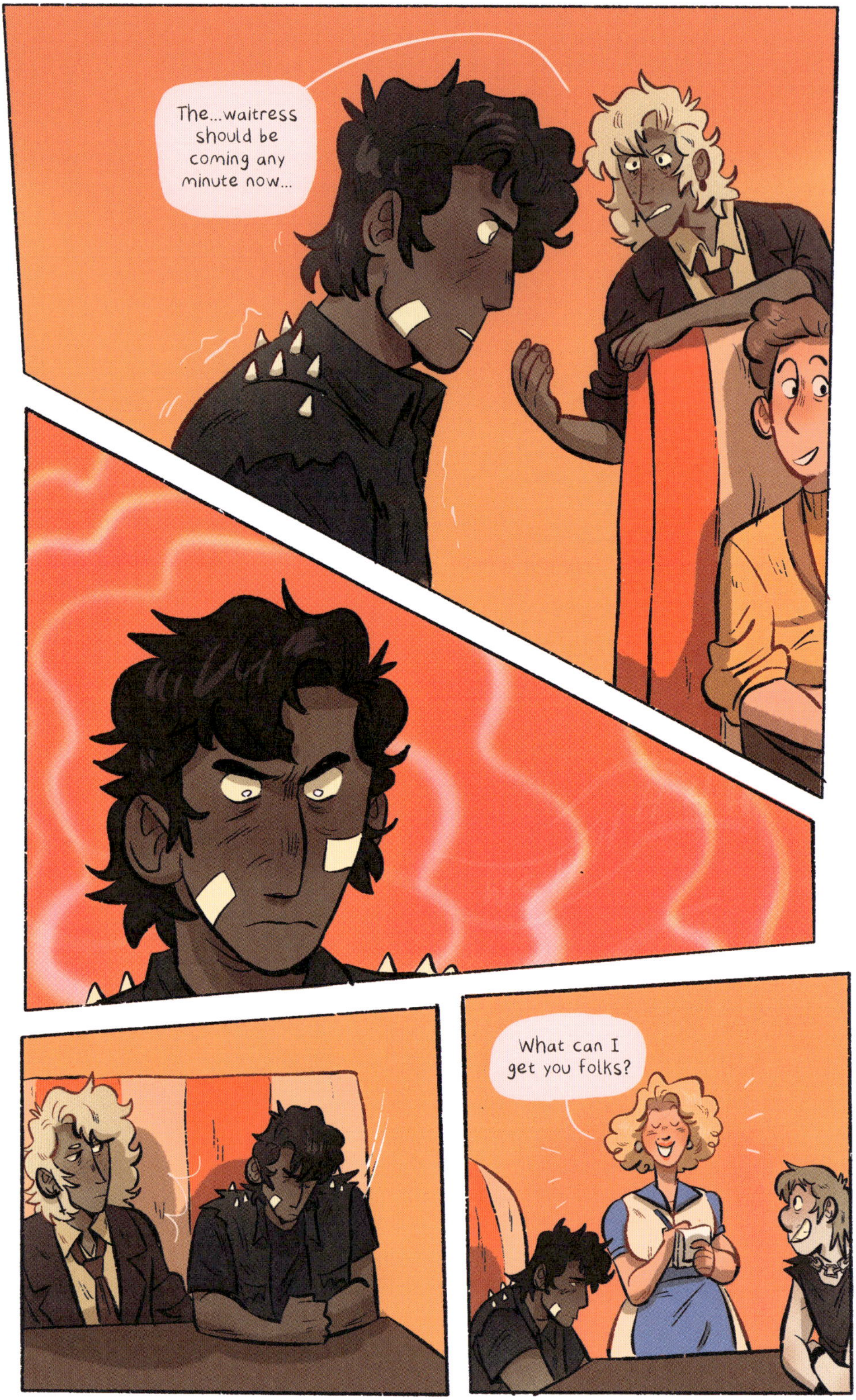
The...waitress should be coming any minute now...
What can I get you folks?

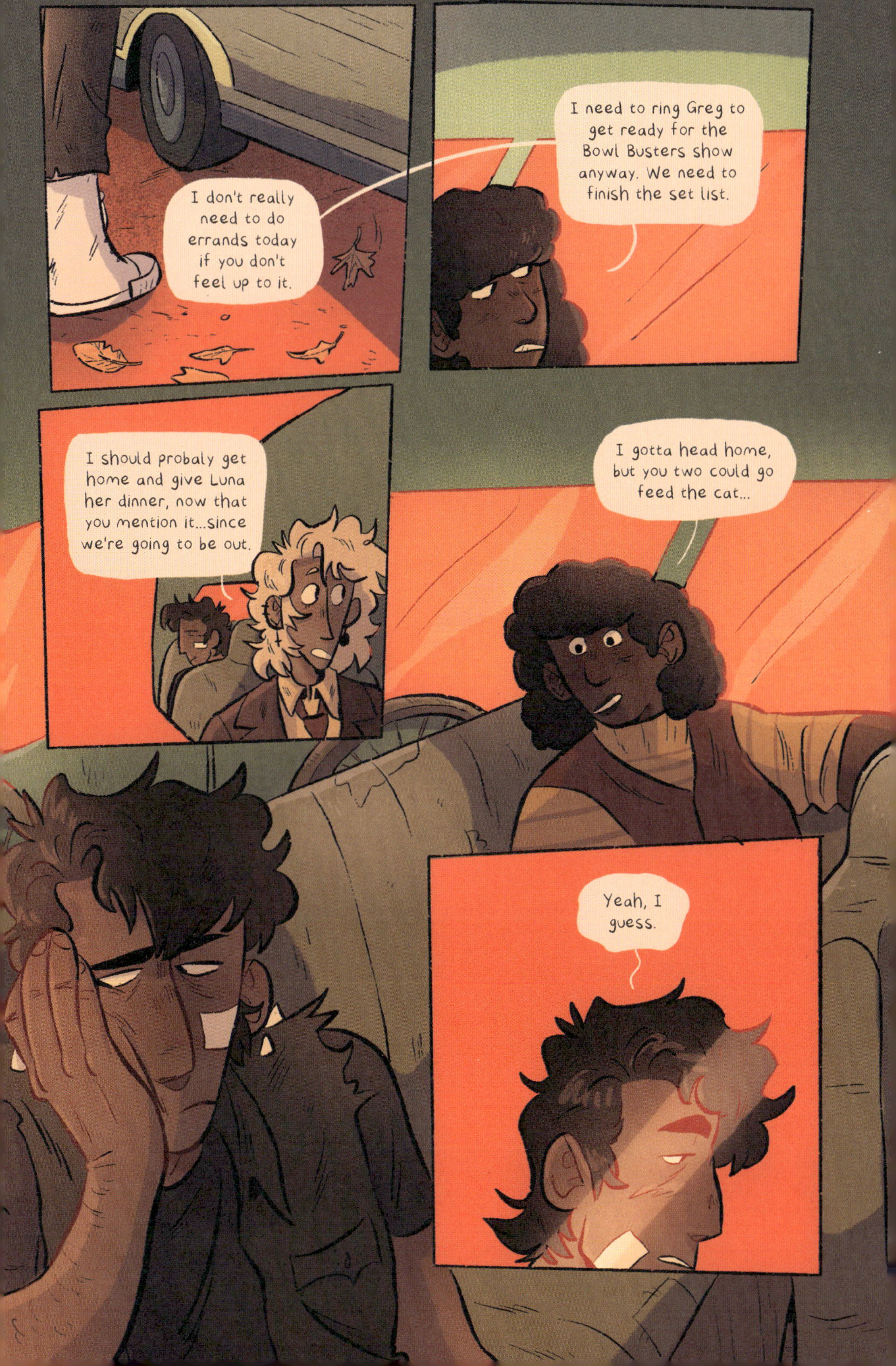
I don't really need to do errands today if you don't feel up to it.
I need to ring Greg to get ready for the Bowl Busters show anyway. We need to finish the set list.
I should probaly get home and give Luna her dinner, now that you mention it...since we're going to be out.
I gotta head home, but you two could go feed the cat...
Yeah, I guess.

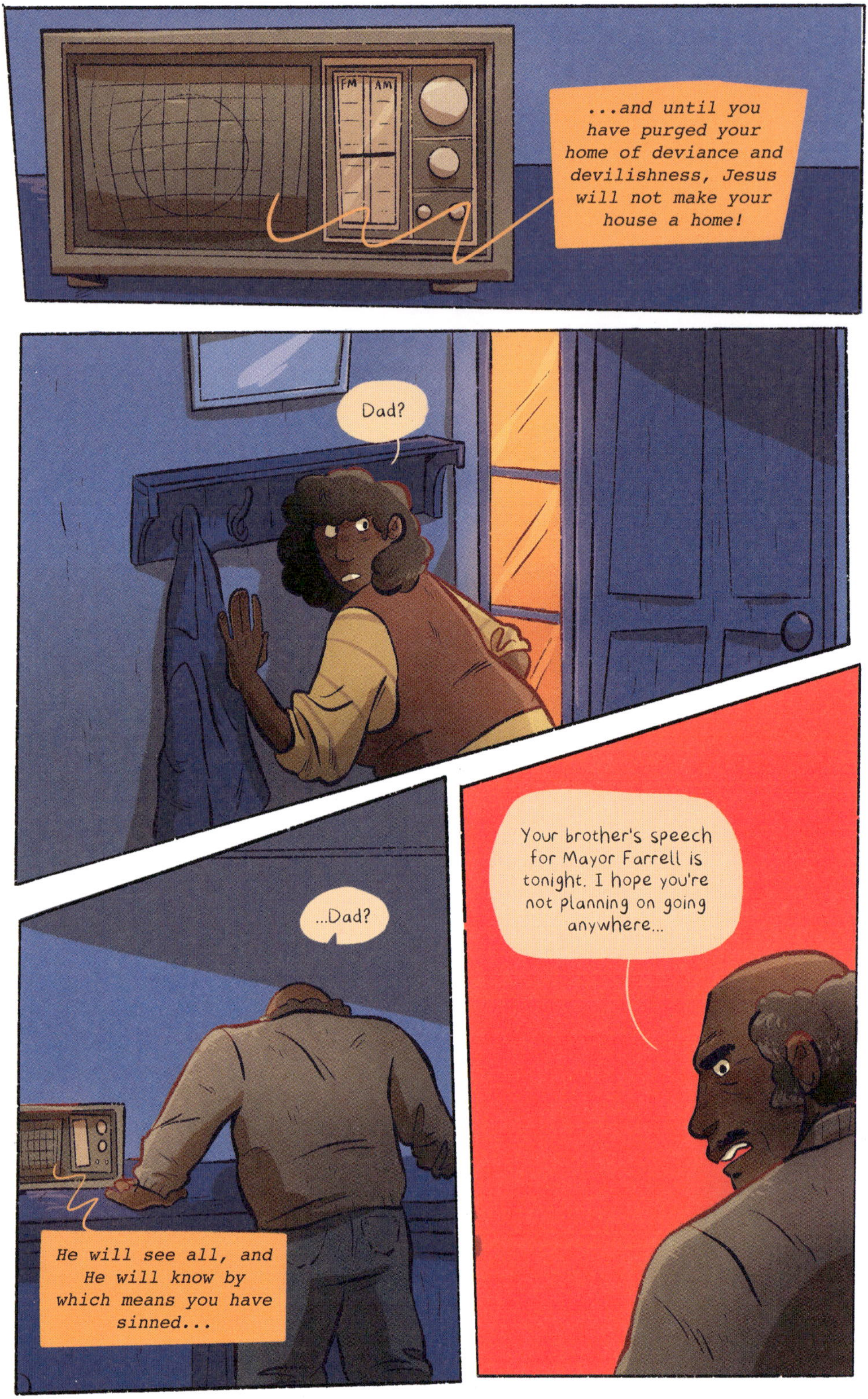

...and until you have purged your home of deviance and devilishness, Jesus will not make your house a home!
Dad?
...Dad?
He will see all, and He will know by which means you have sinned...
Your brother's speech for Mayor Farrell is tonight. I hope you're not planning on going anywhere...

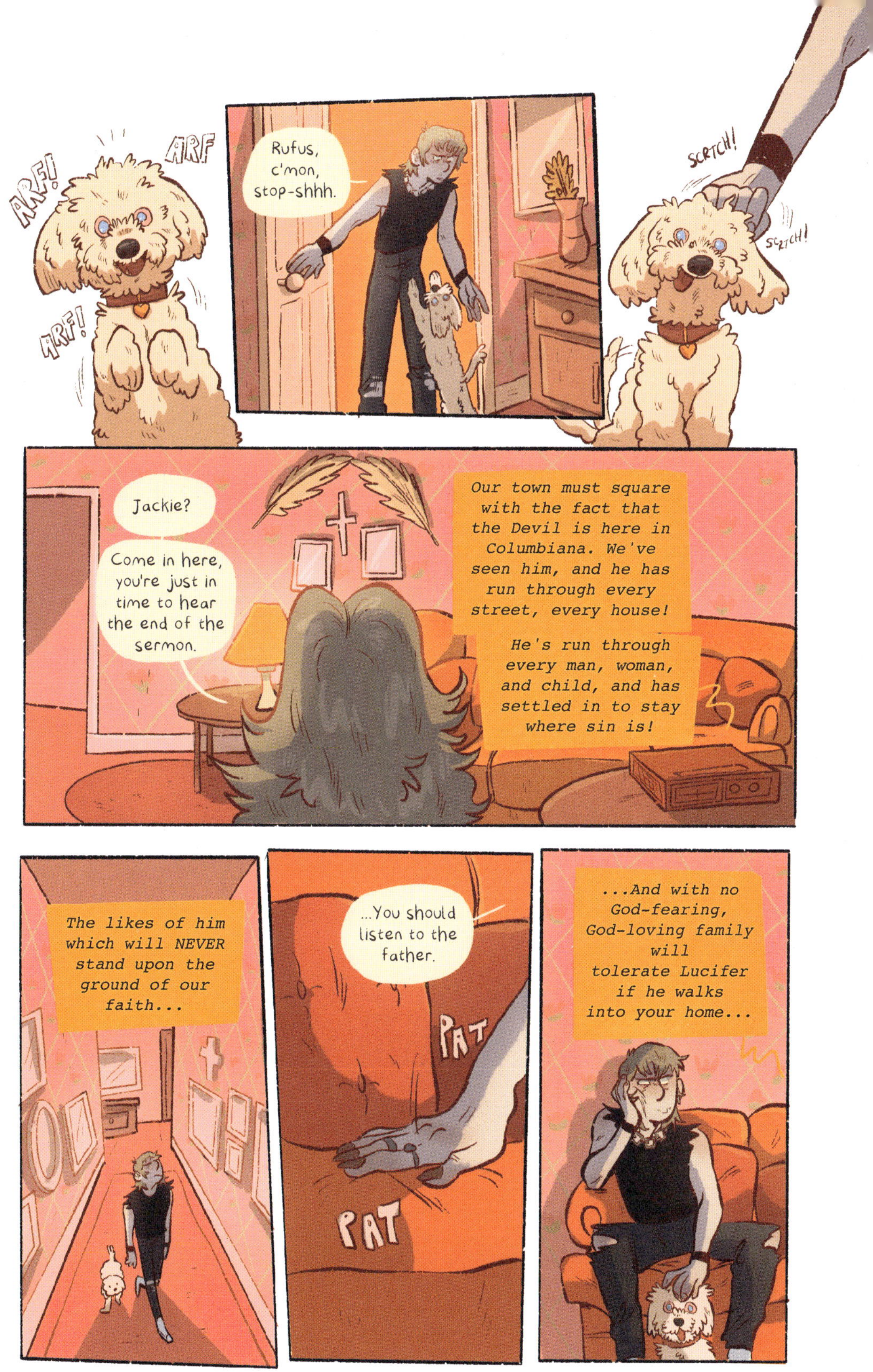

ARF!
ARF
ARF!
Rufus, c'mon, stop-shhh.
SCRTCH!
SCRTCH!
Jackie?
Come in here, you're just in time to hear the end of the sermon.
Our town must square with the fact that the Devil is here in Columbiana. We've seen him, and he has run through every street, every house!
He's run through every man, woman, and child, and has settled in to stay where sin is!
The likes of him which will NEVER stand upon the ground of our faith...
...You should listen to the father.
PAT
PAT
...And with no God-fearing, God-loving family will tolerate Lucifer if he walks into your home...

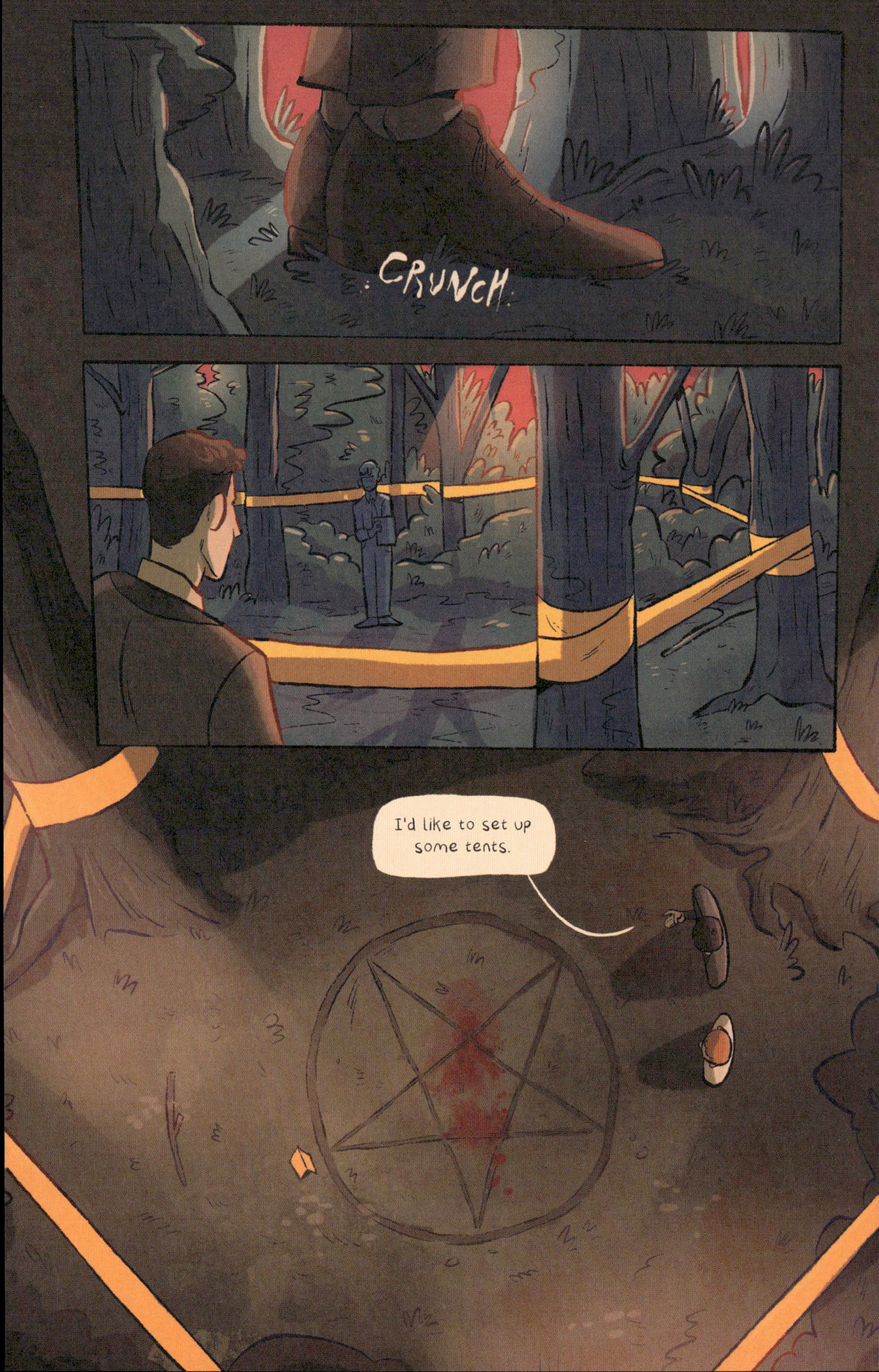
CRUNCH
I'd like to set up some tents.

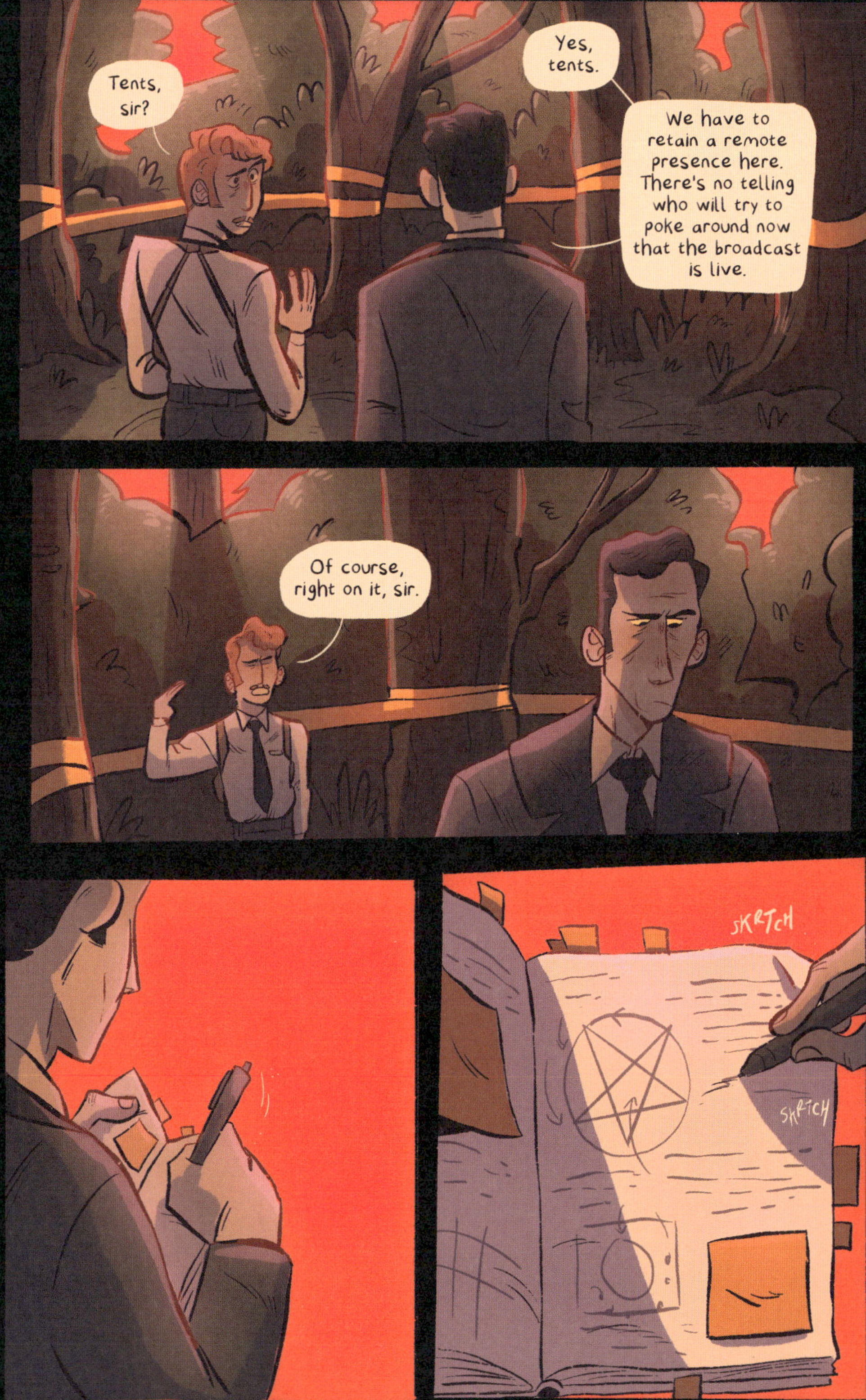
Tents, sir?
Yes, tents.
We have to retain a remote presence here. There's no telling who will try to poke around now that the broadcast is live.
Of course, right on it, sir.
SKRTCH
SKRTCH

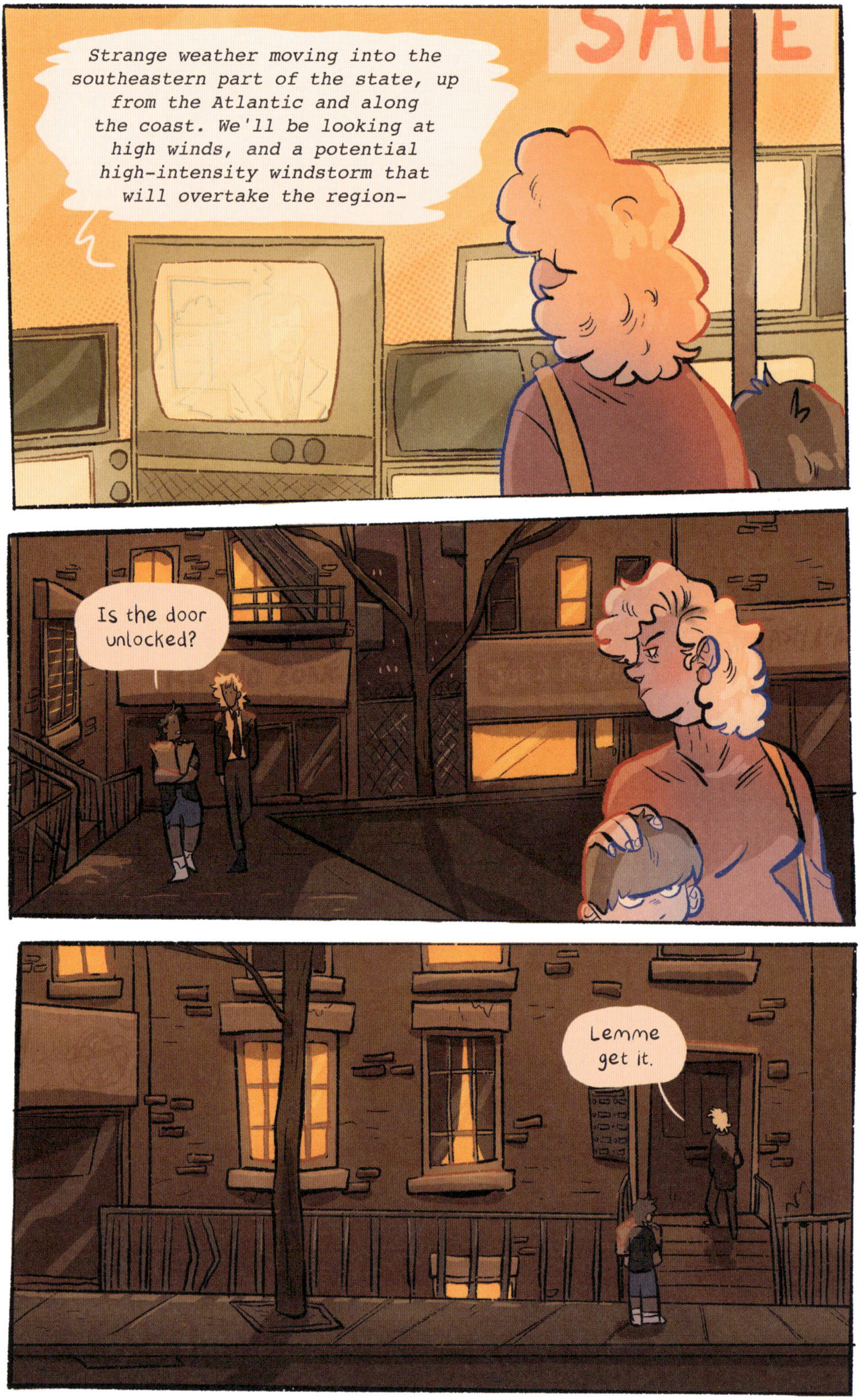
SALE
Strange weather moving into the southeastern part of the state, up from the Atlantic and along the coast. We'll be looking at high winds, and a potential high-intensity windstorm that will overtake the region-
Is the door unlocked?
Lemme get it.

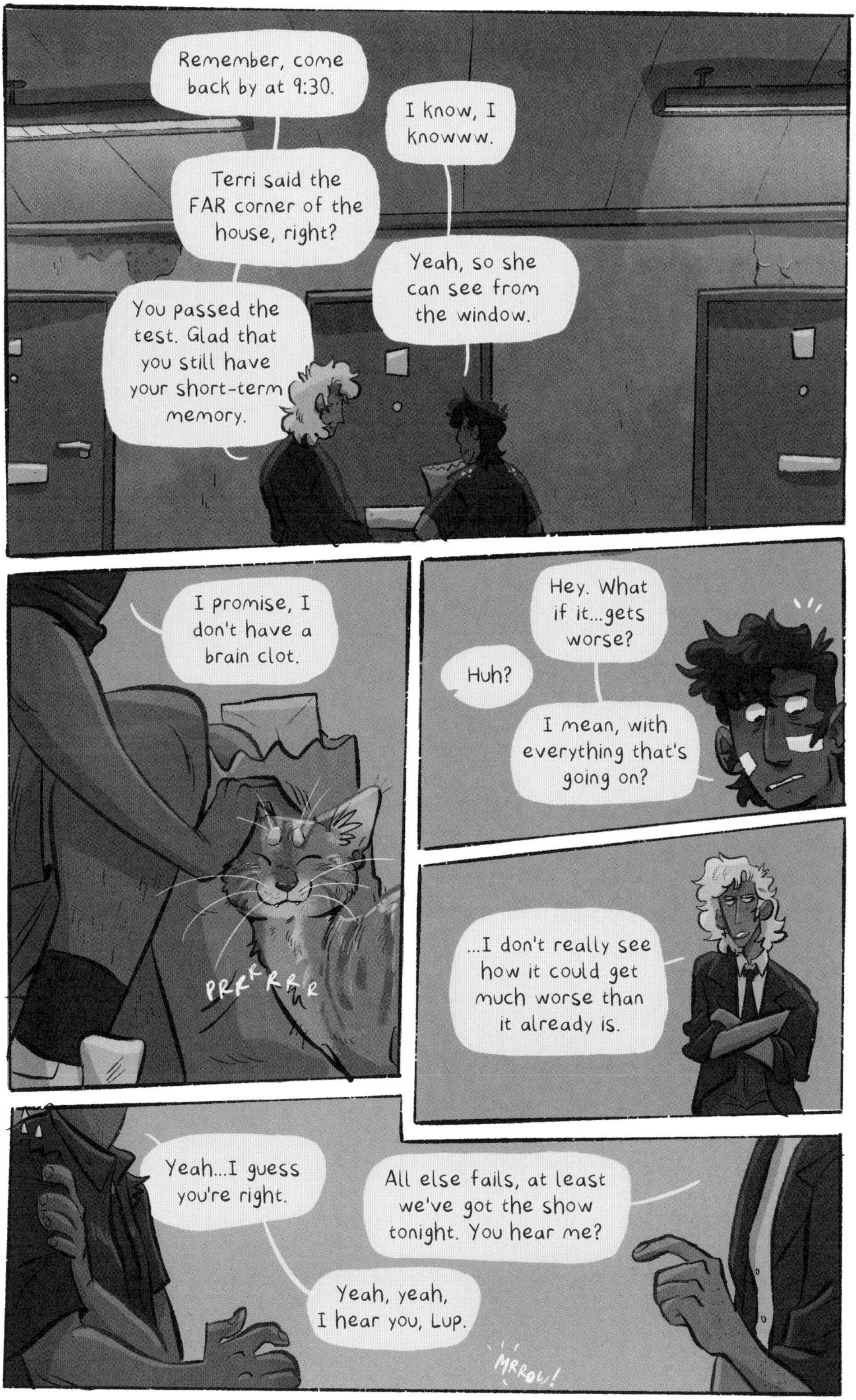

Remember, come back by at 9:30.
Terri said the FAR corner of the house, right?
You passed the test. Glad that you still have your short-term memory.
I know, I knowww.
Yeah, so she can see from the window.
I promise, I don't have a brain clot.
PRRRRRRR
Hey. What if it...gets worse?
Huh?
I mean, with everything that's going on?
...I don't really see how it could get much worse than it already is.
Yeah...I guess you're right.
All else fails, at least we've got the show tonight. You hear me?
Yeah, yeah, I hear you, Lup.
MRROW!

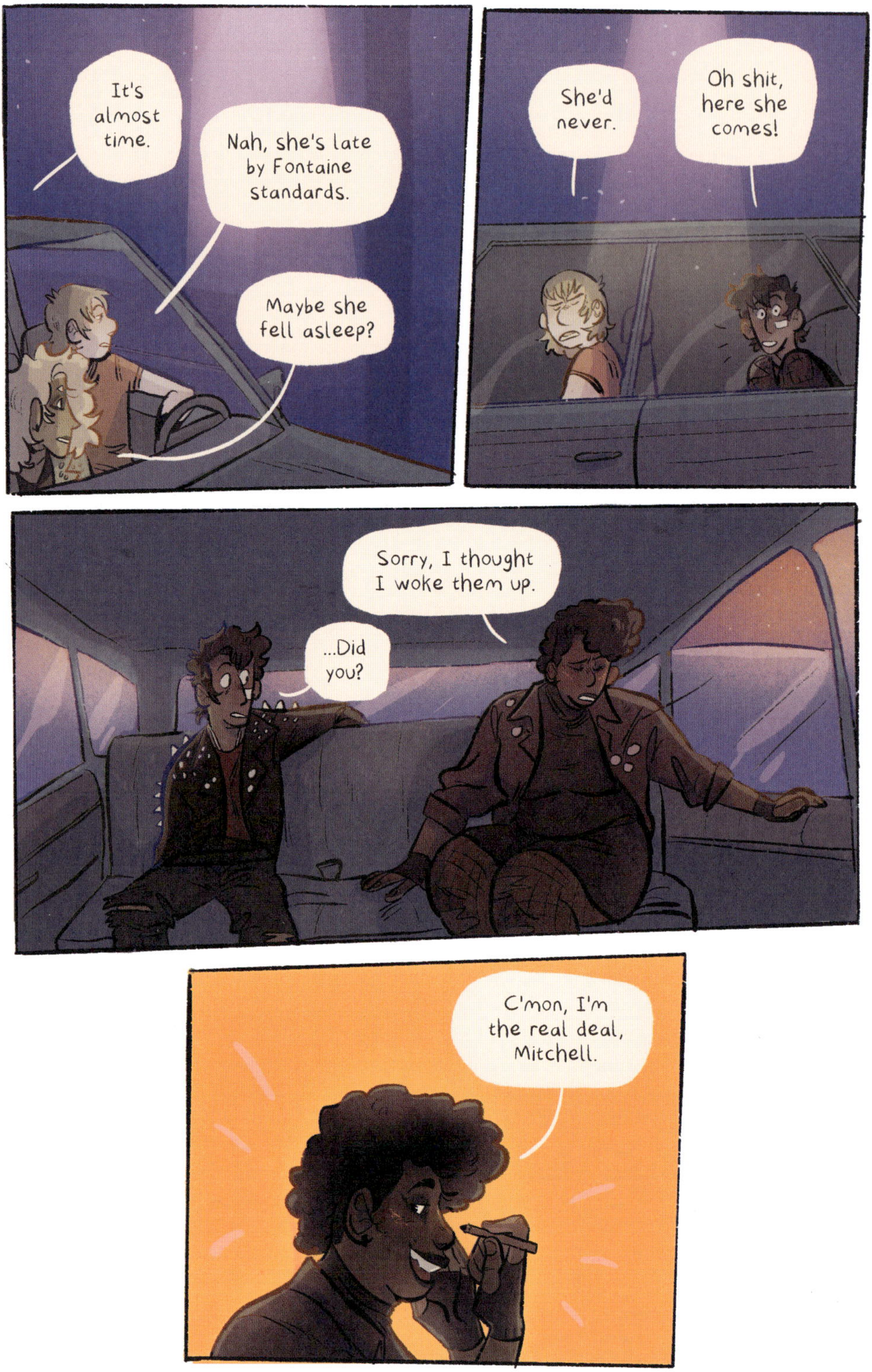
It's almost time.
Nah, she's late by Fontaine standards.
Maybe she fell asleep?
She'd never.
Oh shit, here she comes!
Sorry, I thought I woke them up.
...Did you?
C'mon, I'm the real deal, Mitchell.

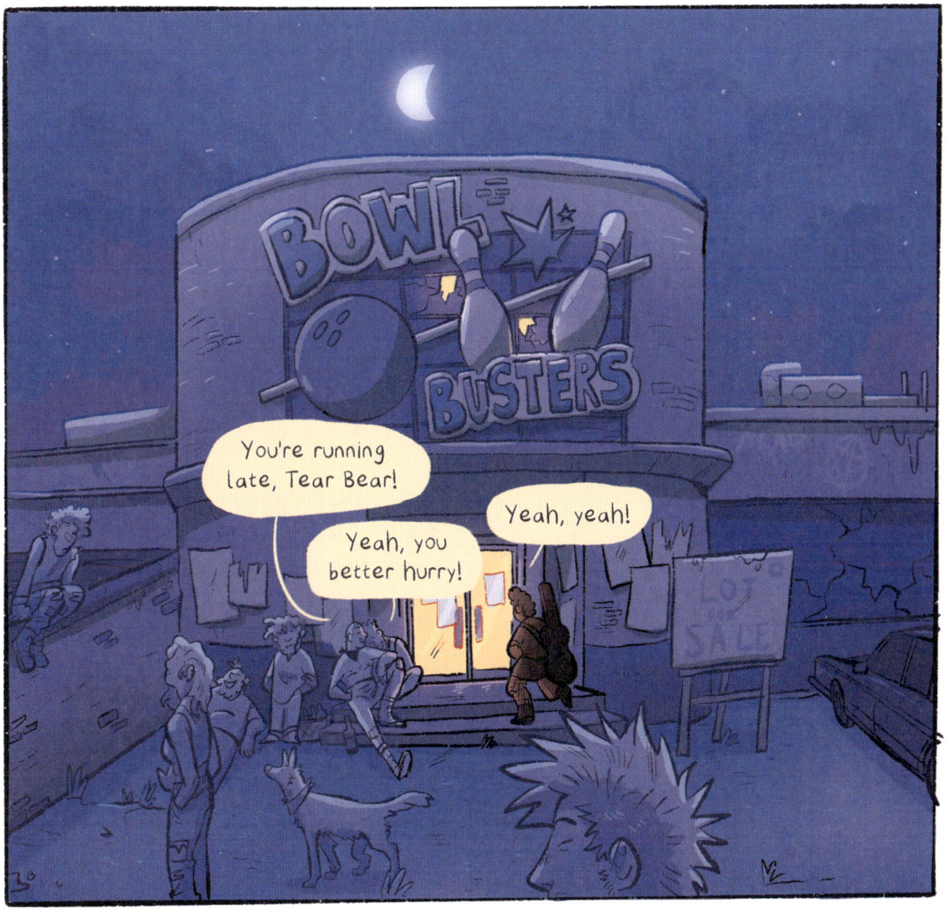
BOWL BUSTERS
You're running late, Tear Bear!
Yeah, you better hurry!
Yeah, yeah!
LOT FOR SALE

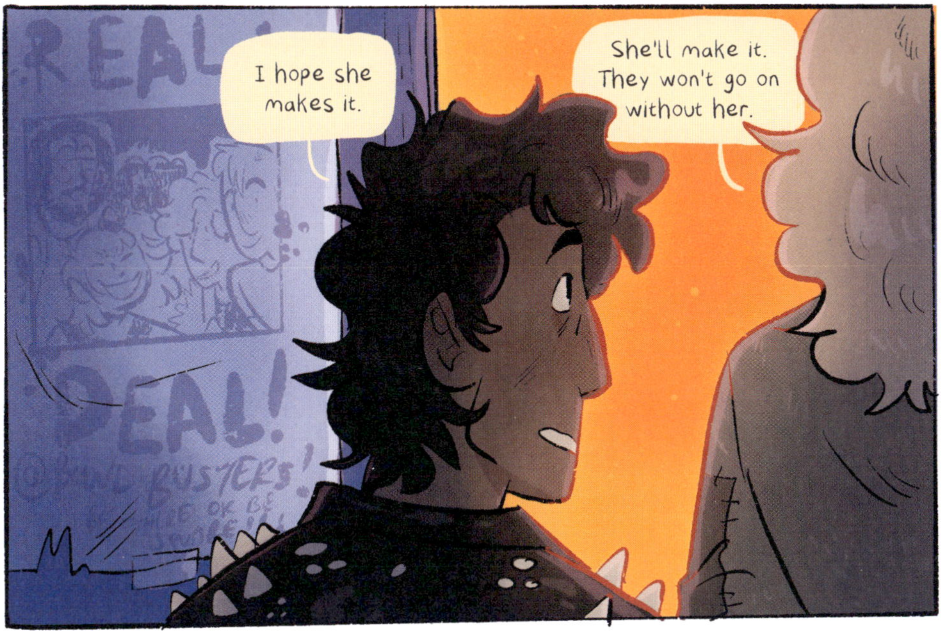
I hope she makes it.
She'll make it. They won't go on without her.

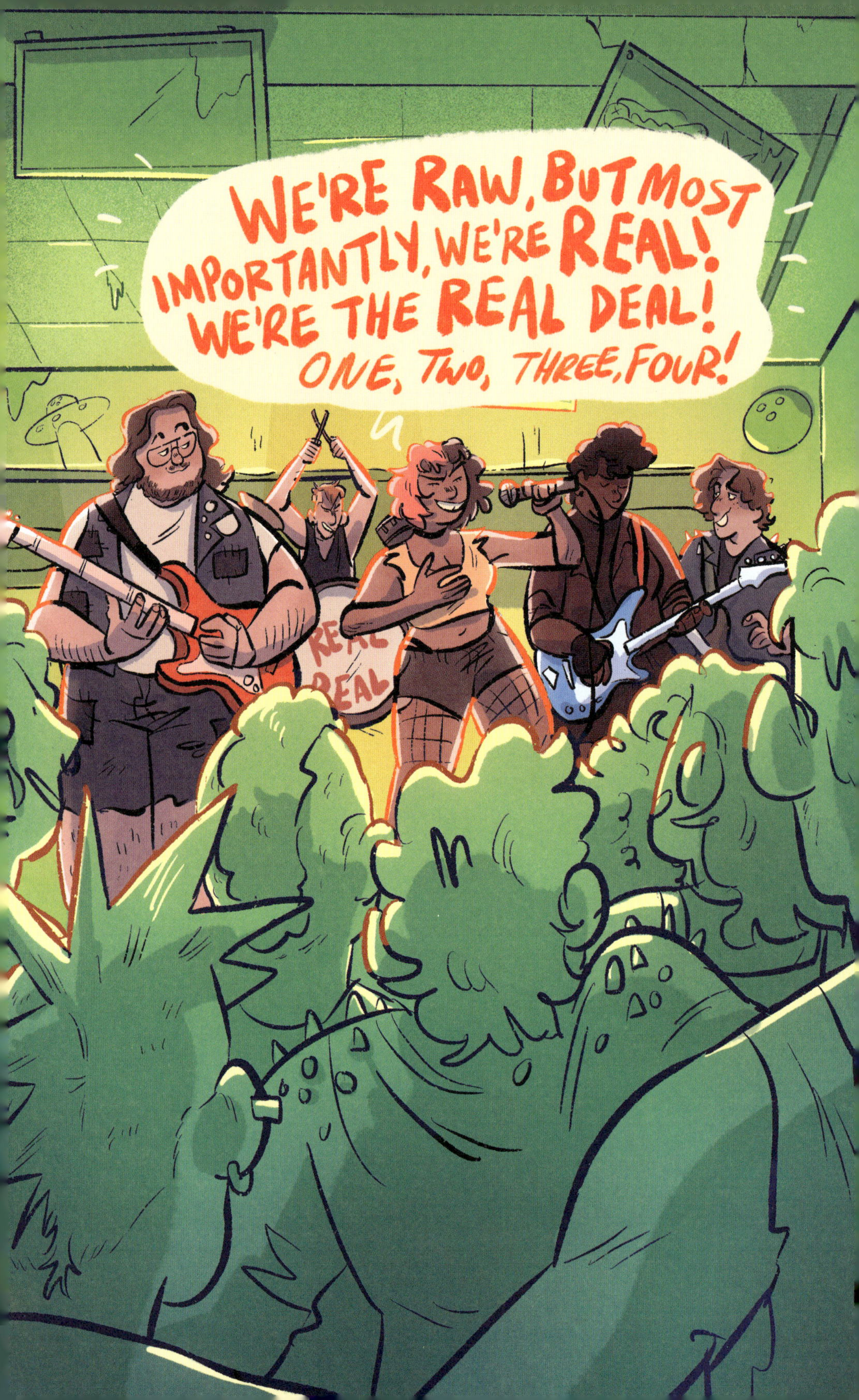
WE'RE RAW, BUT MOST IMPORTANTLY, WE'RE REAL! WE'RE THE REAL DEAL! ONE, TWO, THREE, FOUR!
REAL REAL

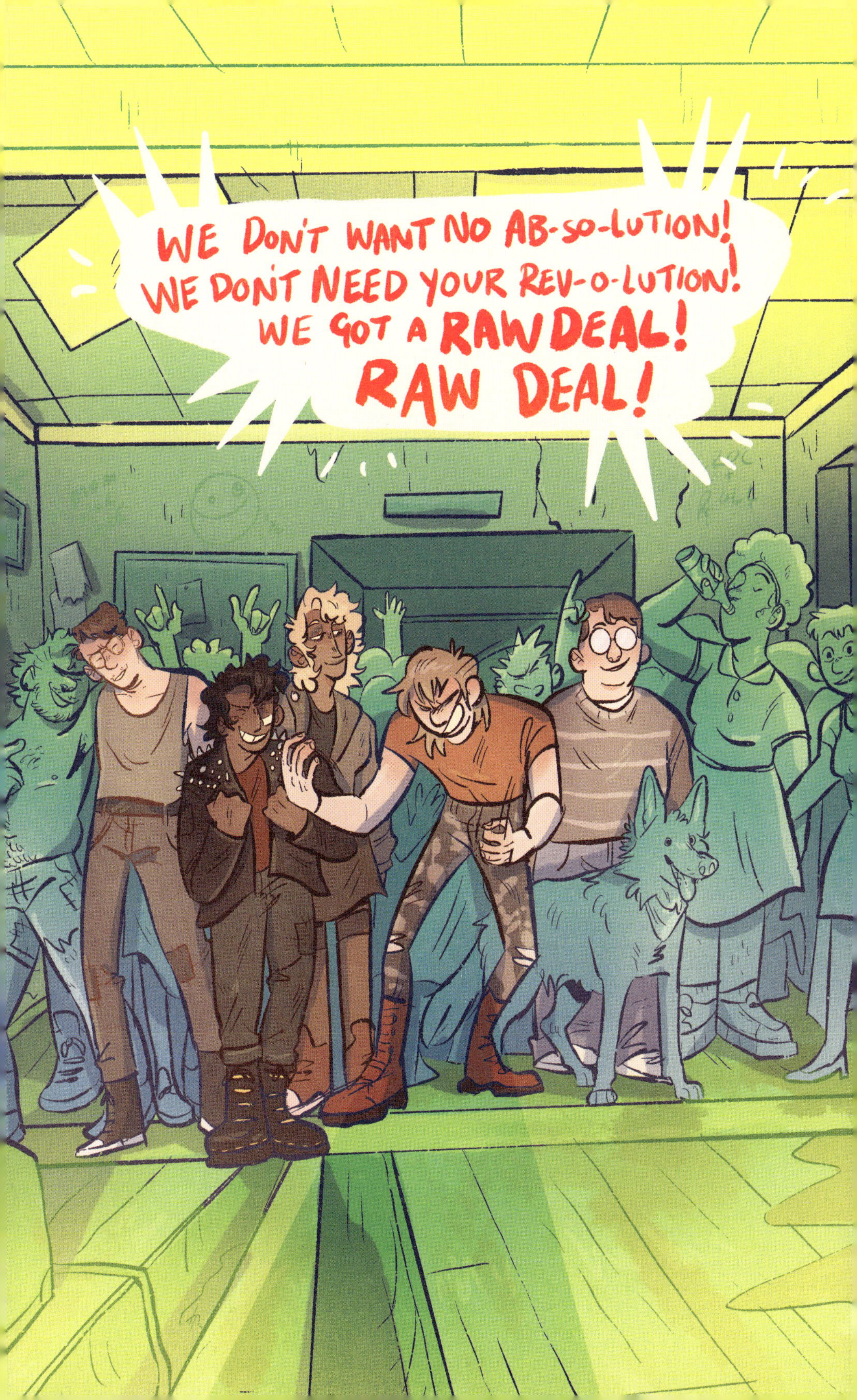
WE DON'T WANT NO AB-SO-LUTION!
WE DON'T NEED YOUR REV-O-LUTION!
WE GOT A RAW DEAL!
RAW DEAL!

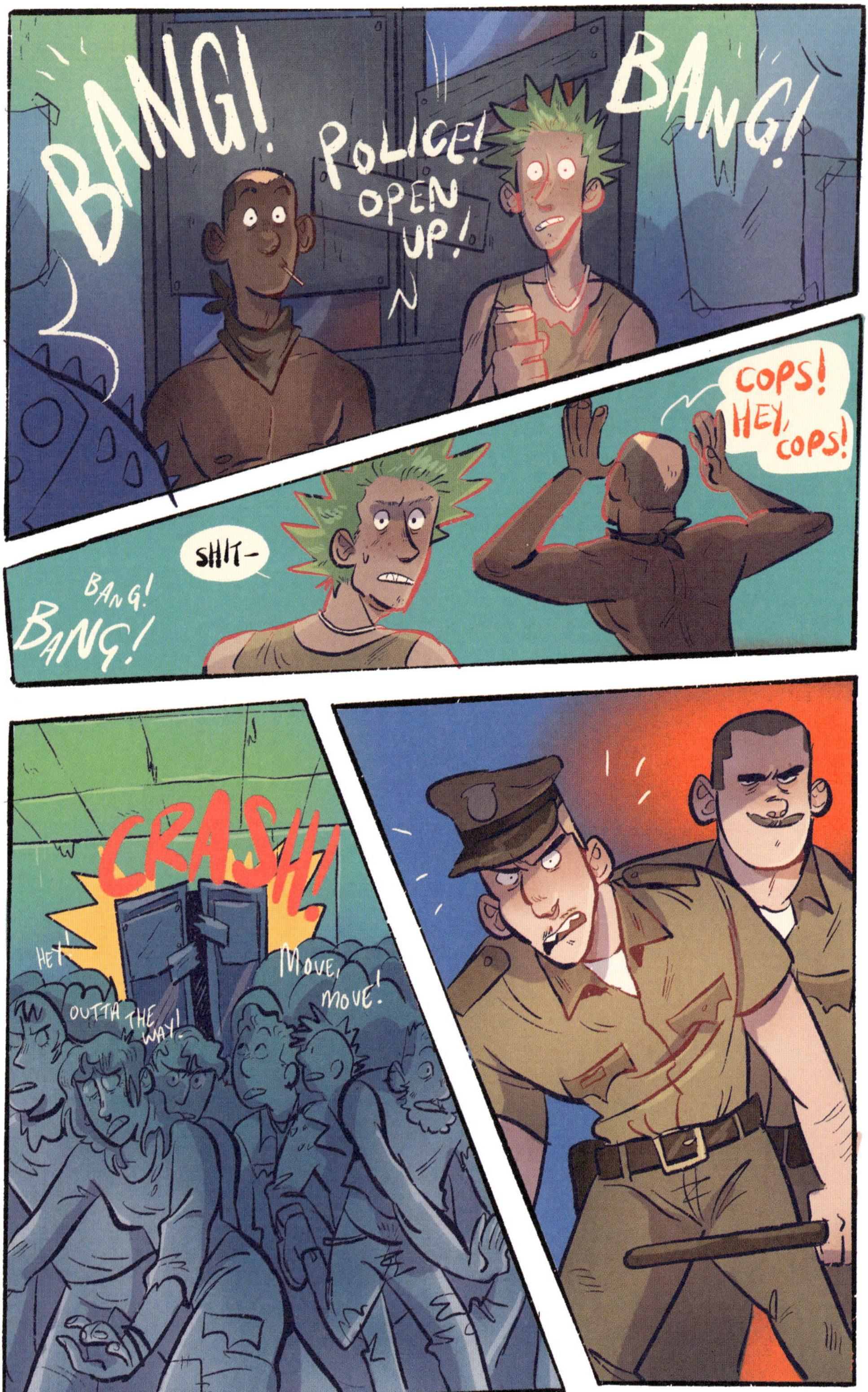
BANG!
POLICE! OPEN UP!
BANG!
COPS! HEY, COPS!
SHIT-
BANG!
BANG!
CRASH!
HEY!
OUTTA THE WAY!
MOVE, MOVE!

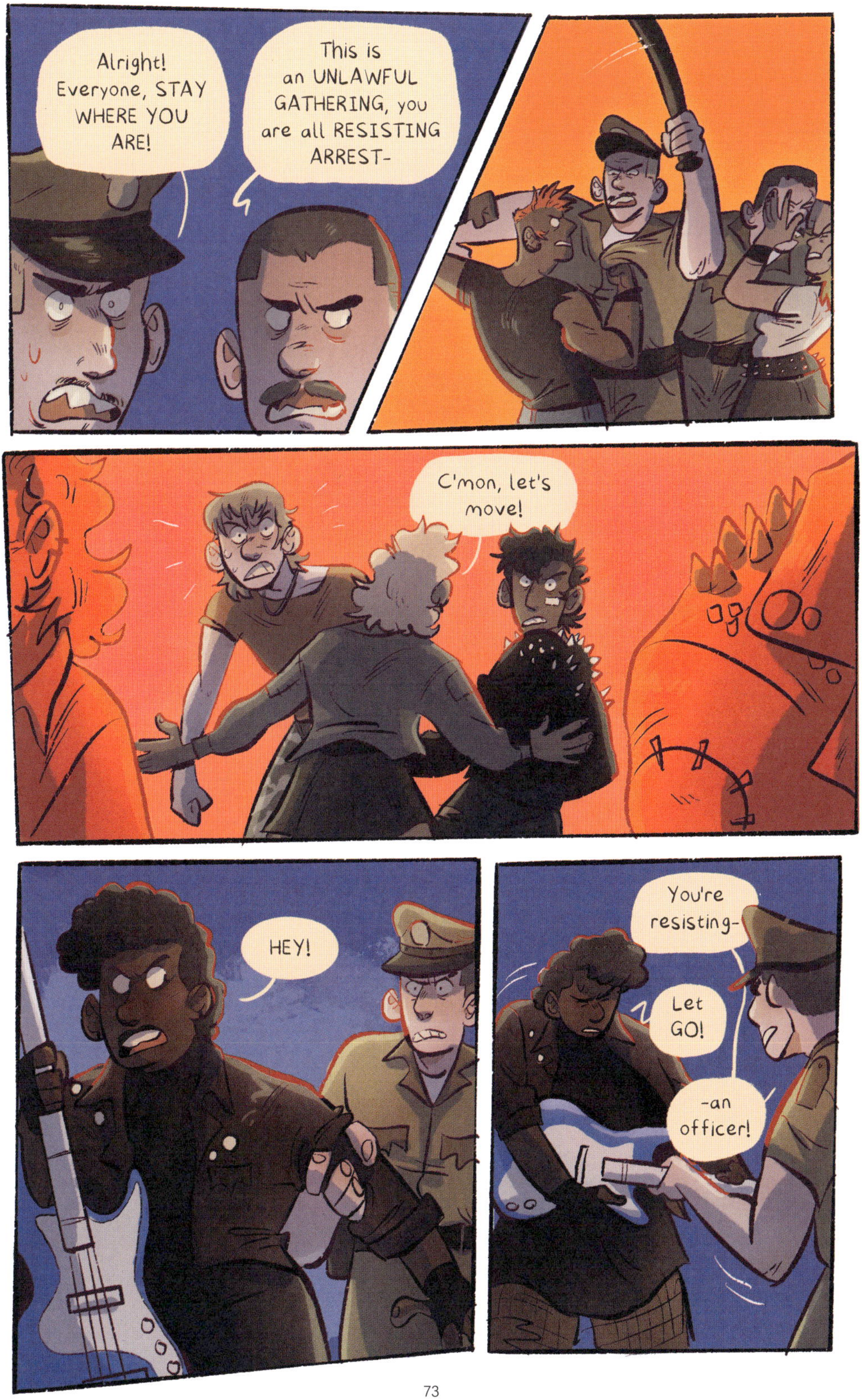
Alright! Everyone, STAY WHERE YOU ARE!
This is an UNLAWFUL GATHERING, you are all RESISTING ARREST-
C'mon, let's move!
HEY!
You're resisting-
Let GO!
-an officer!

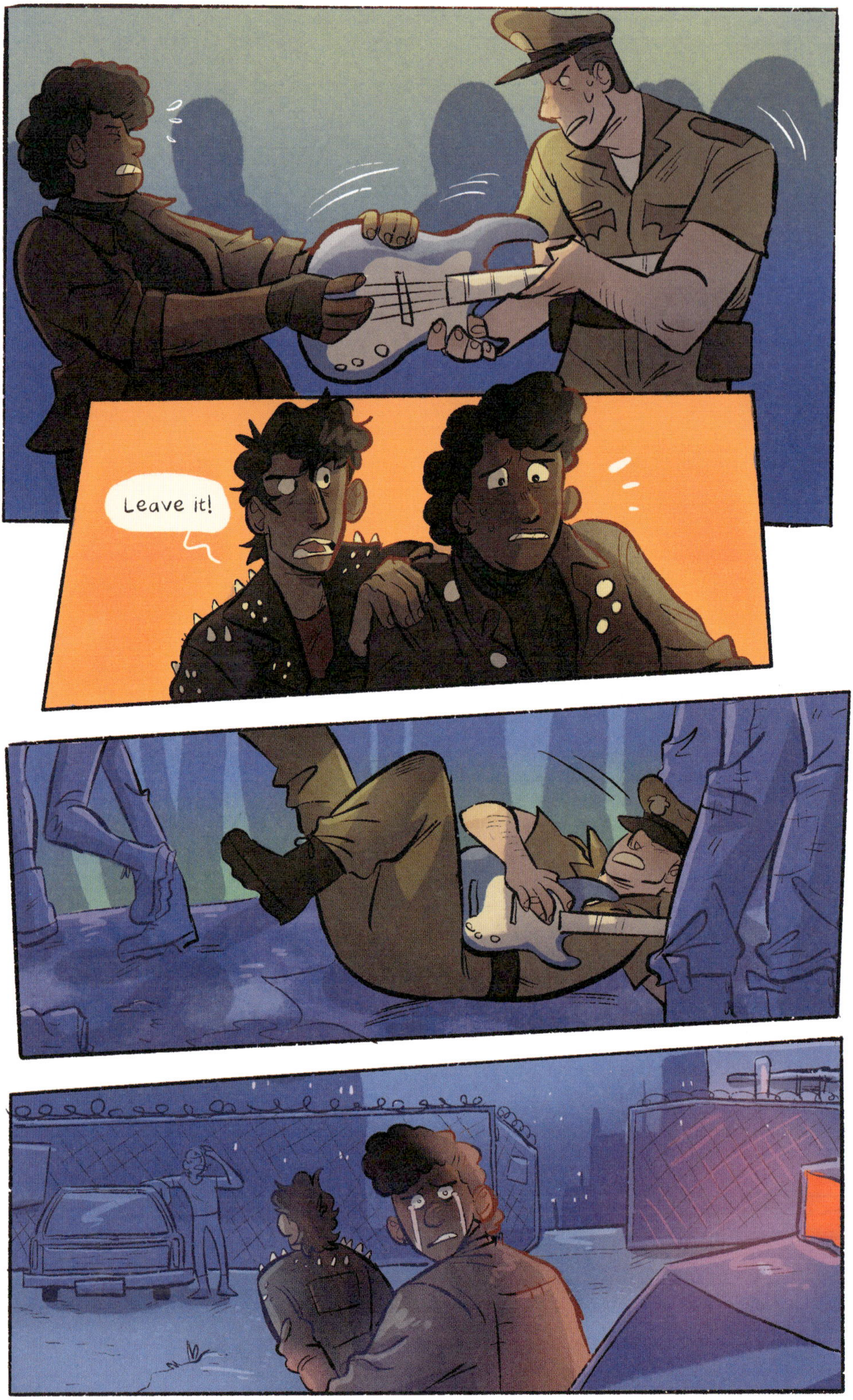
Leave it!

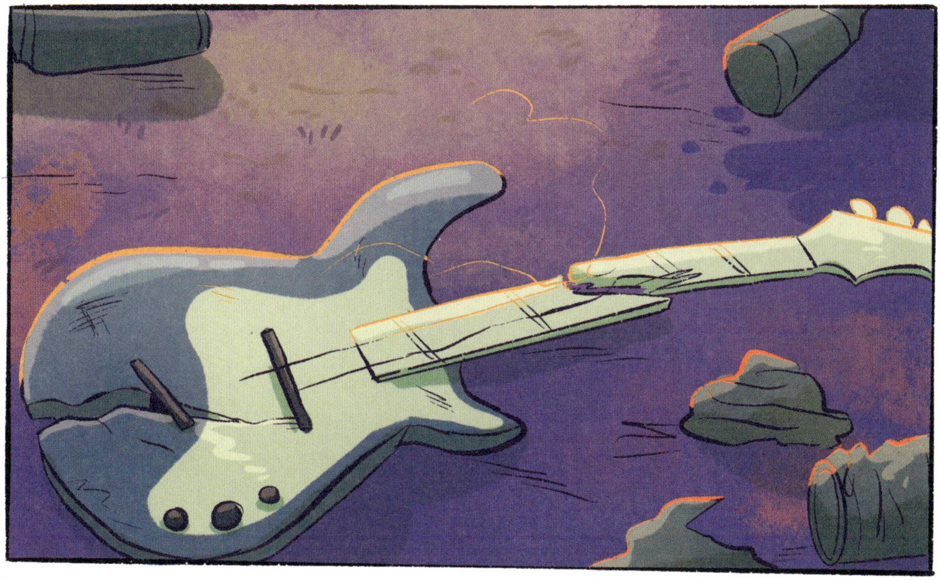

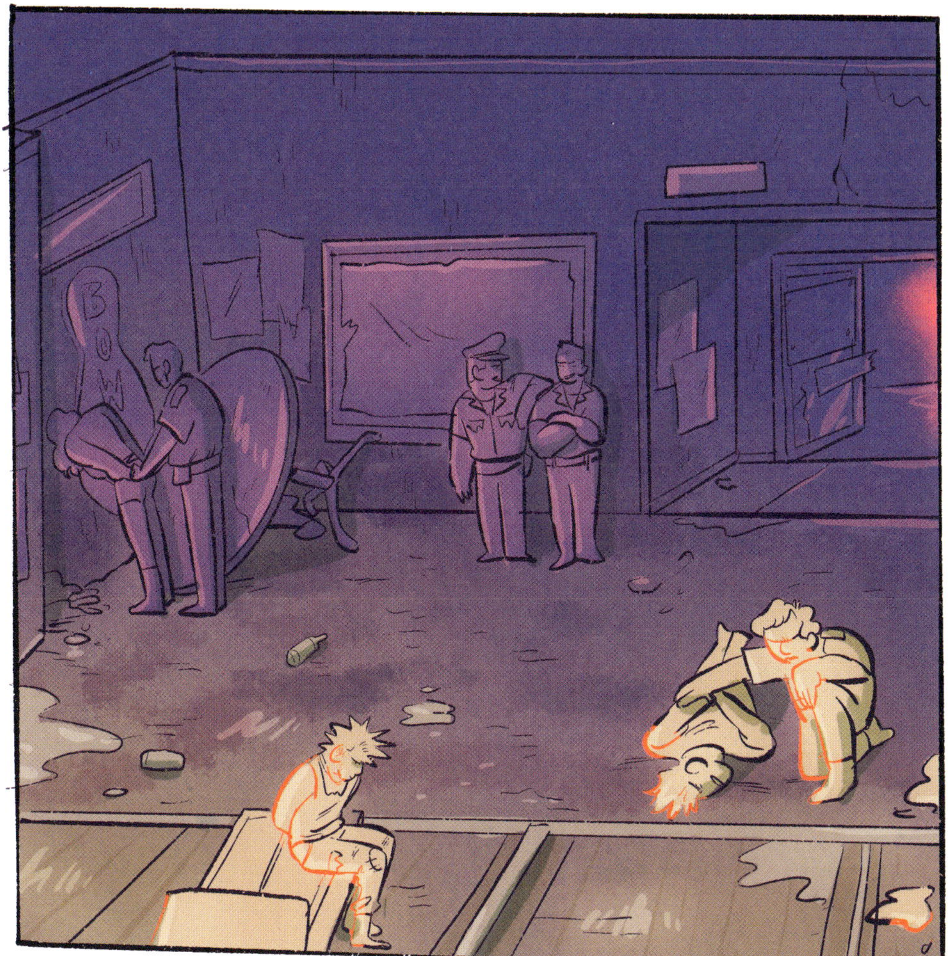

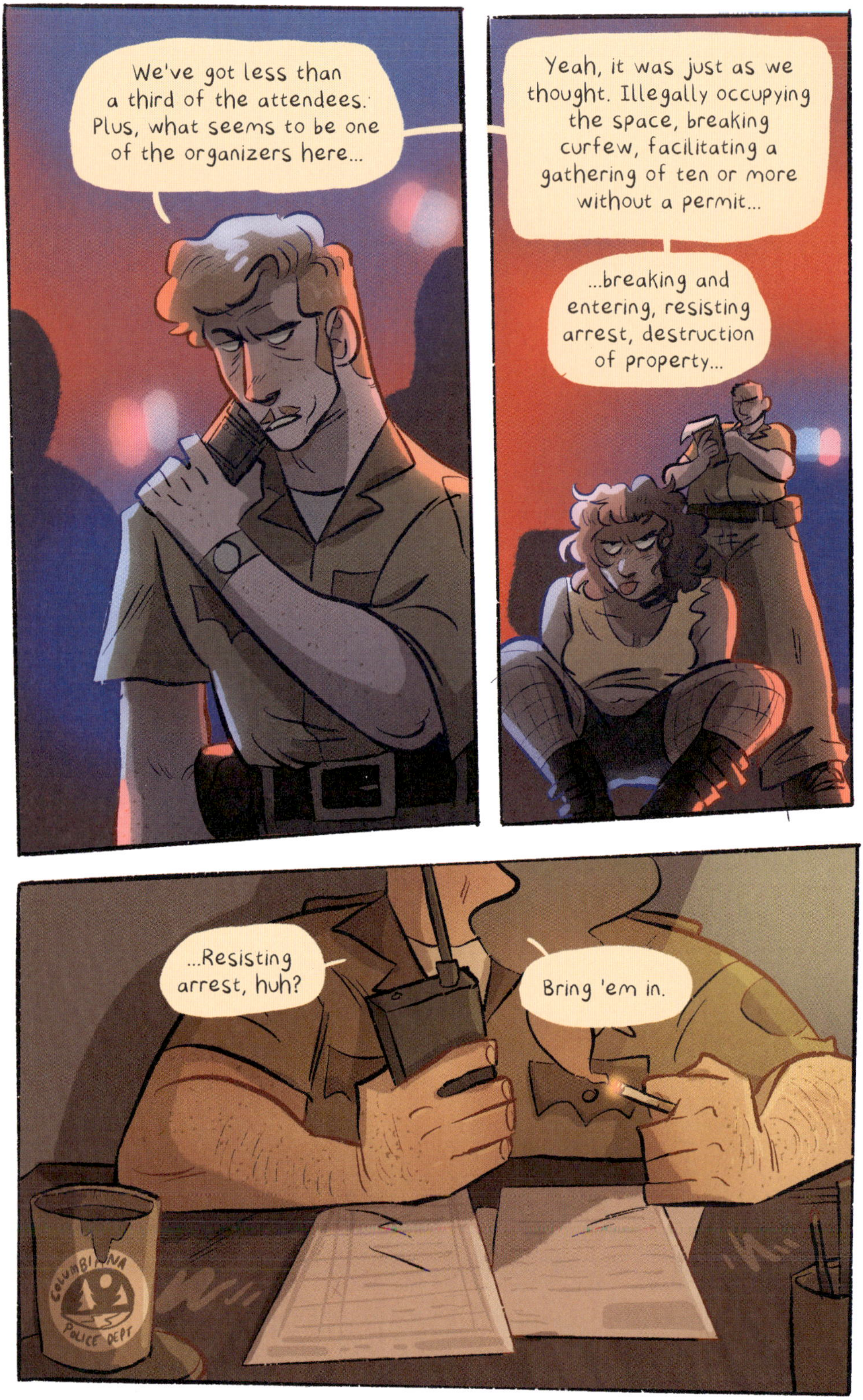
We've got less than a third of the attendees. Plus, what seems to be one of the organizers here...
Yeah, it was just as we thought. Illegally occupying the space, breaking curfew, facilitating a gathering of ten or more without a permit...
...breaking and entering, resisting arrest, destruction of property...
...Resisting arrest, huh?
Bring 'em in.
COLUMBIANA POLICE DEPT

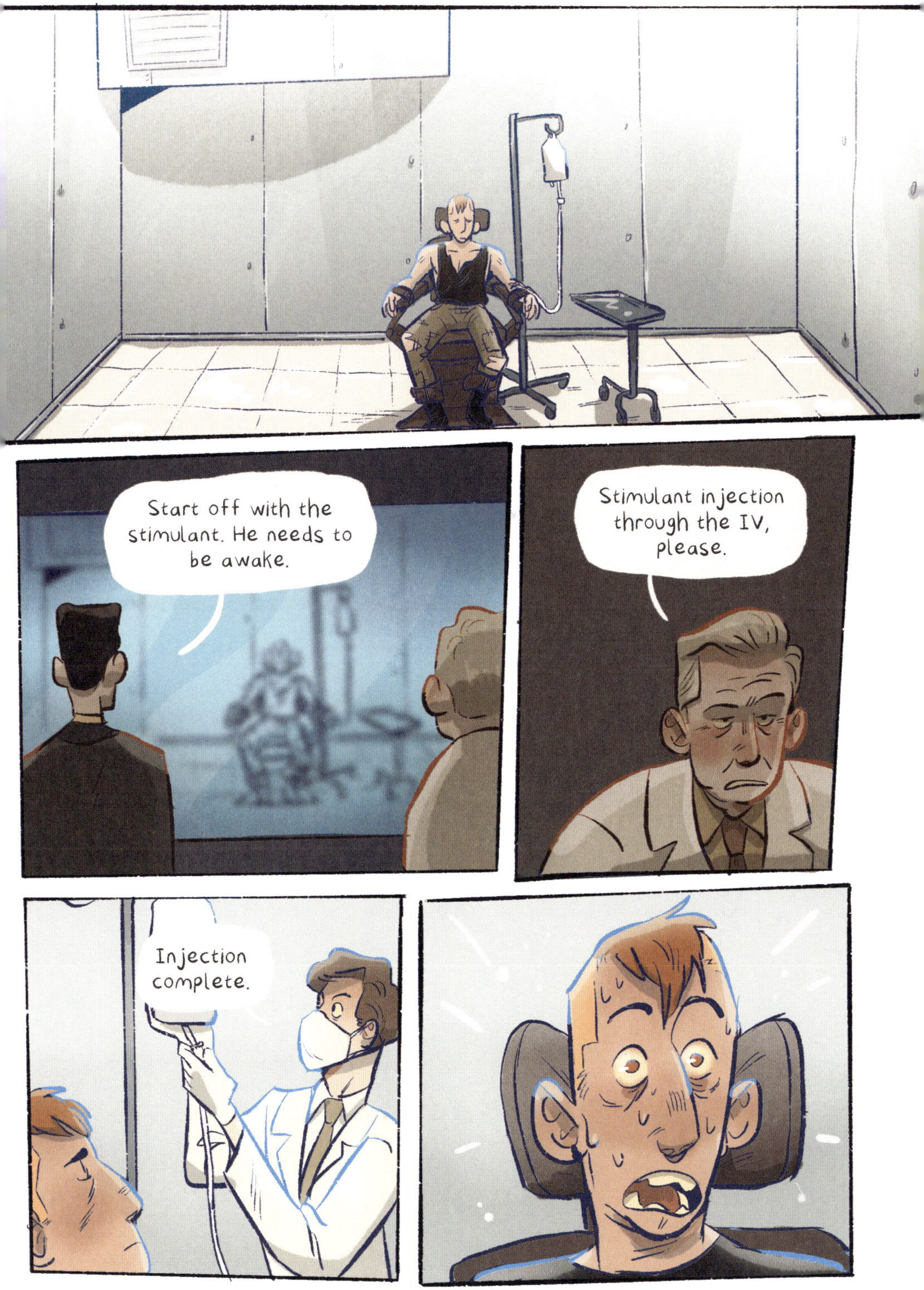
Start off with the stimulant. He needs to be awake.
Stimulant injection through the IV, please.
Injection complete.

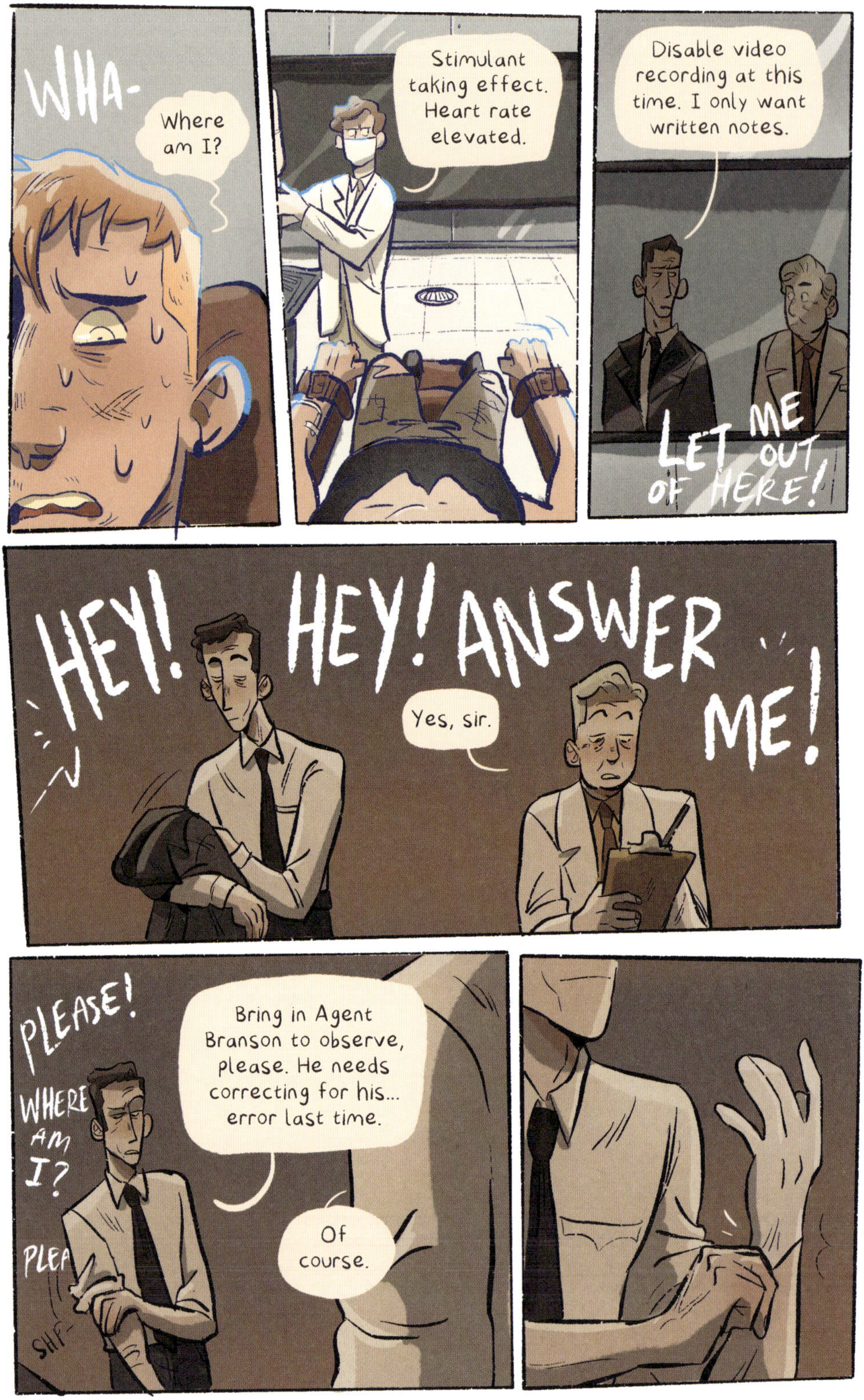
WHA-
Where am I?
Stimulant taking effect. Heart rate elevated.
Disable video recording at this time. I only want written notes.
LET ME OUT OF HERE!
HEY! HEY! ANSWER ME!
Yes, sir.
PLEASE!
WHERE AM I?
PLEA
SHF-
Bring in Agent Branson to observe, please. He needs correcting for his... error last time.
Of course.

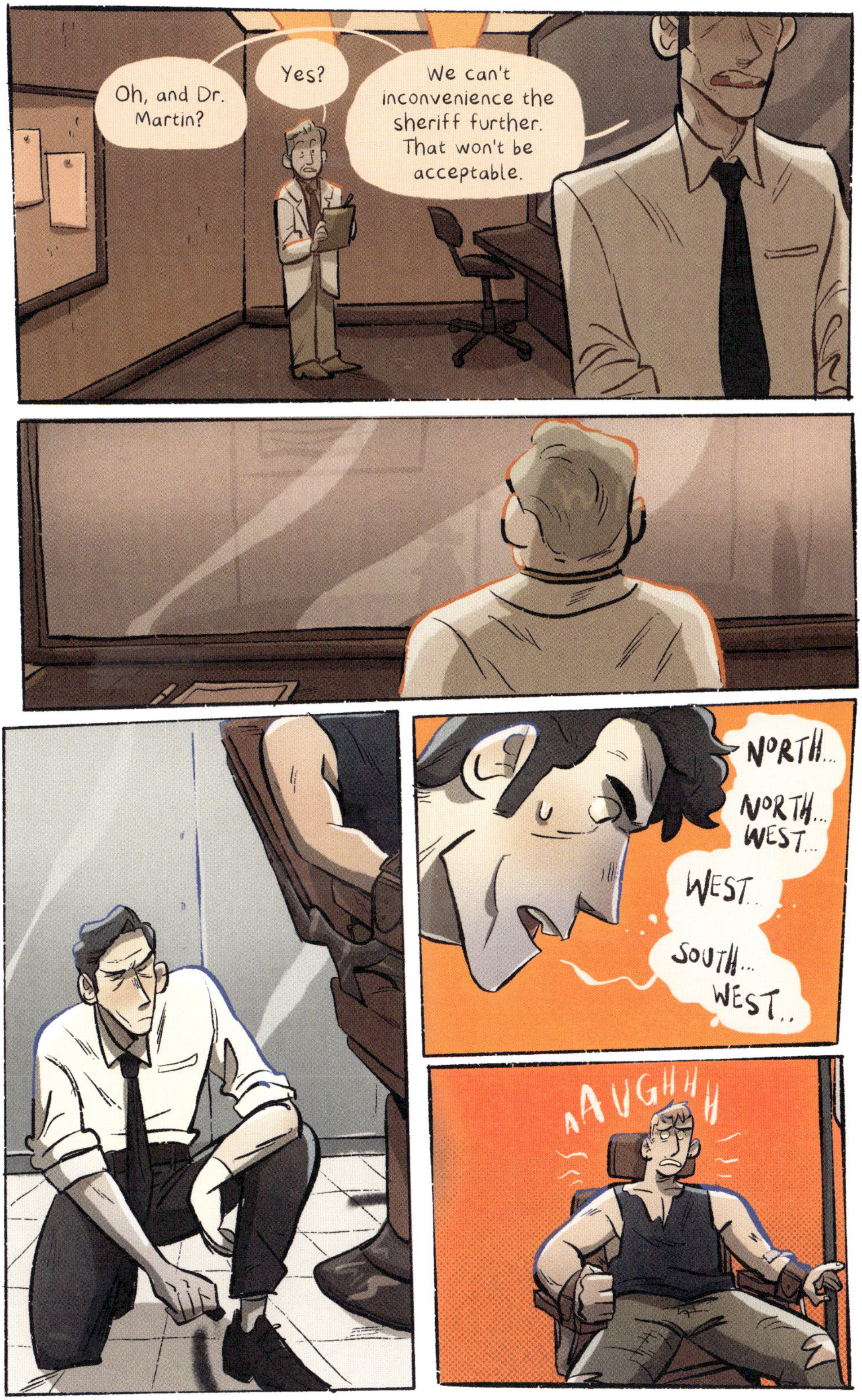

Oh, and Dr. Martin?
Yes?
We can't inconvenience the sheriff further. That won't be acceptable.
NORTH...
NORTH... WEST...
WEST...
SOUTH... WEST..
AAUGHHH

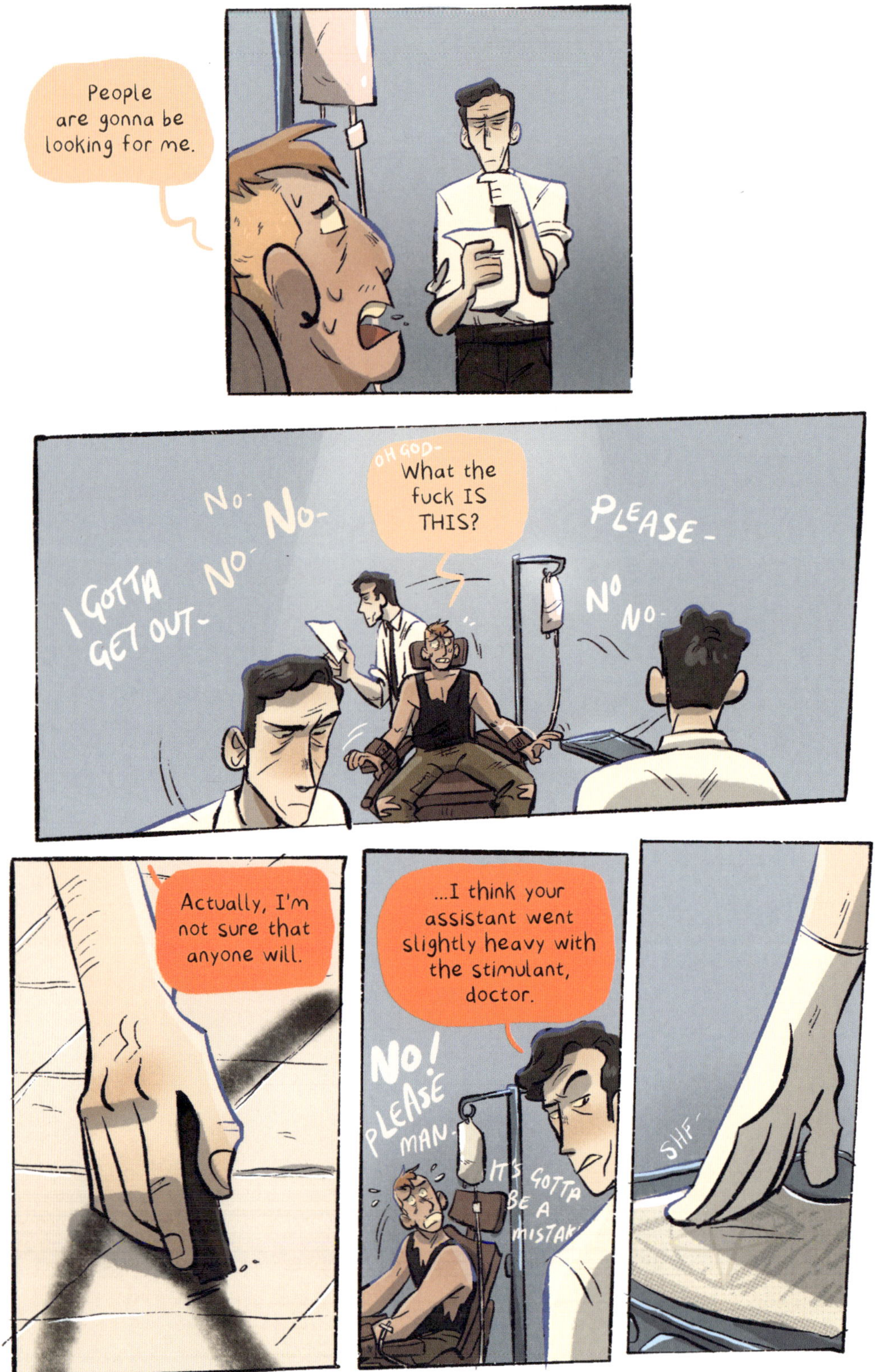
People are gonna be looking for me.
OH GOD-
What the fuck IS THIS?
NO- NO- NO-
I GOTTA GET OUT-
PLEASE-
NO NO-
Actually, I'm not sure that anyone will.
...I think your assistant went slightly heavy with the stimulant, doctor.
NO! PLEASE MAN-
IT'S GOTTA BE A MISTAK-
SHF-

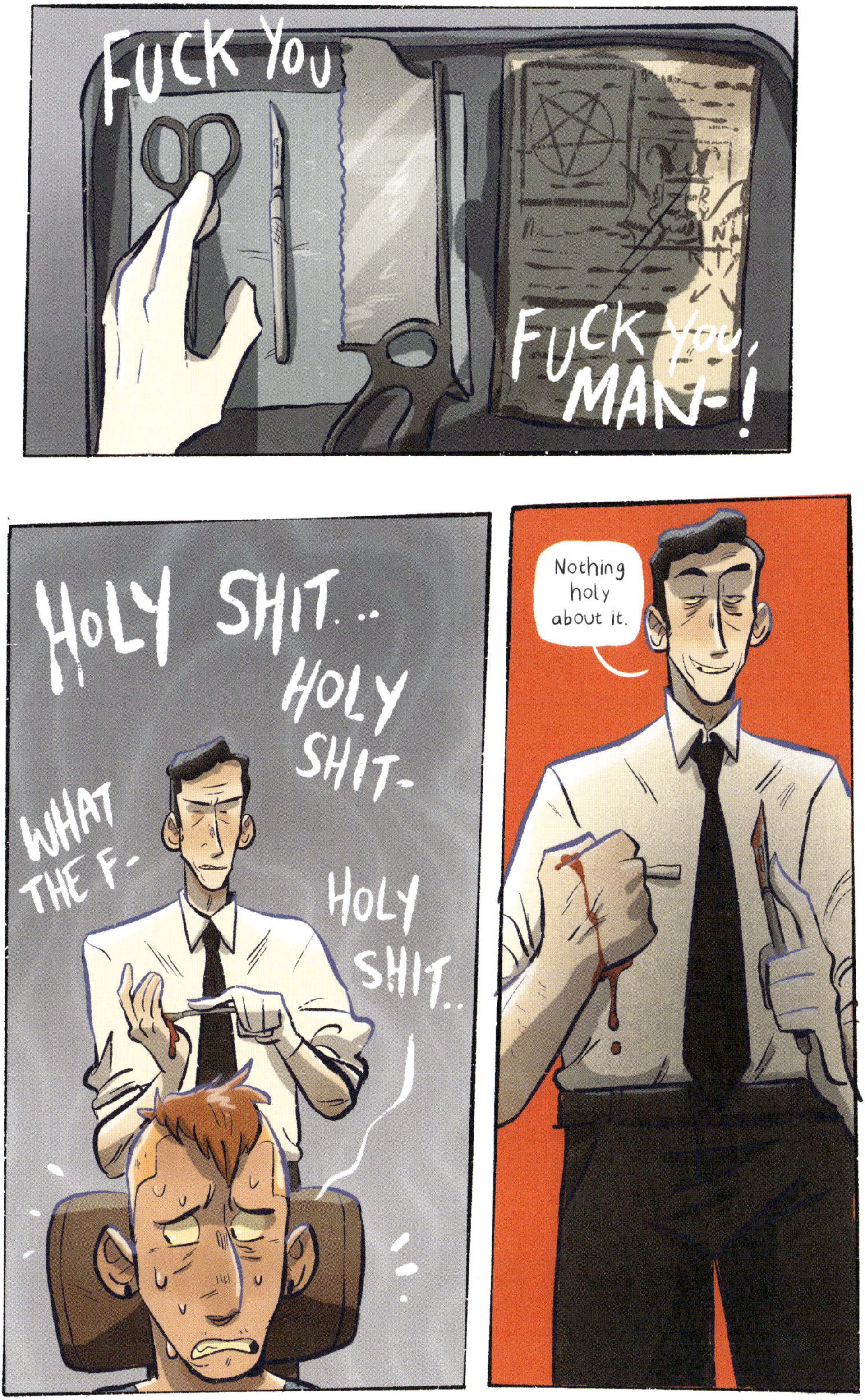
FUCK YOU
FUCK YOU MAN-!
HOLY SHIT...
HOLY SHIT-
WHAT THE F-
HOLY SHIT...
Nothing holy about it.

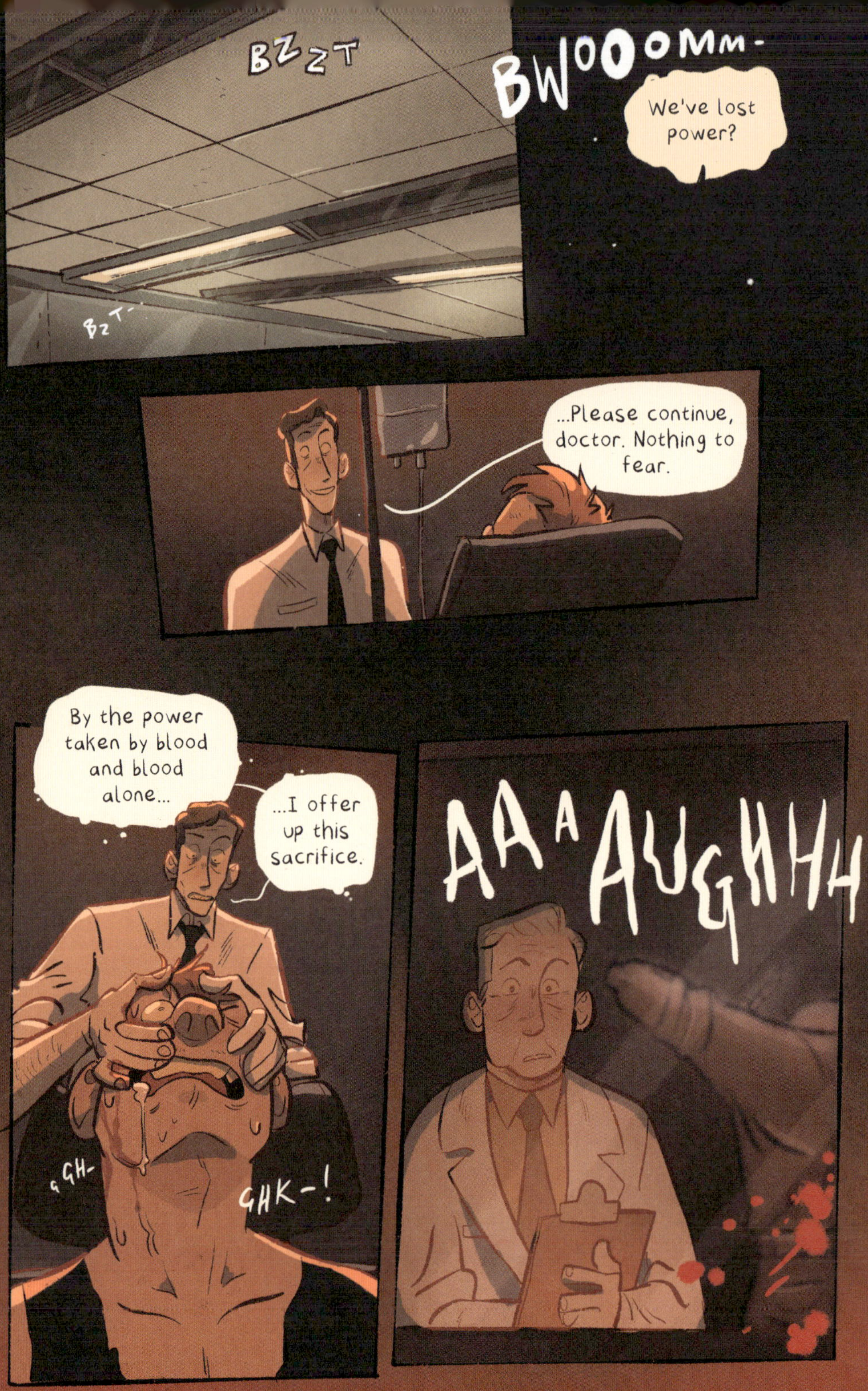
BZZT
BWOOOMM-
We've lost power?
BZT-
...Please continue, doctor. Nothing to fear.
By the power taken by blood and blood alone...
...I offer up this sacrifice.
GGH-
GHK-!
AAAAUGHHH

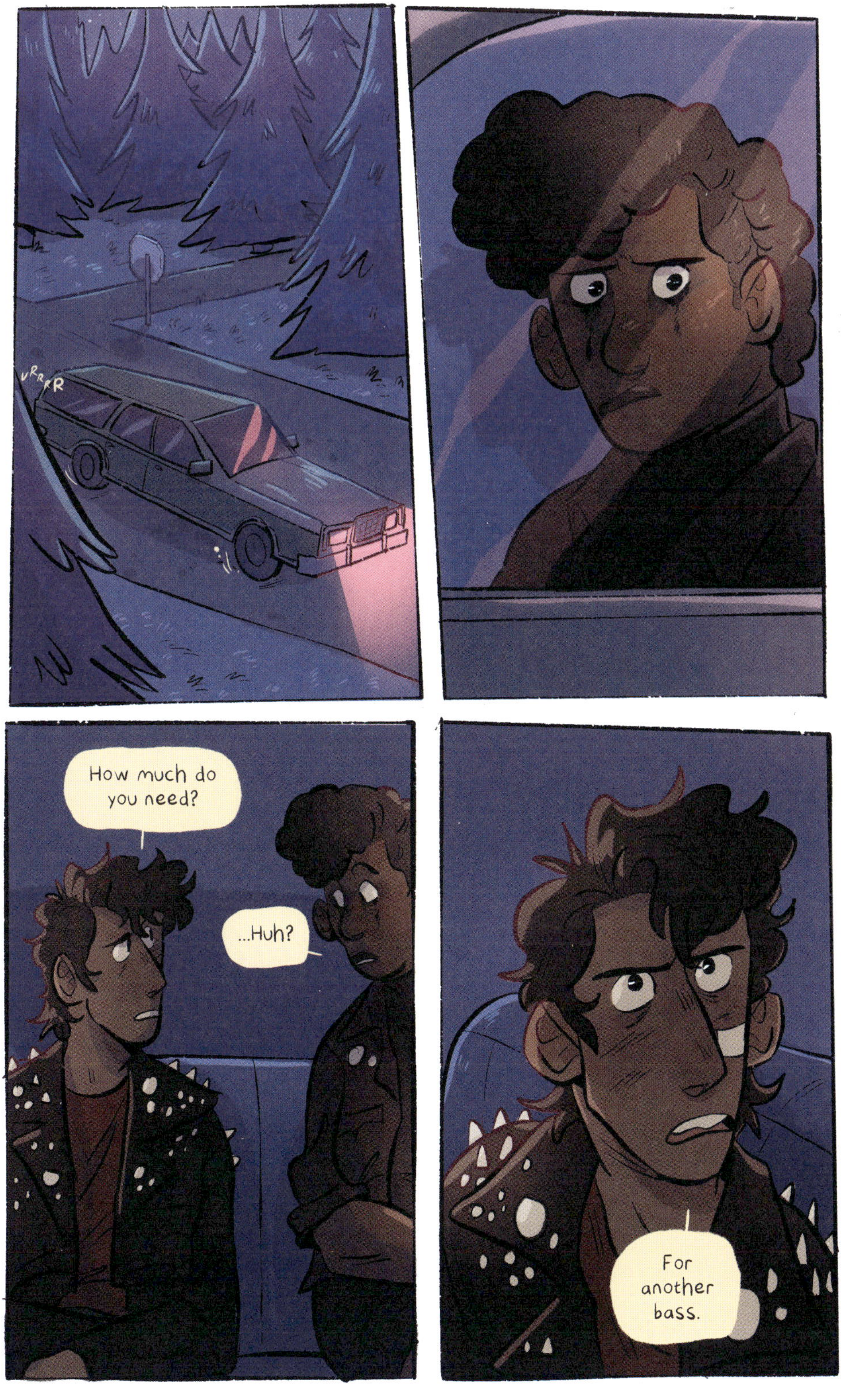
VRRRR
How much do you need?
...Huh?
For another bass.

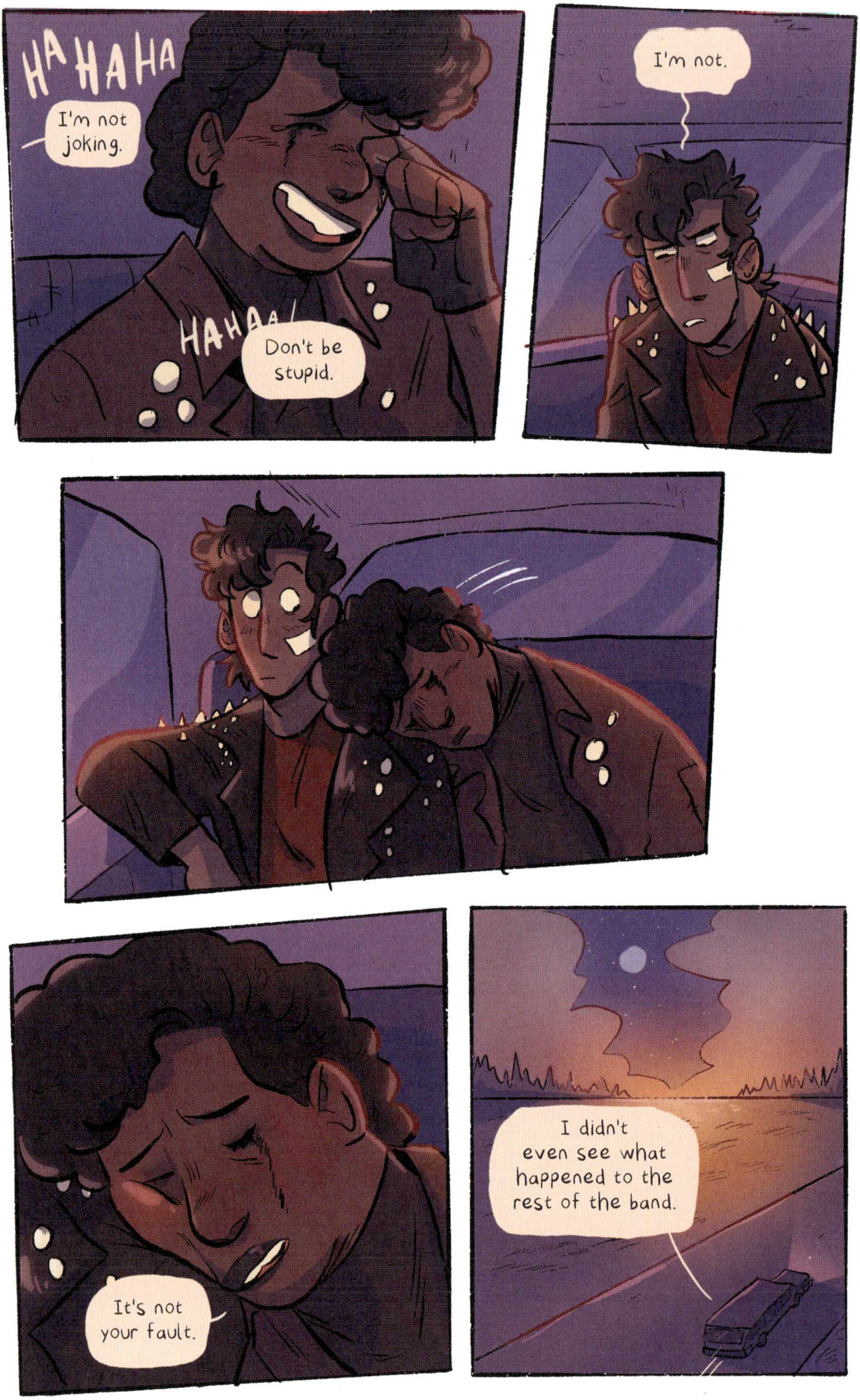
HAHAHAHA
I'm not joking.
HAHAHA!
Don't be stupid.
I'm not.
It's not your fault.
I didn't even see what happened to the rest of the band.

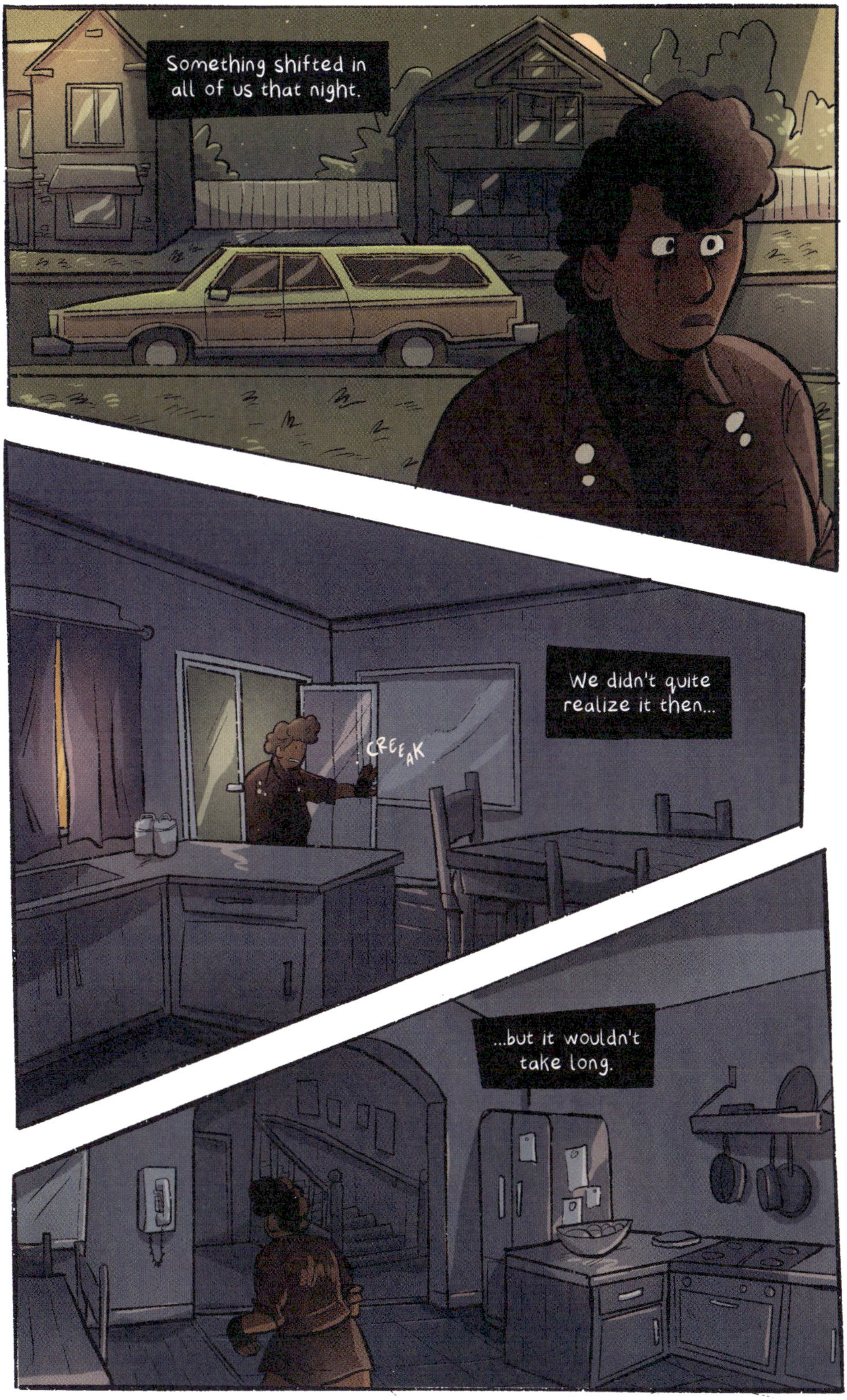
Something shifted in all of us that night.
We didn't quite realize it then...
CREEEAK
...but it wouldn't take long.

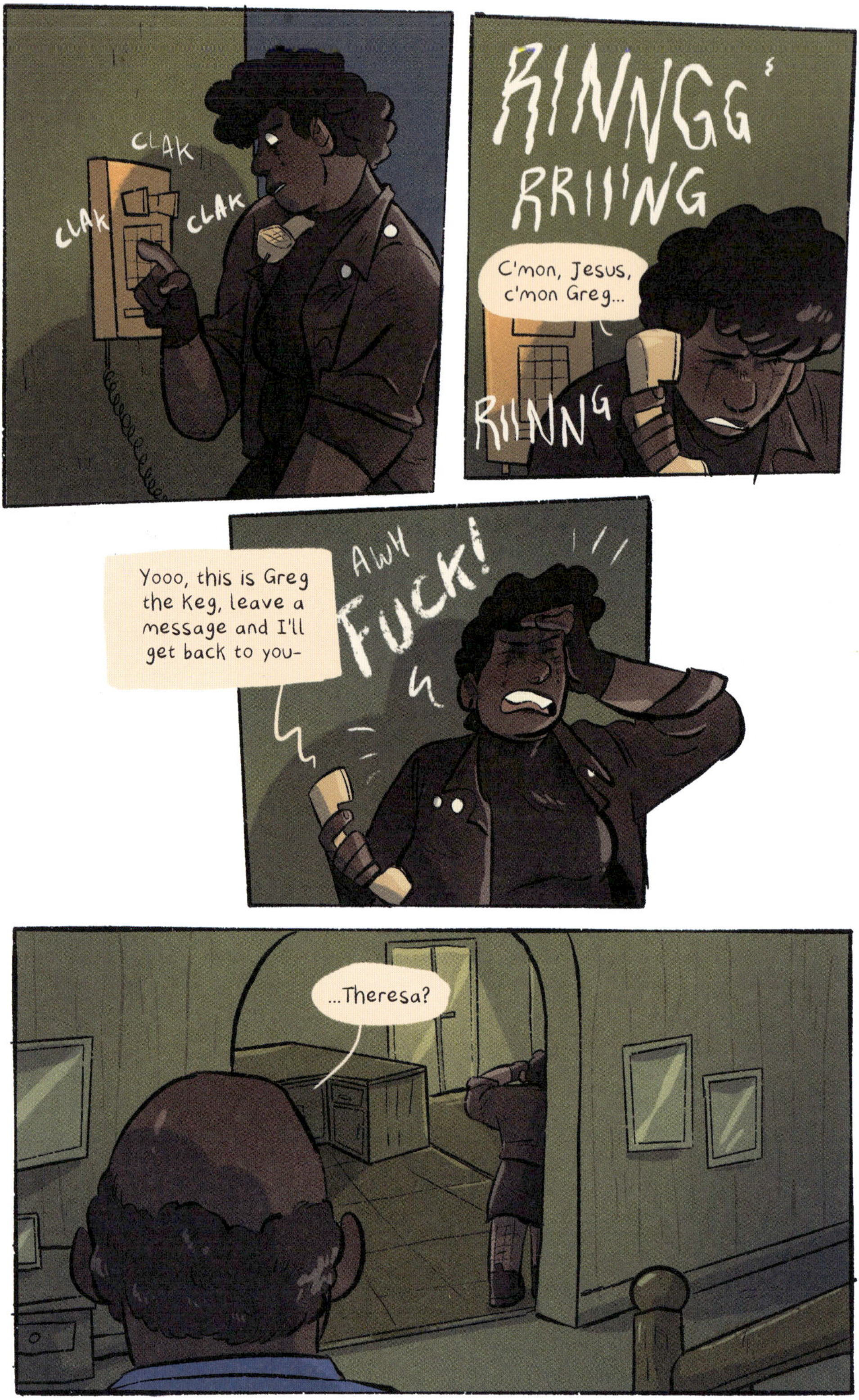
CLAK
CLAK
CLAK
RINNGG
RRII'NG
C'mon, Jesus, c'mon Greg...
RIINNG
Yooo, this is Greg the Keg, leave a message and I'll get back to you-
AWH FUCK!
...Theresa?

Dad, what the hell is going on??
What are you doing up this time of night...and what's on your face?!
Why the hell are your cop friends SO messed up?!
THERESA-
We were just hanging out!! And the cops came and I saw one of them drag off GREG, and now he's not answering his phone and-
Theresa, why were you breaking curfew, the police are specifically looking for-
For WHO, Dad?! I thought they're out trying to find a MURDERER-
...
Go to your room.
DAD!
-NOW!

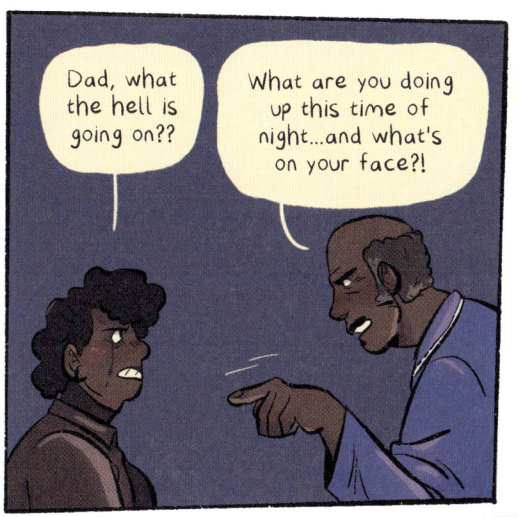

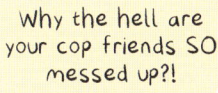

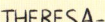

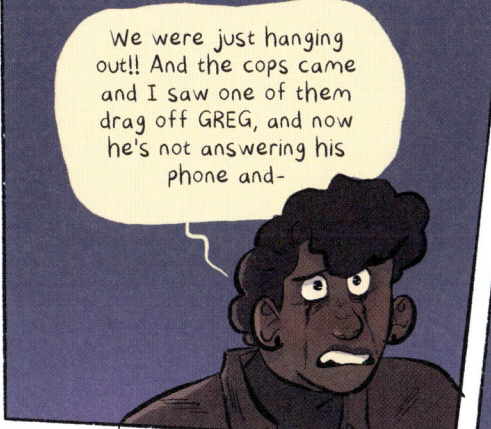

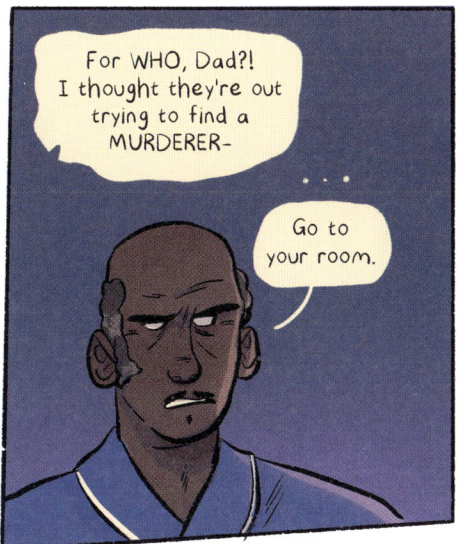

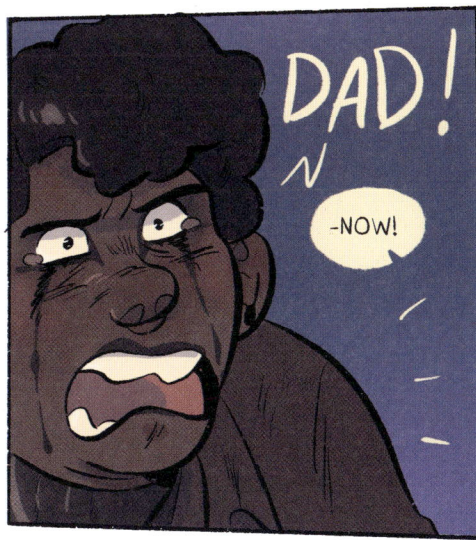

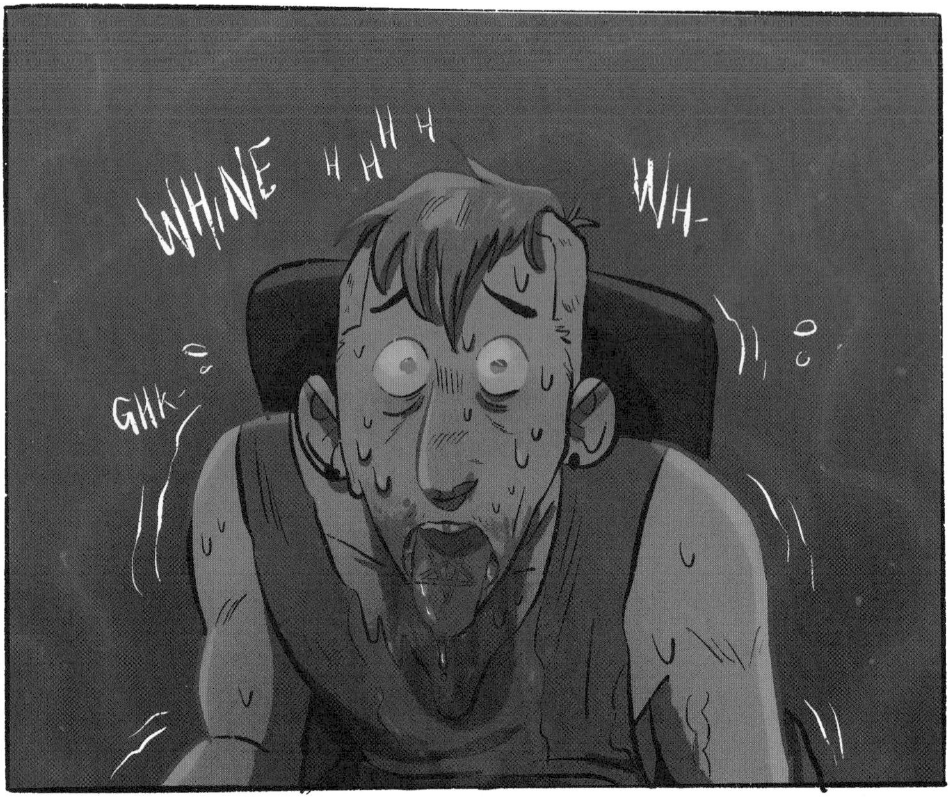
WHINE HHHH
WH-
GHK-

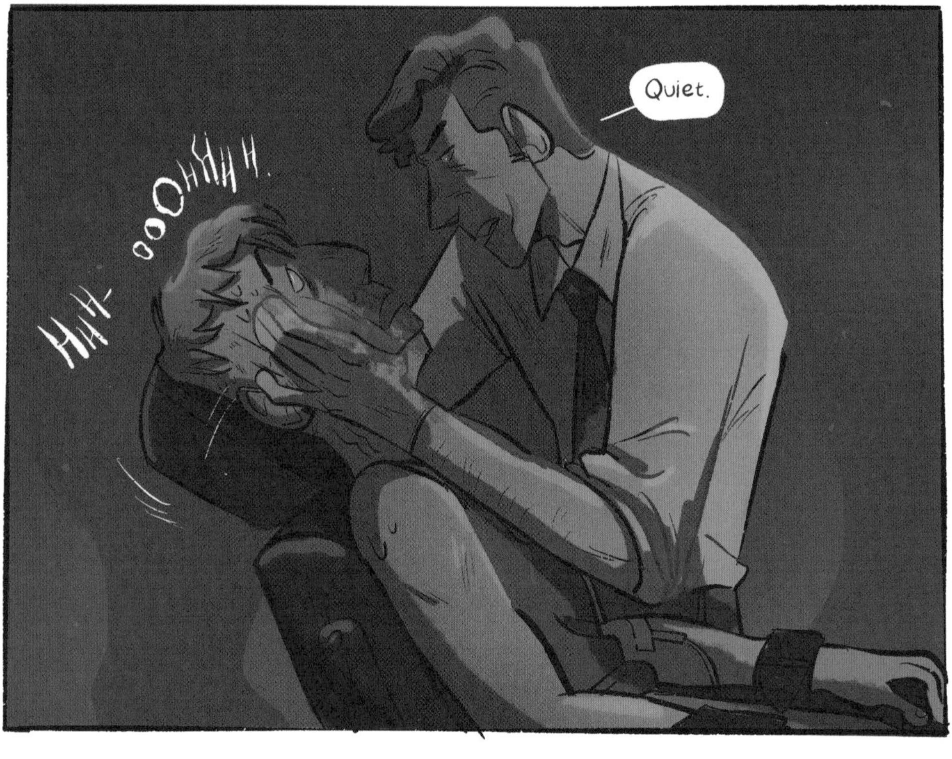
HH- OOOHHHH.
Quiet.

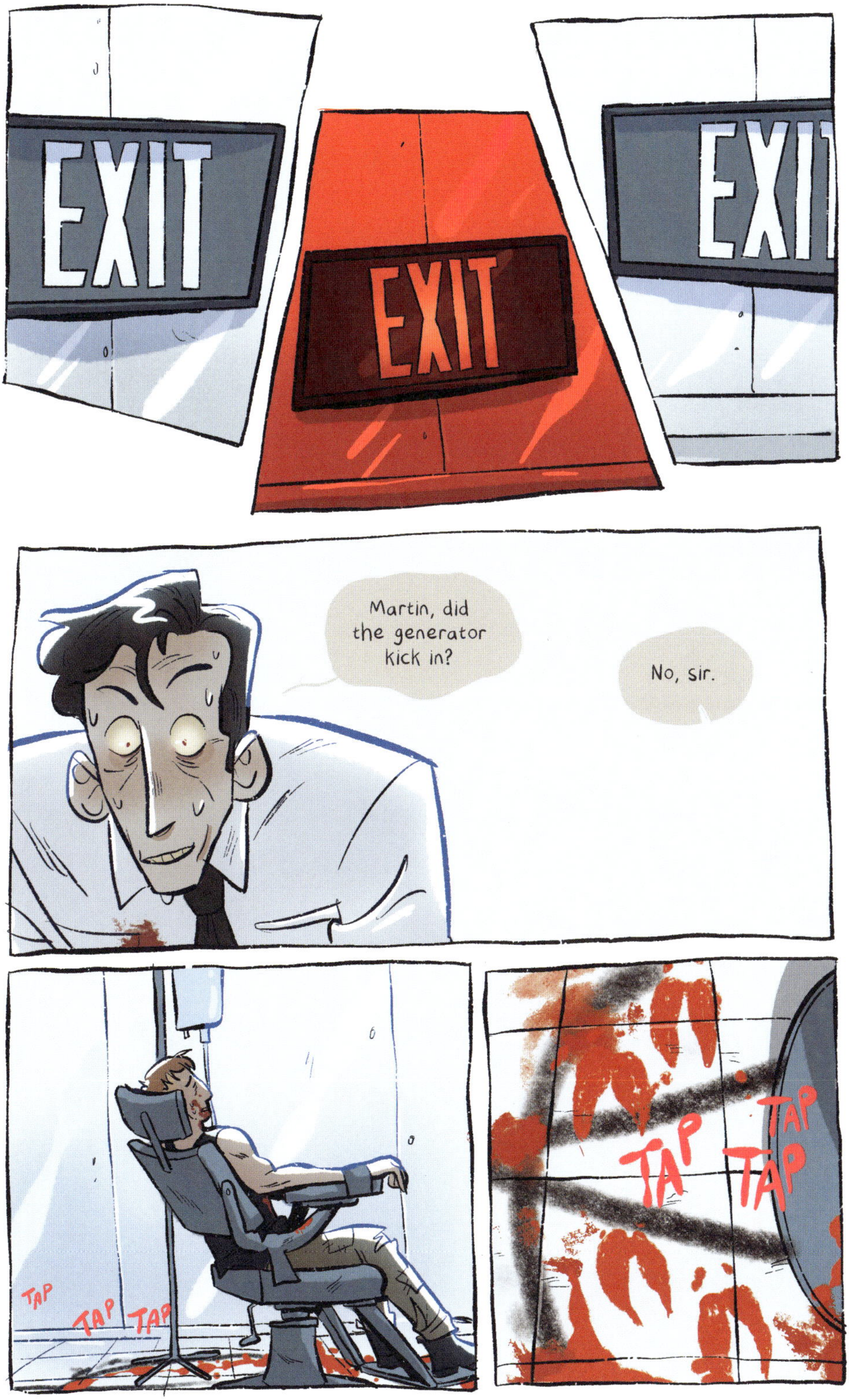
EXIT
EXIT
EXIT
Martin, did the generator kick in?
No, sir.
TAP
TAP
TAP
TAP
TAP
TAP
TAP

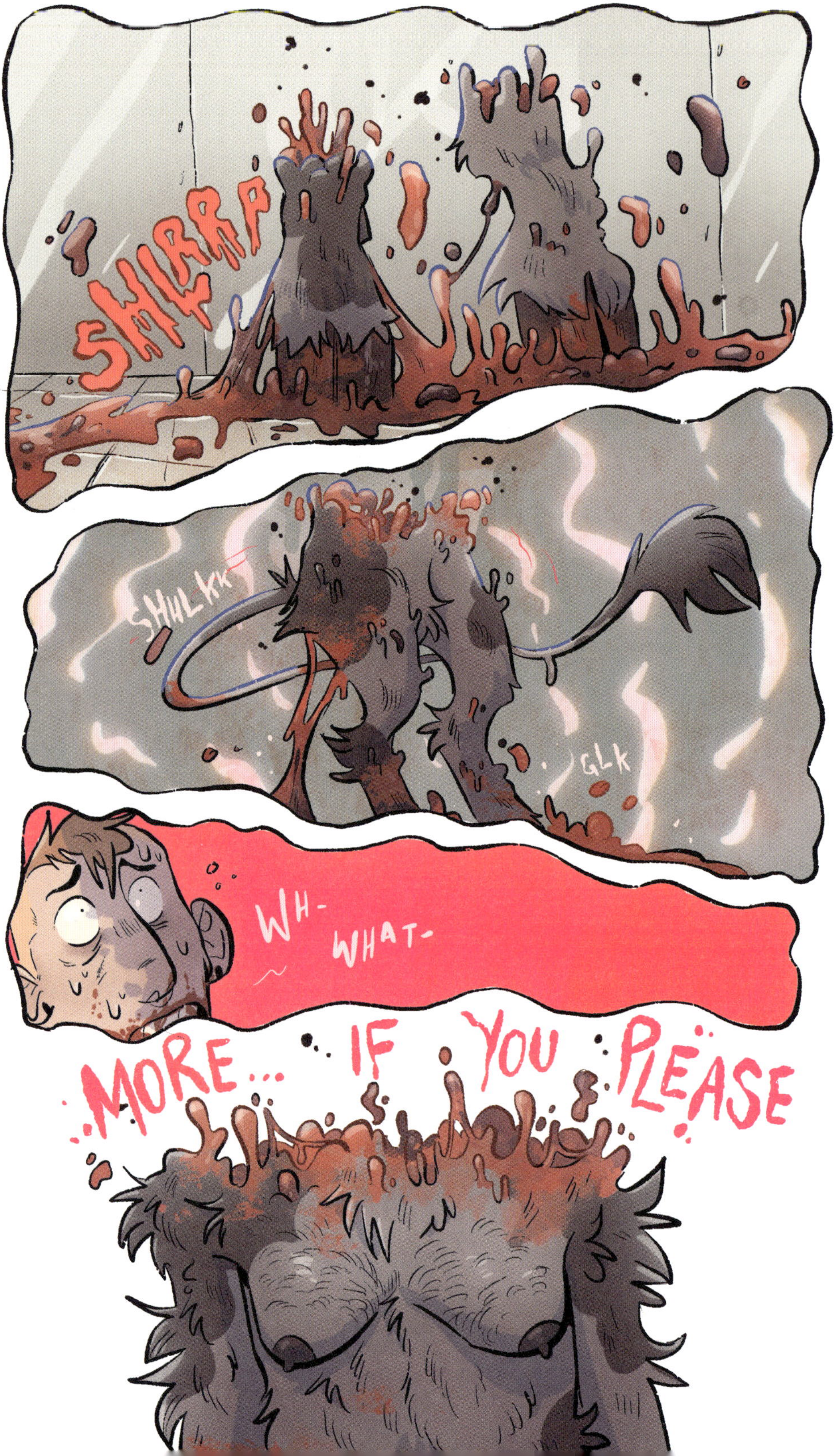
SHRRRP
SHULKK
GLK
WH-
WHAT-
MORE... IF YOU PLEASE

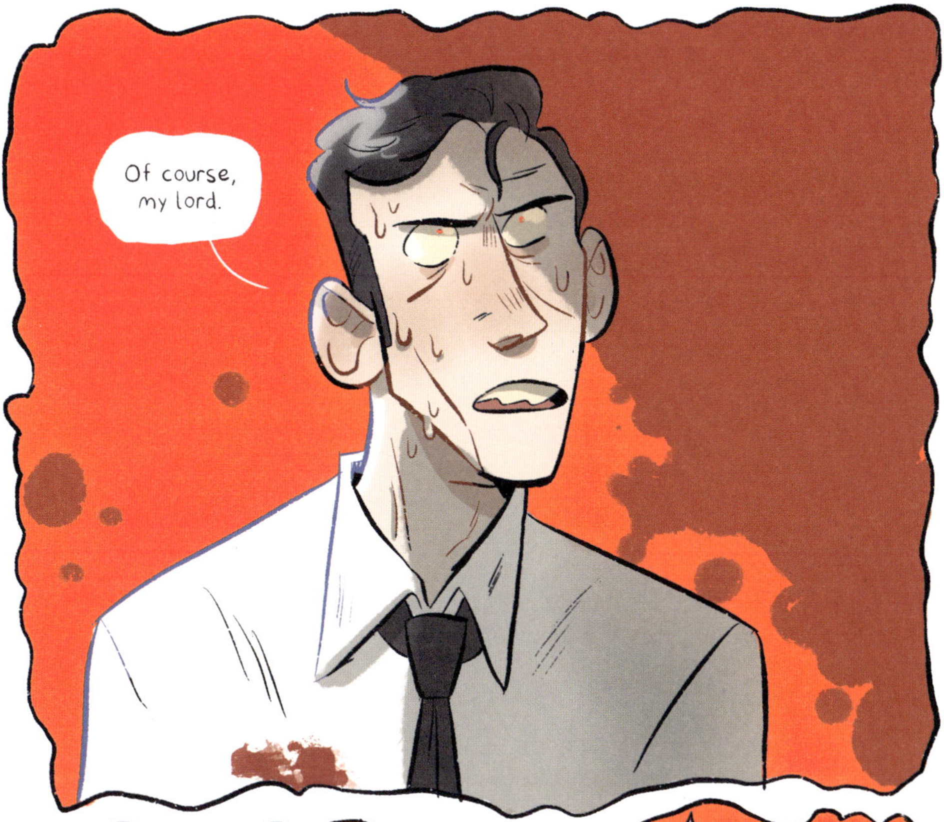
Of course, my lord.

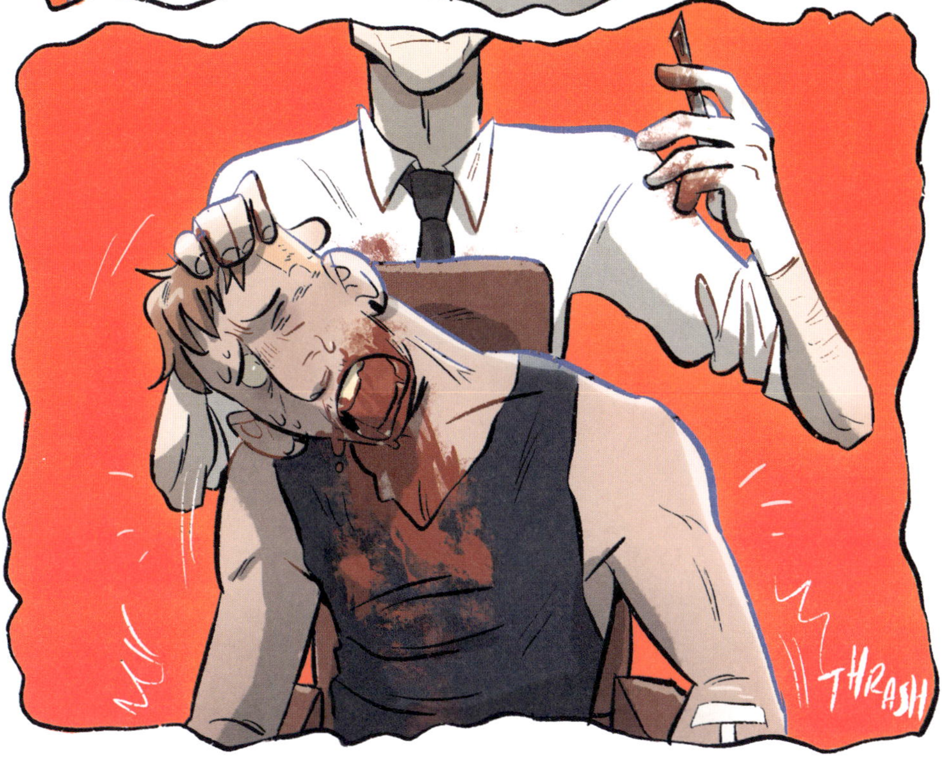
THRASH

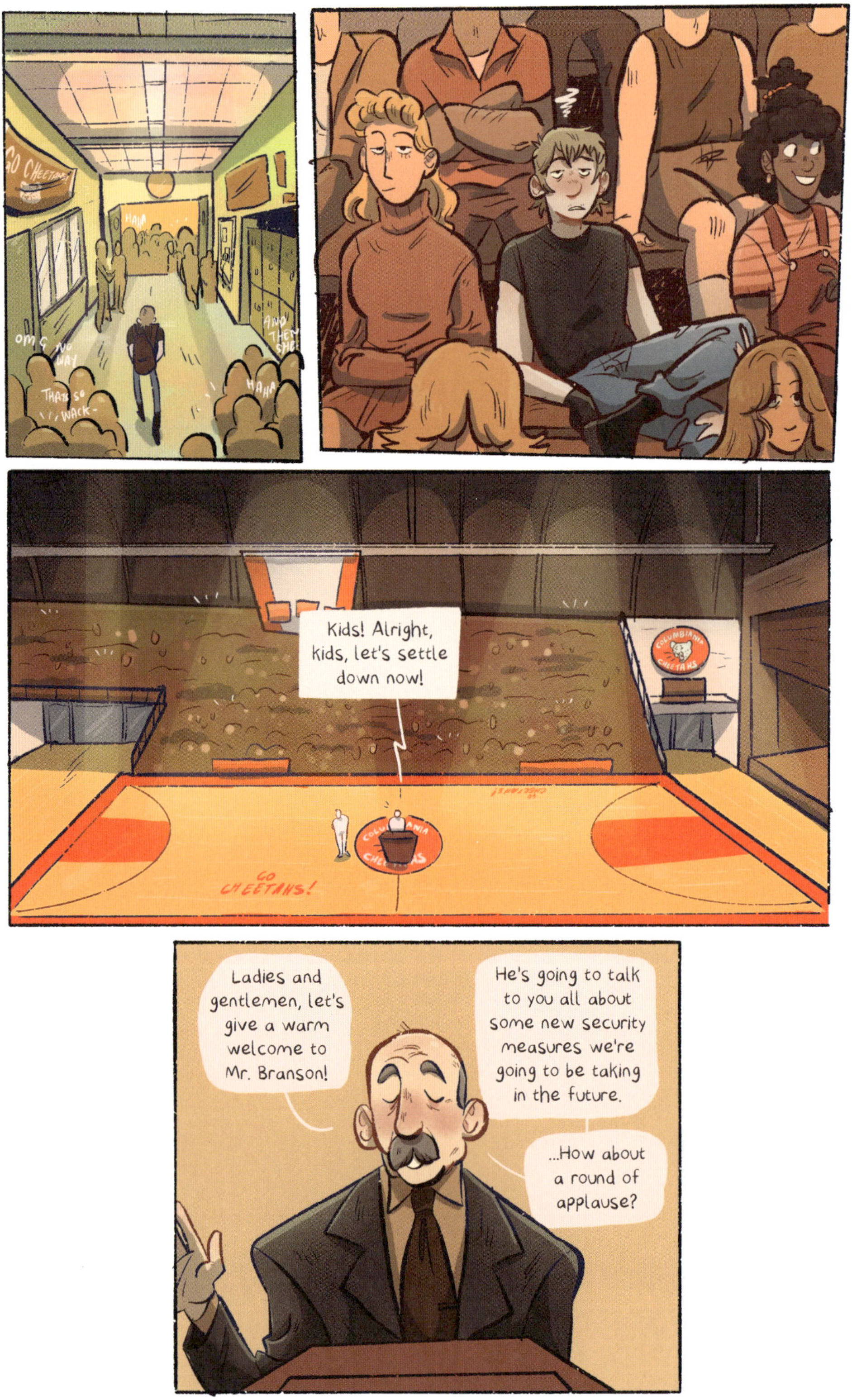
GO CHEETAHS!
HAHA
OMG NO WAY
THAT'S SO WACK-
AND THEN SHE-
HAHA
Kids! Alright, kids, let's settle down now!
COLUMBIANIA CHEETAHS
GO CHEETAHS!
Ladies and gentlemen, let's give a warm welcome to Mr. Branson!
He's going to talk to you all about some new security measures we're going to be taking in the future.
...How about a round of applause?

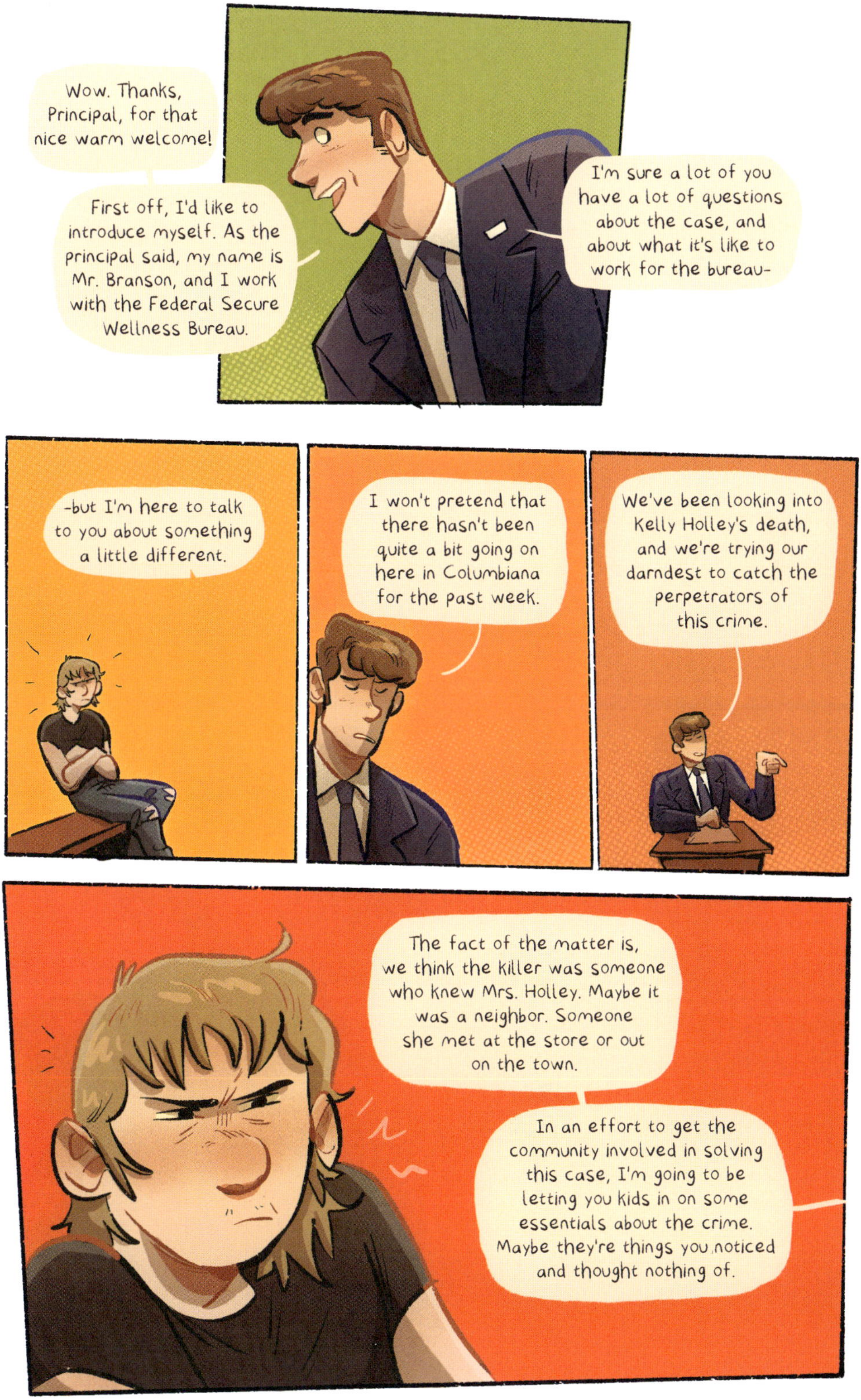

Wow. Thanks, Principal, for that nice warm welcome!
First off, I'd like to introduce myself. As the principal said, my name is Mr. Branson, and I work with the Federal Secure Wellness Bureau.
I'm sure a lot of you have a lot of questions about the case, and about what it's like to work for the bureau-
-but I'm here to talk to you about something a little different.
I won't pretend that there hasn't been quite a bit going on here in Columbiana for the past week.
We've been looking into Kelly Holley's death, and we're trying our darndest to catch the perpetrators of this crime.
The fact of the matter is, we think the killer was someone who knew Mrs. Holley. Maybe it was a neighbor. Someone she met at the store or out on the town.
In an effort to get the community involved in solving this case, I'm going to be letting you kids in on some essentials about the crime. Maybe they're things you noticed and thought nothing of.

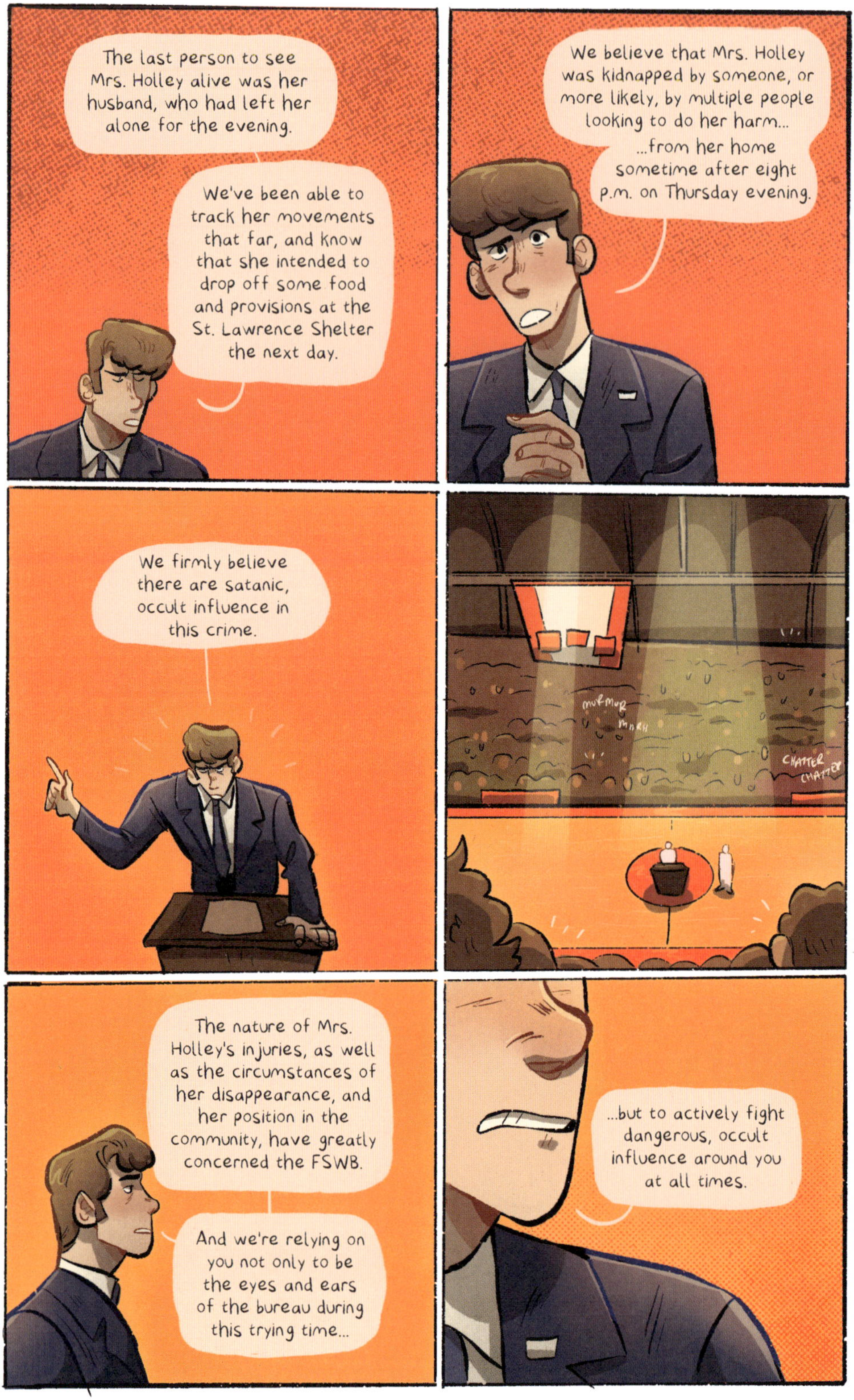

The last person to see Mrs. Holley alive was her husband, who had left her alone for the evening.
We've been able to track her movements that far, and know that she intended to drop off some food and provisions at the St. Lawrence Shelter the next day.
We believe that Mrs. Holley was kidnapped by someone, or more likely, by multiple people looking to do her harm...
...from her home sometime after eight p.m. on Thursday evening.
We firmly believe there are satanic, occult influence in this crime.
murmur
mnrh
CHATTER
CHATTER
The nature of Mrs. Holley's injuries, as well as the circumstances of her disappearance, and her position in the community, have greatly concerned the FSWB.
And we're relying on you not only to be the eyes and ears of the bureau during this trying time...
...but to actively fight dangerous, occult influence around you at all times.

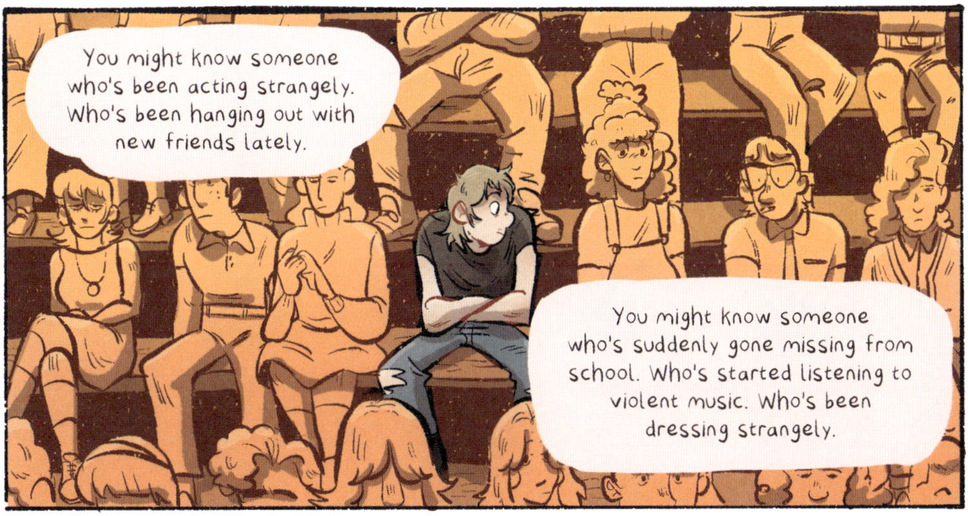
You might know someone who's been acting strangely. Who's been hanging out with new friends lately.
You might know someone who's suddenly gone missing from school. Who's started listening to violent music. Who's been dressing strangely.

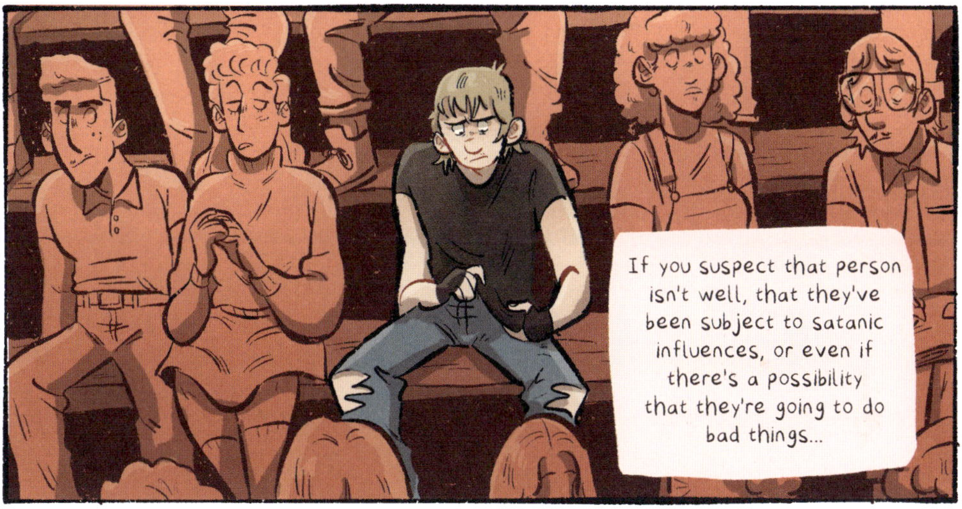
If you suspect that person isn't well, that they've been subject to satanic influences, or even if there's a possibility that they're going to do bad things...

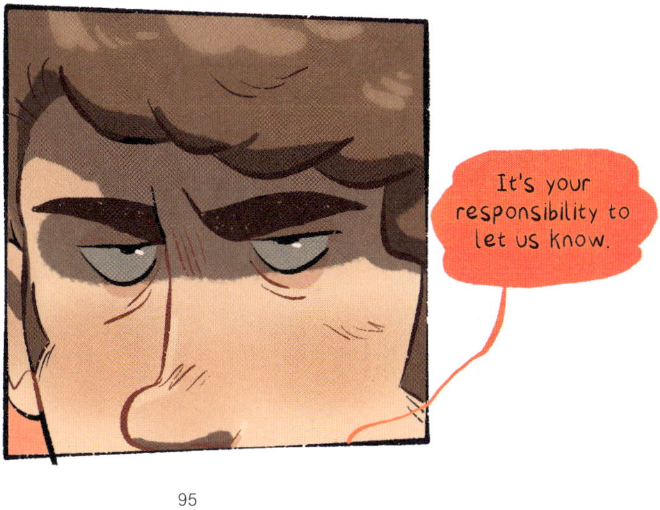
It's your responsibility to let us know.

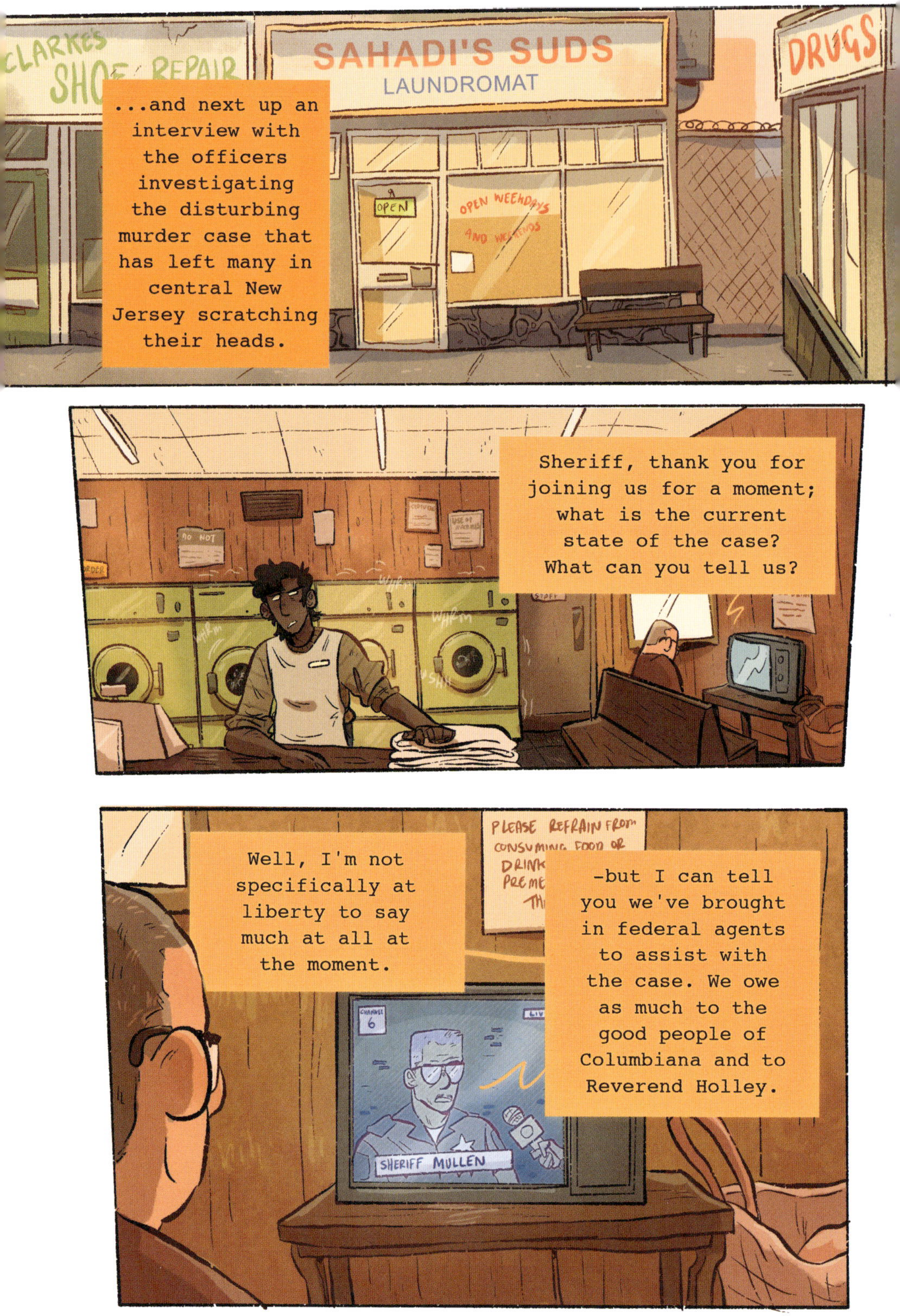
SAHADI'S SUDS
LAUNDROMAT
DRUGS
...and next up an interview with the officers investigating the disturbing murder case that has left many in central New Jersey scratching their heads.
OPEN
OPEN WEEKDAYS
Sheriff, thank you for joining us for a moment; what is the current state of the case? What can you tell us?
Well, I'm not specifically at liberty to say much at all at the moment.
-but I can tell you we've brought in federal agents to assist with the case. We owe as much to the good people of Columbiana and to Reverend Holley.
PLEASE REFRAIN FROM
6
SHERIFF MULLEN

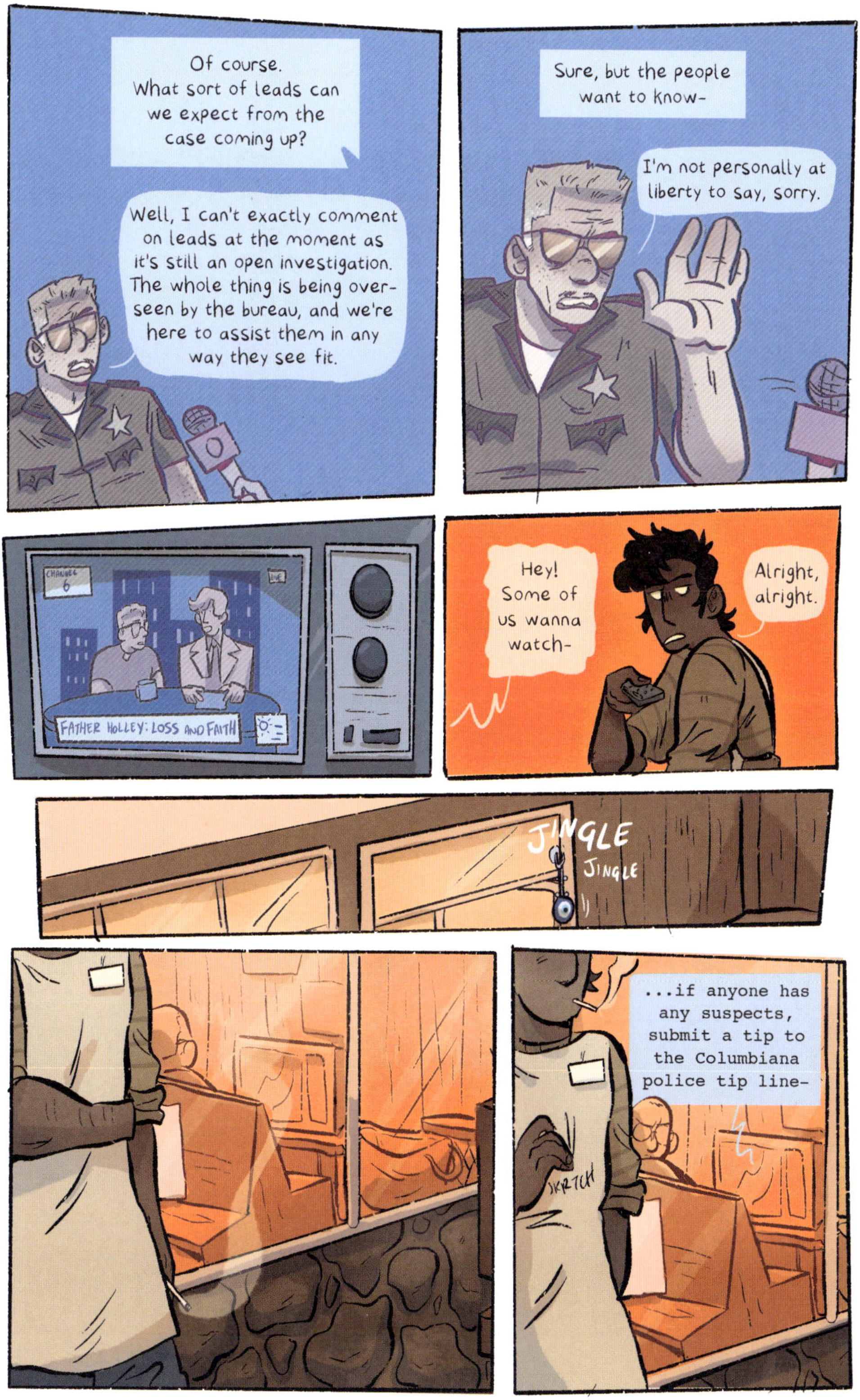
Of course.
What sort of leads can we expect from the case coming up?
Well, I can't exactly comment on leads at the moment as it's still an open investigation. The whole thing is being over-seen by the bureau, and we're here to assist them in any way they see fit.
Sure, but the people want to know-
I'm not personally at liberty to say, sorry.
FATHER HOLLEY: LOSS AND FAITH
Hey! Some of us wanna watch-
Alright, alright.
JINGLE
JINGLE
SKRTCH
...if anyone has any suspects, submit a tip to the Columbiana police tip line-

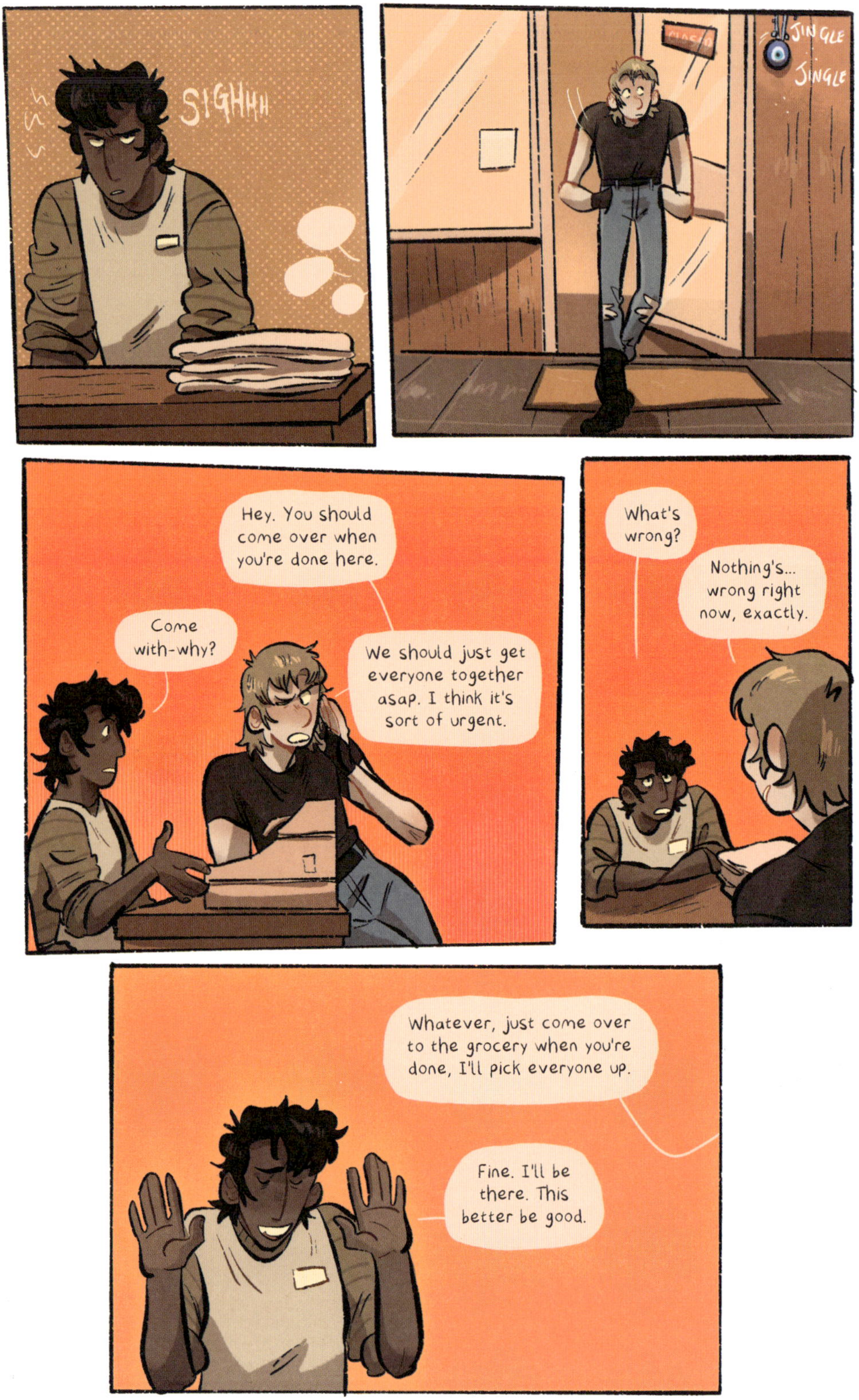
SIGHHH
JINGLE
JINGLE
Hey. You should come over when you're done here.
Come with-why?
We should just get everyone together asap. I think it's sort of urgent.
What's wrong?
Nothing's... wrong right now, exactly.
Whatever, just come over to the grocery when you're done, I'll pick everyone up.
Fine. I'll be there. This better be good.

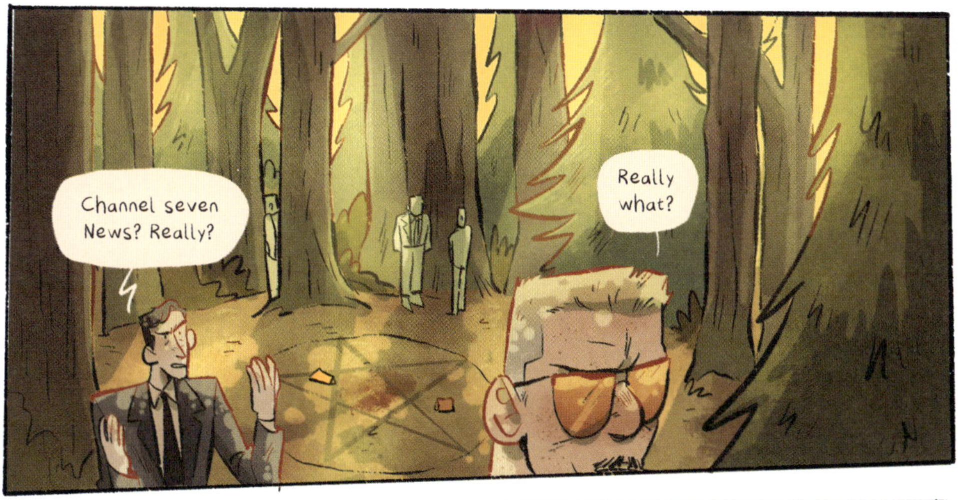
Channel seven News? Really?
Really what?

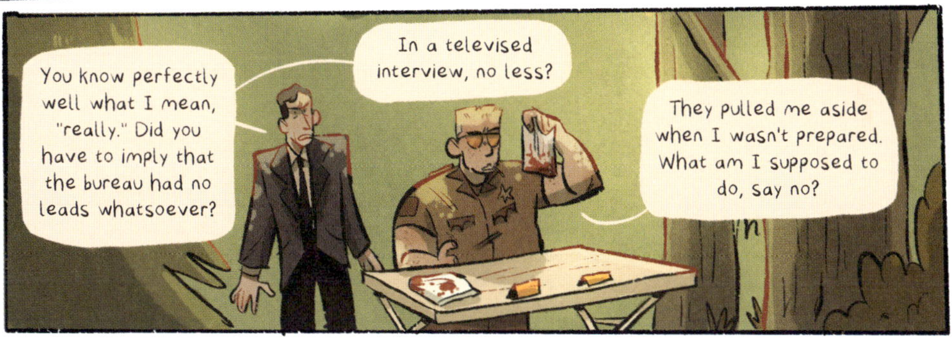
You know perfectly well what I mean, "really." Did you have to imply that the bureau had no leads whatsoever?
In a televised interview, no less?
They pulled me aside when I wasn't prepared. What am I supposed to do, say no?

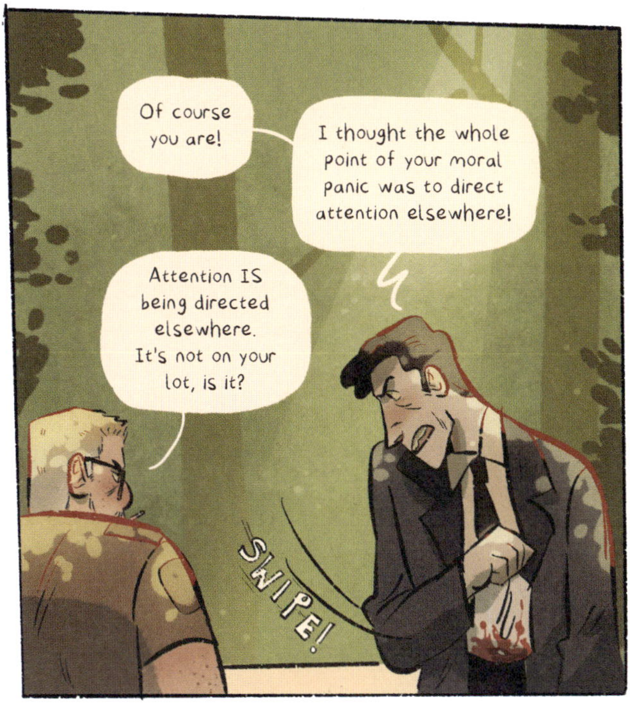
Of course you are!
I thought the whole point of your moral panic was to direct attention elsewhere!
Attention IS being directed elsewhere. It's not on your lot, is it?
SWIPE!

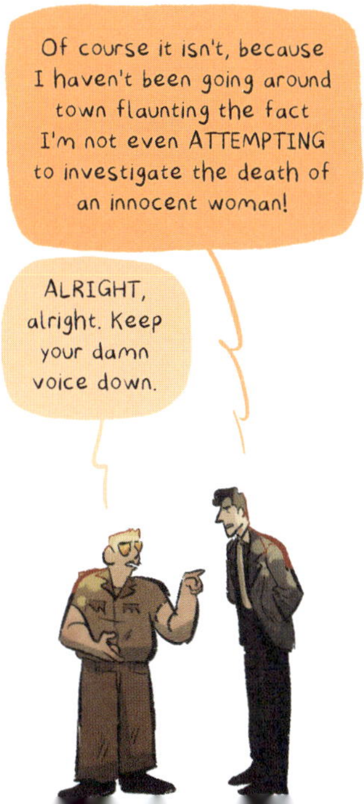
Of course it isn't, because I haven't been going around town flaunting the fact I'm not even ATTEMPTING to investigate the death of an innocent woman!
ALRIGHT, alright. Keep your damn voice down.

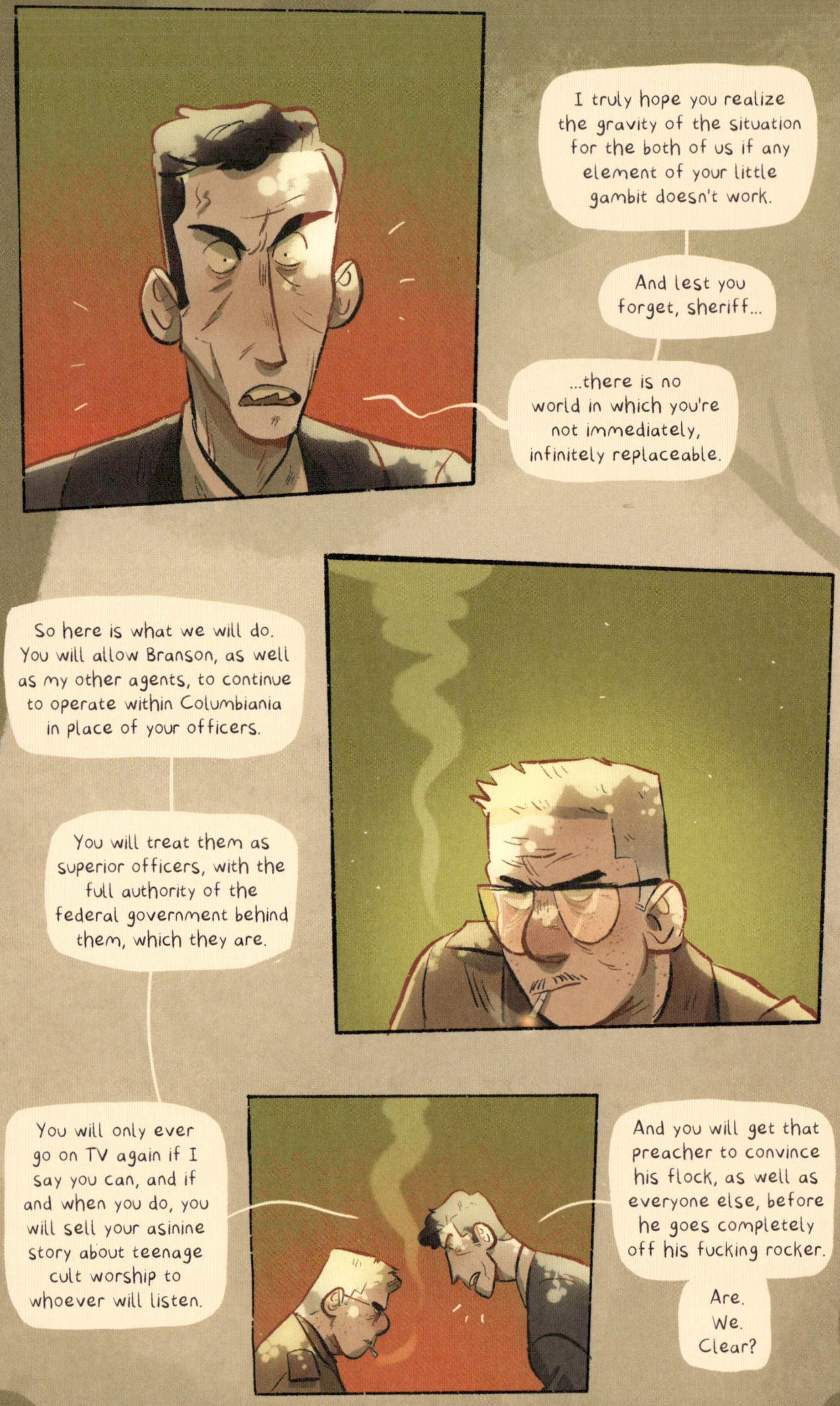
I truly hope you realize the gravity of the situation for the both of us if any element of your little gambit doesn't work.
And lest you forget, sheriff...
...there is no world in which you're not immediately, infinitely replaceable.
So here is what we will do. You will allow Branson, as well as my other agents, to continue to operate within Columbiania in place of your officers.
You will treat them as superior officers, with the full authority of the federal government behind them, which they are.
You will only ever go on TV again if I say you can, and if and when you do, you will sell your asinine story about teenage cult worship to whoever will listen.
And you will get that preacher to convince his flock, as well as everyone else, before he goes completely off his fucking rocker.
Are. We. Clear?

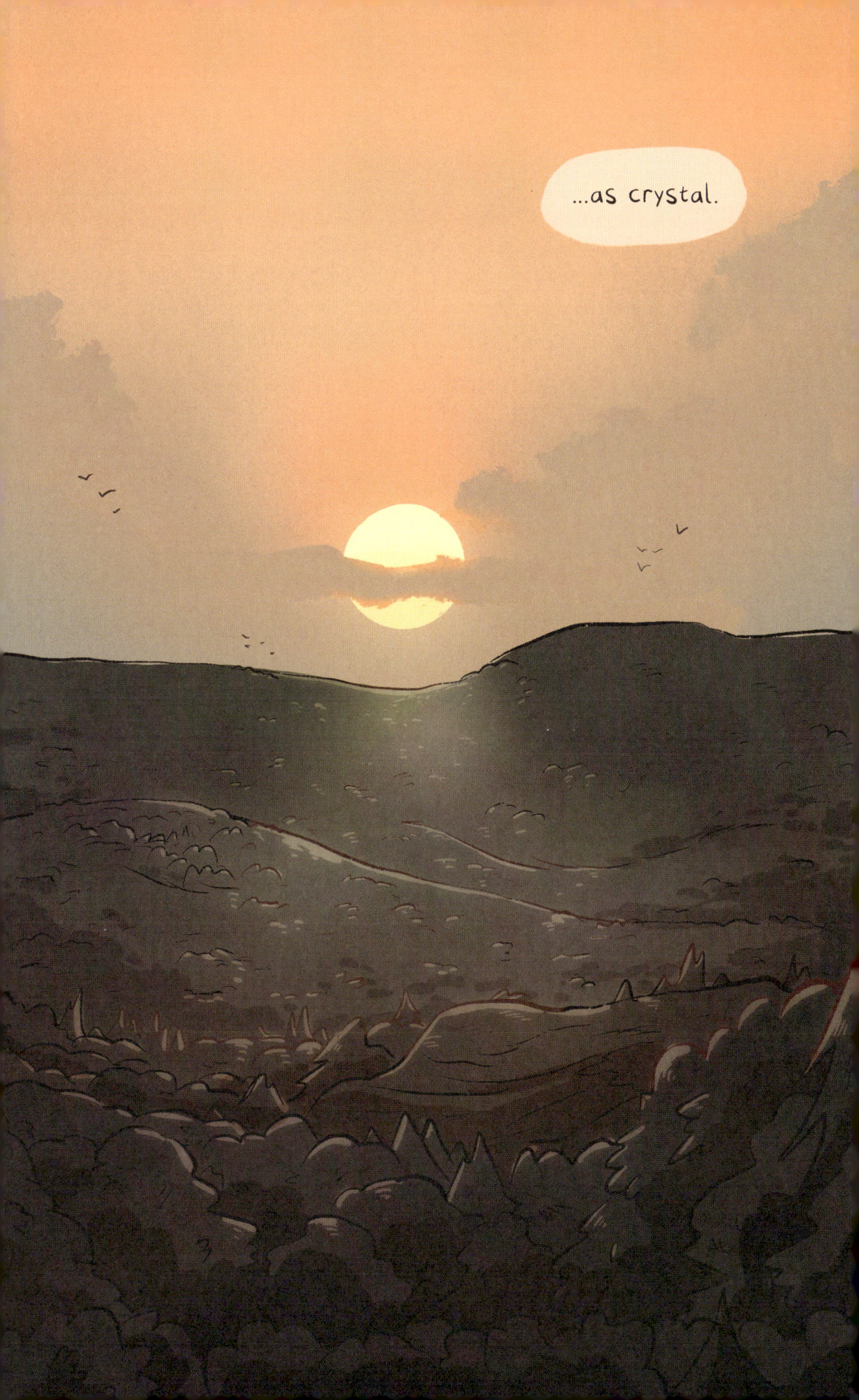
...as crystal.

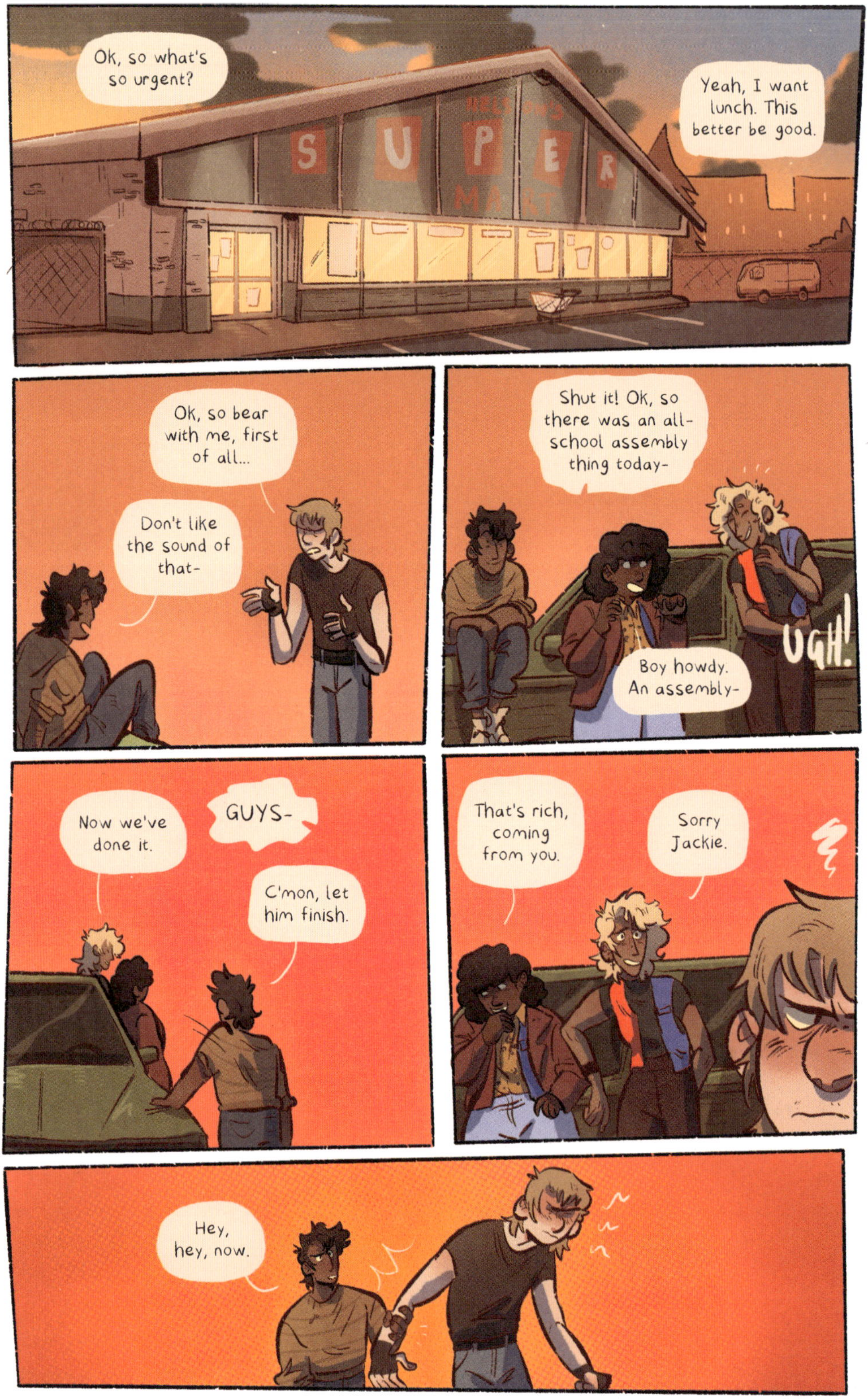
SUPER MART
Ok, so what's so urgent?
Yeah, I want lunch. This better be good.
Ok, so bear with me, first of all...
Don't like the sound of that-
Shut it! Ok, so there was an all-school assembly thing today-
UGH!
Boy howdy. An assembly-
Now we've done it.
GUYS-
C'mon, let him finish.
That's rich, coming from you.
Sorry Jackie.
Hey, hey, now.

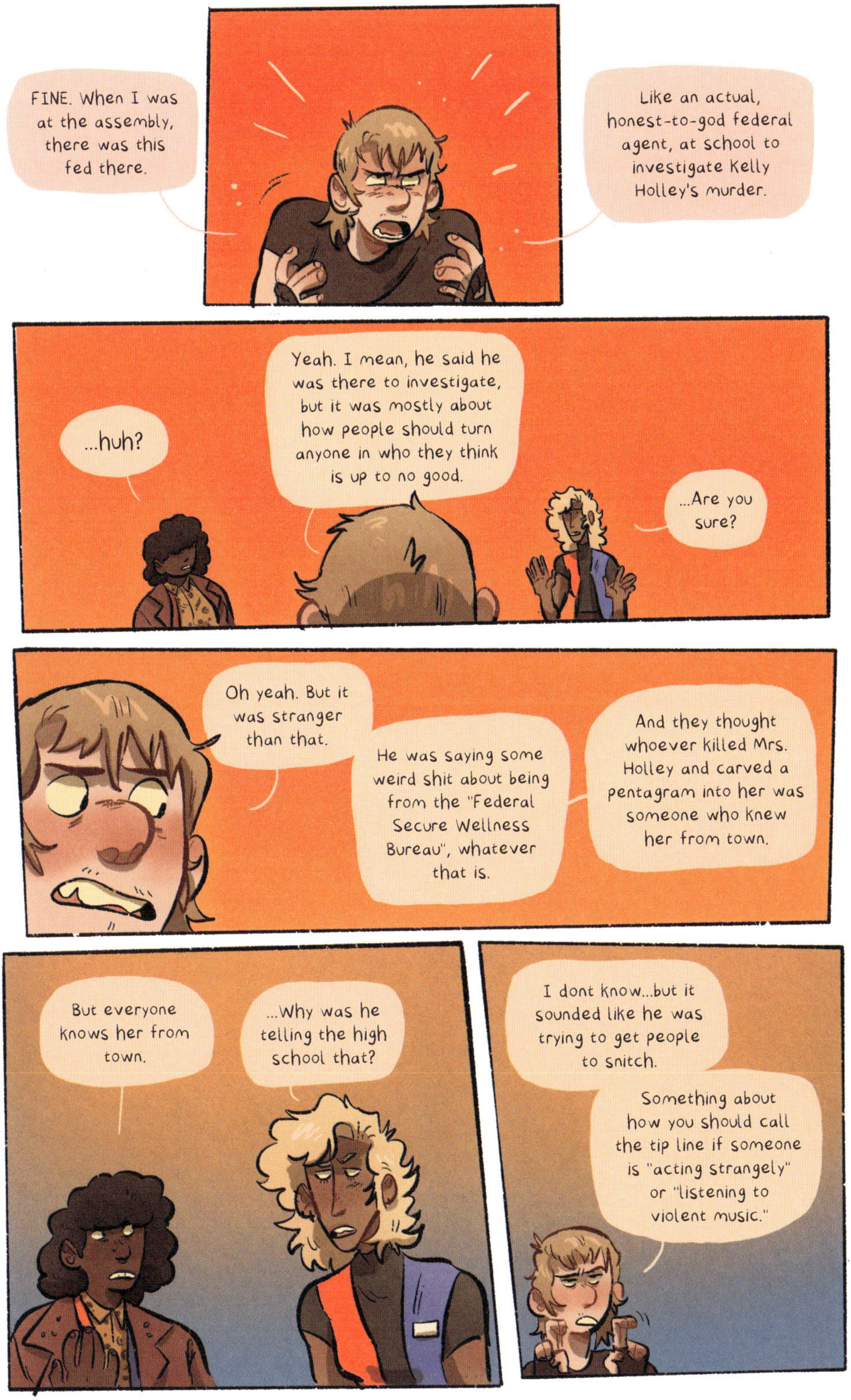
FINE. When I was at the assembly, there was this fed there.
Like an actual, honest-to-god federal agent, at school to investigate Kelly Holley's murder.
...huh?
Yeah. I mean, he said he was there to investigate, but it was mostly about how people should turn anyone in who they think is up to no good.
...Are you sure?
Oh yeah. But it was stranger than that.
He was saying some weird shit about being from the "Federal Secure Wellness Bureau", whatever that is.
And they thought whoever killed Mrs. Holley and carved a pentagram into her was someone who knew her from town.
But everyone knows her from town.
...Why was he telling the high school that?
I dont know...but it sounded like he was trying to get people to snitch.
Something about how you should call the tip line if someone is "acting strangely" or "listening to violent music."

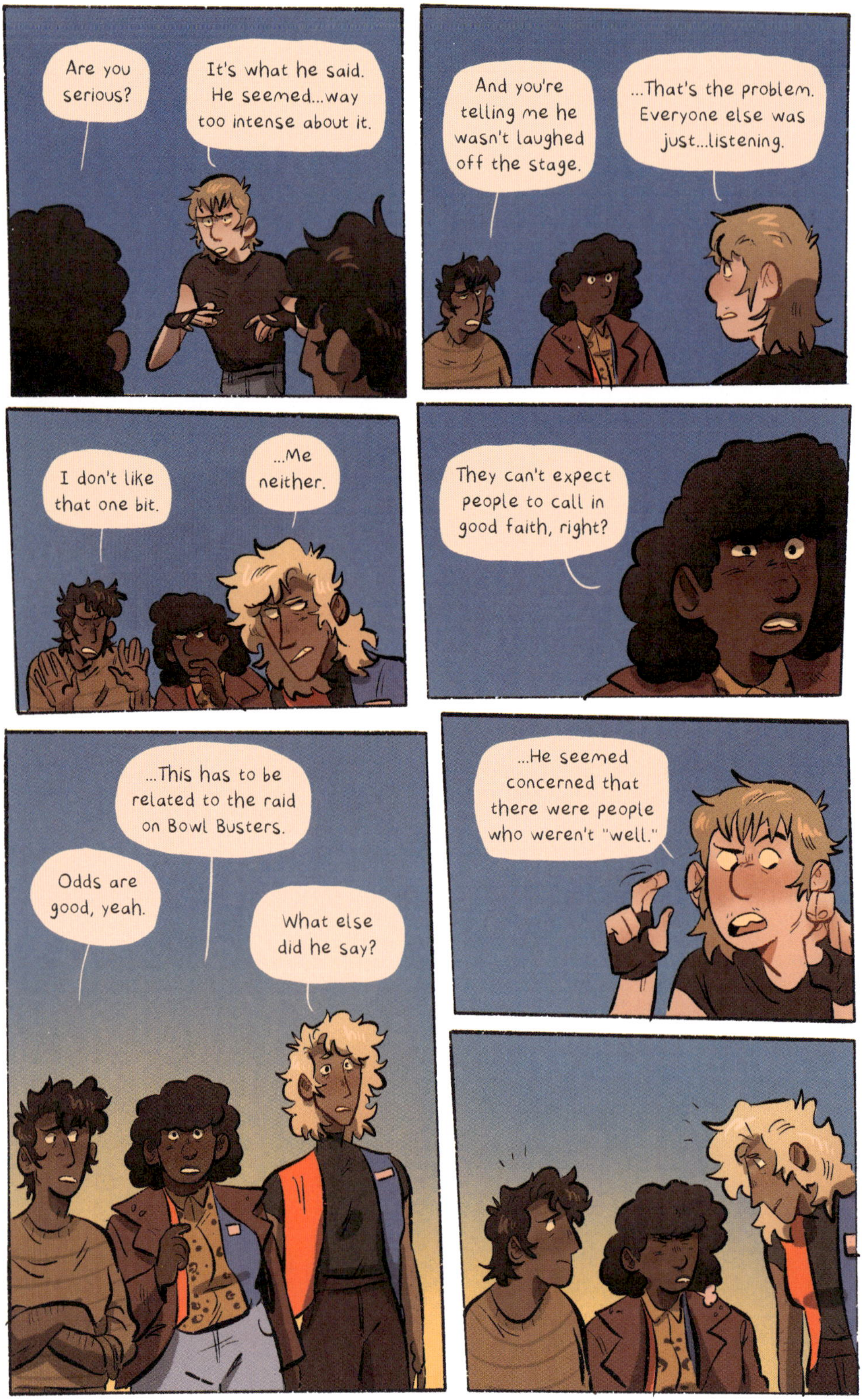
Are you serious?
It's what he said. He seemed...way too intense about it.
And you're telling me he wasn't laughed off the stage.
...That's the problem. Everyone else was just...listening.
I don't like that one bit.
...Me neither.
They can't expect people to call in good faith, right?
...This has to be related to the raid on Bowl Busters.
Odds are good, yeah.
What else did he say?
...He seemed concerned that there were people who weren't "well."

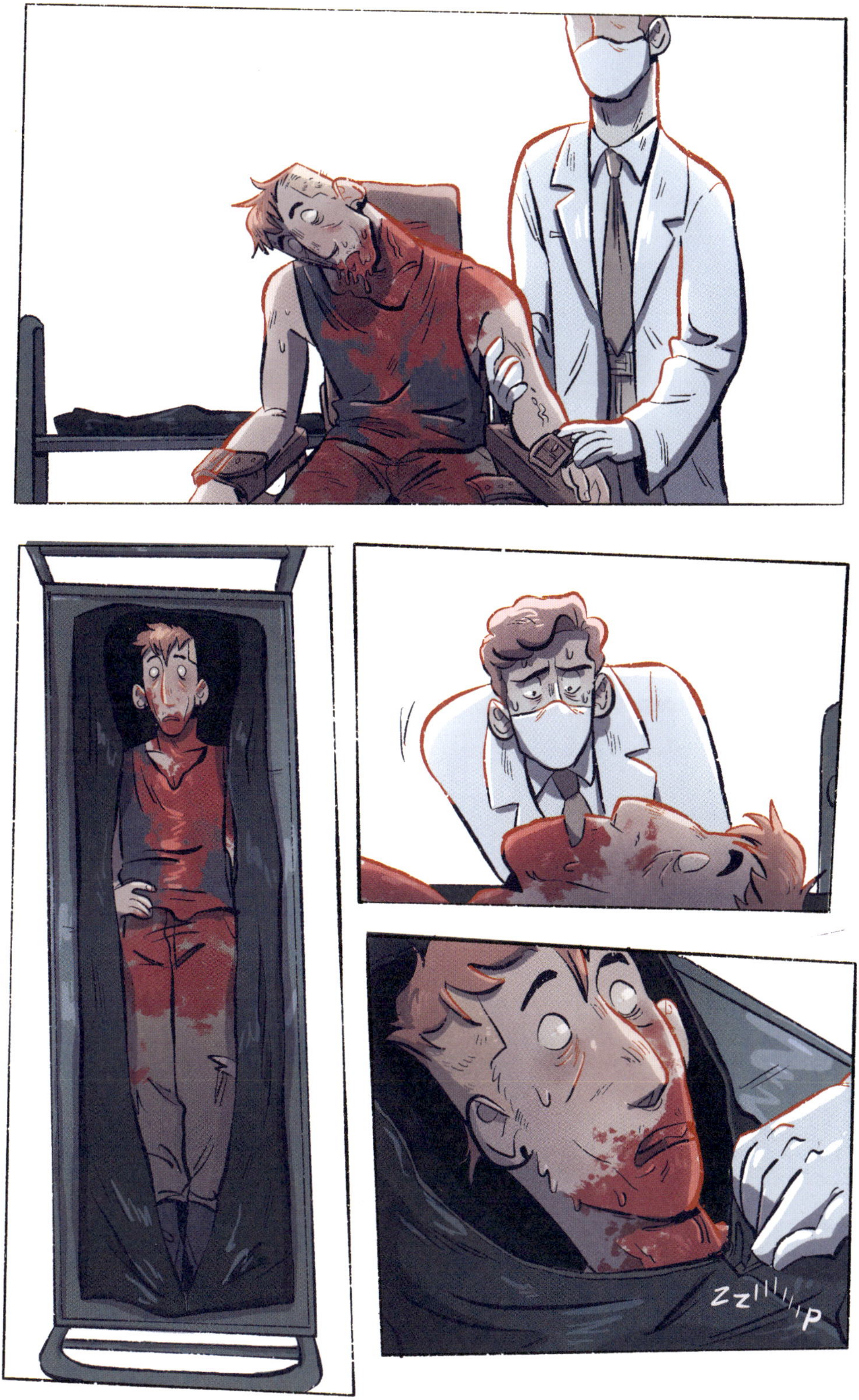
ZZIIIIIIP

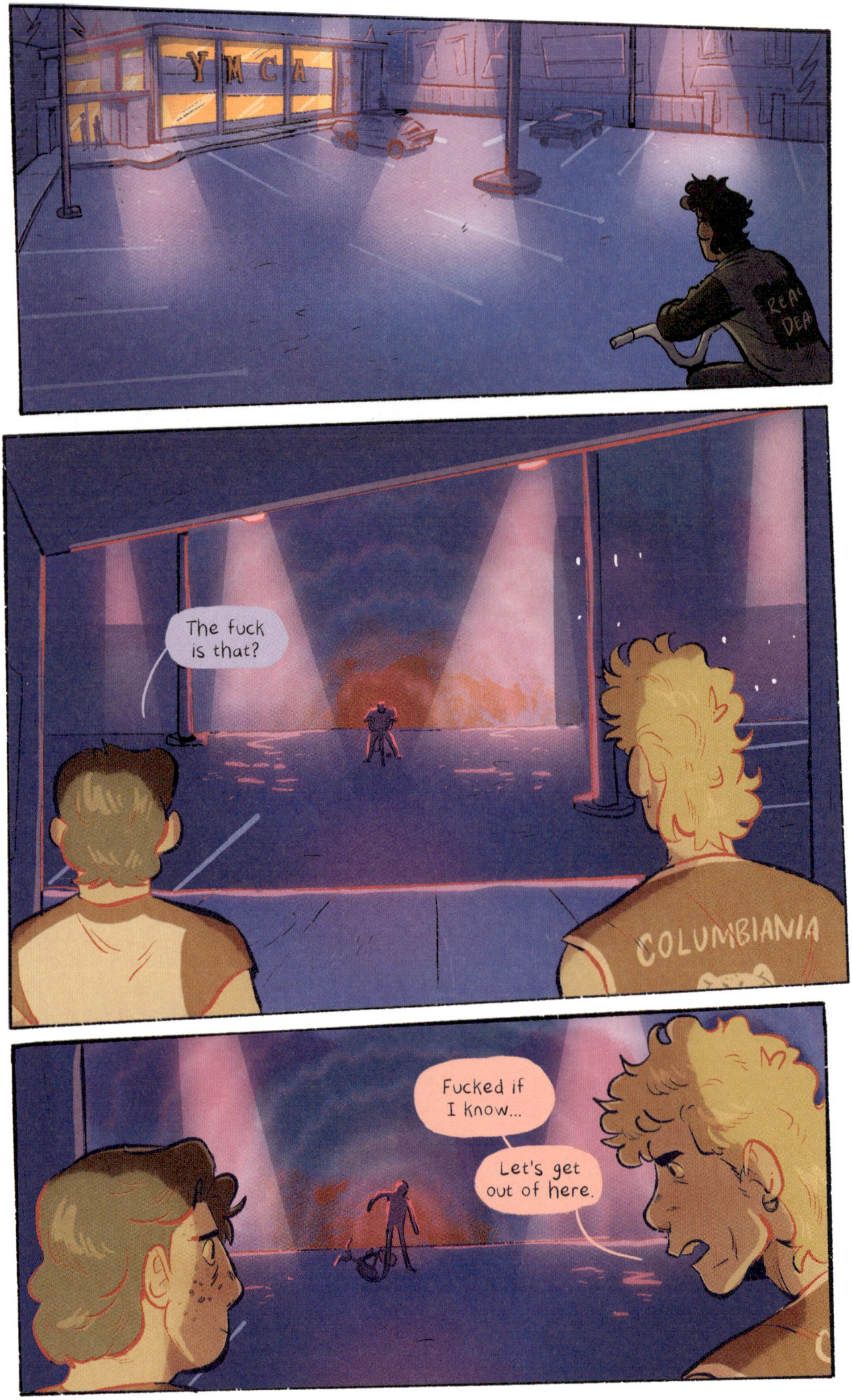
YMCA
The fuck is that?
COLUMBIANIA
Fucked if I know...
Let's get out of here.

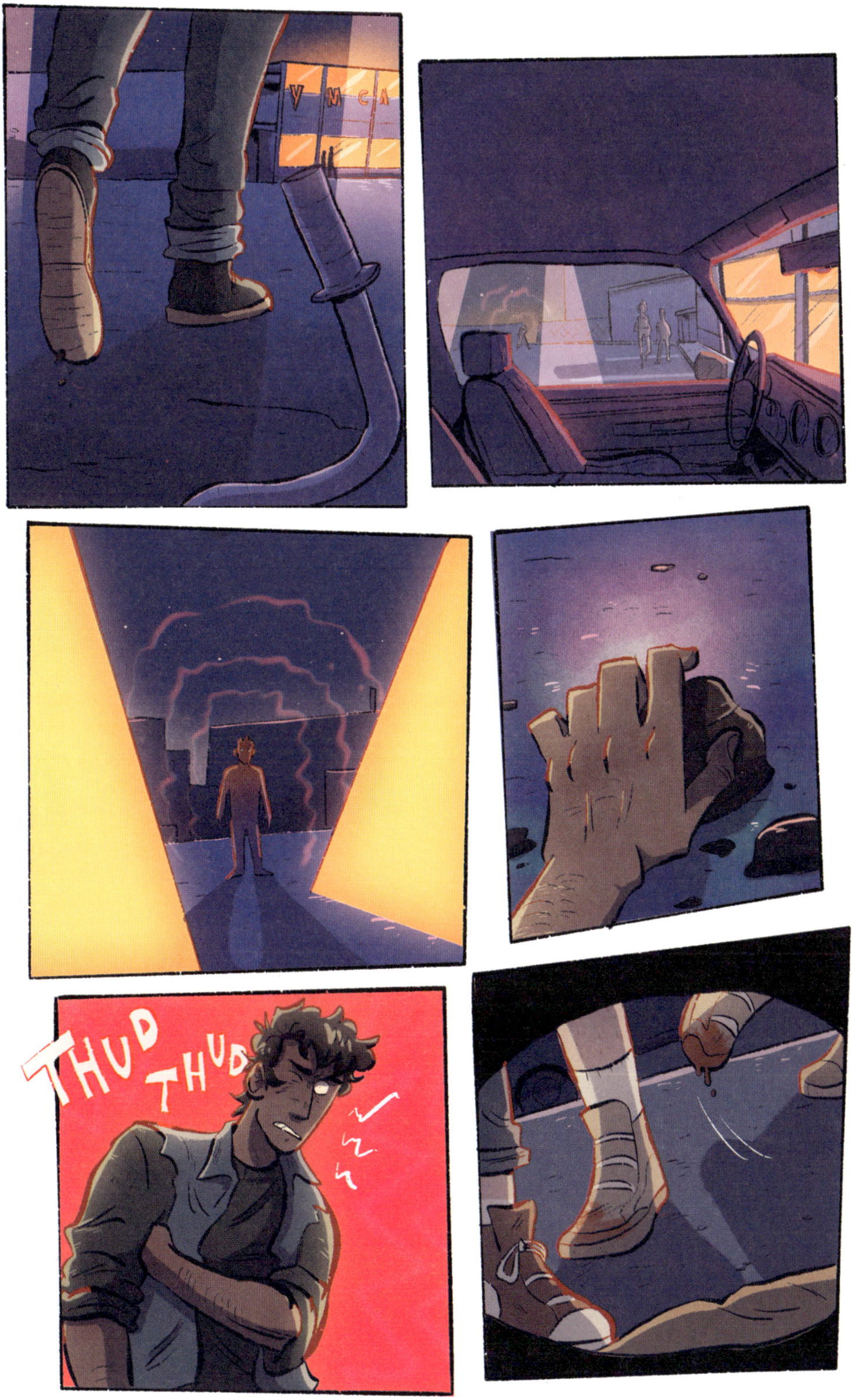
YMCA
THUD THUD

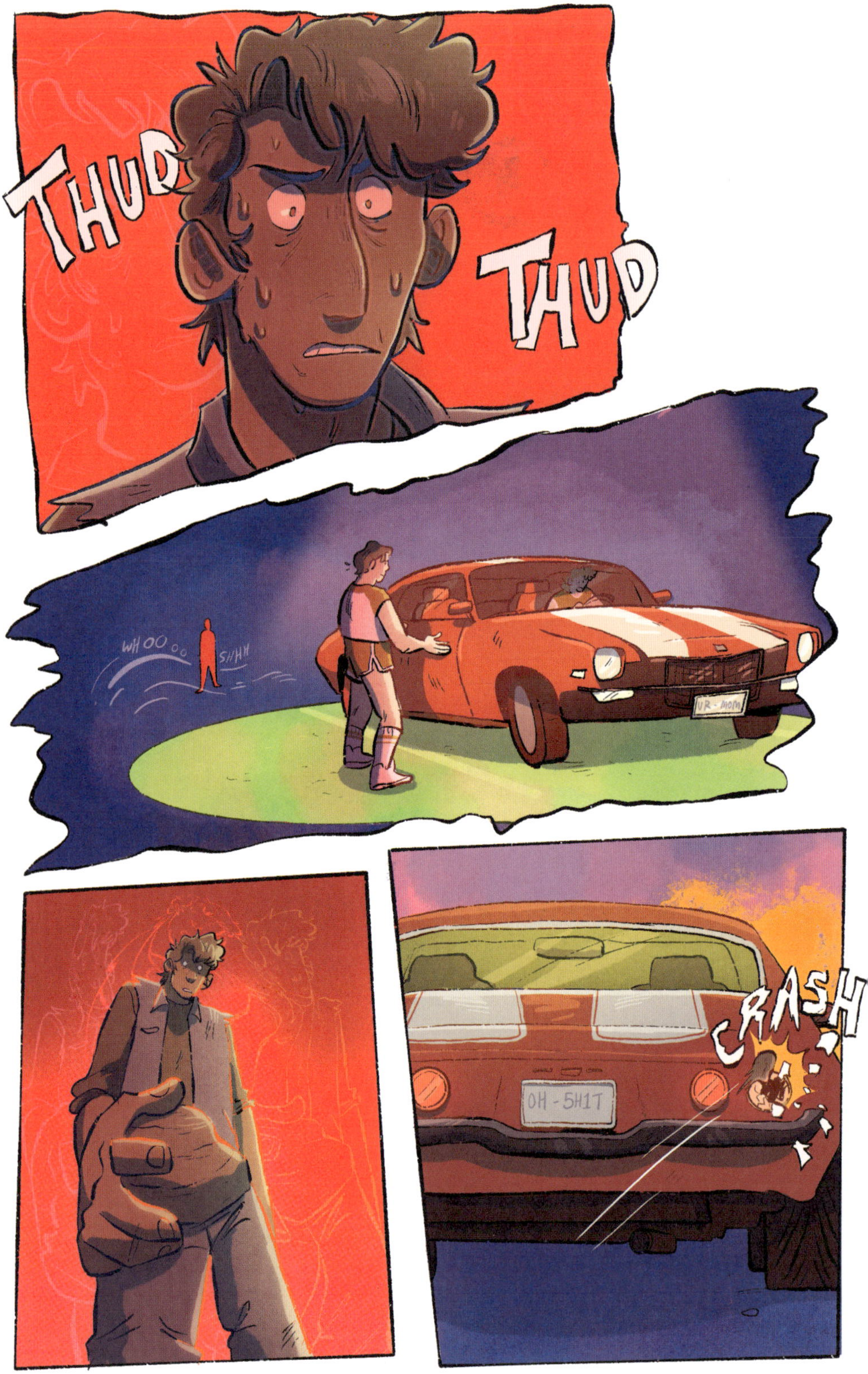
THUD
THUD
WHOOoo
SHHH
UR-MOM
OH-5H1T
CRASH

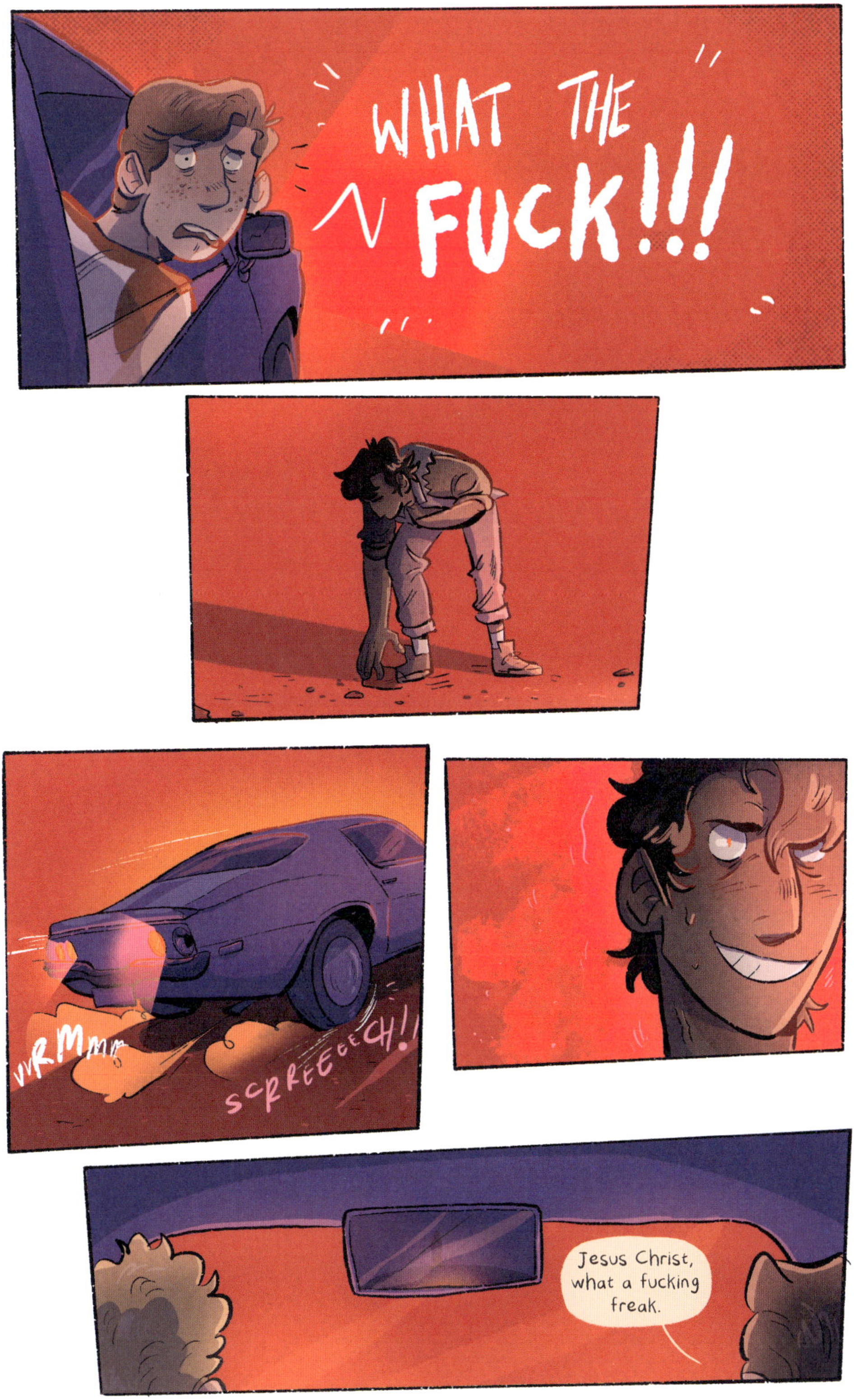
WHAT THE FUCK!!!
VVRMMM
SCREEEECH!!
Jesus Christ, what a fucking freak.

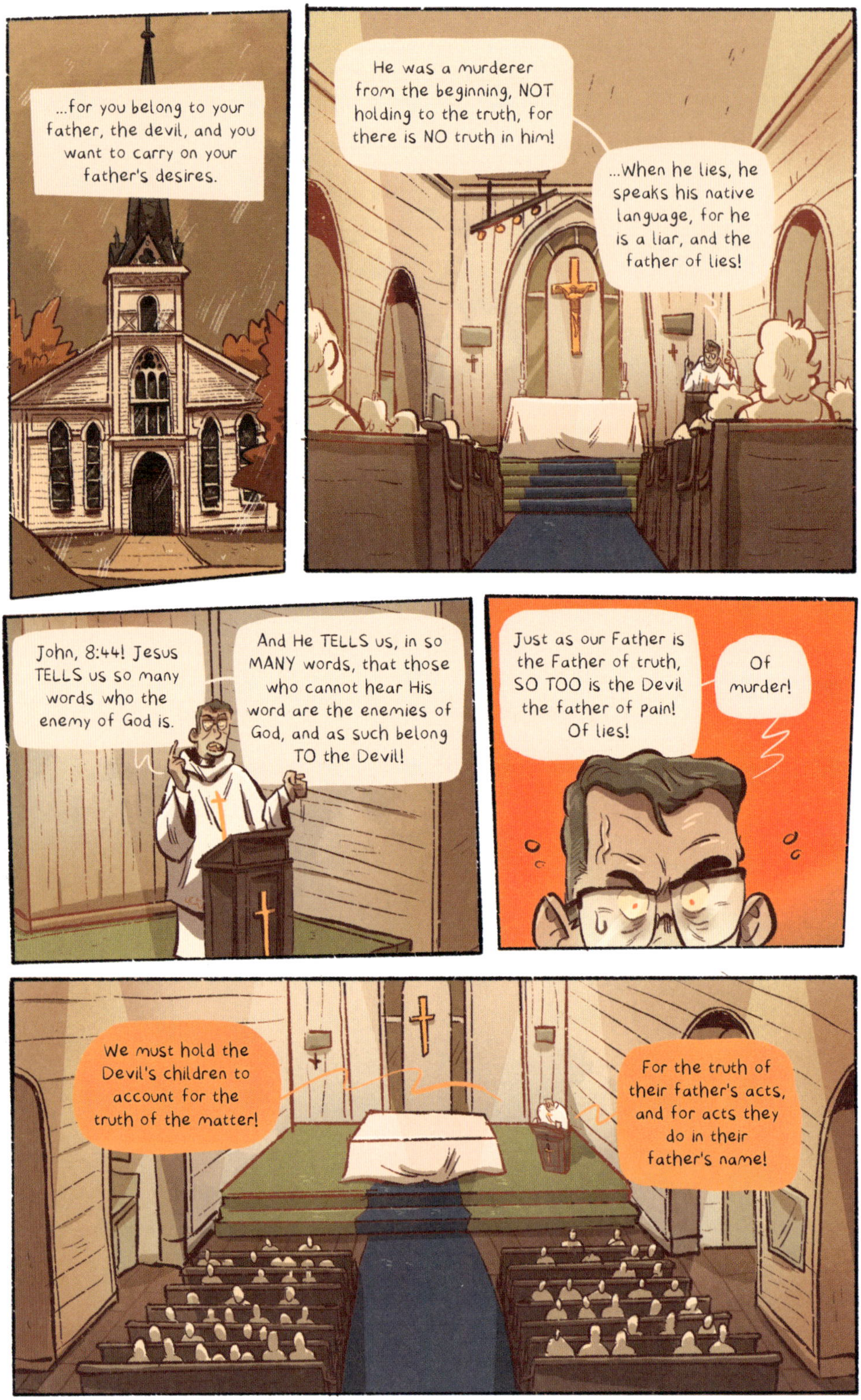

...for you belong to your father, the devil, and you want to carry on your father's desires.
He was a murderer from the beginning, NOT holding to the truth, for there is NO truth in him!
...When he lies, he speaks his native language, for he is a liar, and the father of lies!
John, 8:44! Jesus TELLS us so many words who the enemy of God is.
And He TELLS us, in so MANY words, that those who cannot hear His word are the enemies of God, and as such belong TO the Devil!
Just as our Father is the Father of truth, SO TOO is the Devil the father of pain! Of lies!
Of murder!
We must hold the Devil's children to account for the truth of the matter!
For the truth of their father's acts, and for acts they do in their father's name!

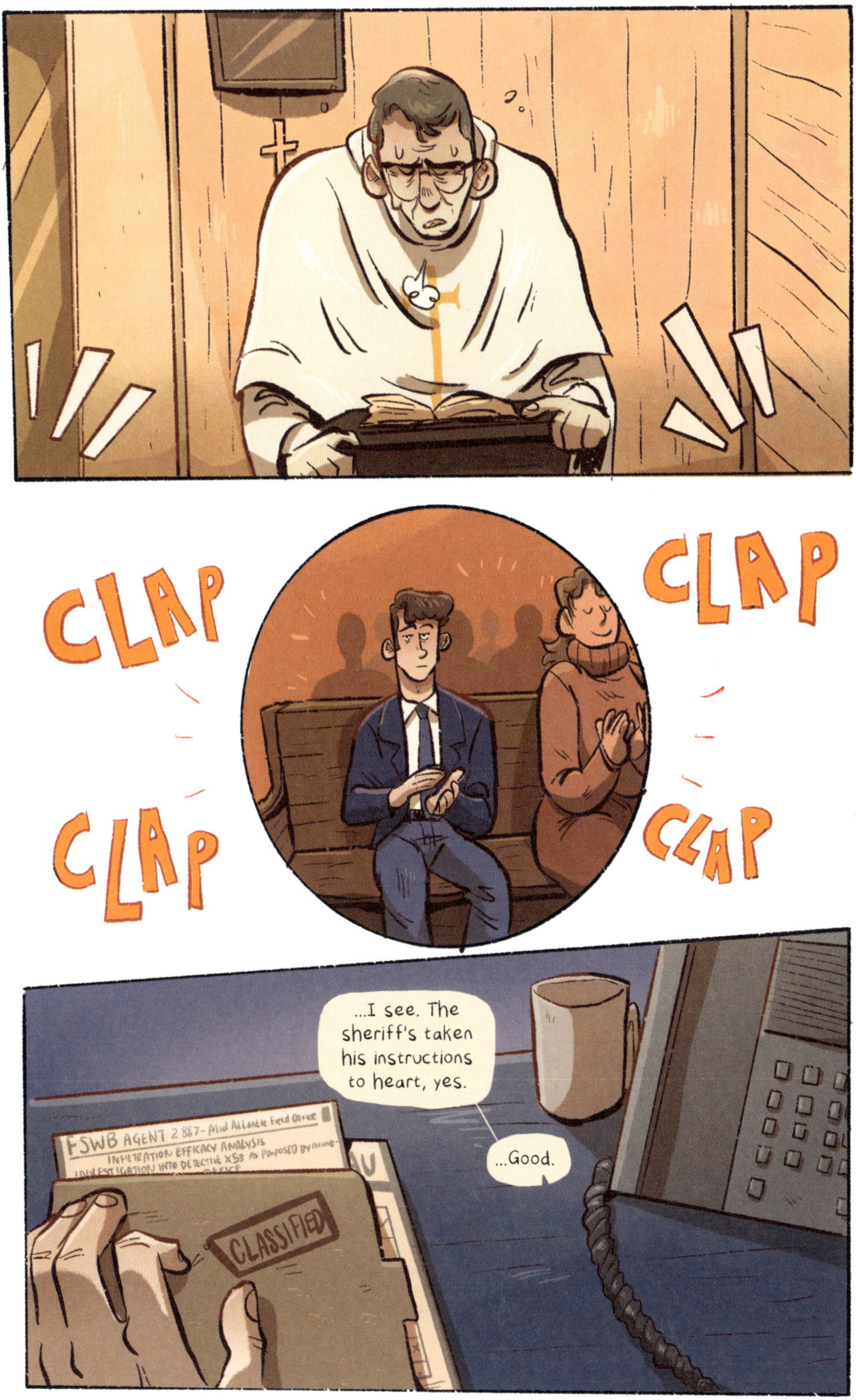
CLAP
CLAP
CLAP
CLAP
...I see. The sheriff's taken his instructions to heart, yes.
FSWB AGENT 2 887 - Mid Atlantic Field Office
INFILTRATION EFFICACY ANALYSIS
CLASSIFIED
...Good.

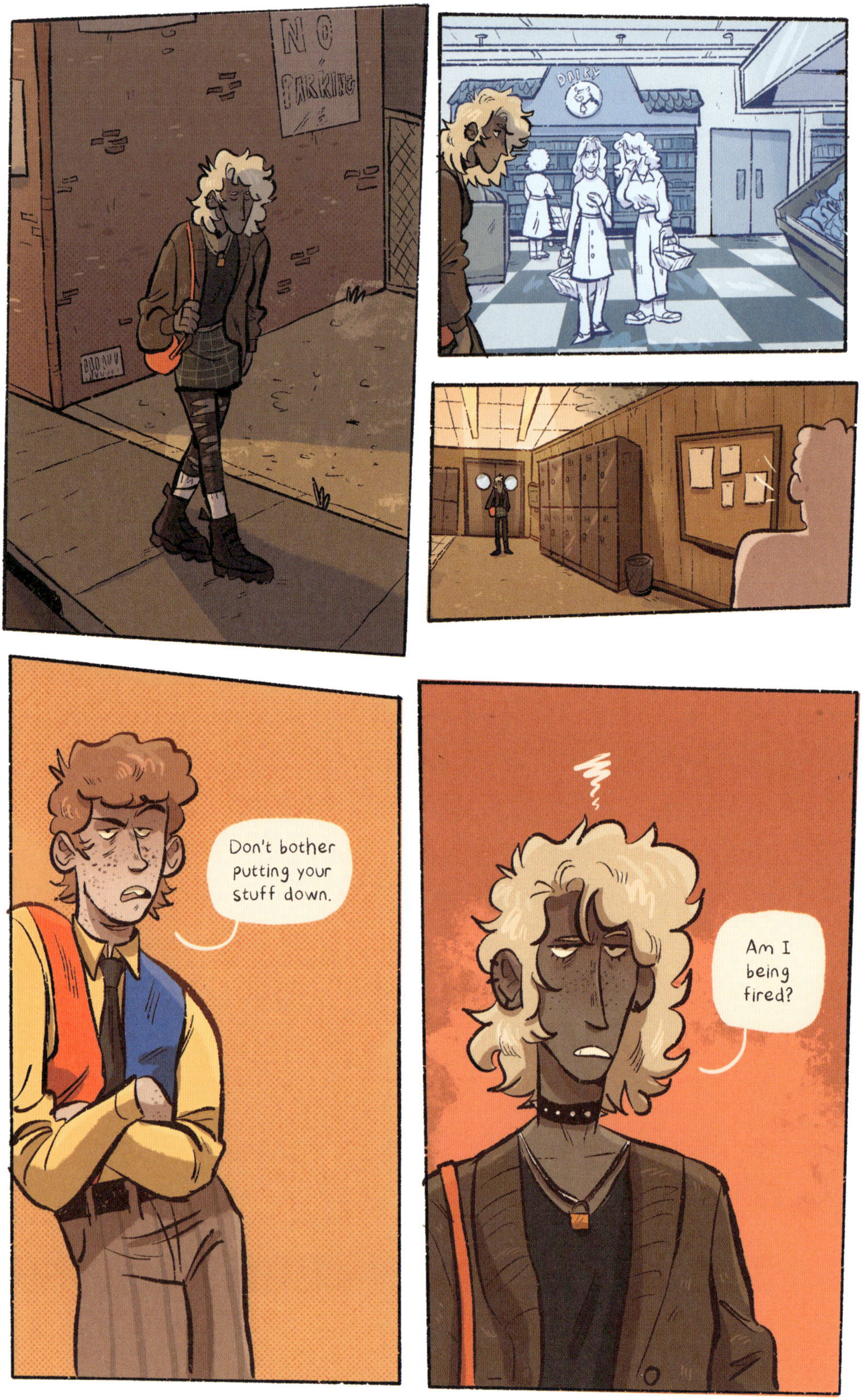
NO PARKING
DAIRY
Don't bother putting your stuff down.
Am I being fired?

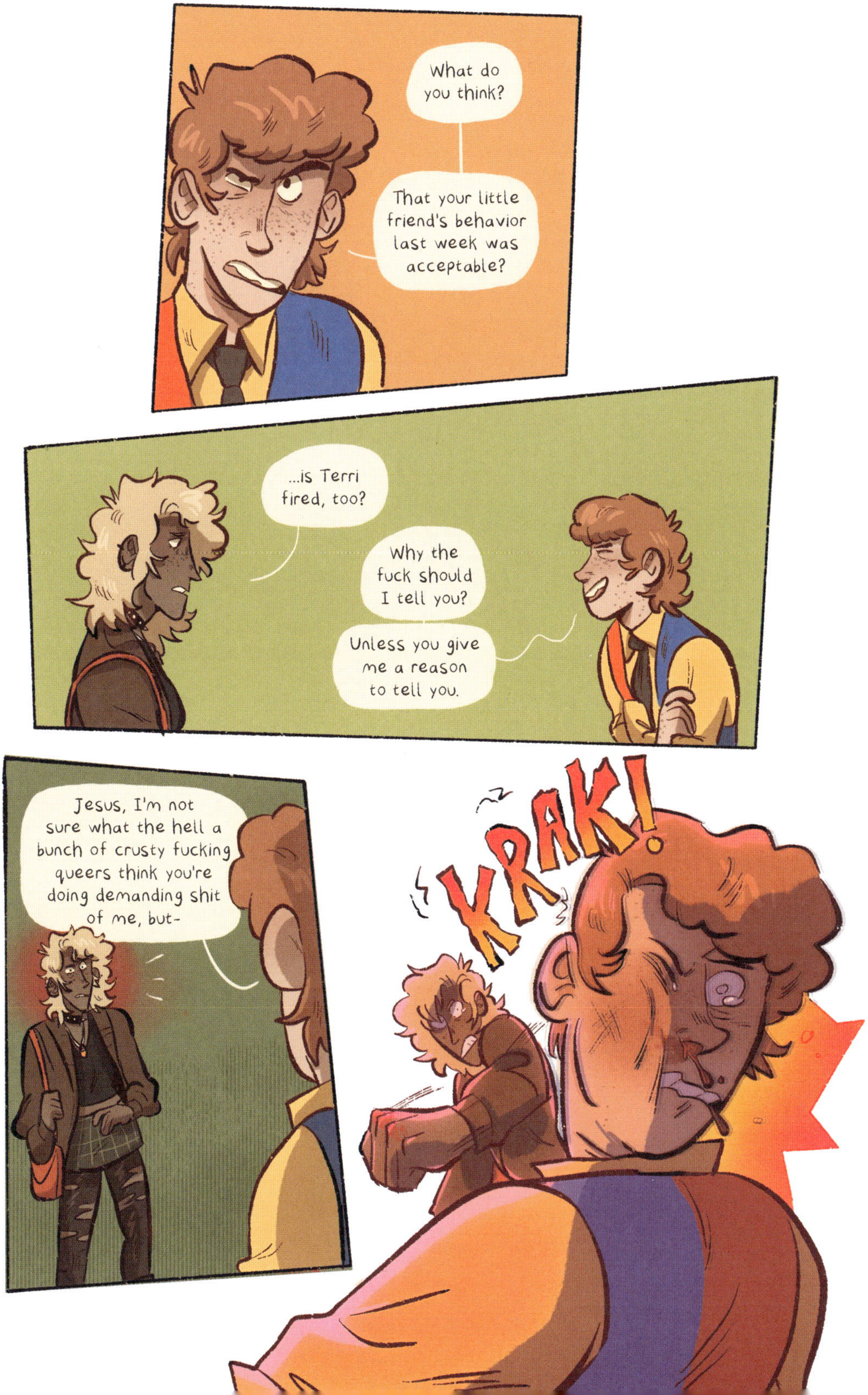
What do you think?
That your little friend's behavior last week was acceptable?
...is Terri fired, too?
Why the fuck should I tell you?
Unless you give me a reason to tell you.
Jesus, I'm not sure what the hell a bunch of crusty fucking queers think you're doing demanding shit of me, but-
KRAK!

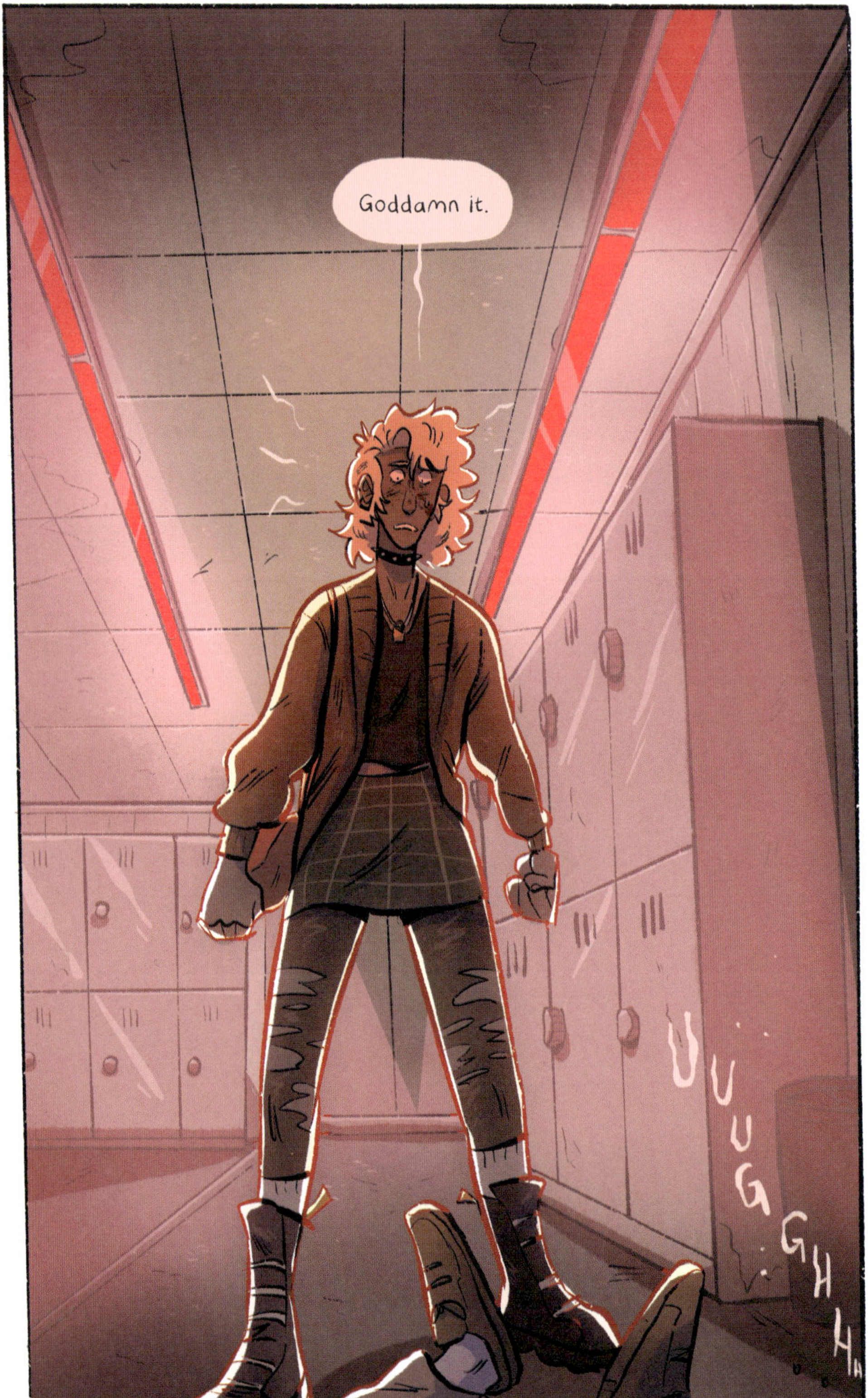
Goddamn it.
UUUGGGHHHA

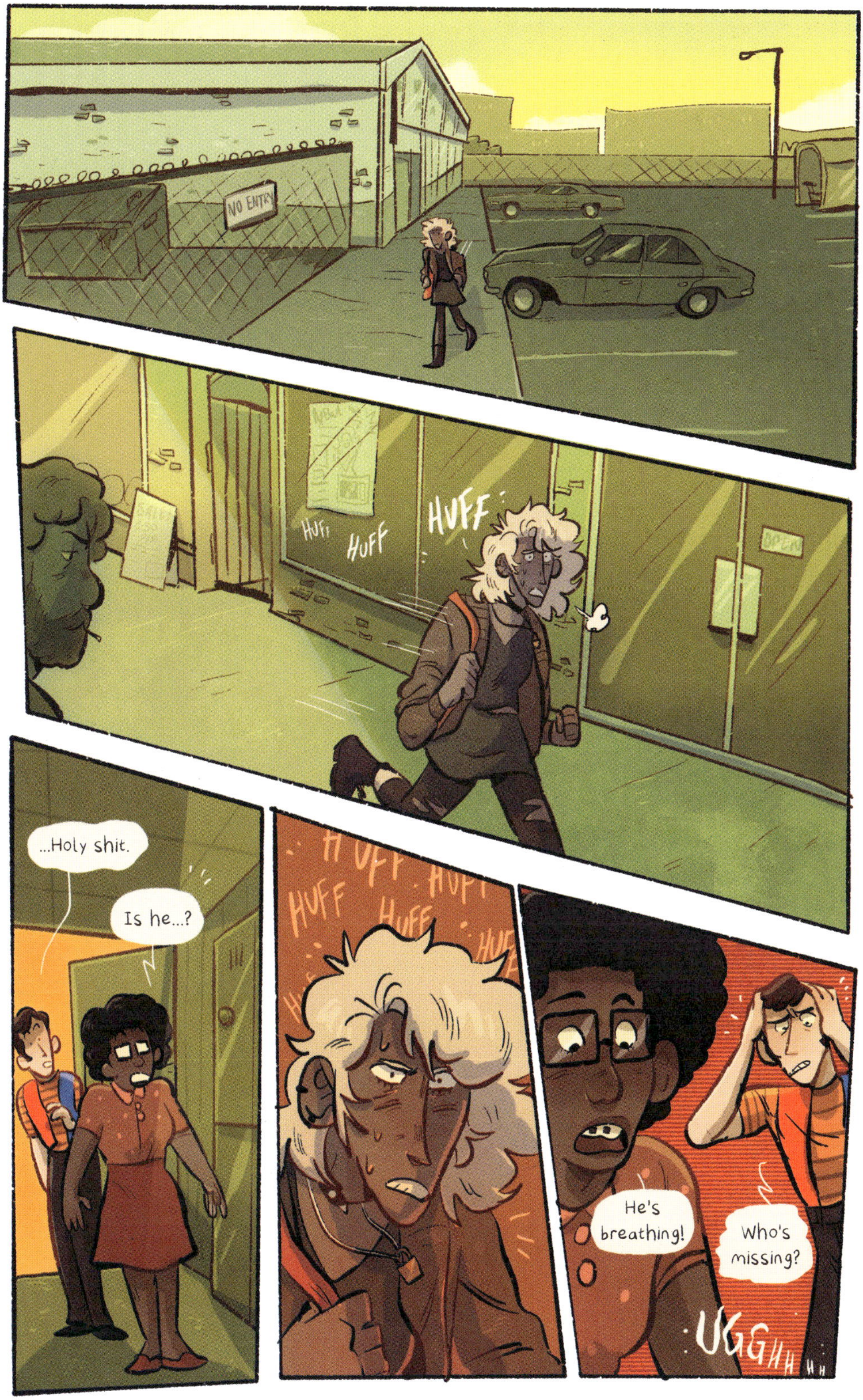
NO ENTRY
HUFF
HUFF
HUFF
OPEN
...Holy shit.
Is he...?
HUFF
HUFF
HUFF
He's breathing!
Who's missing?
UGGHH HH

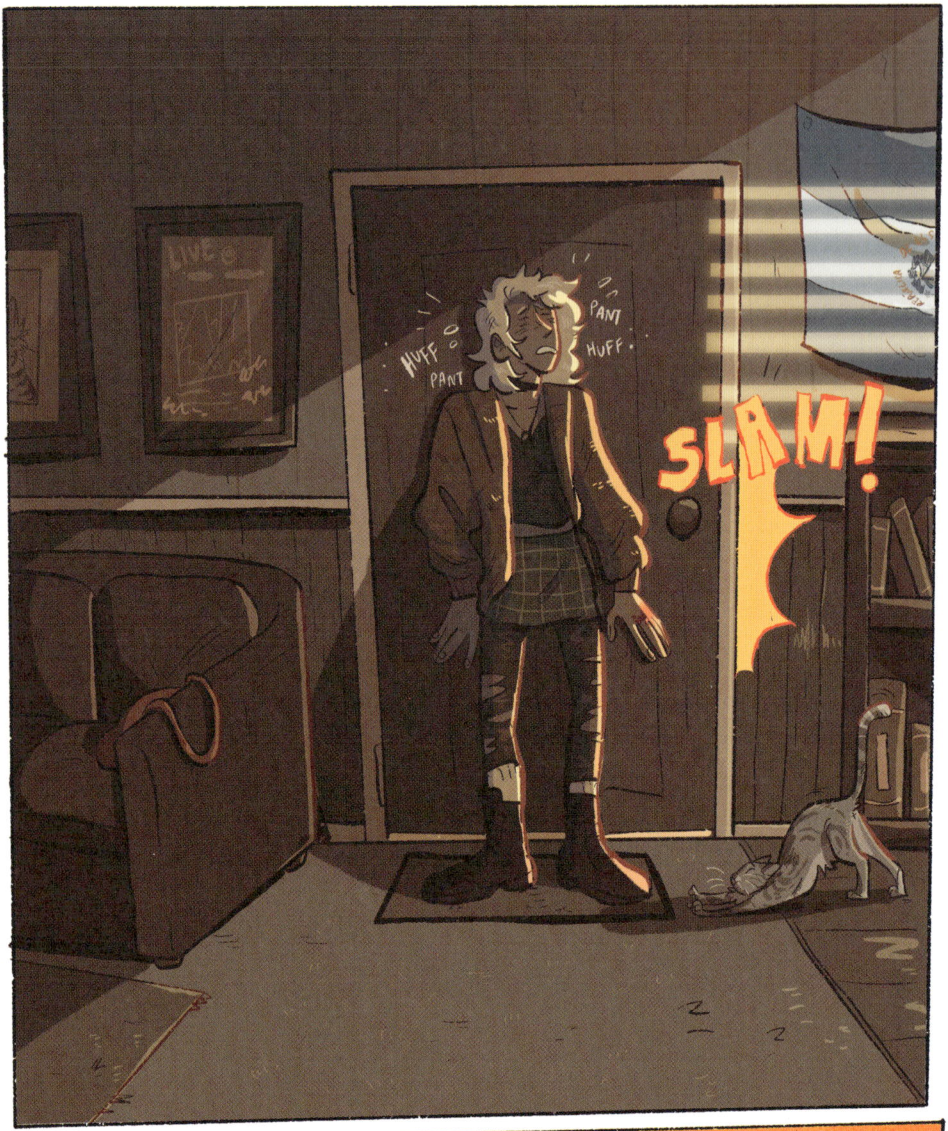
HUFF PANT
PANT HUFF
SLAM!

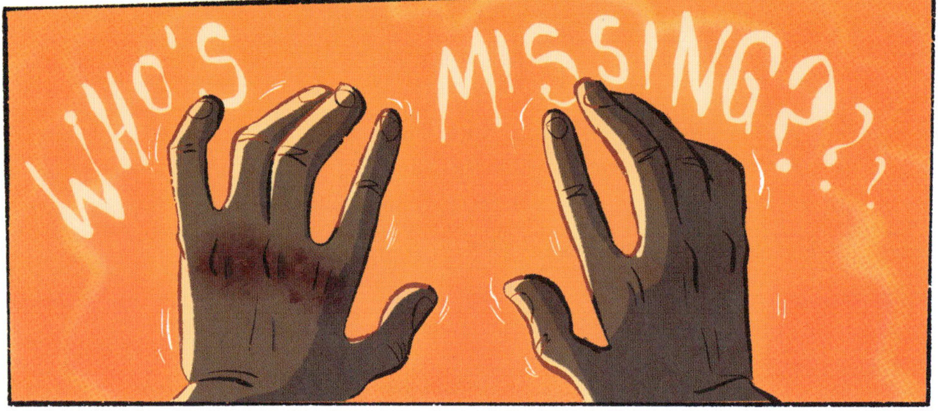
WHO'S MISSING???

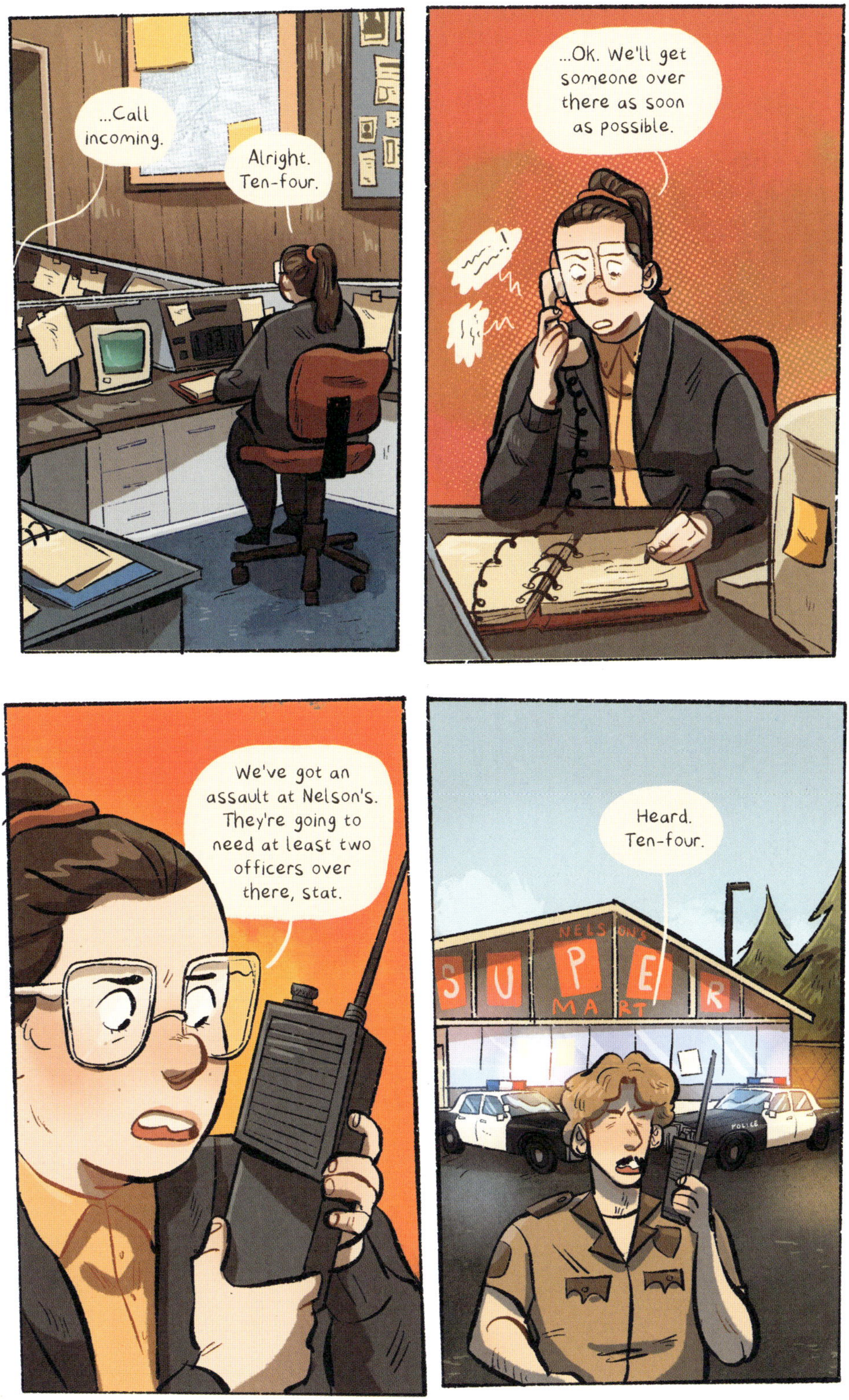
...Call incoming.
Alright. Ten-four.
...Ok. We'll get someone over there as soon as possible.
We've got an assault at Nelson's. They're going to need at least two officers over there, stat.
Heard. Ten-four.
NELSON'S SUPER MART

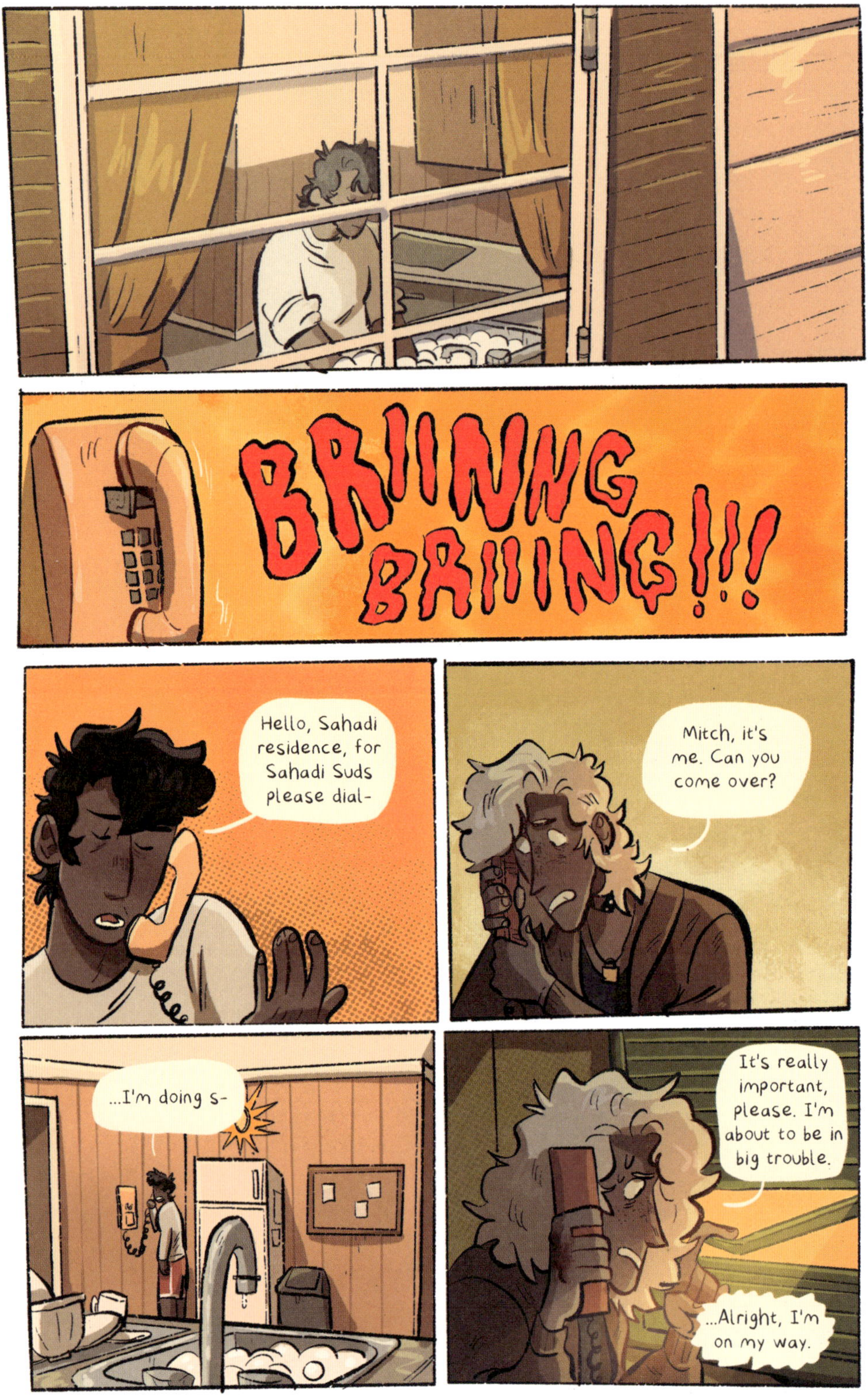
BRIINNG
BRIIING!!!
Hello, Sahadi residence, for Sahadi Suds please dial-
Mitch, it's me. Can you come over?
...I'm doing s-
It's really important, please. I'm about to be in big trouble.
...Alright, I'm on my way.

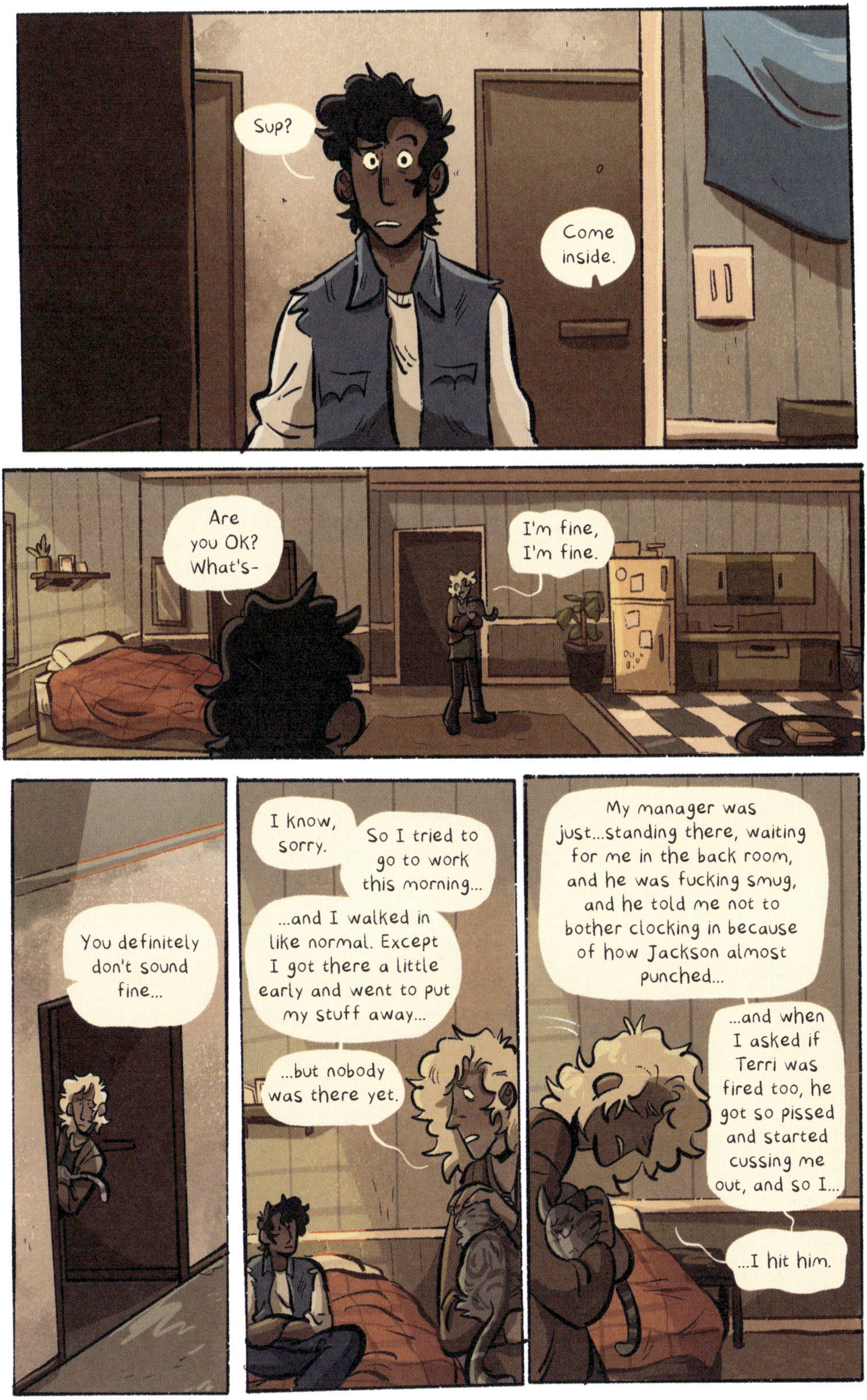
Sup?
Come inside.
Are you OK? What's-
I'm fine, I'm fine.
You definitely don't sound fine...
I know, sorry.
So I tried to go to work this morning...
...and I walked in like normal. Except I got there a little early and went to put my stuff away...
...but nobody was there yet.
My manager was just...standing there, waiting for me in the back room, and he was fucking smug, and he told me not to bother clocking in because of how Jackson almost punched...
...and when I asked if Terri was fired too, he got so pissed and started cussing me out, and so I...
...I hit him.

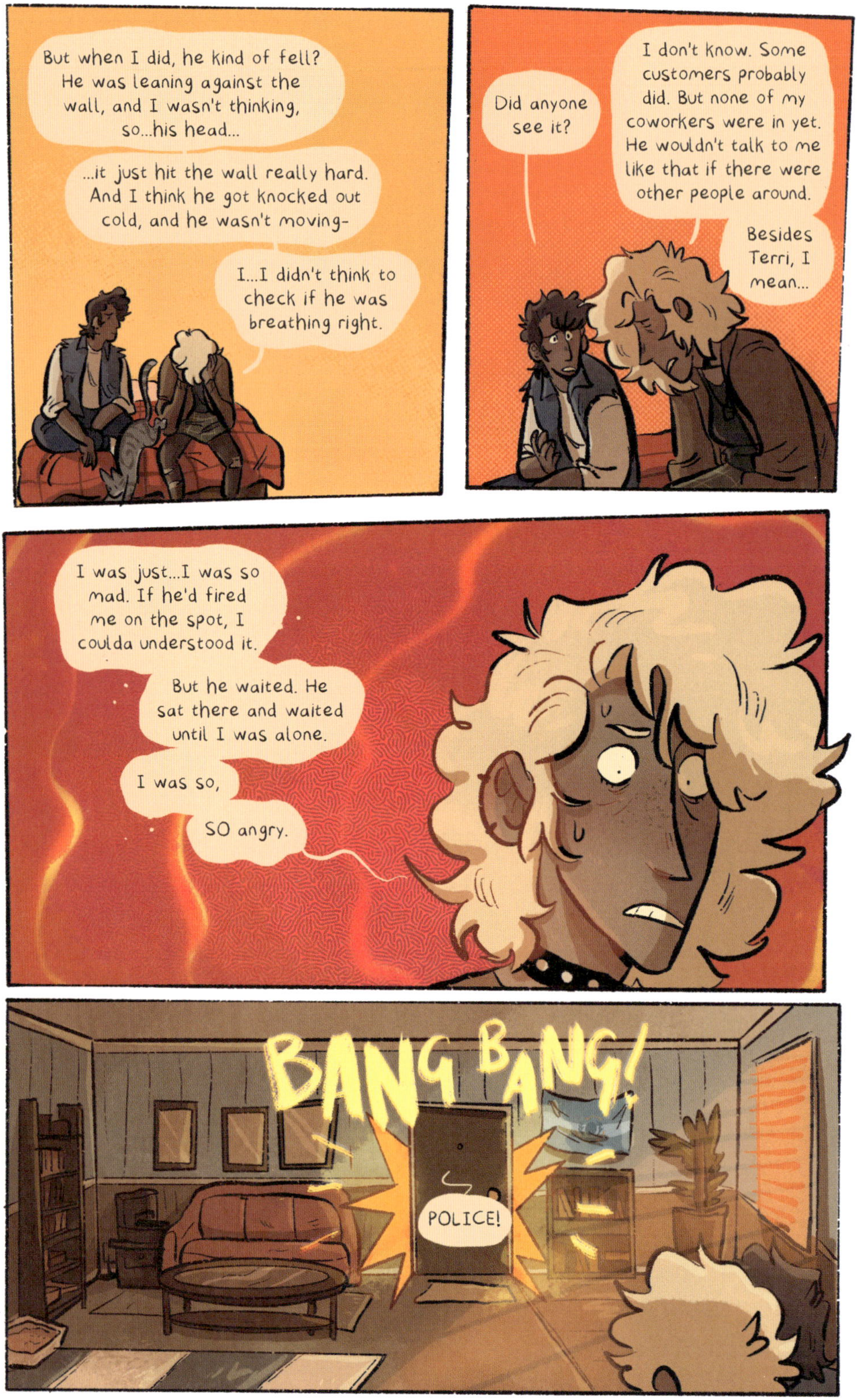
But when I did, he kind of fell? He was leaning against the wall, and I wasn't thinking, so...his head...
...it just hit the wall really hard. And I think he got knocked out cold, and he wasn't moving-
I...I didn't think to check if he was breathing right.
Did anyone see it?
I don't know. Some customers probably did. But none of my coworkers were in yet. He wouldn't talk to me like that if there were other people around.
Besides Terri, I mean...
I was just...I was so mad. If he'd fired me on the spot, I coulda understood it.
But he waited. He sat there and waited until I was alone.
I was so,
SO angry.
BANG BANG!
POLICE!

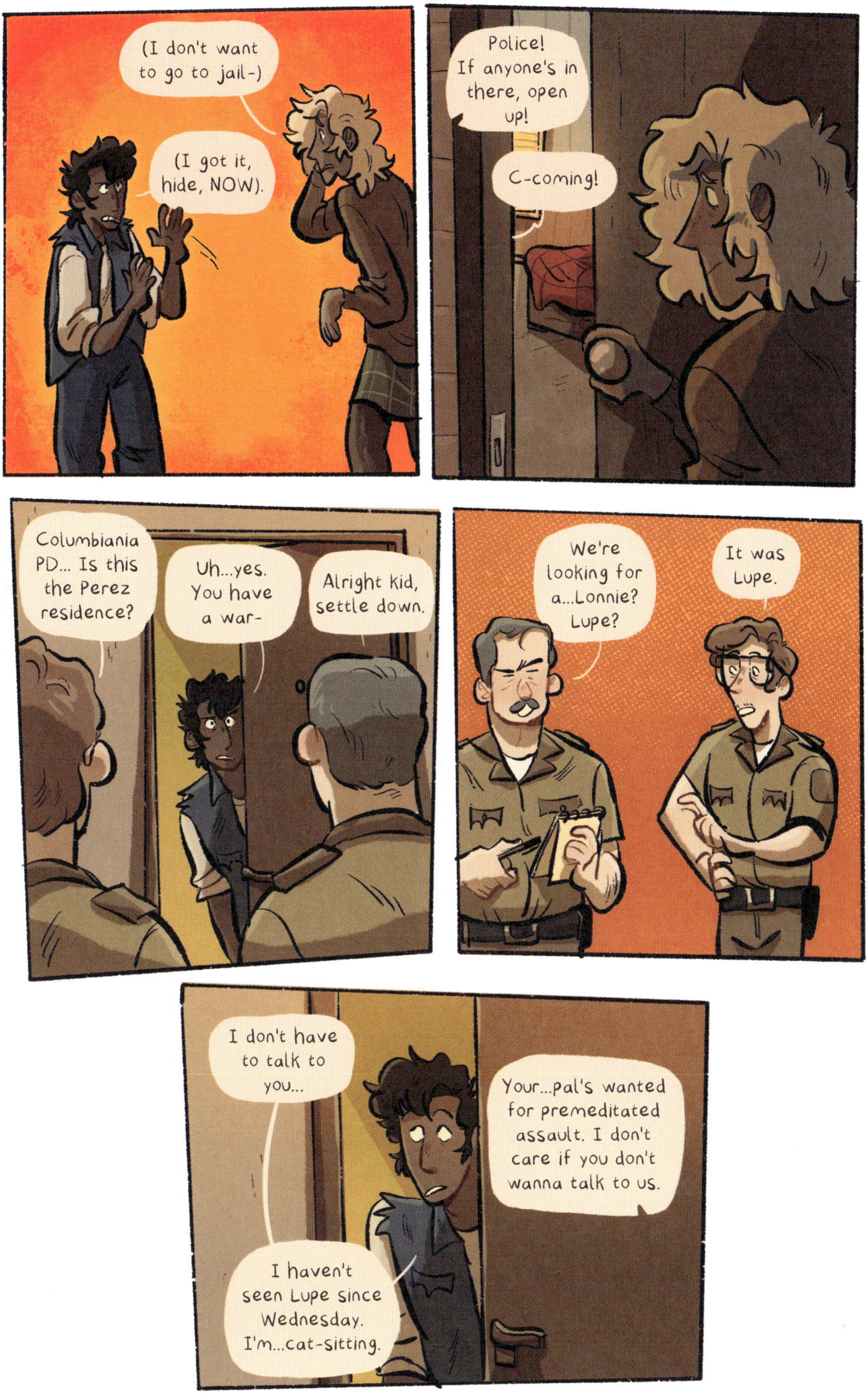
(I don't want to go to jail-)
(I got it, hide, NOW).
Police! If anyone's in there, open up!
C-coming!
Columbiania PD... Is this the Perez residence?
Uh...yes. You have a war-
Alright kid, settle down.
We're looking for a...Lonnie? Lupe?
It was Lupe.
I don't have to talk to you...
Your...pal's wanted for premeditated assault. I don't care if you don't wanna talk to us.
I haven't seen Lupe since Wednesday. I'm...cat-sitting.

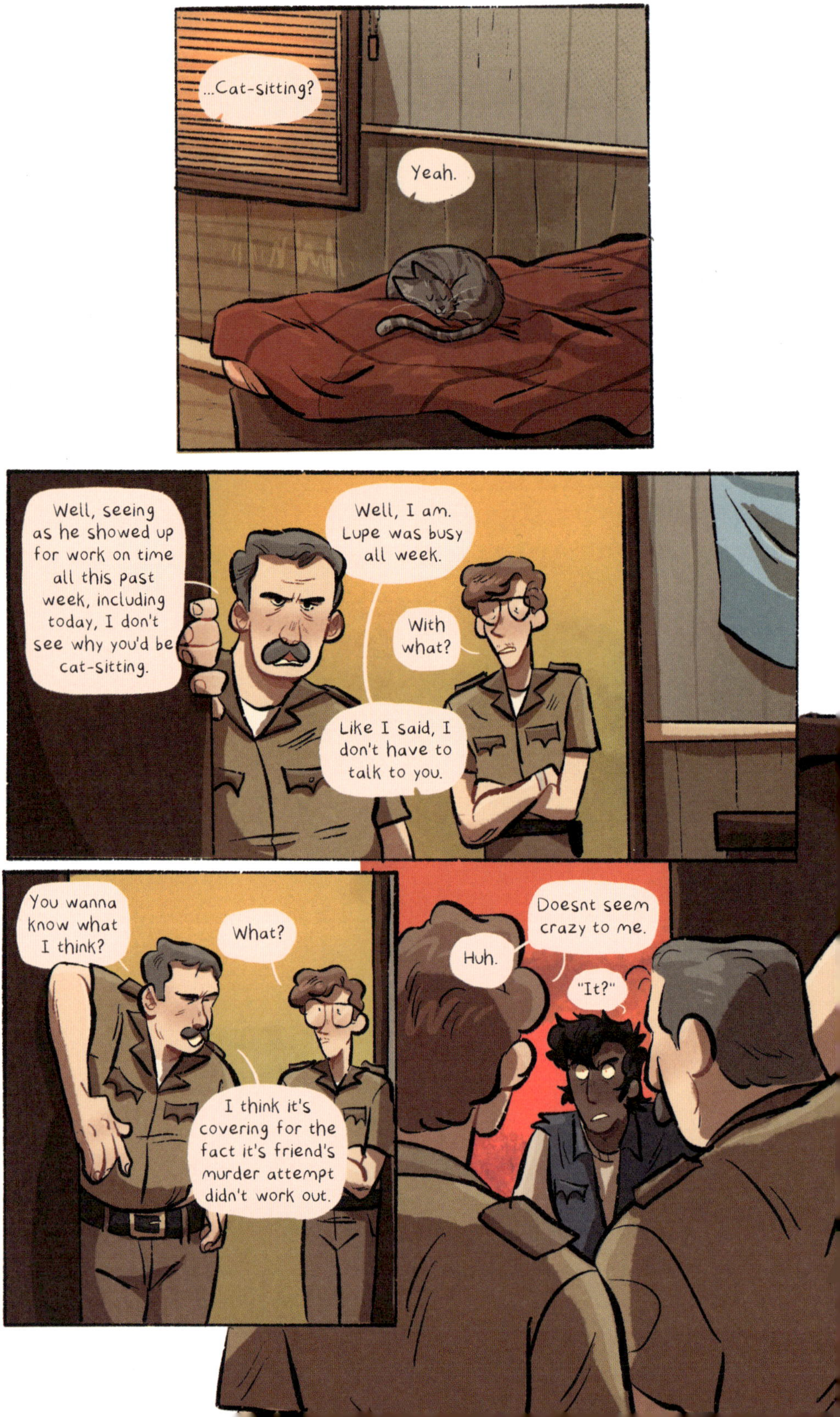
...Cat-sitting?
Yeah.
Well, seeing as he showed up for work on time all this past week, including today, I don't see why you'd be cat-sitting.
Well, I am. Lupe was busy all week.
With what?
Like I said, I don't have to talk to you.
You wanna know what I think?
What?
I think it's covering for the fact it's friend's murder attempt didn't work out.
Doesnt seem crazy to me.
Huh.
"It?"

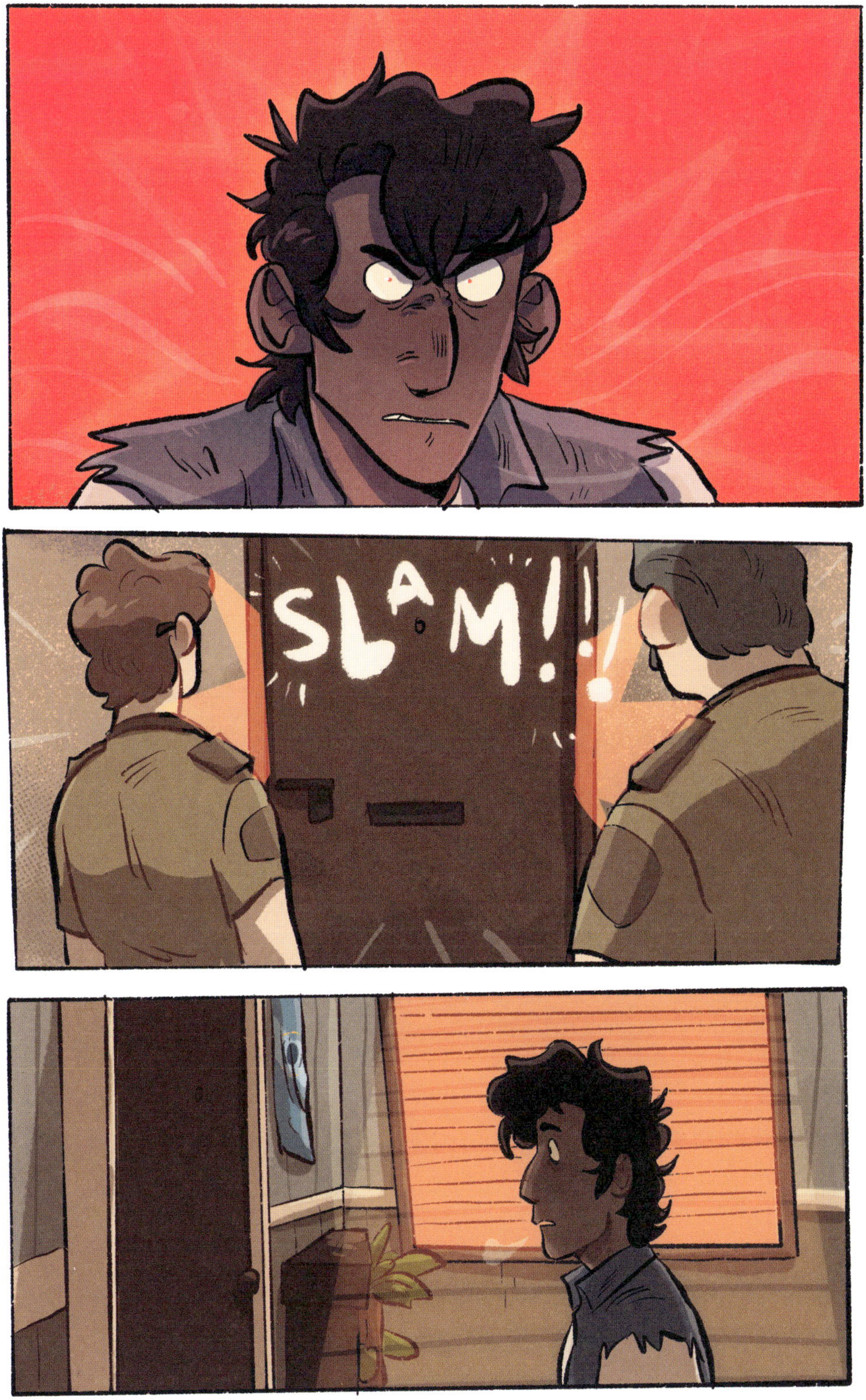
SLAM!!

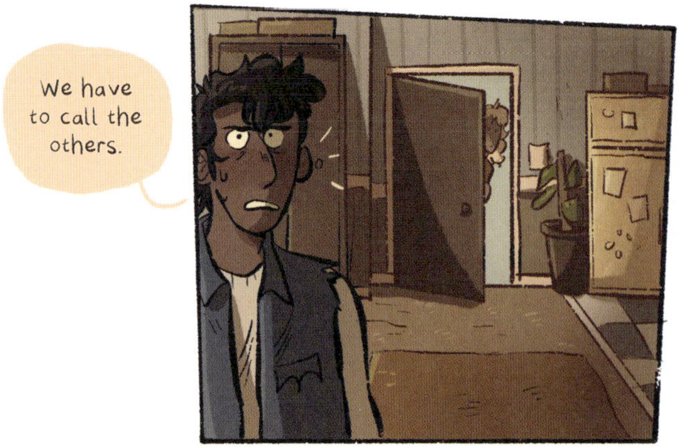
We have to call the others.

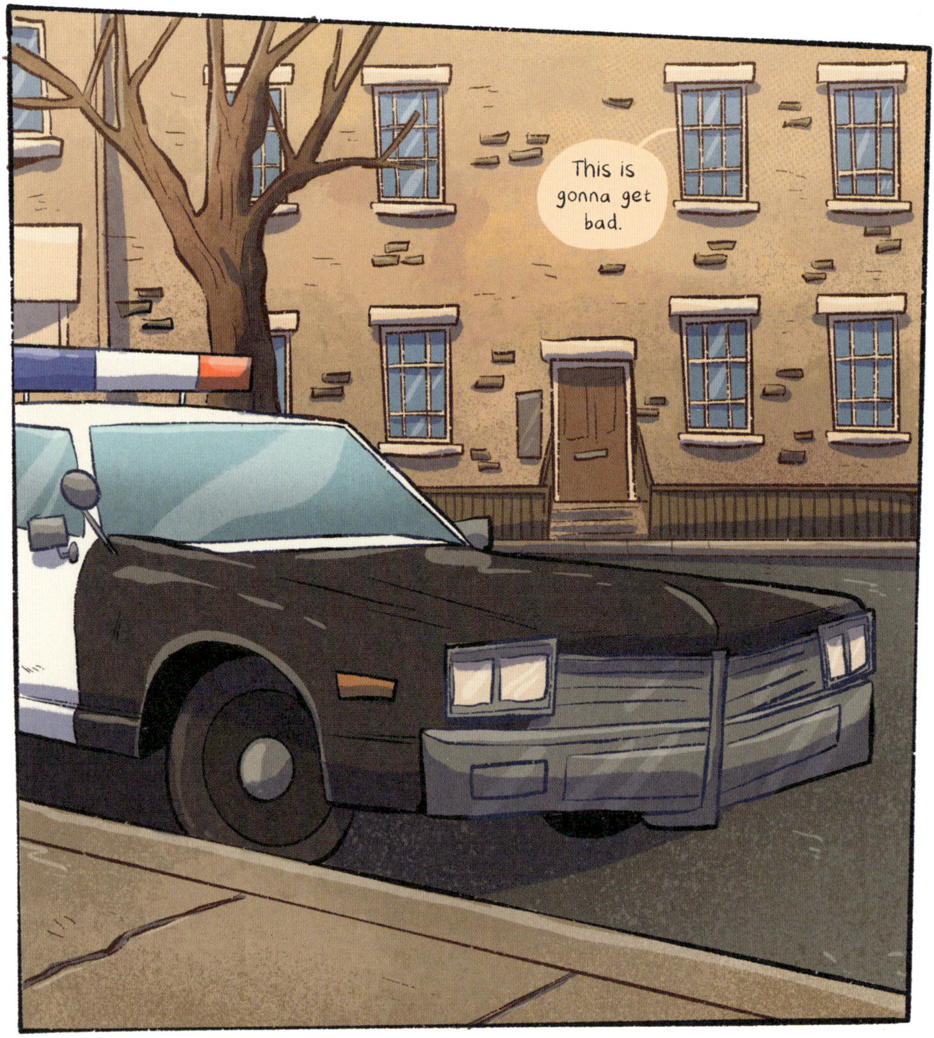
This is gonna get bad.

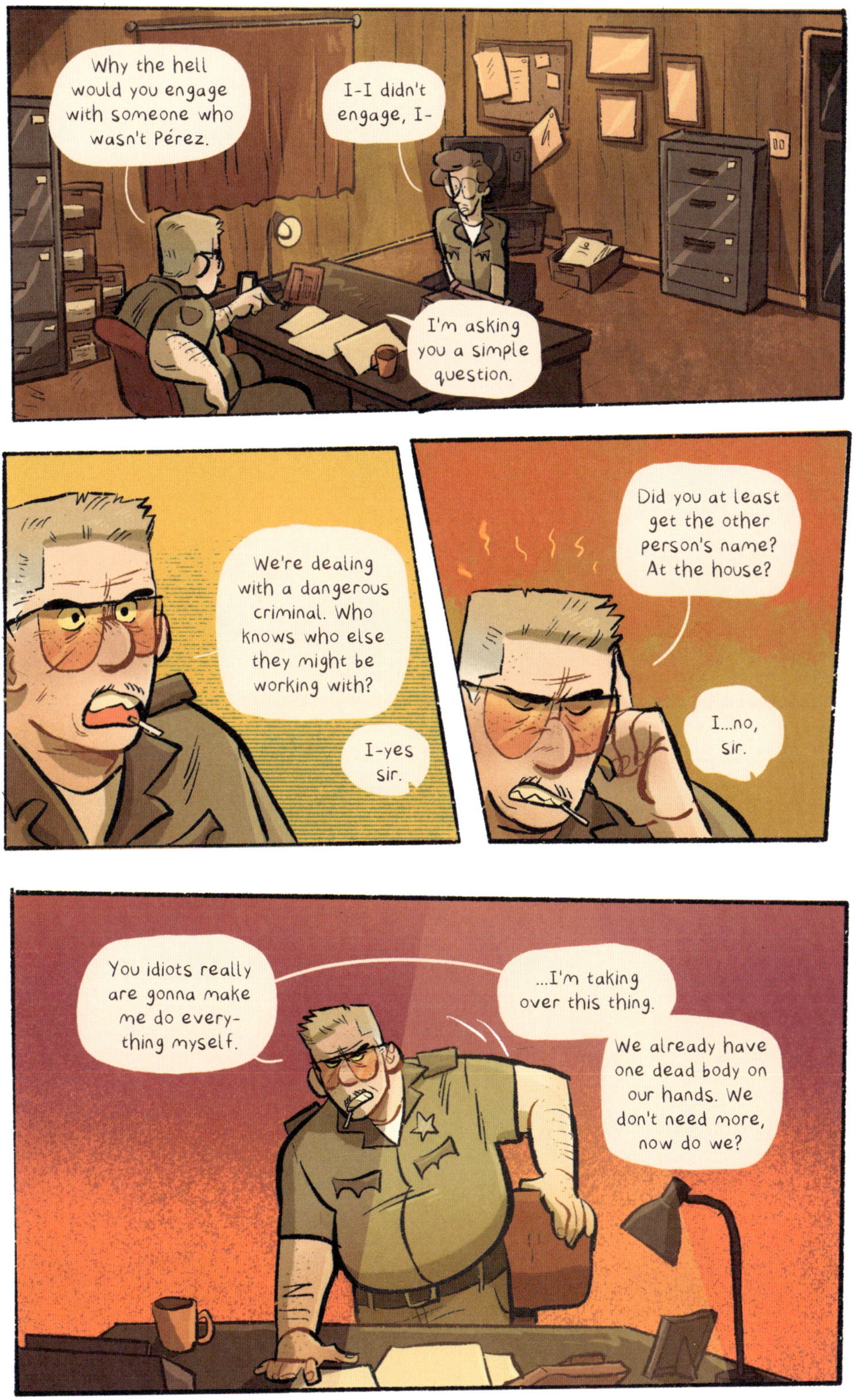
Why the hell would you engage with someone who wasn't Pérez.
I-I didn't engage, I-
I'm asking you a simple question.
We're dealing with a dangerous criminal. Who knows who else they might be working with?
I-yes sir.
Did you at least get the other person's name? At the house?
I...no, sir.
You idiots really are gonna make me do every-thing myself.
...I'm taking over this thing.
We already have one dead body on our hands. We don't need more, now do we?

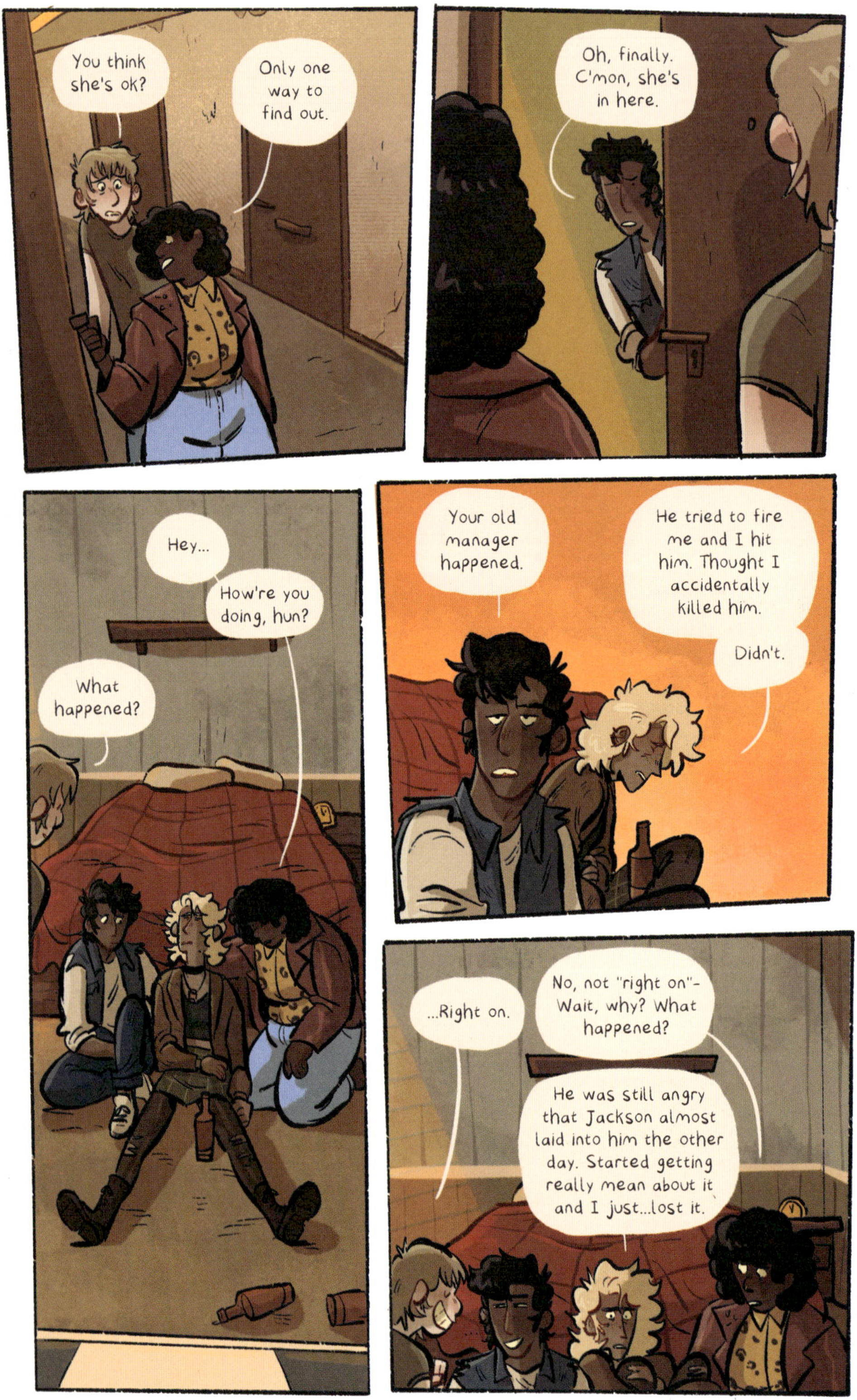
You think she's ok?
Only one way to find out.
Oh, finally. C'mon, she's in here.
Hey...
How're you doing, hun?
What happened?
Your old manager happened.
He tried to fire me and I hit him. Thought I accidentally killed him.
Didn't.
...Right on.
No, not "right on"- Wait, why? What happened?
He was still angry that Jackson almost laid into him the other day. Started getting really mean about it and I just...lost it.

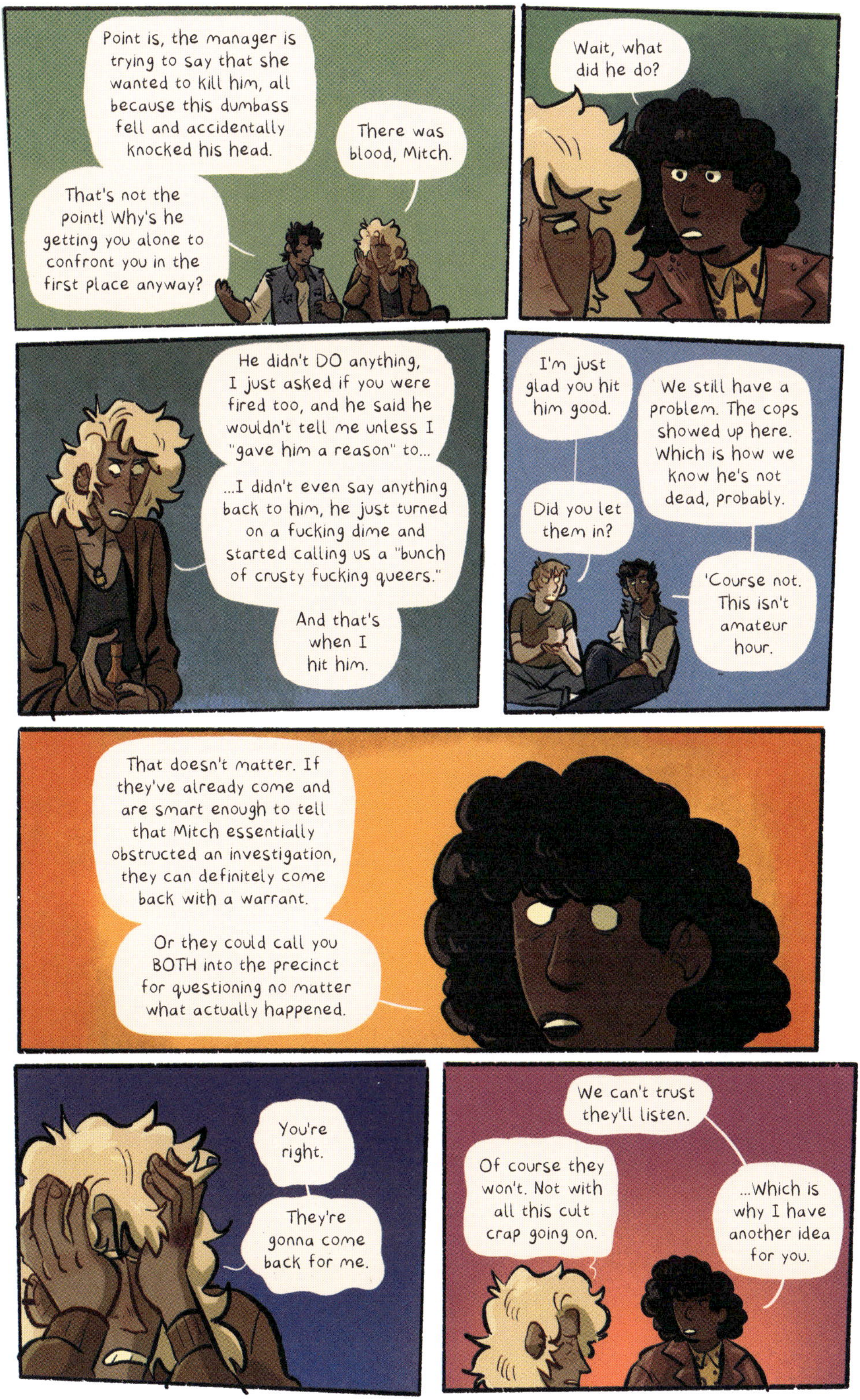
Point is, the manager is trying to say that she wanted to kill him, all because this dumbass fell and accidentally knocked his head.
There was blood, Mitch.
That's not the point! Why's he getting you alone to confront you in the first place anyway?
Wait, what did he do?
He didn't DO anything, I just asked if you were fired too, and he said he wouldn't tell me unless I "gave him a reason" to...
...I didn't even say anything back to him, he just turned on a fucking dime and started calling us a "bunch of crusty fucking queers."
And that's when I hit him.
I'm just glad you hit him good.
We still have a problem. The cops showed up here. Which is how we know he's not dead, probably.
Did you let them in?
'Course not. This isn't amateur hour.
That doesn't matter. If they've already come and are smart enough to tell that Mitch essentially obstructed an investigation, they can definitely come back with a warrant.
Or they could call you BOTH into the precinct for questioning no matter what actually happened.
You're right.
They're gonna come back for me.
We can't trust they'll listen.
Of course they won't. Not with all this cult crap going on.
...Which is why I have another idea for you.

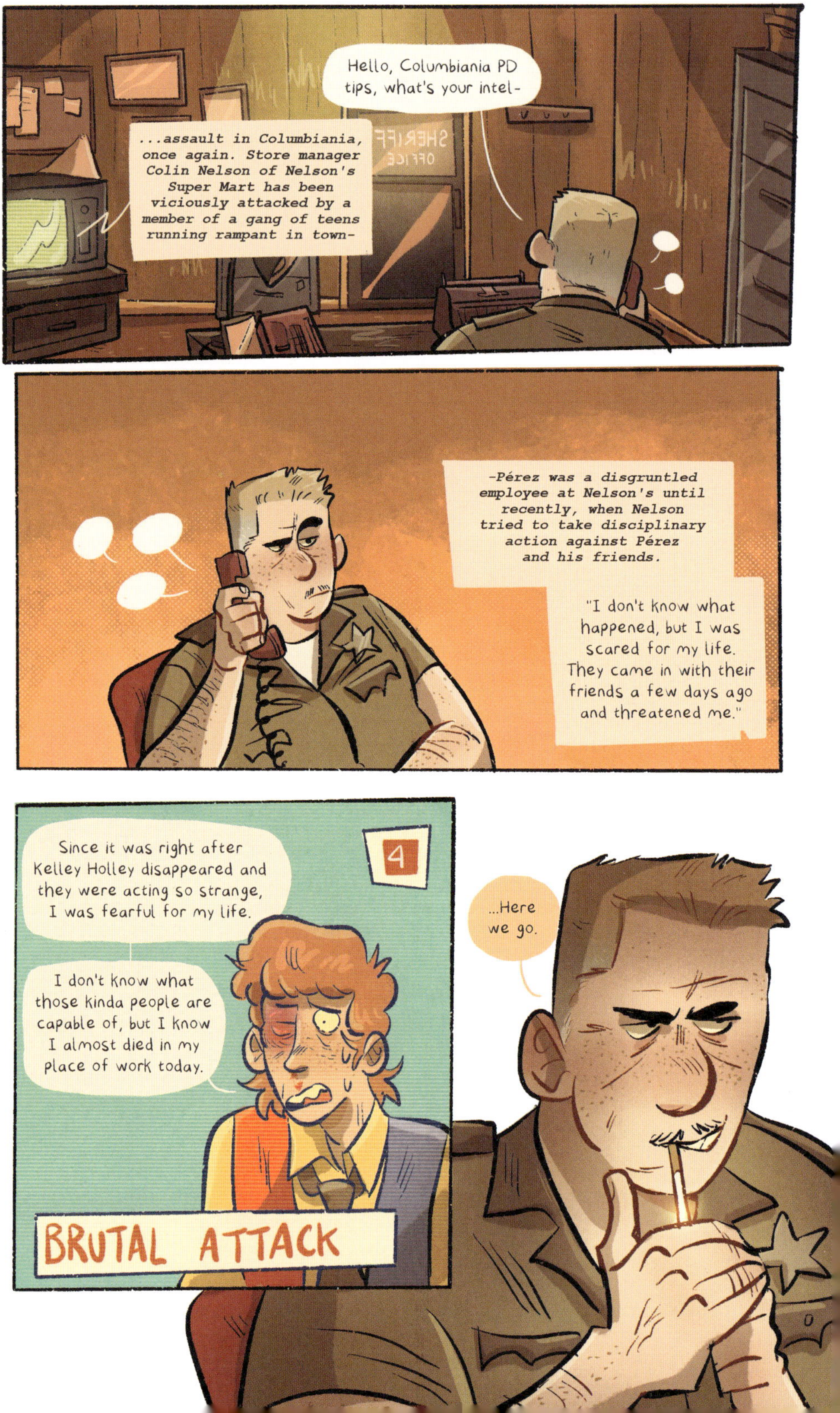
Hello, Columbiania PD tips, what's your intel-
...assault in Columbiania, once again. Store manager Colin Nelson of Nelson's Super Mart has been viciously attacked by a member of a gang of teens running rampant in town-
SHERIFF OFFICE
-Pérez was a disgruntled employee at Nelson's until recently, when Nelson tried to take disciplinary action against Pérez and his friends.
"I don't know what happened, but I was scared for my life. They came in with their friends a few days ago and threatened me."
Since it was right after Kelley Holley disappeared and they were acting so strange, I was fearful for my life.
I don't know what those kinda people are capable of, but I know I almost died in my place of work today.
4
BRUTAL ATTACK
...Here we go.

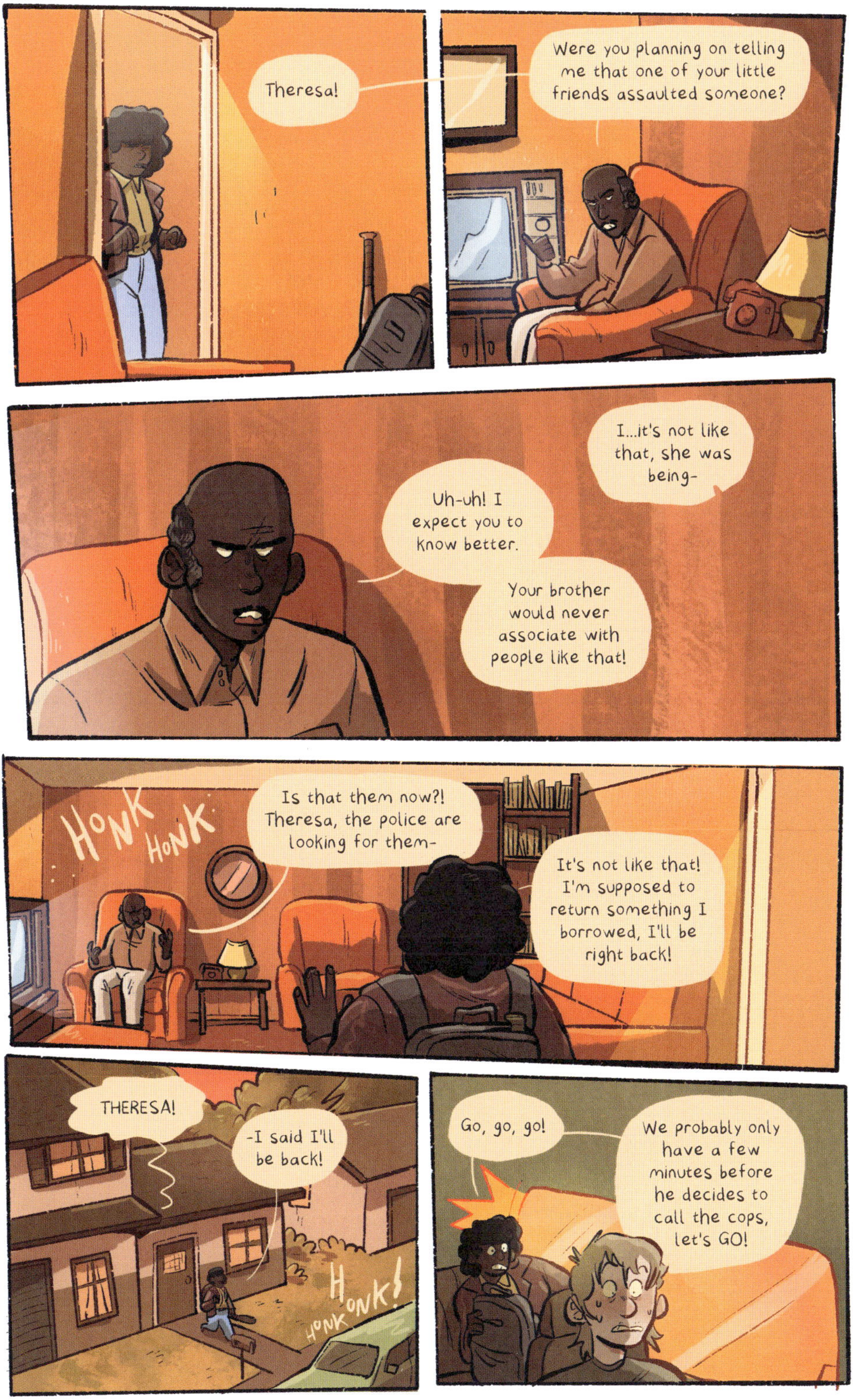
Theresa!
Were you planning on telling me that one of your little friends assaulted someone?
I...it's not like that, she was being-
Uh-uh! I expect you to know better.
Your brother would never associate with people like that!
HONK HONK
Is that them now?! Theresa, the police are looking for them-
It's not like that! I'm supposed to return something I borrowed, I'll be right back!
THERESA!
-I said I'll be back!
HONK! HONK
Go, go, go!
We probably only have a few minutes before he decides to call the cops, let's GO!

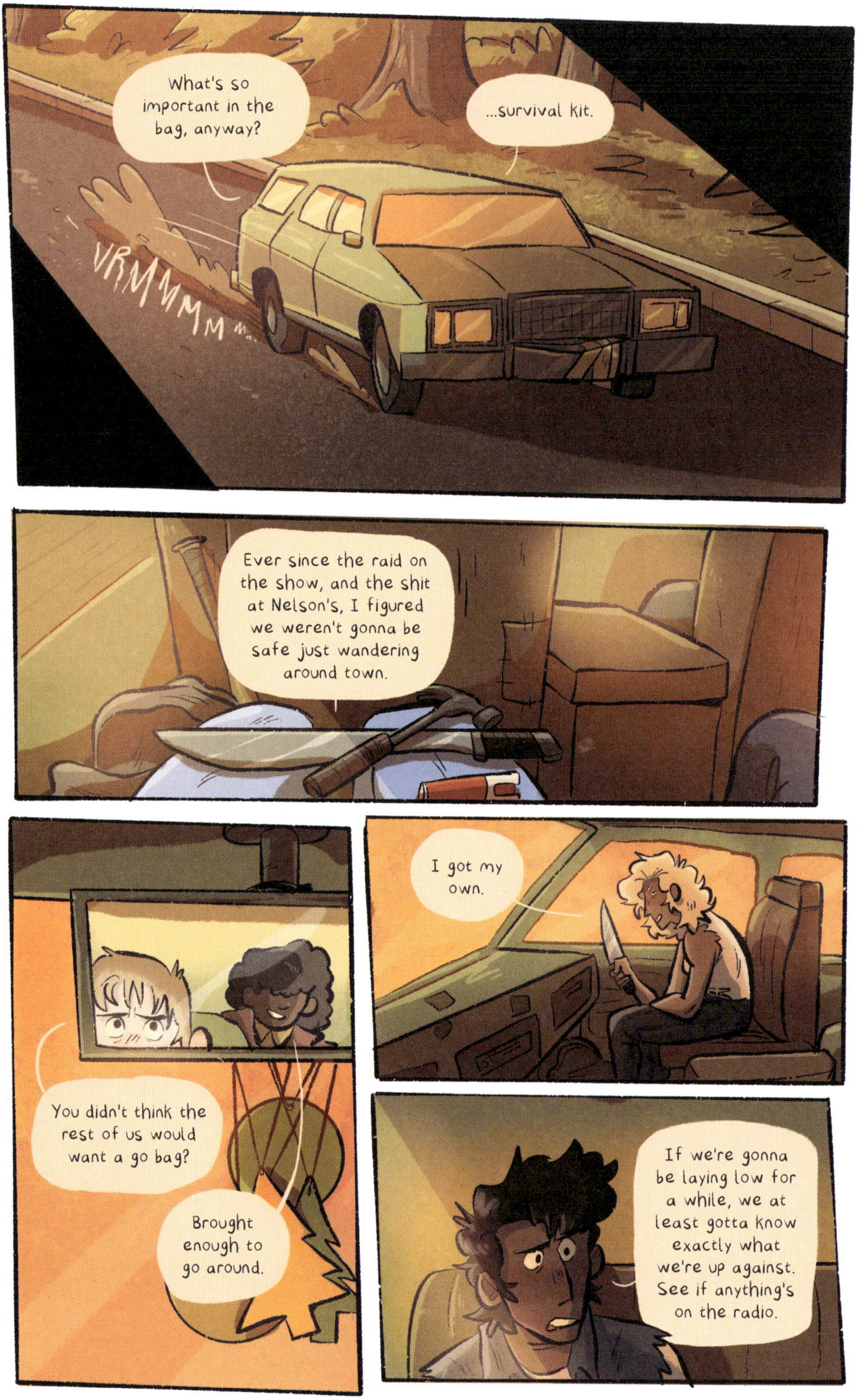
What's so important in the bag, anyway?
...survival kit.
VRMMMMm...
Ever since the raid on the show, and the shit at Nelson's, I figured we weren't gonna be safe just wandering around town.
You didn't think the rest of us would want a go bag?
Brought enough to go around.
I got my own.
If we're gonna be laying low for a while, we at least gotta know exactly what we're up against. See if anything's on the radio.

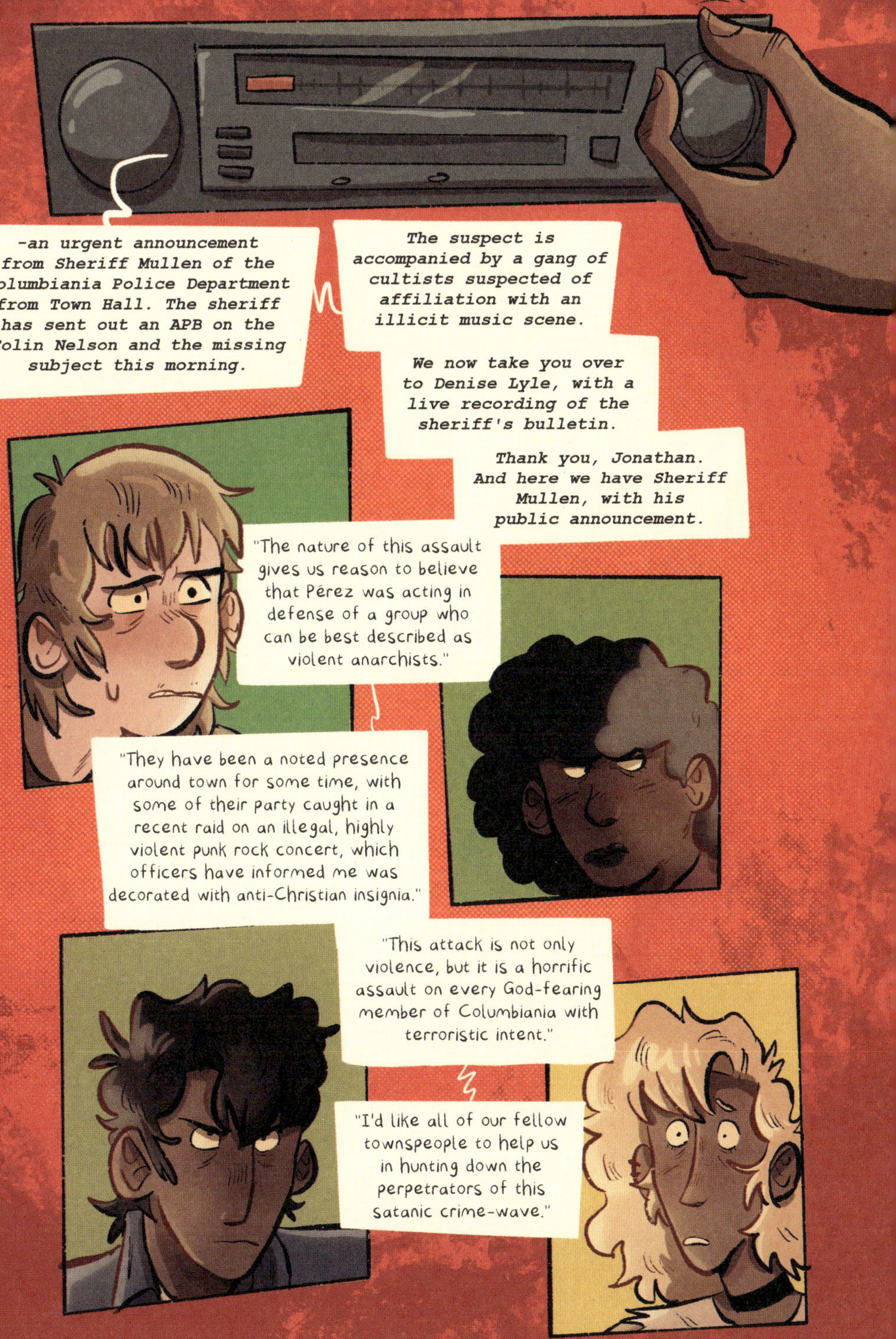
-an urgent announcement from Sheriff Mullen of the Columbiania Police Department from Town Hall. The sheriff has sent out an APB on the Colin Nelson and the missing subject this morning.
The suspect is accompanied by a gang of cultists suspected of affiliation with an illicit music scene.
We now take you over to Denise Lyle, with a live recording of the sheriff's bulletin.
Thank you, Jonathan. And here we have Sheriff Mullen, with his public announcement.
"The nature of this assault gives us reason to believe that Pérez was acting in defense of a group who can be best described as violent anarchists."
"They have been a noted presence around town for some time, with some of their party caught in a recent raid on an illegal, highly violent punk rock concert, which officers have informed me was decorated with anti-Christian insignia."
"This attack is not only violence, but it is a horrific assault on every God-fearing member of Columbiania with terroristic intent."
"I'd like all of our fellow townspeople to help us in hunting down the perpetrators of this satanic crime-wave."

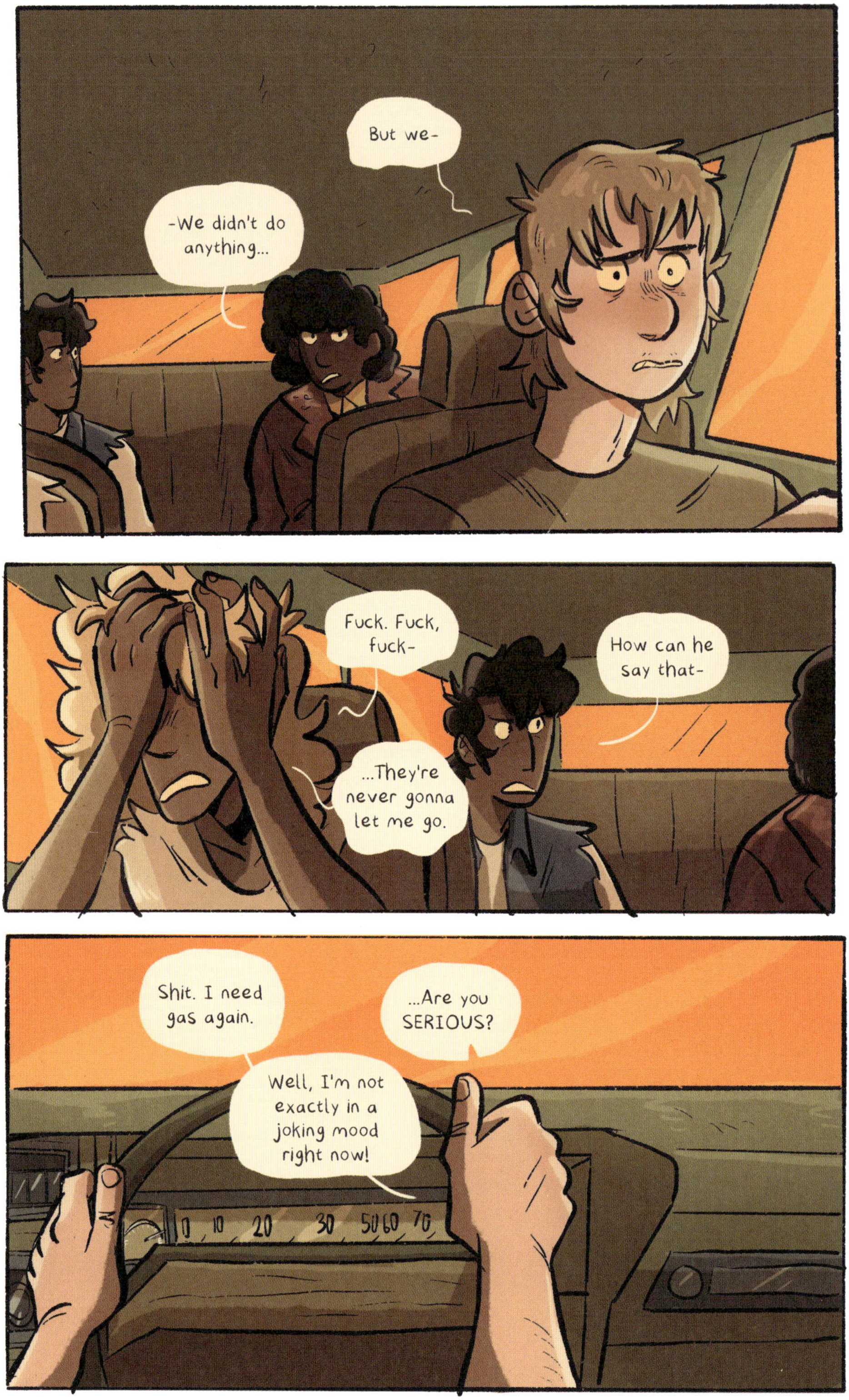
-We didn't do anything...
But we-
Fuck. Fuck, fuck-
...They're never gonna let me go.
How can he say that-
Shit. I need gas again.
...Are you SERIOUS?
Well, I'm not exactly in a joking mood right now!
0 10 20 30 50 60 70

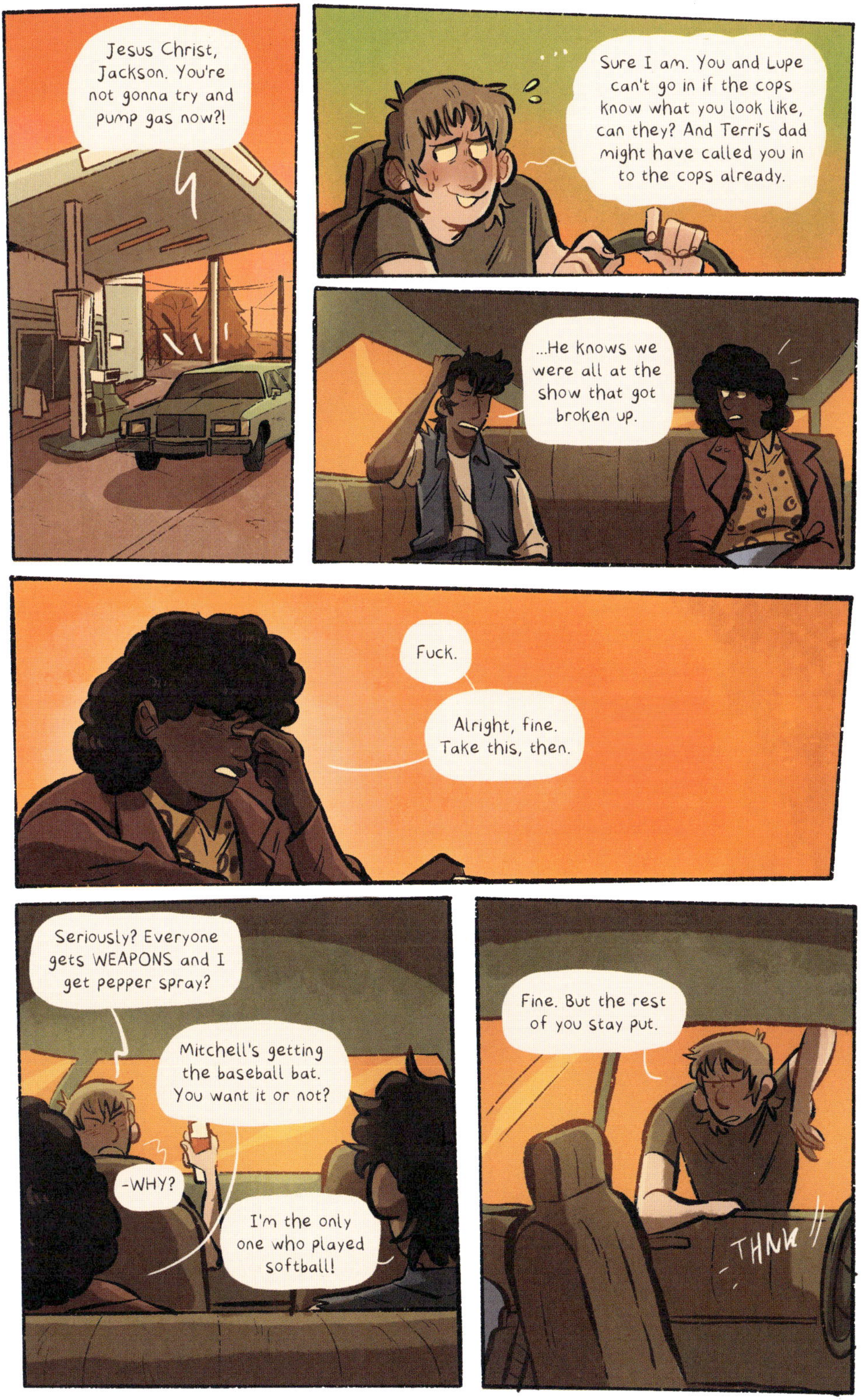

Jesus Christ, Jackson. You're not gonna try and pump gas now?!
Sure I am. You and Lupe can't go in if the cops know what you look like, can they? And Terri's dad might have called you in to the cops already.
...He knows we were all at the show that got broken up.
Fuck.
Alright, fine. Take this, then.
Seriously? Everyone gets WEAPONS and I get pepper spray?
Mitchell's getting the baseball bat. You want it or not?
-WHY?
I'm the only one who played softball!
Fine. But the rest of you stay put.
THNK

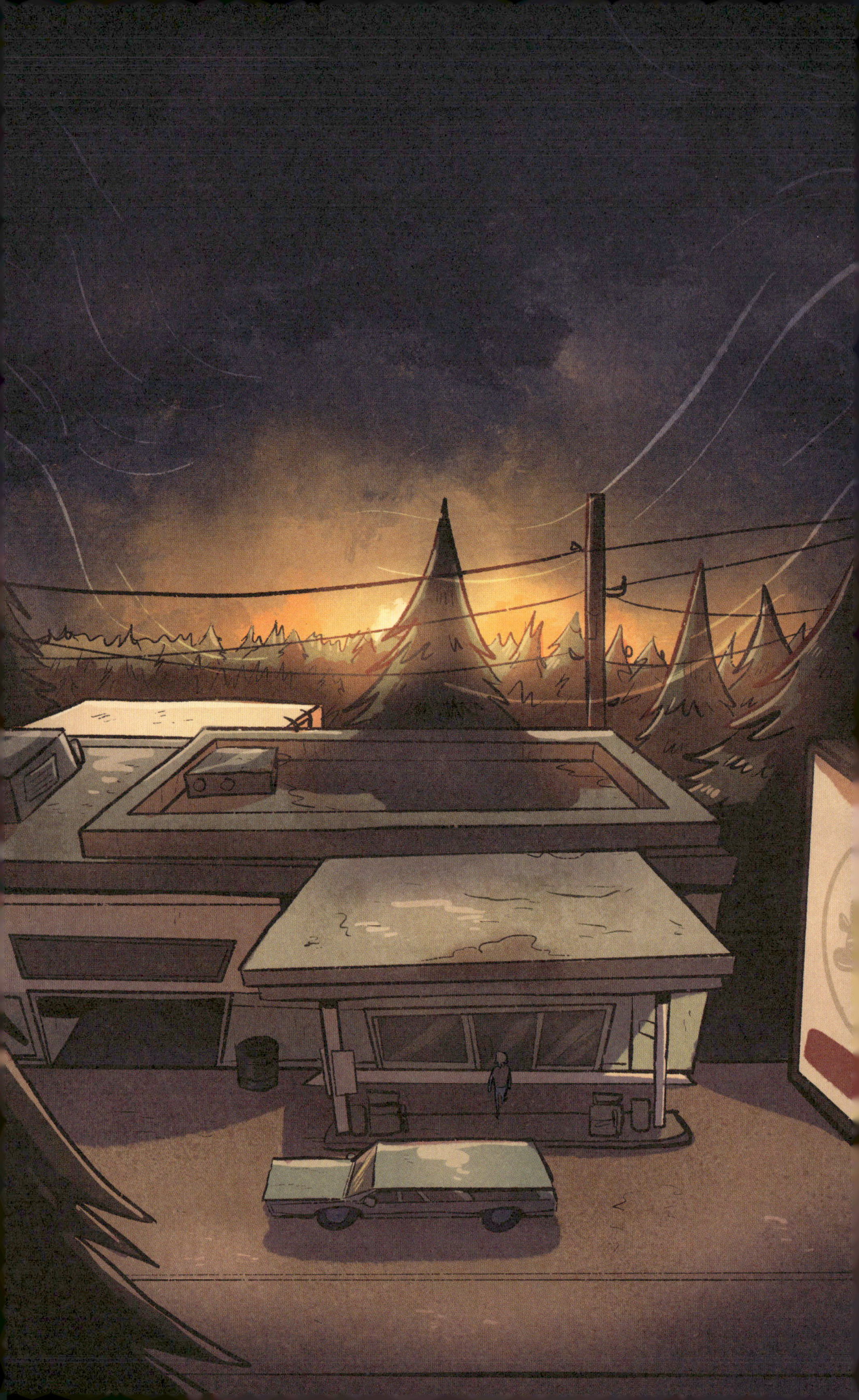

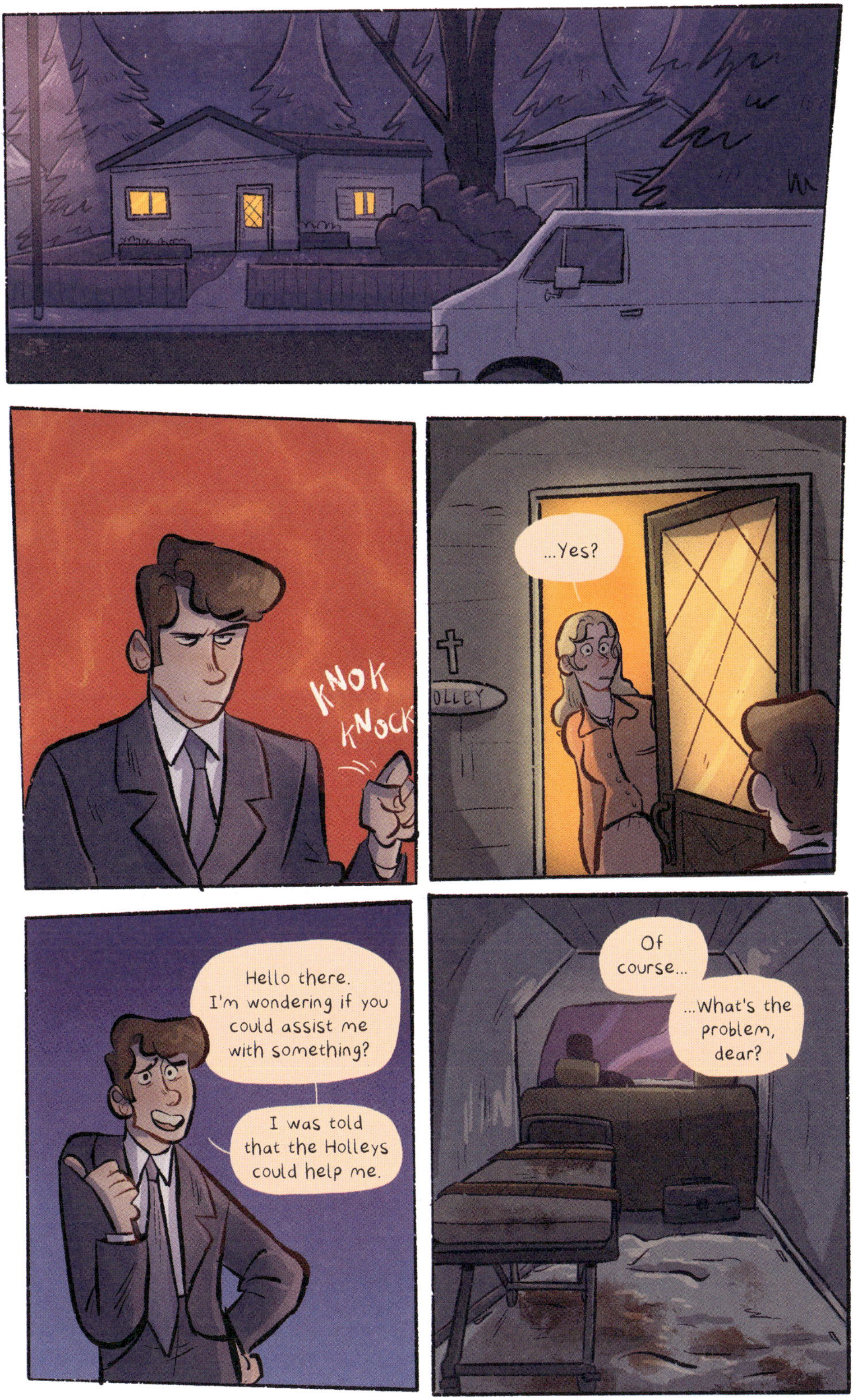
KNOK
KNOCK
...Yes?
Hello there. I'm wondering if you could assist me with something?
I was told that the Holleys could help me.
Of course...
...What's the problem, dear?

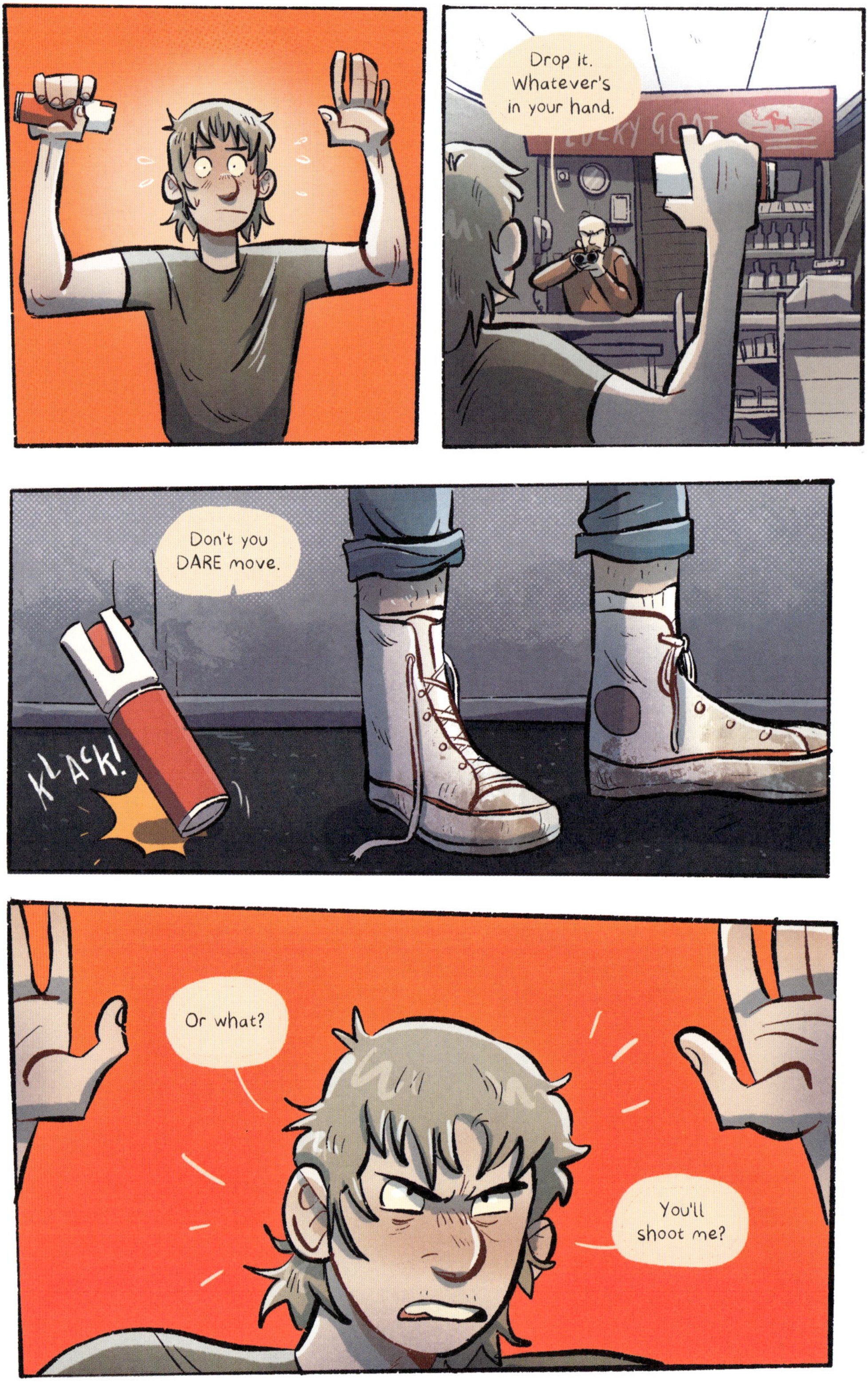
Drop it. Whatever's in your hand.
Don't you DARE move.
KLACK!
Or what?
You'll shoot me?

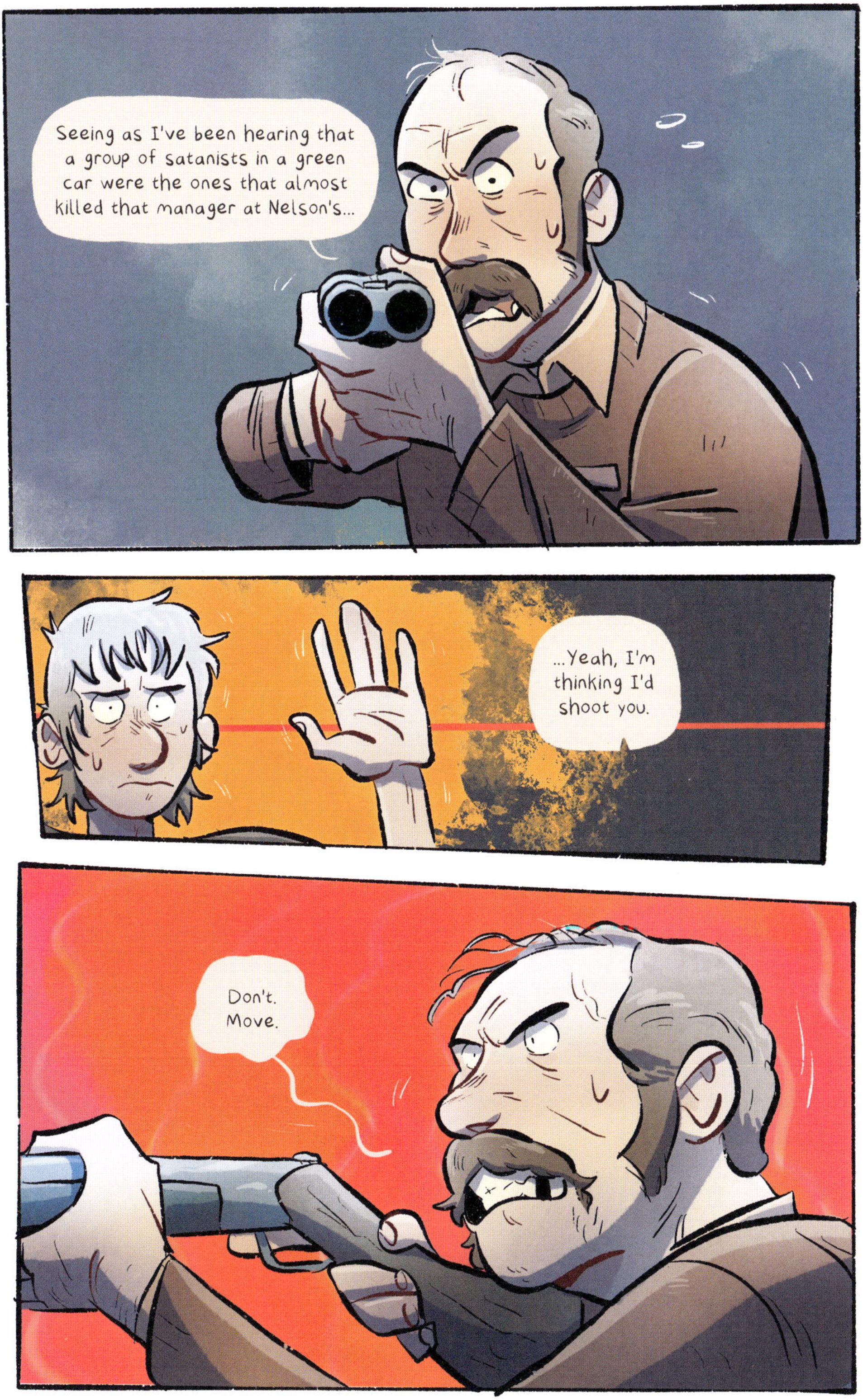
Seeing as I've been hearing that a group of satanists in a green car were the ones that almost killed that manager at Nelson's...
...Yeah, I'm thinking I'd shoot you.
Don't. Move.

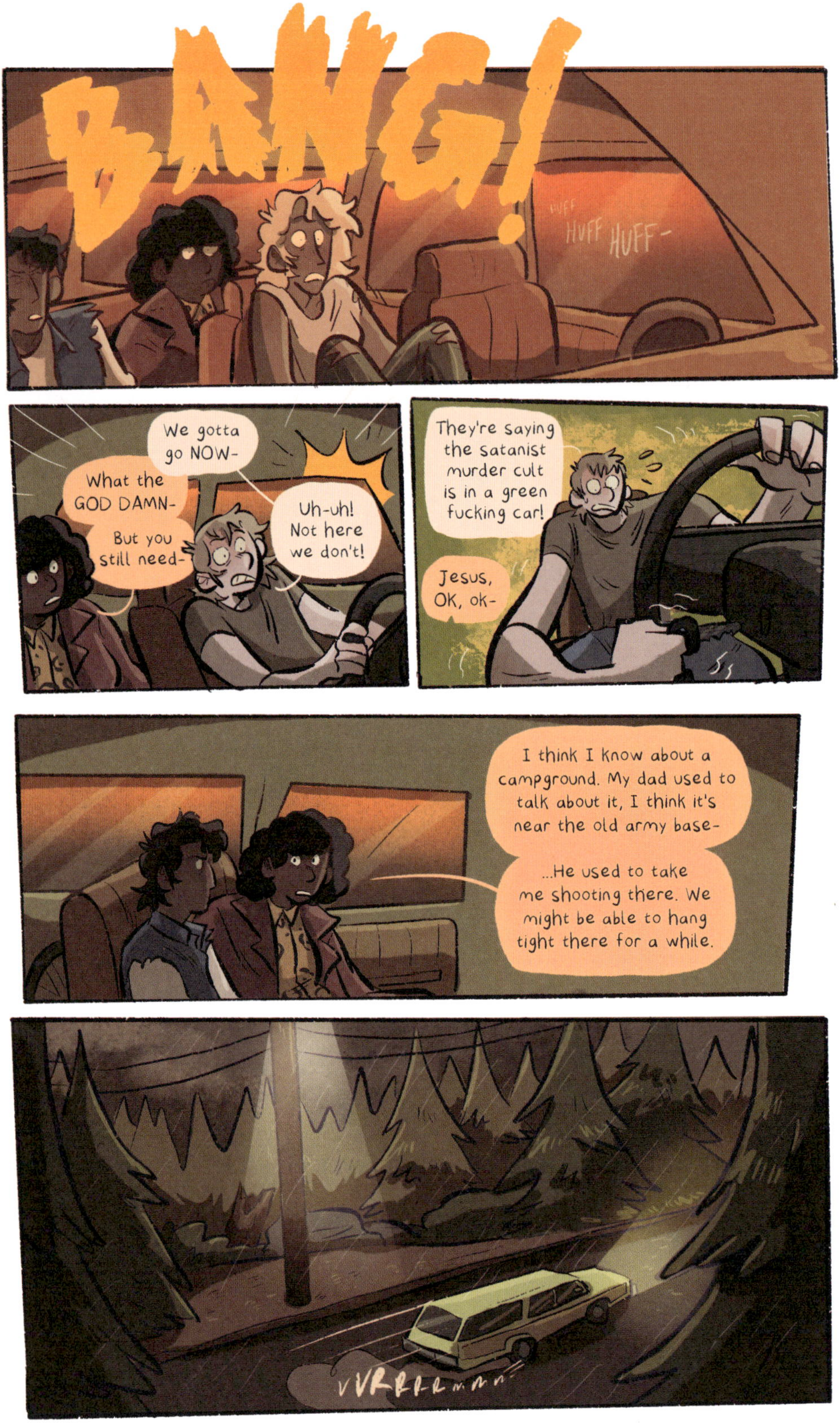
BANG!
HUFF
HUFF
HUFF-
What the GOD DAMN-
We gotta go NOW-
But you still need-
Uh-uh! Not here we don't!
They're saying the satanist murder cult is in a green fucking car!
Jesus, OK, ok-
I think I know about a campground. My dad used to talk about it, I think it's near the old army base-
...He used to take me shooting there. We might be able to hang tight there for a while.
VVRRRRRmmm-

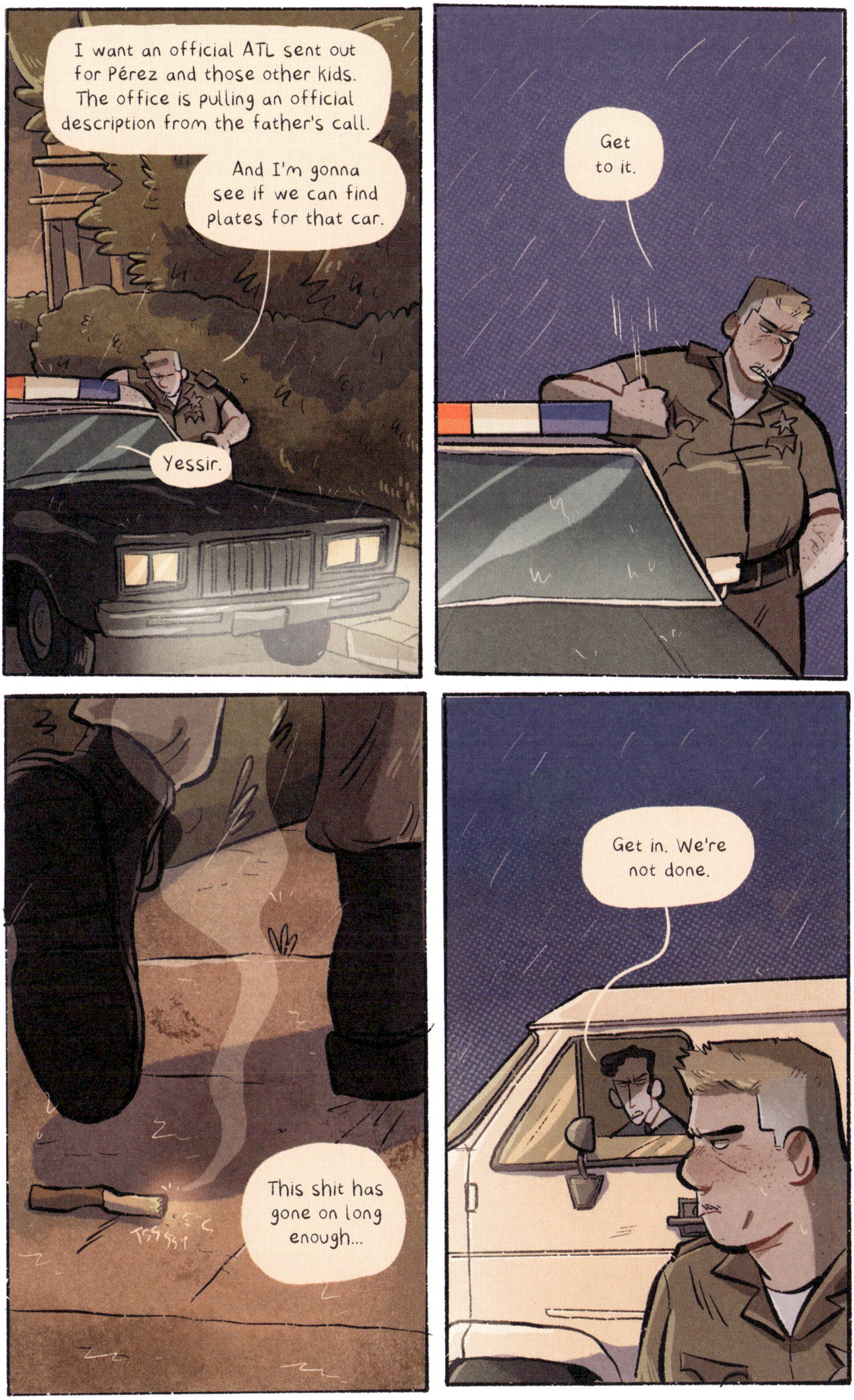
I want an official ATL sent out for Pérez and those other kids. The office is pulling an official description from the father's call.
And I'm gonna see if we can find plates for that car.
Yessir.
Get to it.
This shit has gone on long enough...
Get in. We're not done.

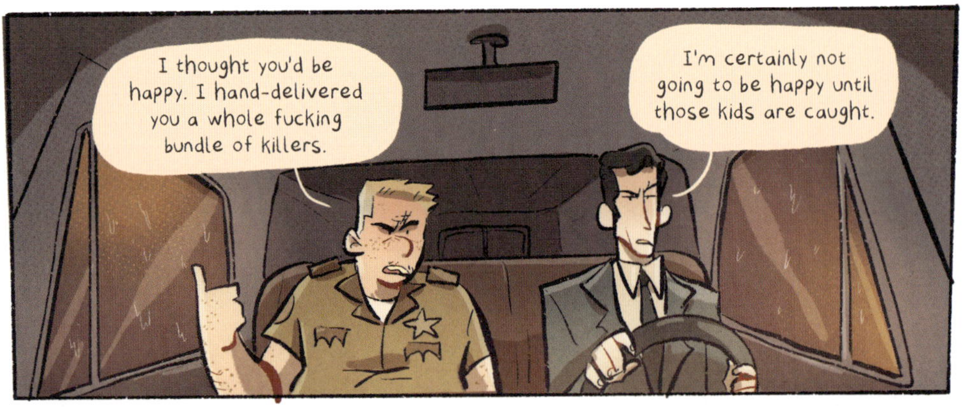
I thought you'd be happy. I hand-delivered you a whole fucking bundle of killers.
I'm certainly not going to be happy until those kids are caught.

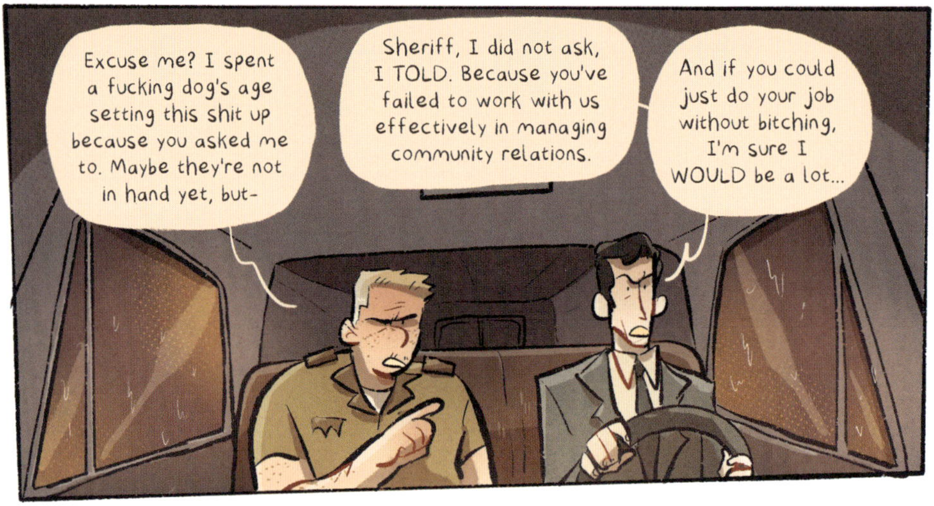
Excuse me? I spent a fucking dog's age setting this shit up because you asked me to. Maybe they're not in hand yet, but-
Sheriff, I did not ask, I TOLD. Because you've failed to work with us effectively in managing community relations.
And if you could just do your job without bitching, I'm sure I WOULD be a lot...

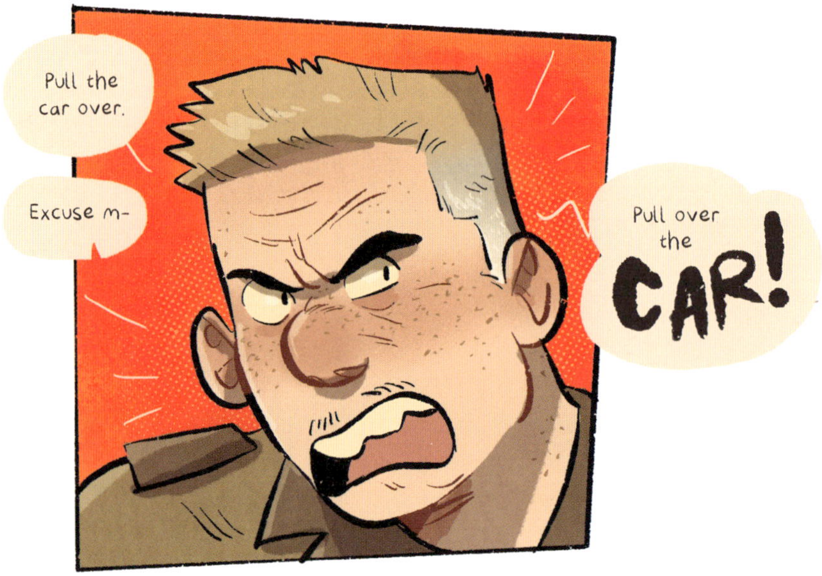
Pull the car over.
Excuse m-
Pull over the CAR!

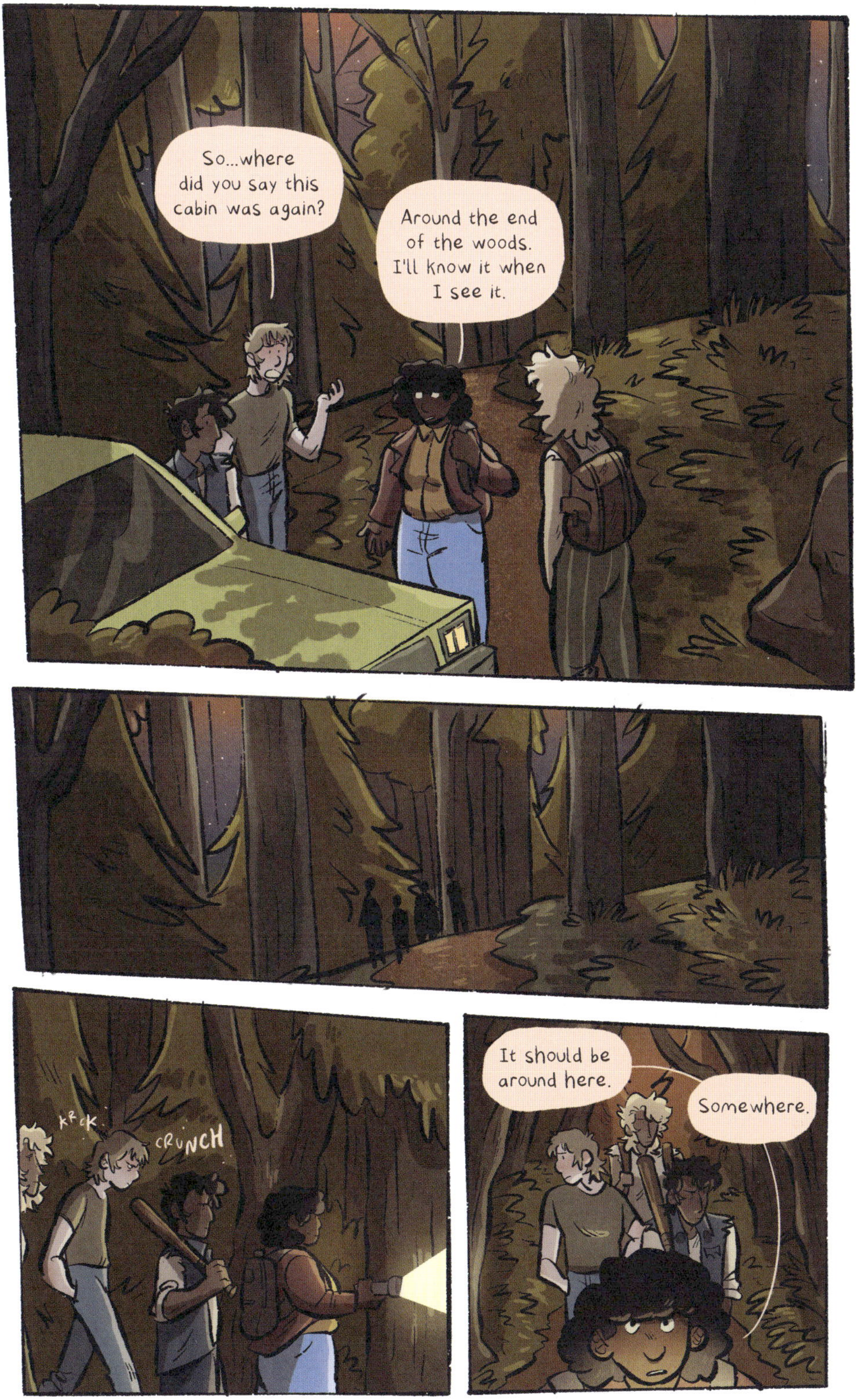
So...where did you say this cabin was again?
Around the end of the woods. I'll know it when I see it.
KRCK
CRUNCH
It should be around here.
Somewhere.

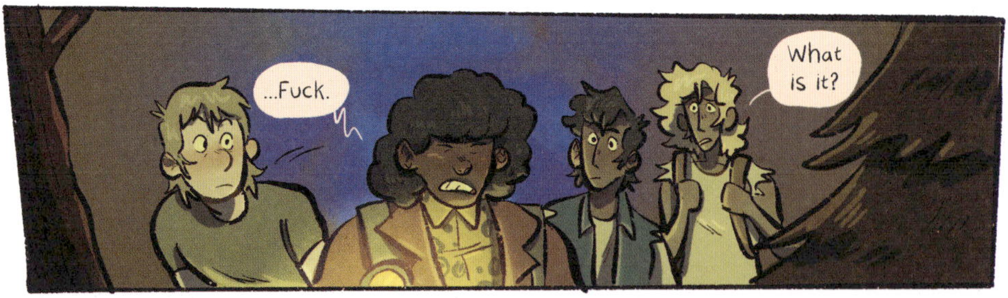
...Fuck.
What is it?

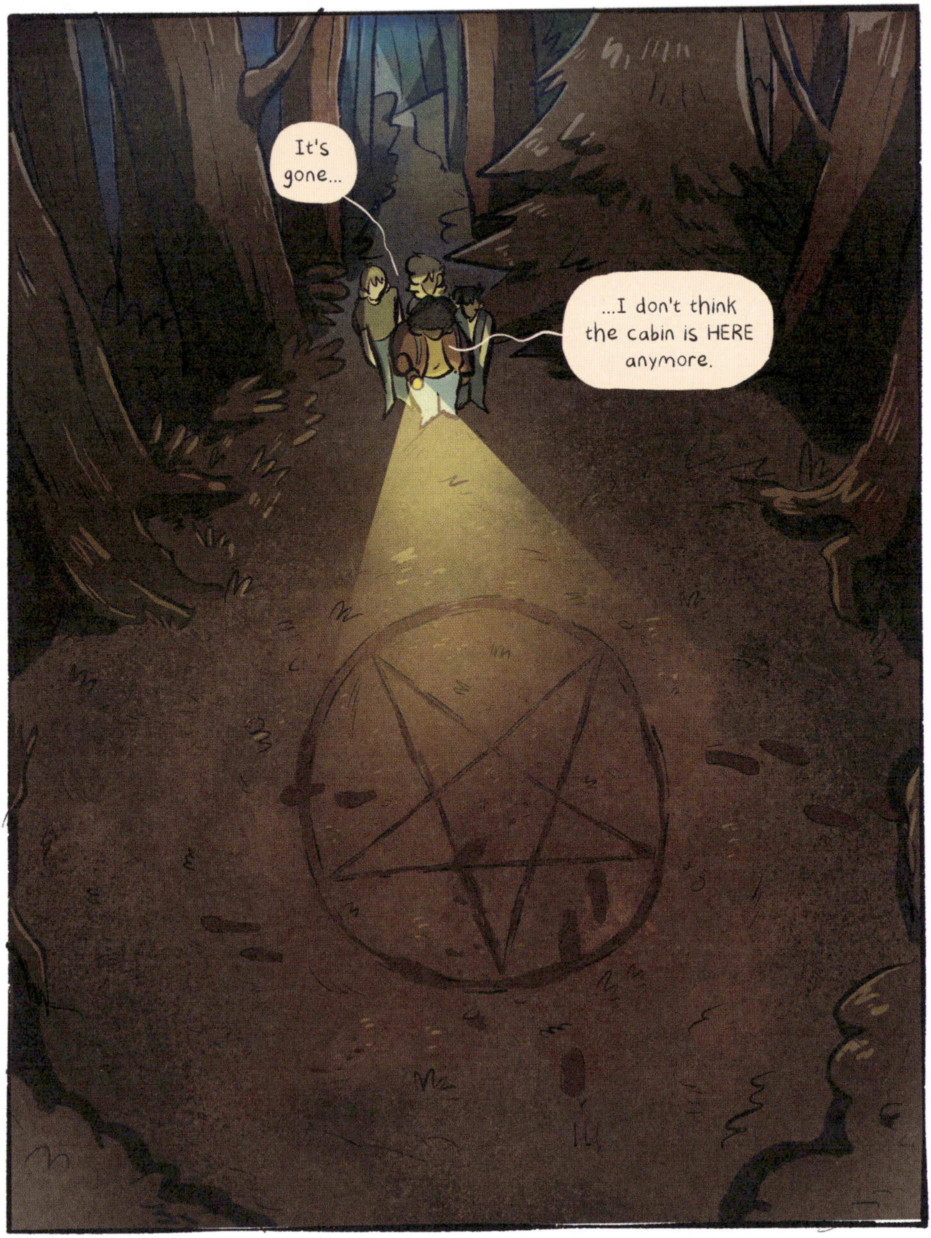
It's gone...
...I don't think the cabin is HERE anymore.

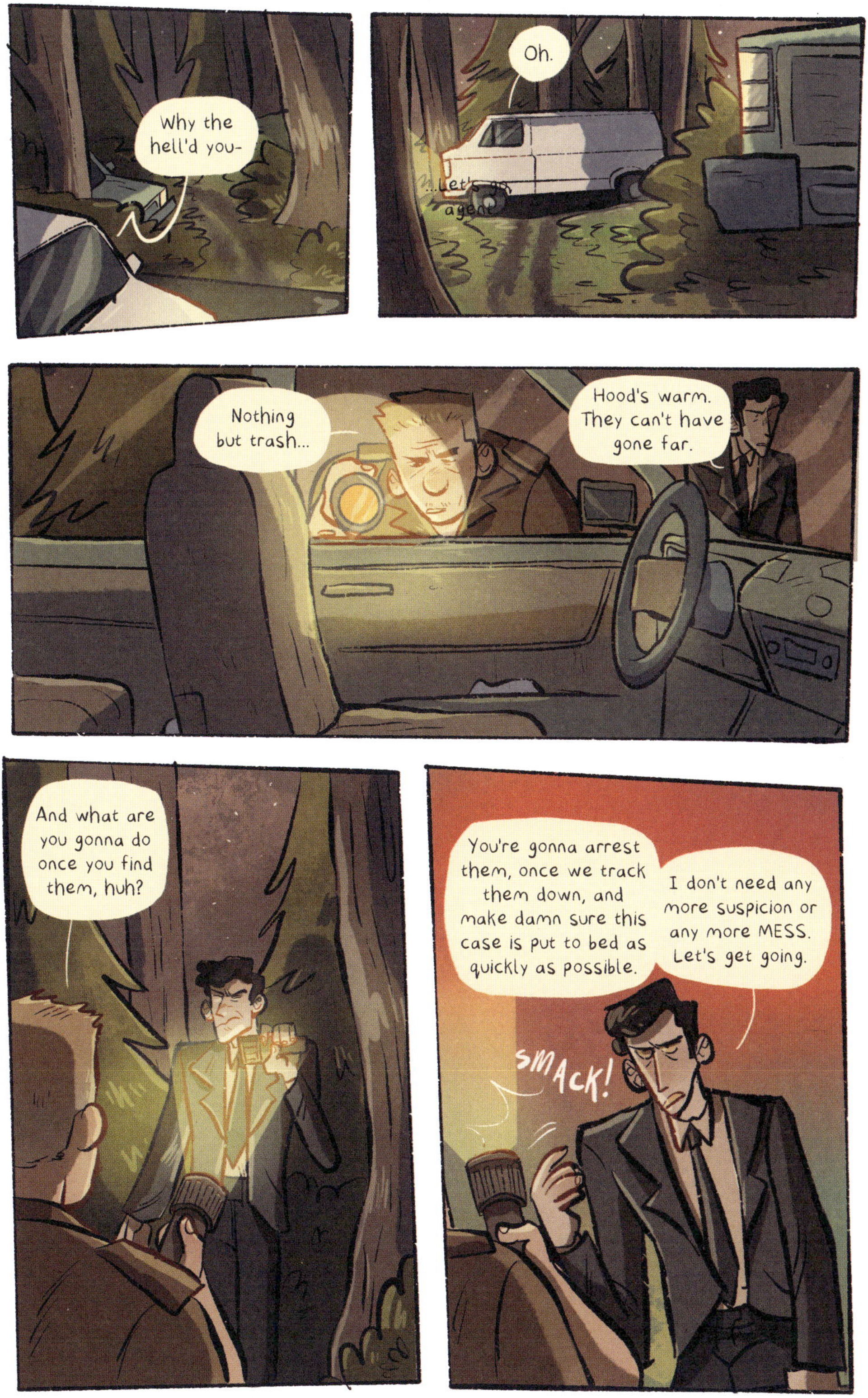
Why the hell'd you-
Oh.
...Let's go, agent
Nothing but trash...
Hood's warm. They can't have gone far.
And what are you gonna do once you find them, huh?
You're gonna arrest them, once we track them down, and make damn sure this case is put to bed as quickly as possible.
I don't need any more suspicion or any more MESS. Let's get going.
SMACK!

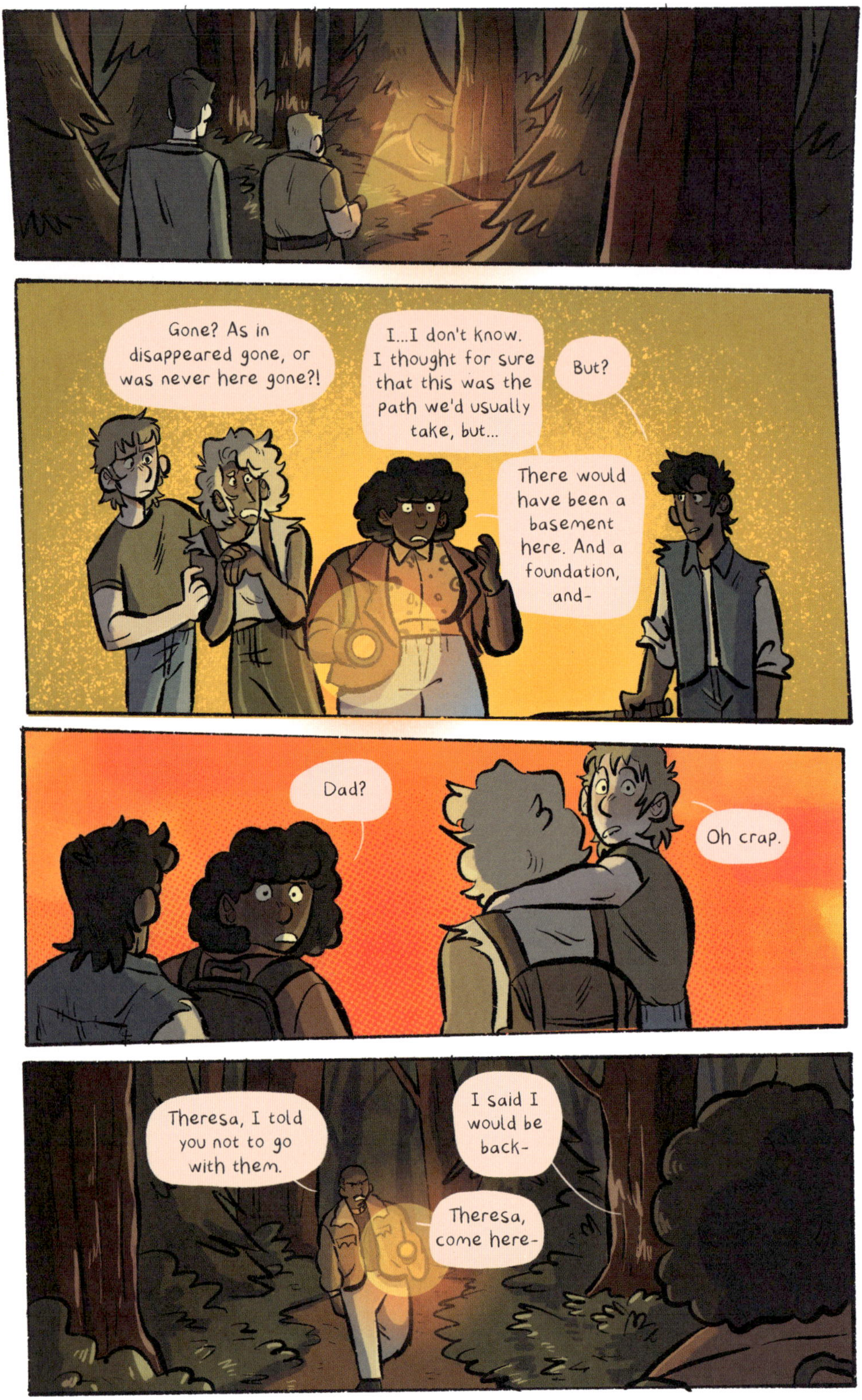

Gone? As in disappeared gone, or was never here gone?!
I...I don't know. I thought for sure that this was the path we'd usually take, but...
But?
There would have been a basement here. And a foundation, and-
Dad?
Oh crap.
Theresa, I told you not to go with them.
I said I would be back-
Theresa, come here-

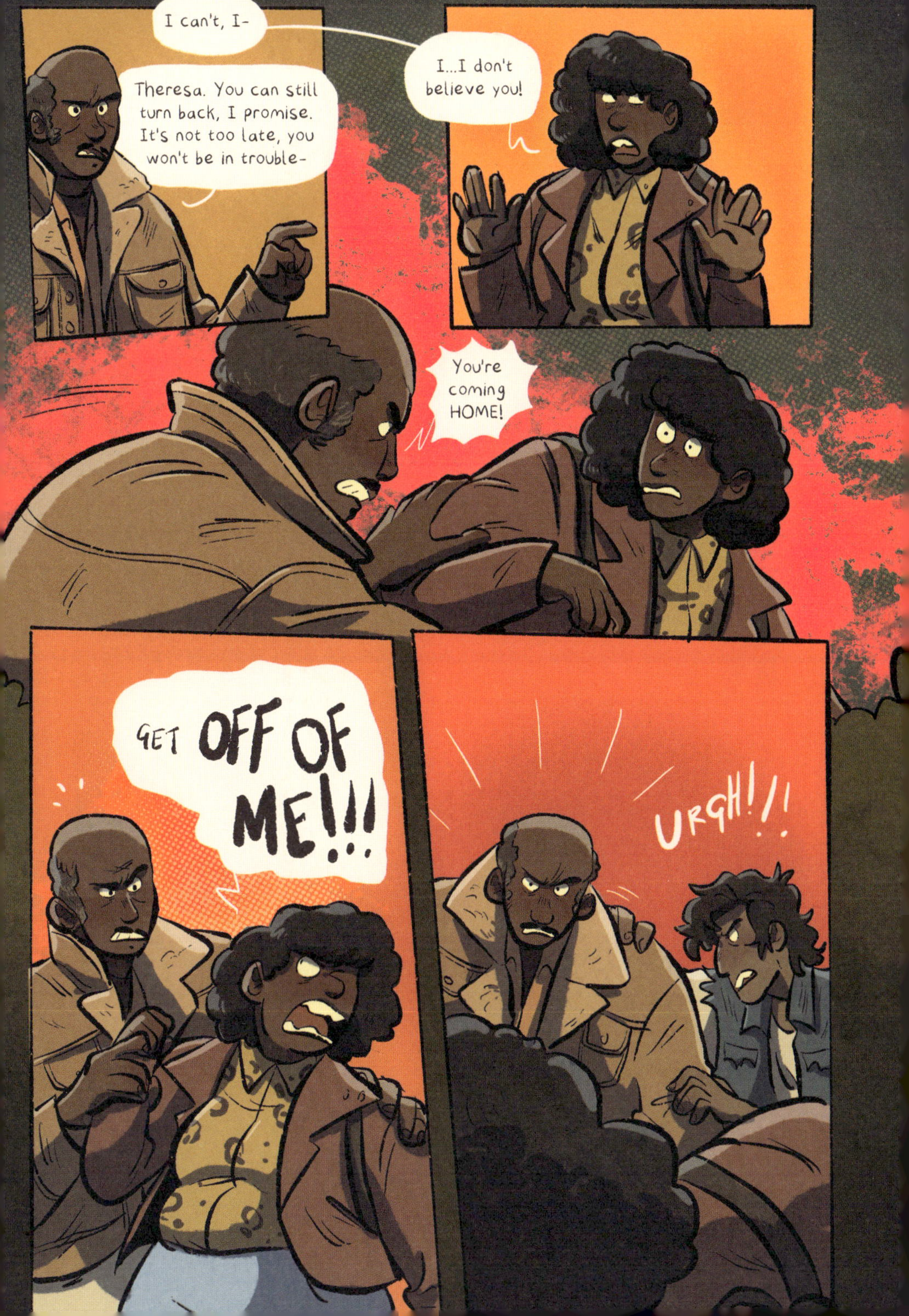
I can't, I-
Theresa. You can still turn back, I promise. It's not too late, you won't be in trouble-
I...I don't believe you!
You're coming HOME!
GET OFF OF ME!!!
URGH!!!

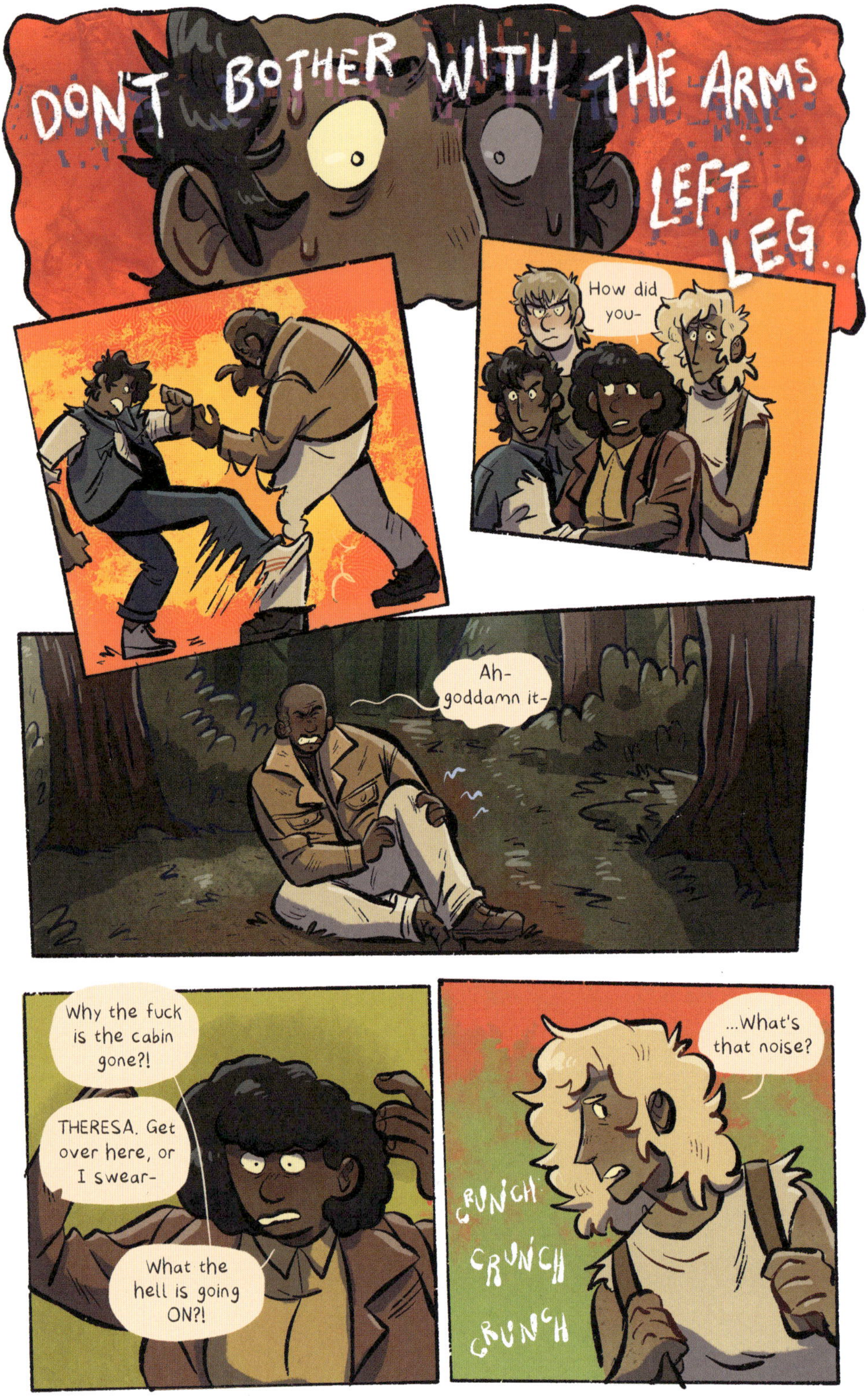
DON'T BOTHER WITH THE ARMS
LEFT LEG...
How did you-
Ah- goddamn it-
Why the fuck is the cabin gone?!
THERESA. Get over here, or I swear-
What the hell is going ON?!
...What's that noise?
CRUNCH
CRUNCH
CRUNCH

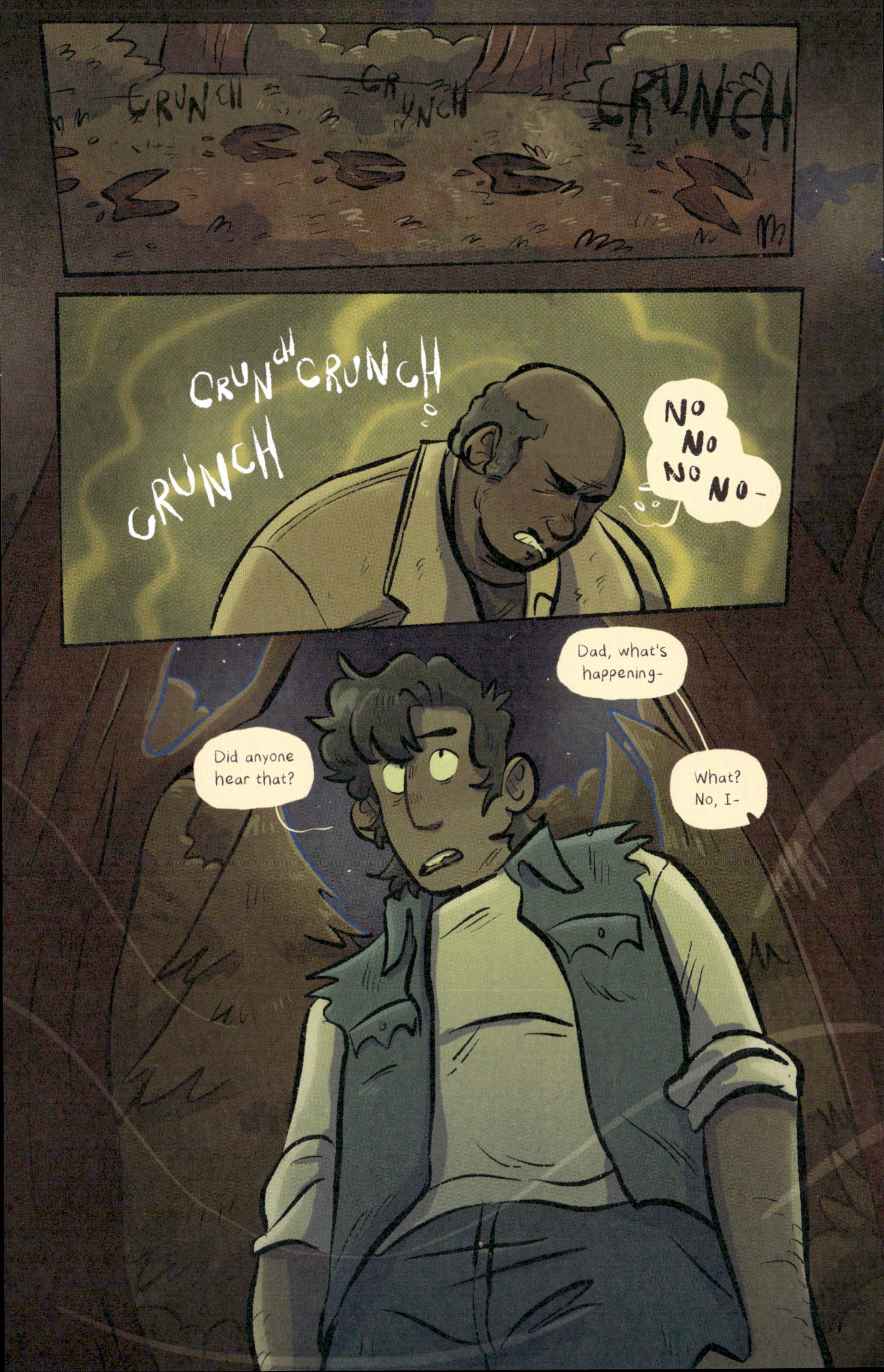

CRUNCH
CRUNCH
CRUNCH
CRUNCH CRUNCH
CRUNCH
NO NO NO NO-
Dad, what's happening-
Did anyone hear that?
What? No, I-

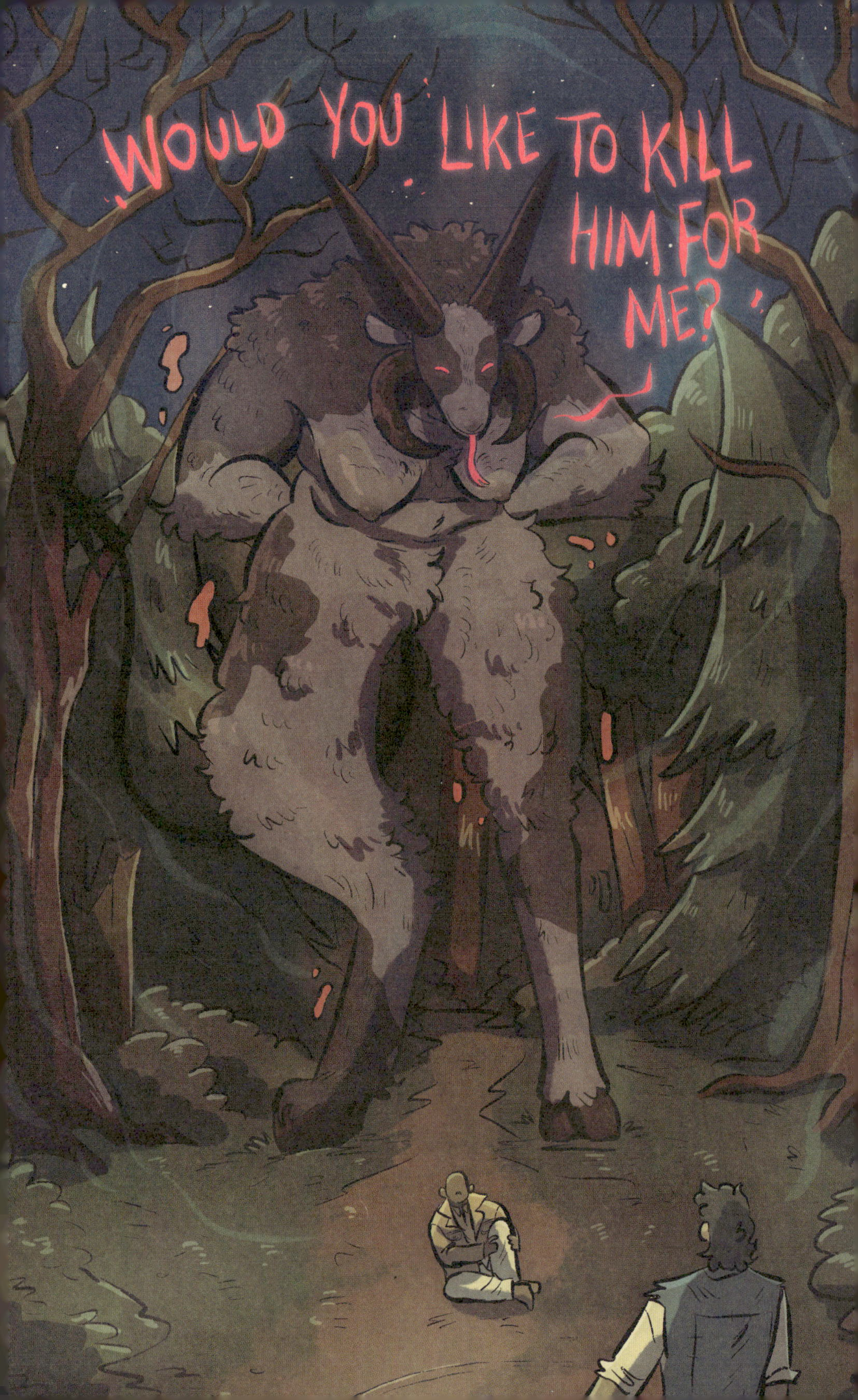
WOULD YOU LIKE TO KILL HIM FOR ME?

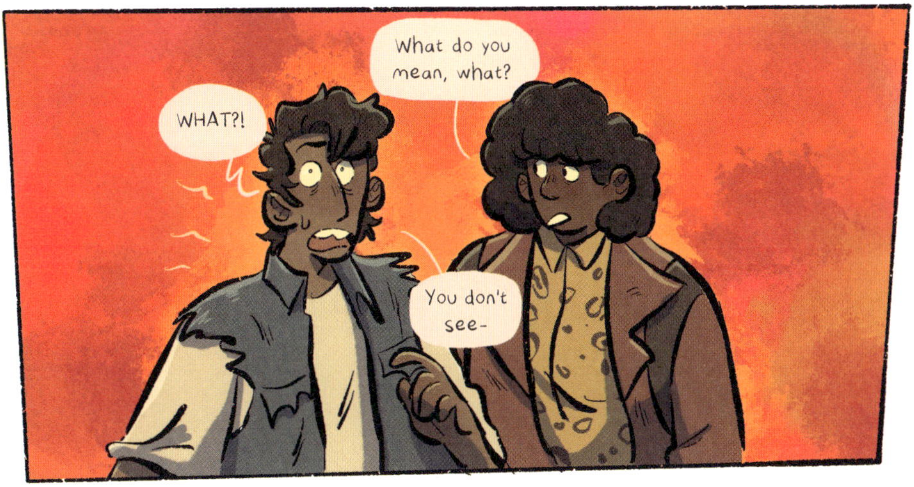
WHAT?!
What do you mean, what?
You don't see-

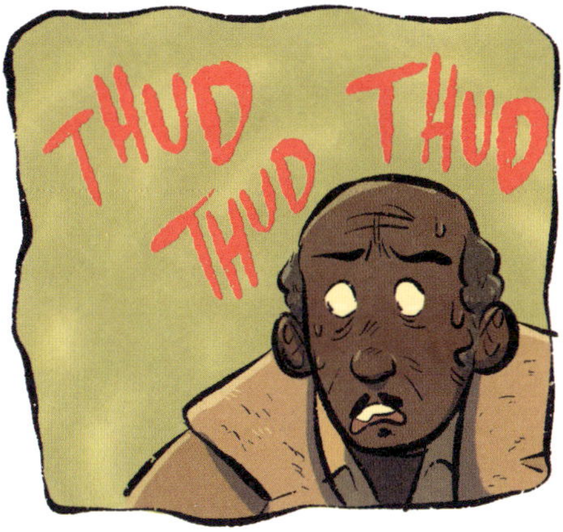
THUD
THUD
THUD

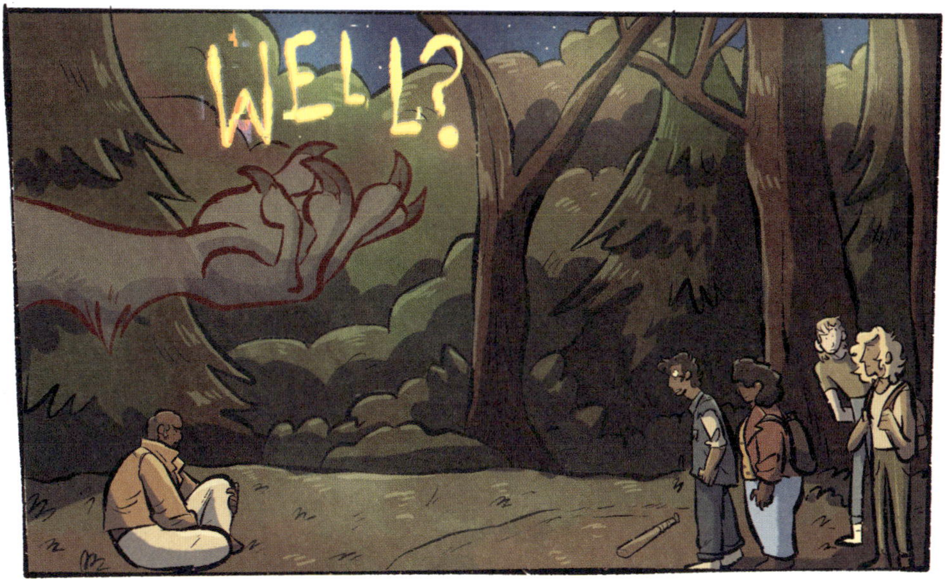
WELL?

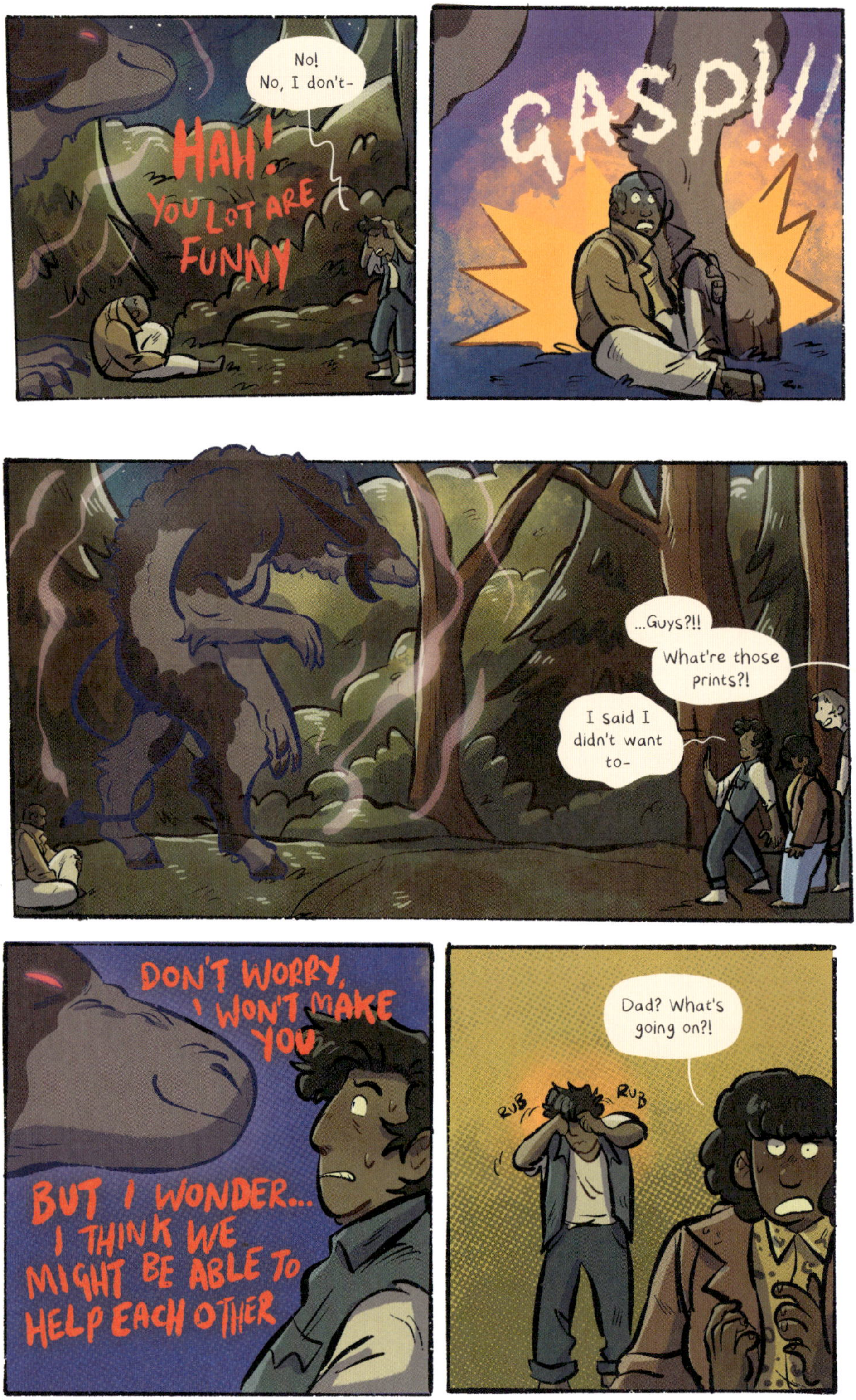
No!
No, I don't-
HAH! YOU LOT ARE FUNNY
GASP!!!
...Guys?!!
What're those prints?!
I said I didn't want to-
DON'T WORRY, I WON'T MAKE YOU
BUT I WONDER... I THINK WE MIGHT BE ABLE TO HELP EACH OTHER
Dad? What's going on?!
RUB
RUB

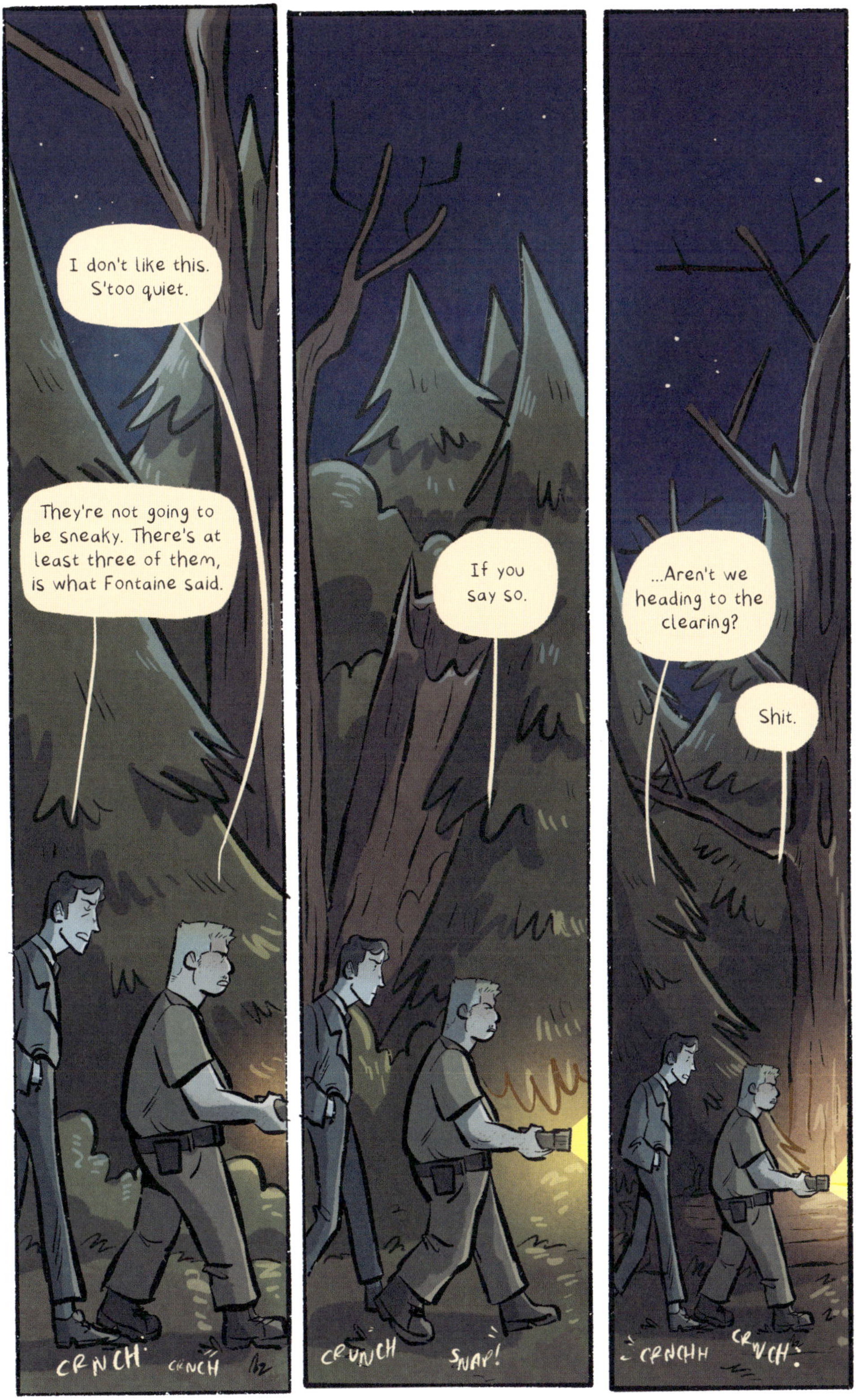
I don't like this. S'too quiet.
They're not going to be sneaky. There's at least three of them, is what Fontaine said.
CRNCH
CRNCH
If you say so.
CRUNCH
SNAP!
...Aren't we heading to the clearing?
Shit.
CRNCHH
CRNCH

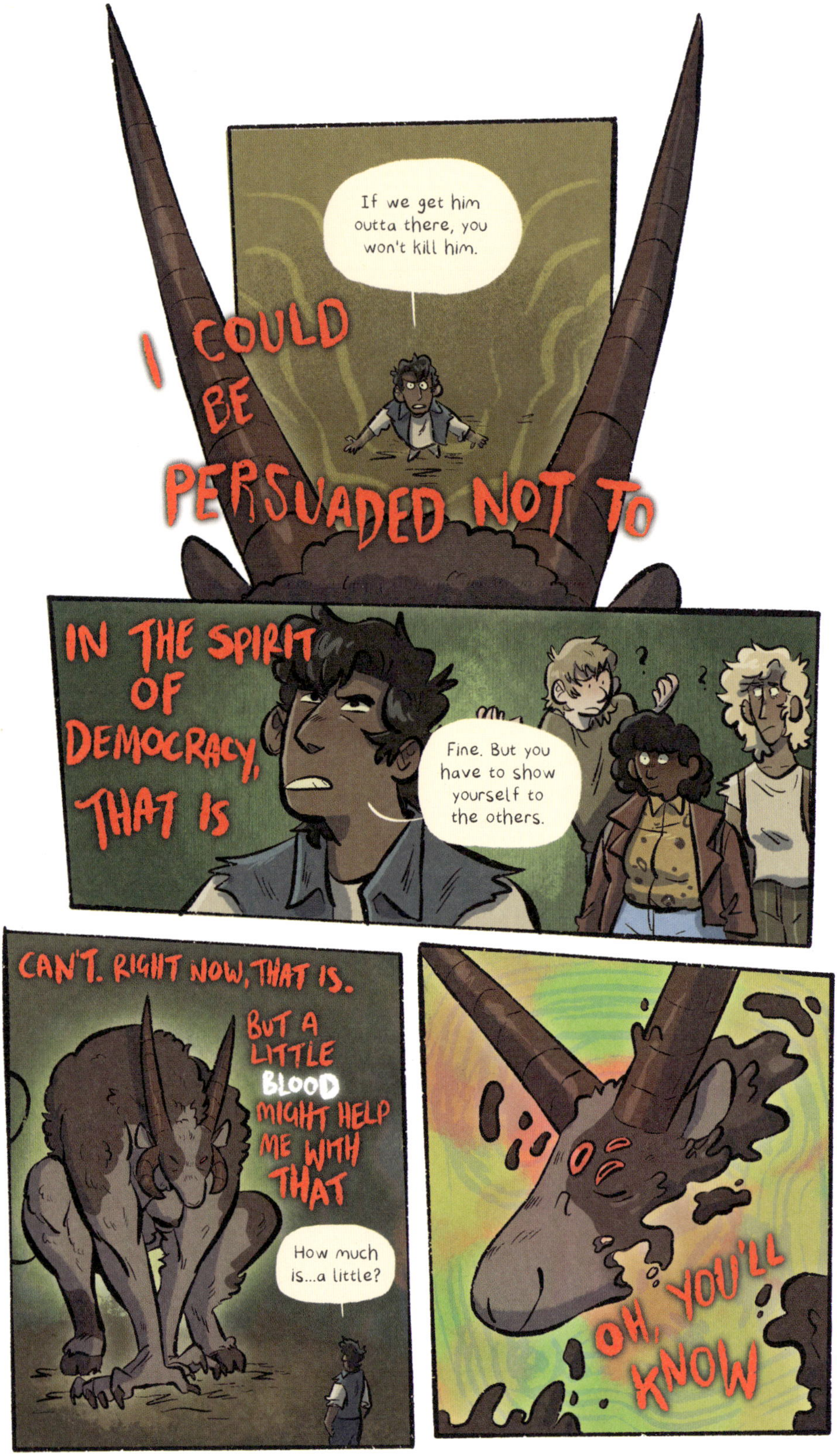
If we get him outta there, you won't kill him.
I COULD BE PERSUADED NOT TO
IN THE SPIRIT OF DEMOCRACY, THAT IS
Fine. But you have to show yourself to the others.
?
?
CAN'T. RIGHT NOW, THAT IS.
BUT A LITTLE BLOOD MIGHT HELP ME WITH THAT
How much is...a little?
OH, YOU'LL KNOW

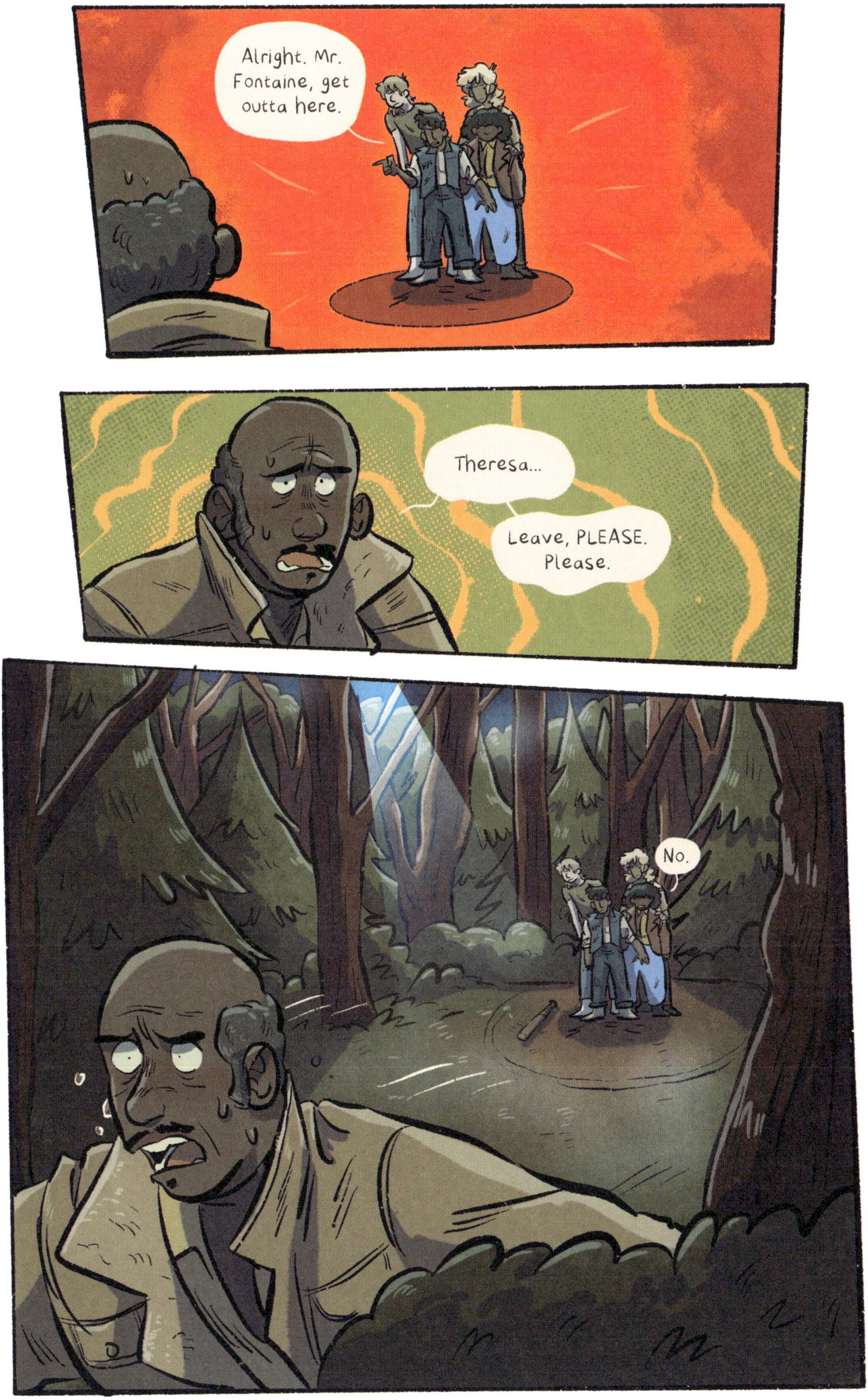
Alright. Mr. Fontaine, get outta here.
Theresa...
Leave, PLEASE. Please.
No.

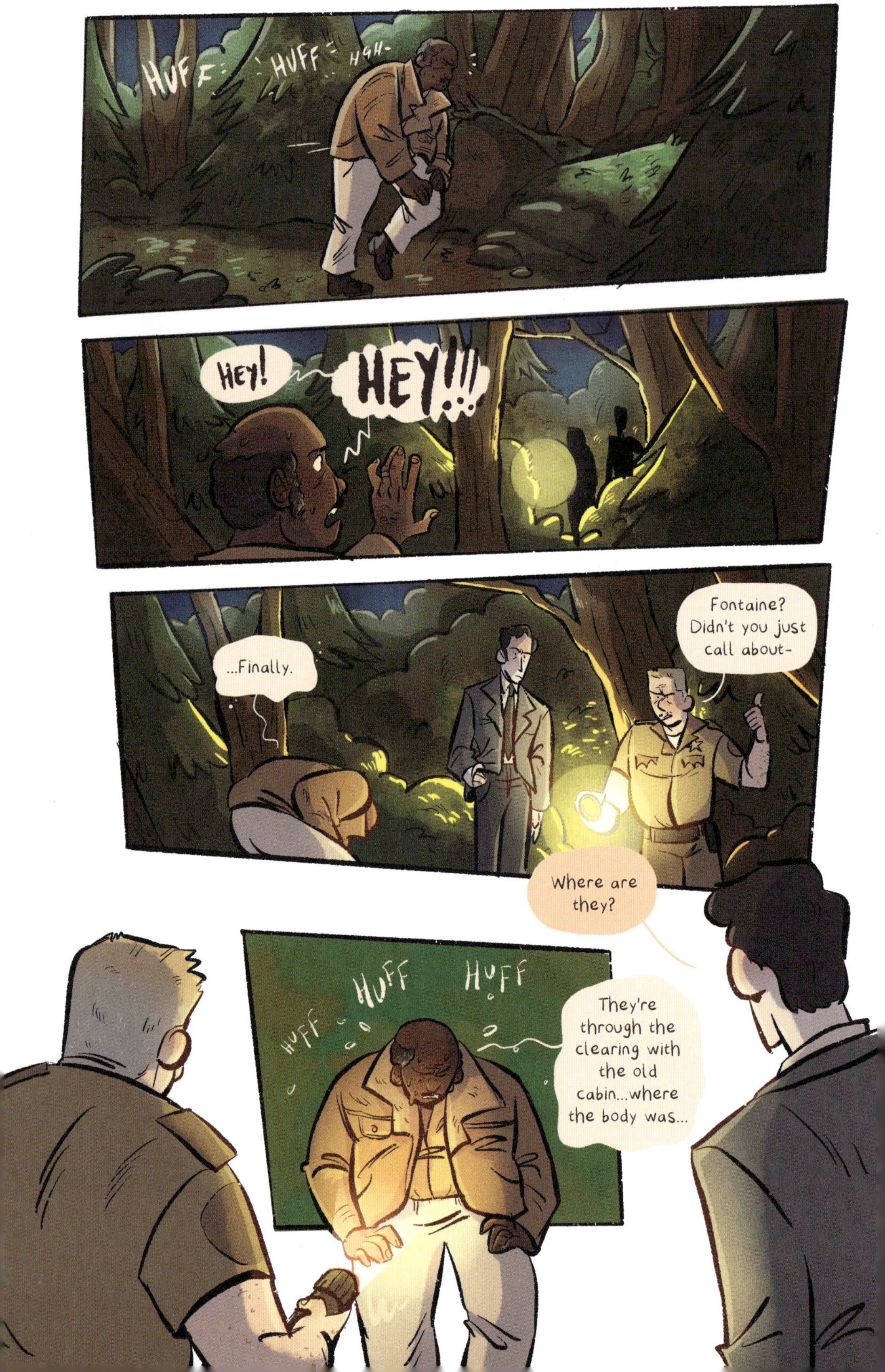
HUFF
HUFF
HGH
HEY!
HEY!!!
...Finally.
Fontaine? Didn't you just call about-
Where are they?
HUFF
HUFF
HUFF
They're through the clearing with the old cabin...where the body was...

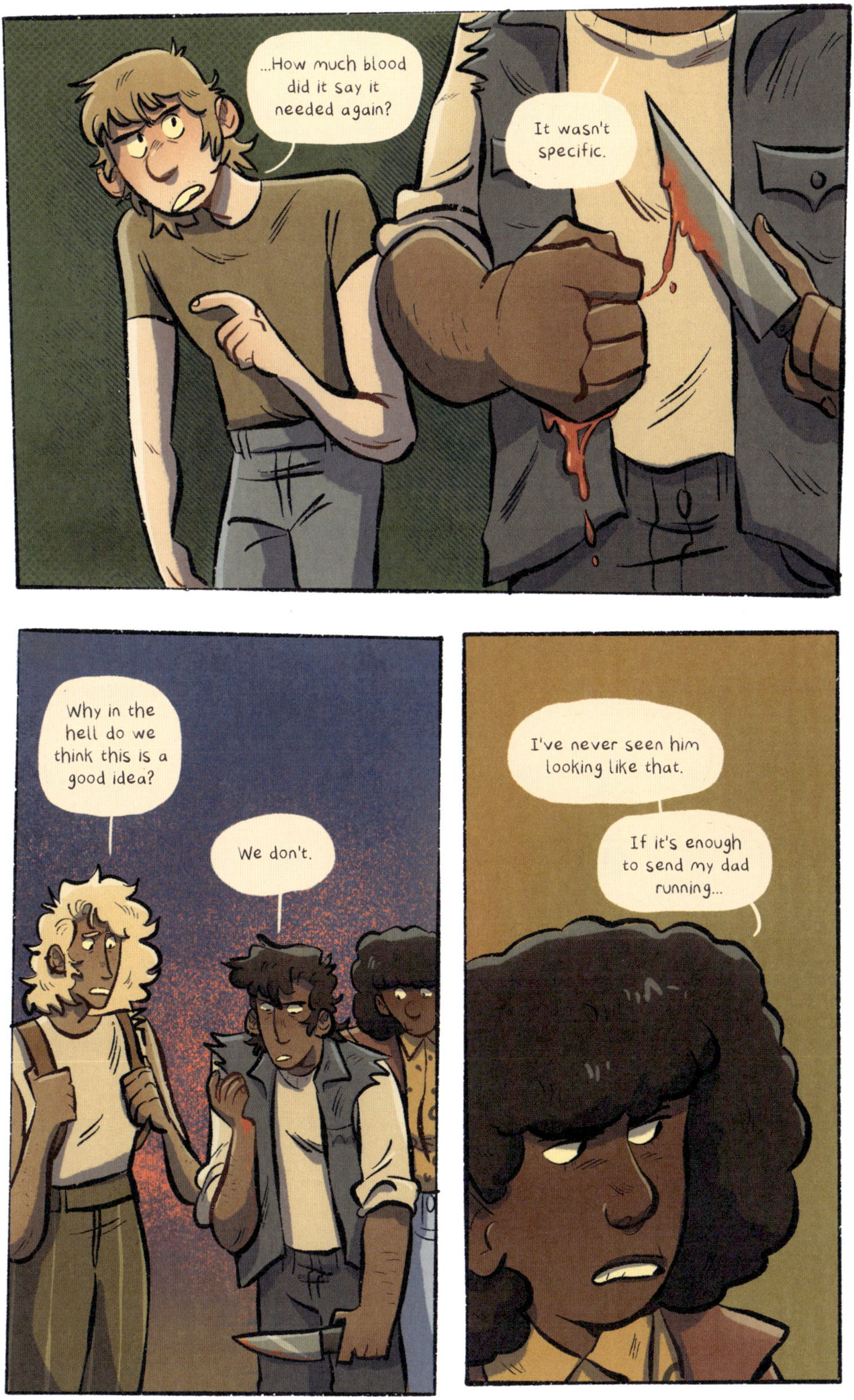
...How much blood did it say it needed again?
It wasn't specific.
Why in the hell do we think this is a good idea?
We don't.
I've never seen him looking like that.
If it's enough to send my dad running...

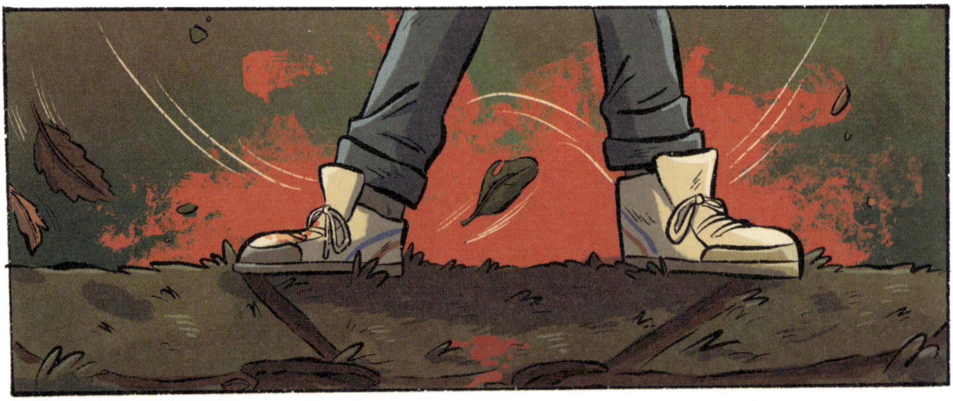

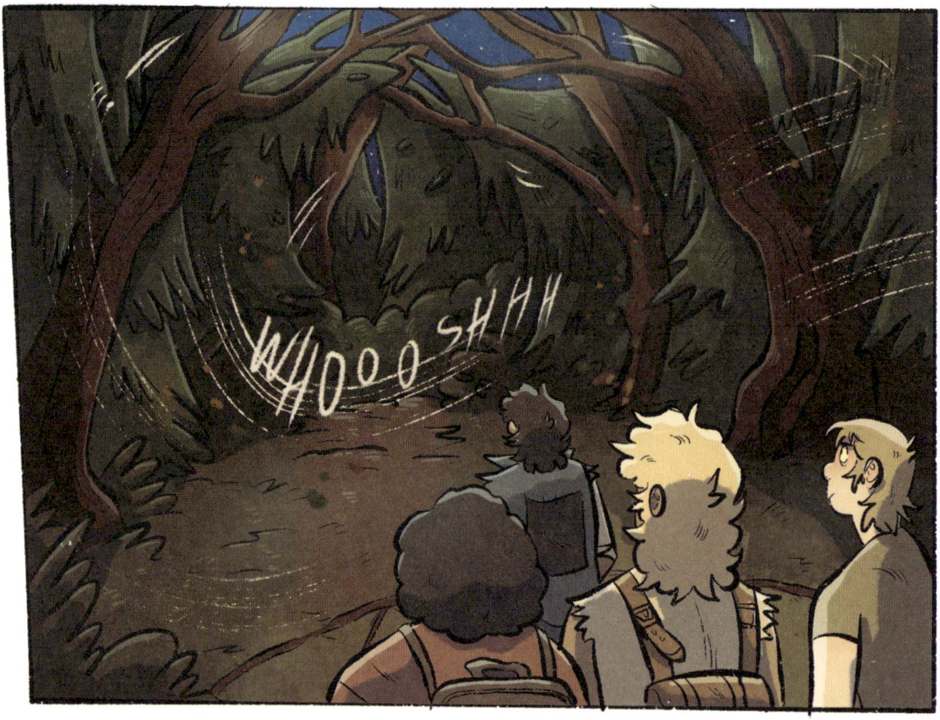
WHOOOOSHHH

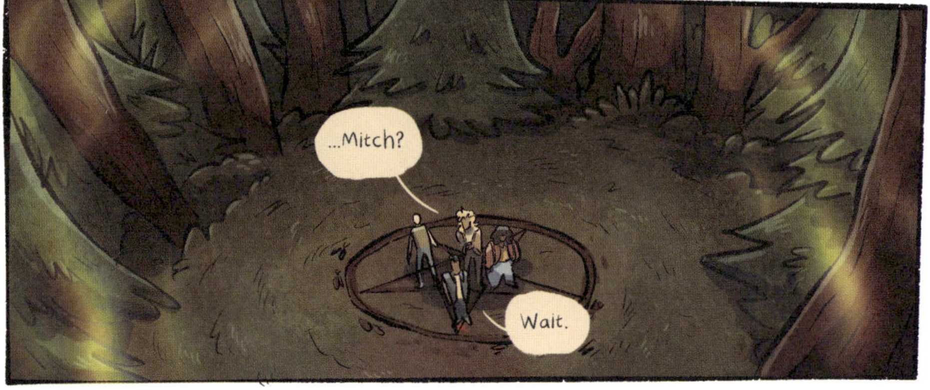
...Mitch?
Wait.

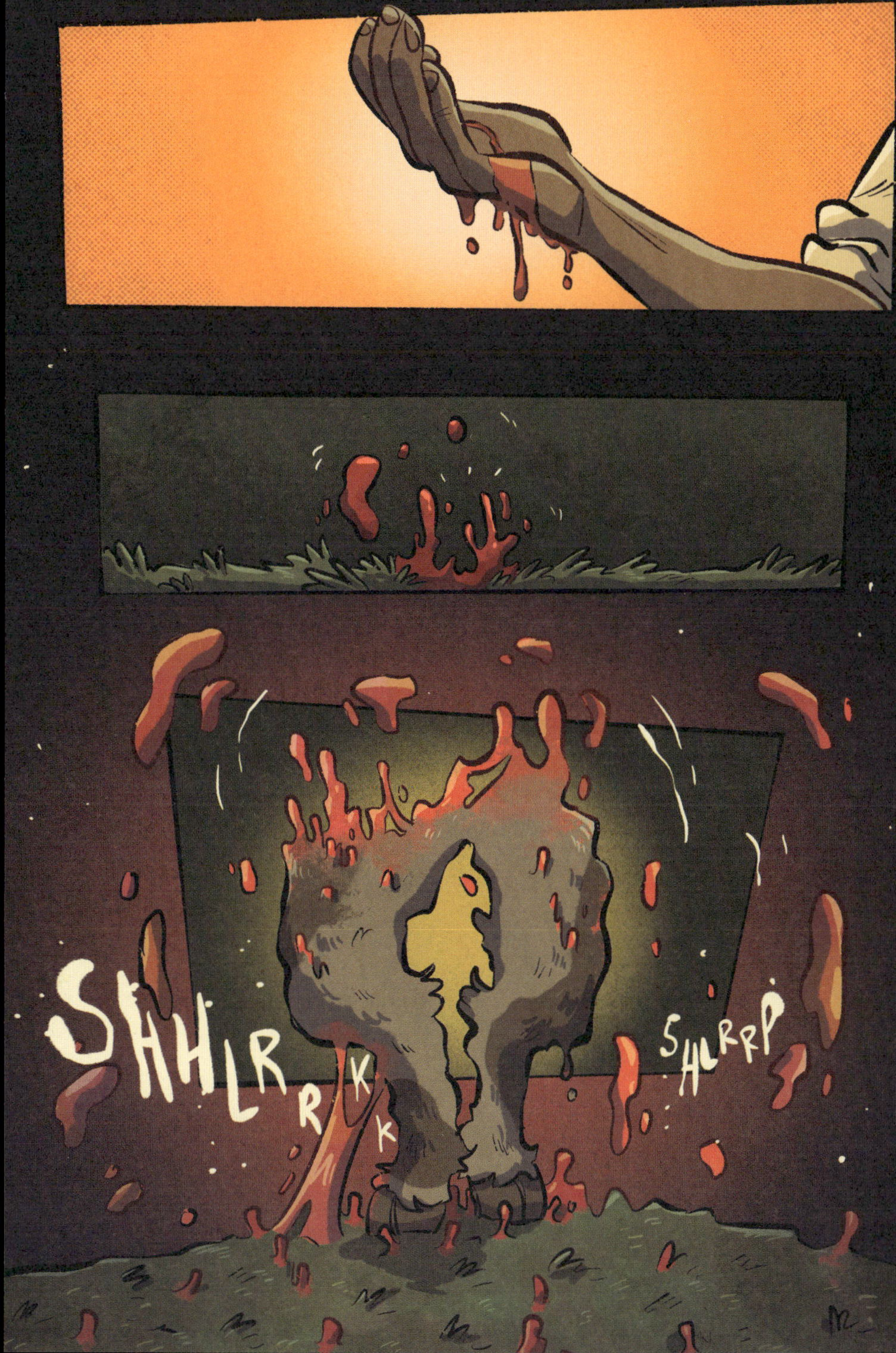
SHHLRRKK
SHLRRP

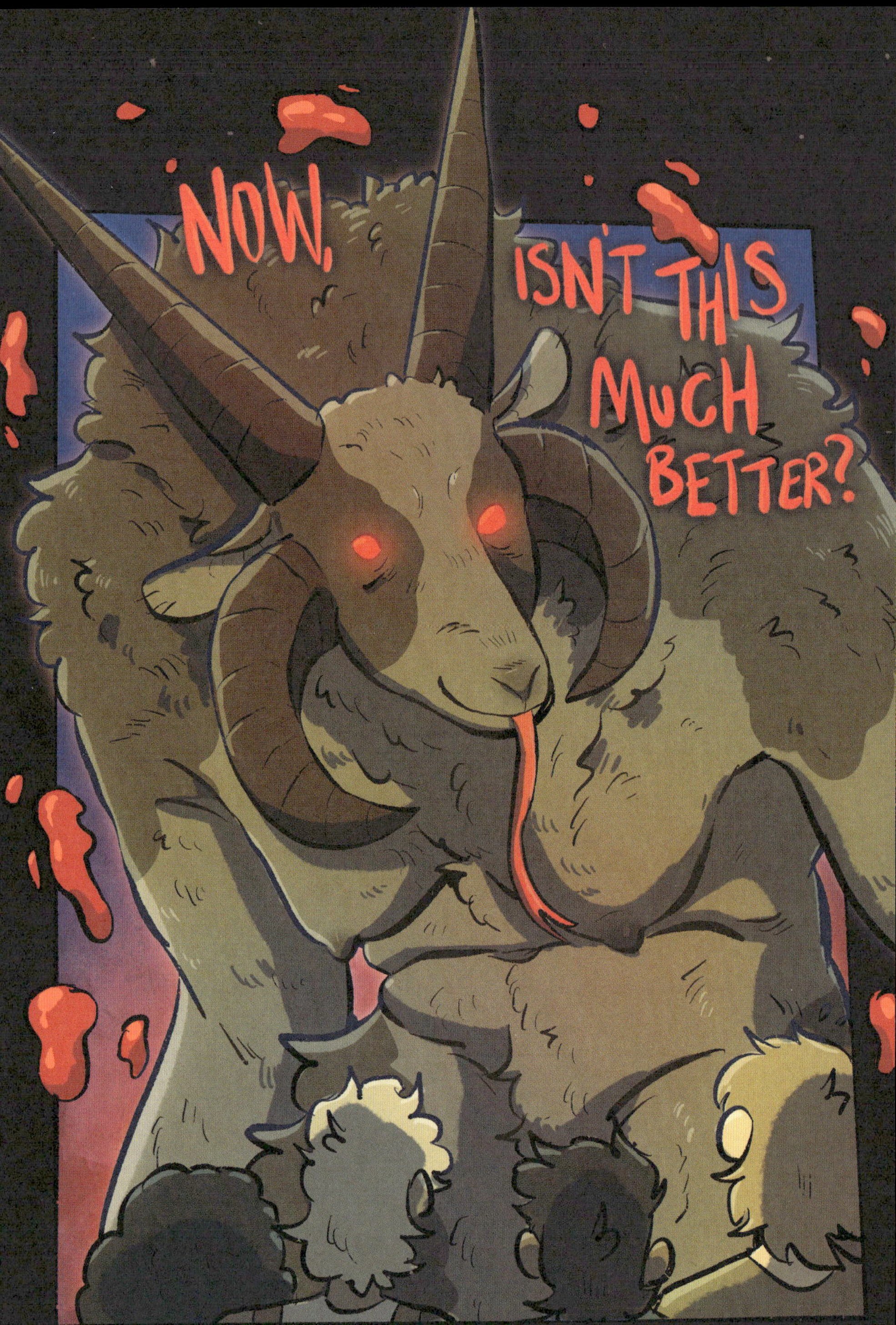
NOW,
ISN'T THIS MUCH BETTER?

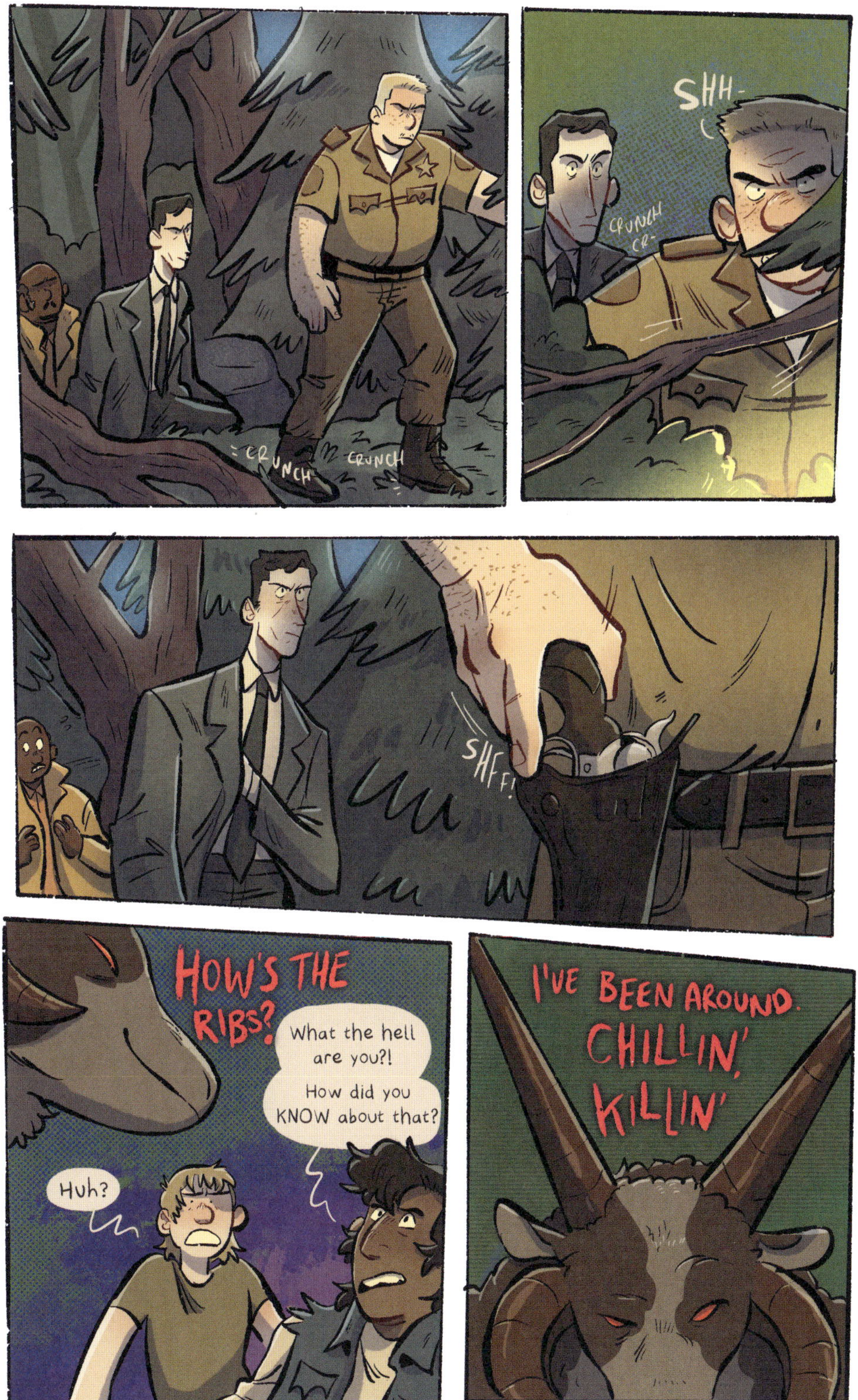
CRUNCH
CRUNCH
SHH-
CRUNCH CR-
SHFF!
HOW'S THE RIBS?
What the hell are you?!
How did you KNOW about that?
Huh?
I'VE BEEN AROUND. CHILLIN', KILLIN'

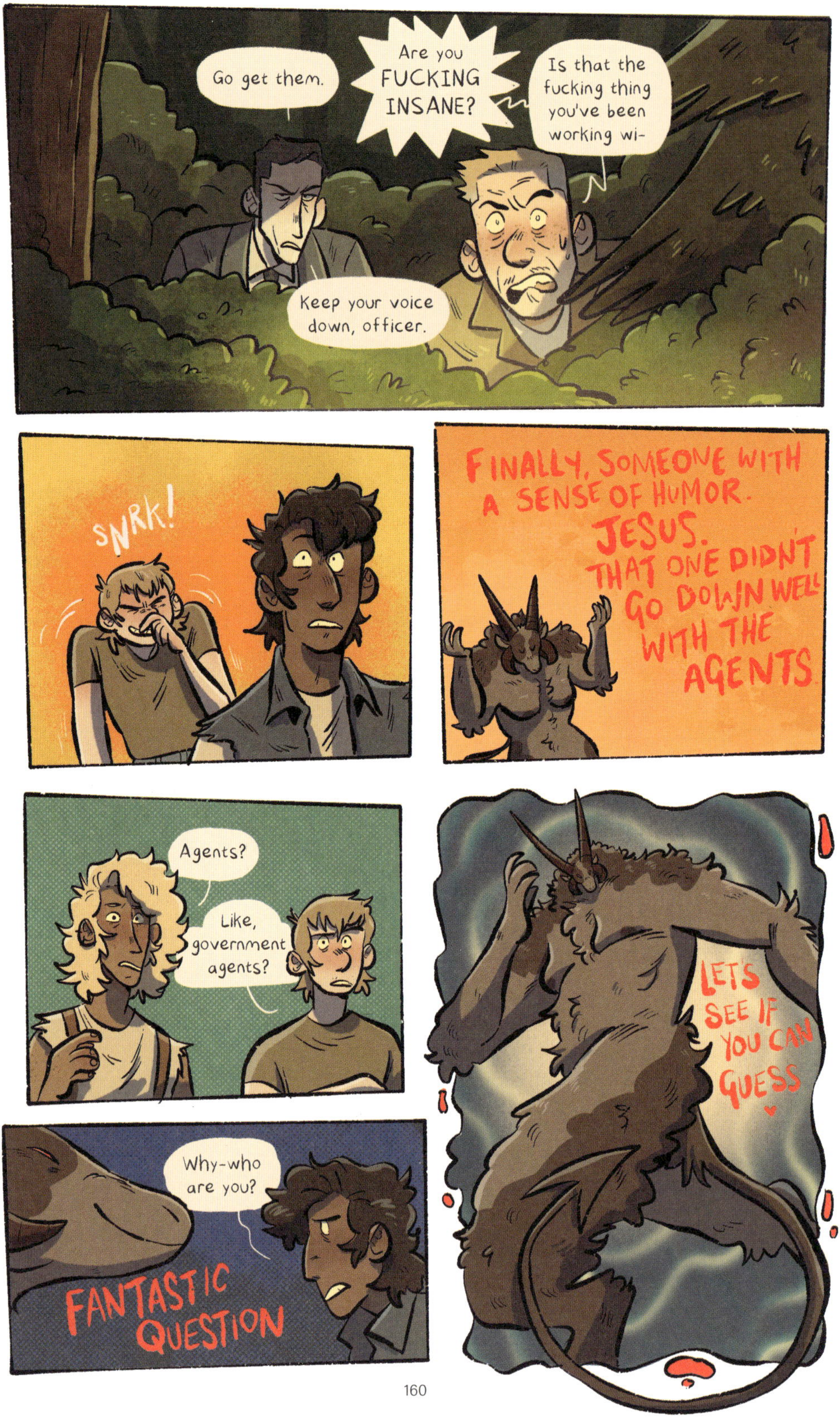

Go get them.
Are you FUCKING INSANE?
Is that the fucking thing you've been working wi-
Keep your voice down, officer.
SNRK!
FINALLY, SOMEONE WITH A SENSE OF HUMOR.
JESUS.
THAT ONE DIDN'T GO DOWN WELL WITH THE AGENTS
Agents?
Like, government agents?
LET'S SEE IF YOU CAN GUESS
Why-who are you?
FANTASTIC QUESTION

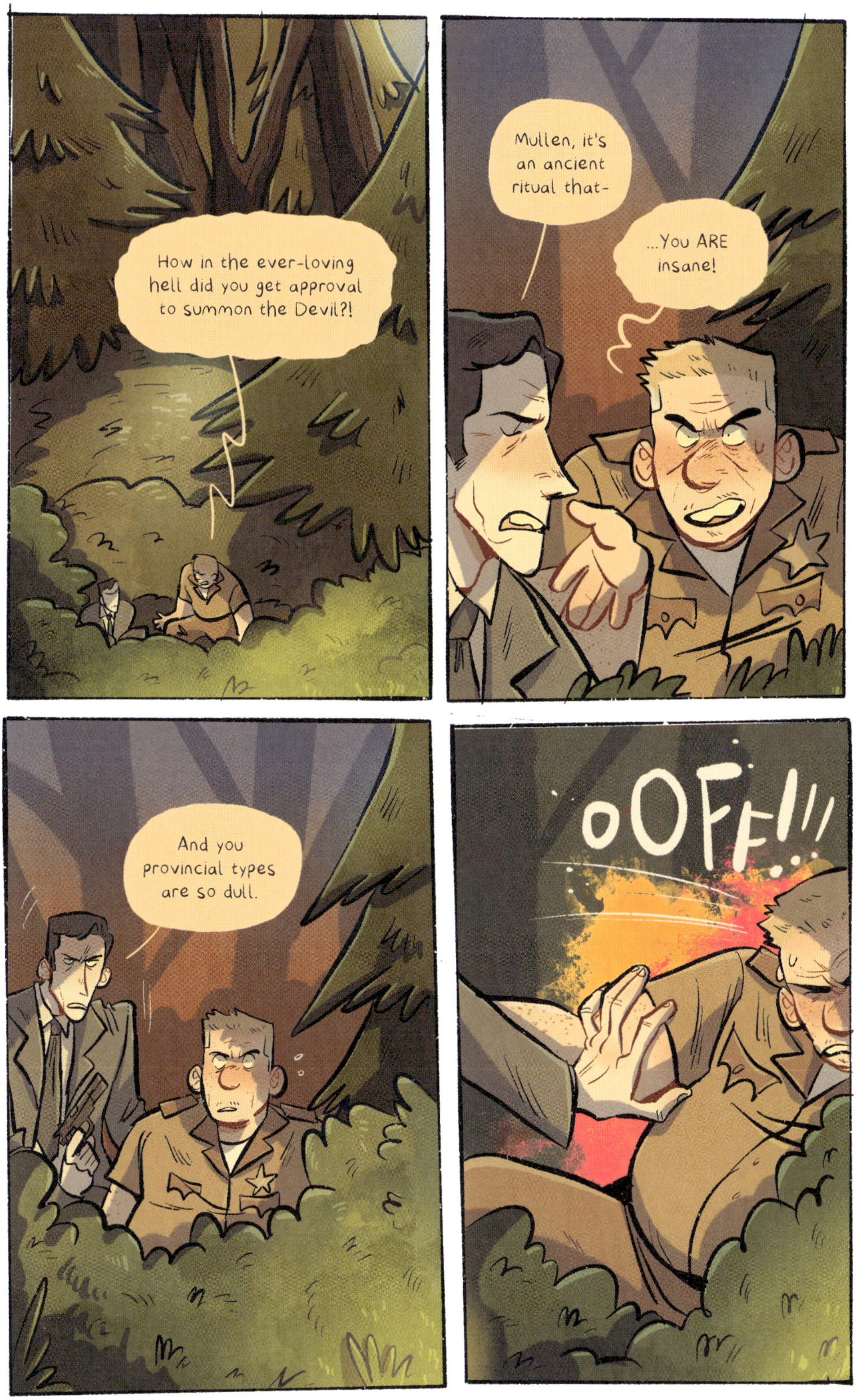
How in the ever-loving hell did you get approval to summon the Devil?!
Mullen, it's an ancient ritual that-
...You ARE insane!
And you provincial types are so dull.
OOFF!!!

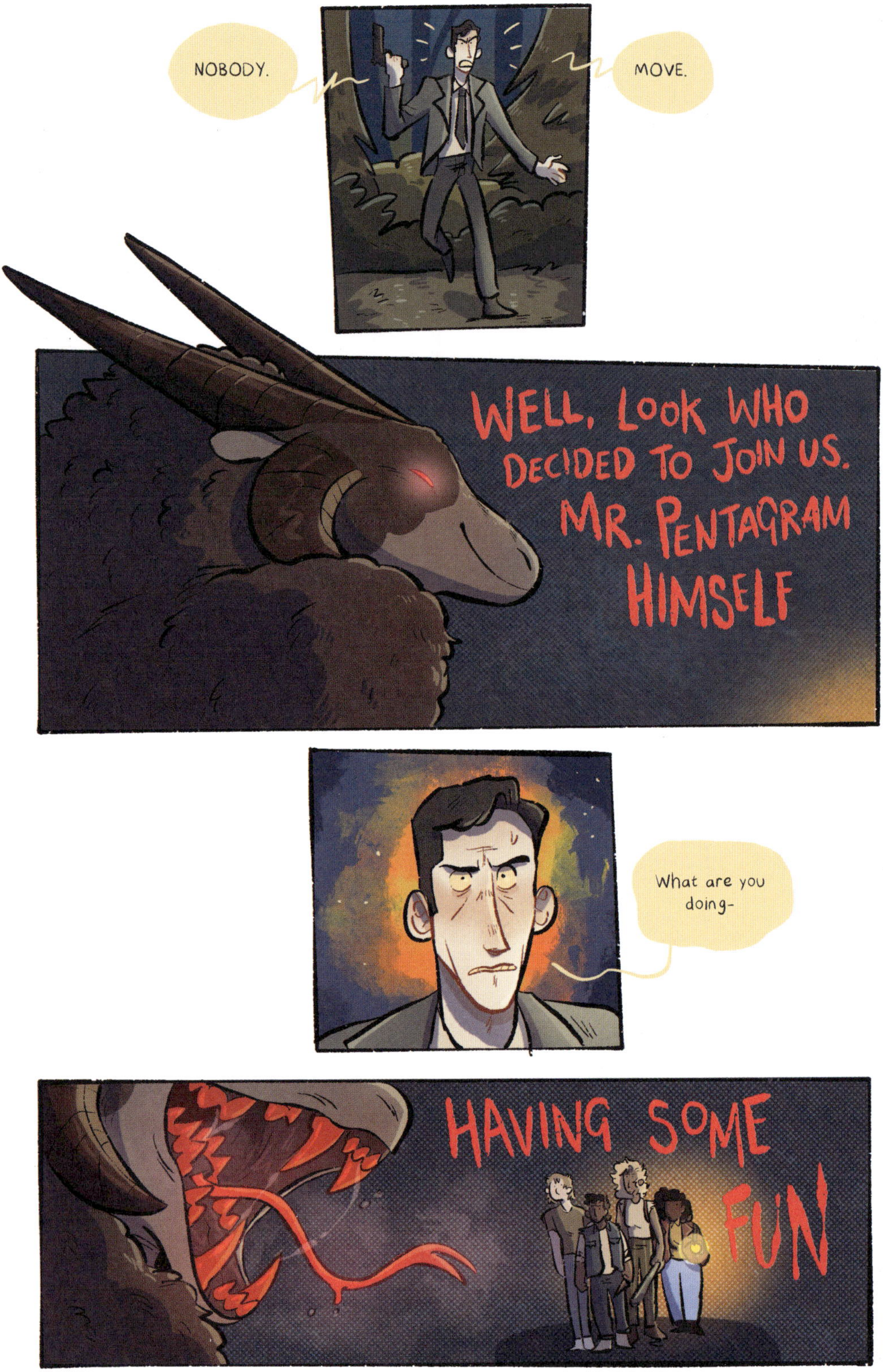
NOBODY.
MOVE.
WELL, LOOK WHO DECIDED TO JOIN US. MR. PENTAGRAM HIMSELF
What are you doing-
HAVING SOME FUN

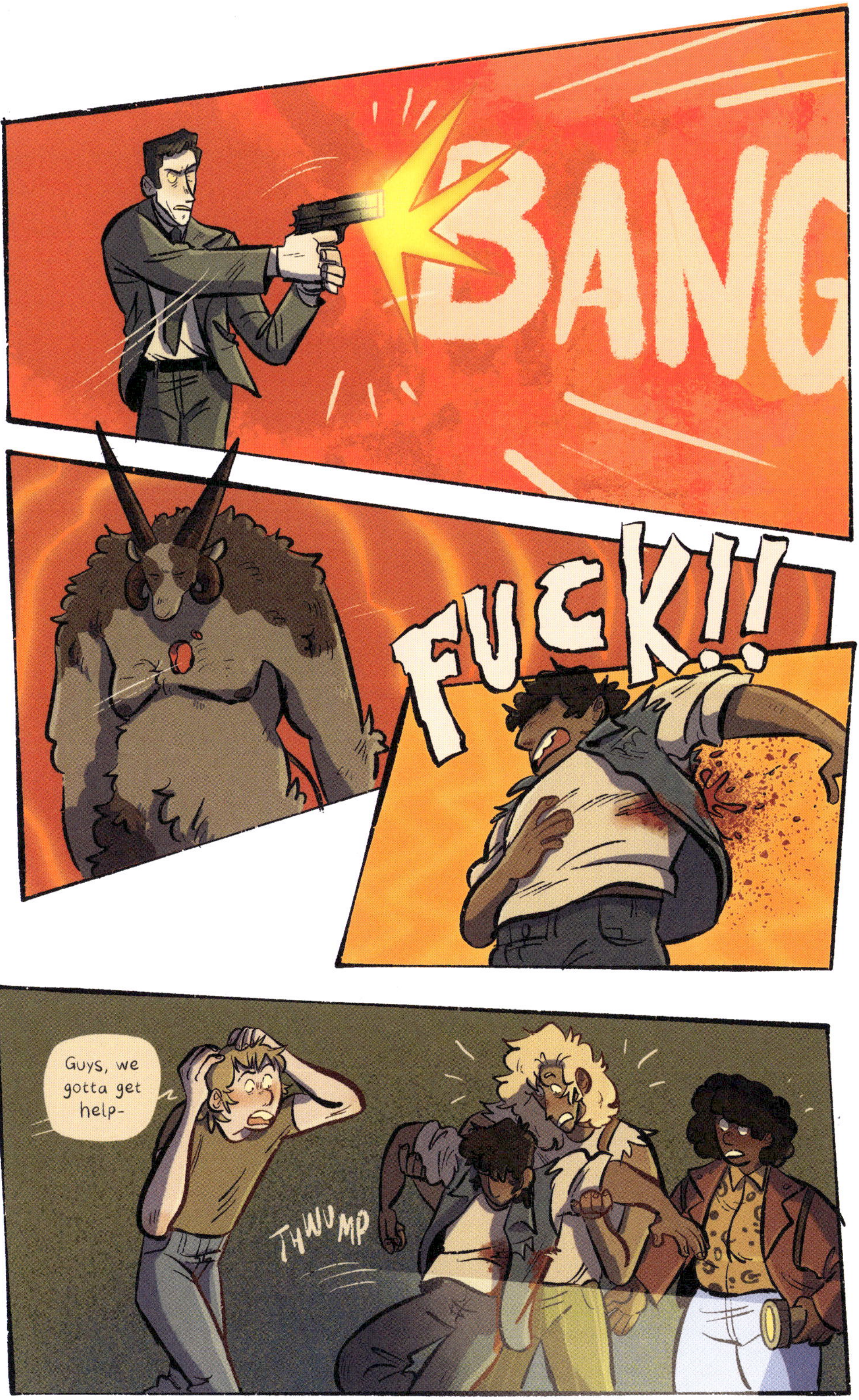
BANG
FUCK!!
Guys, we gotta get help-
THWUMP

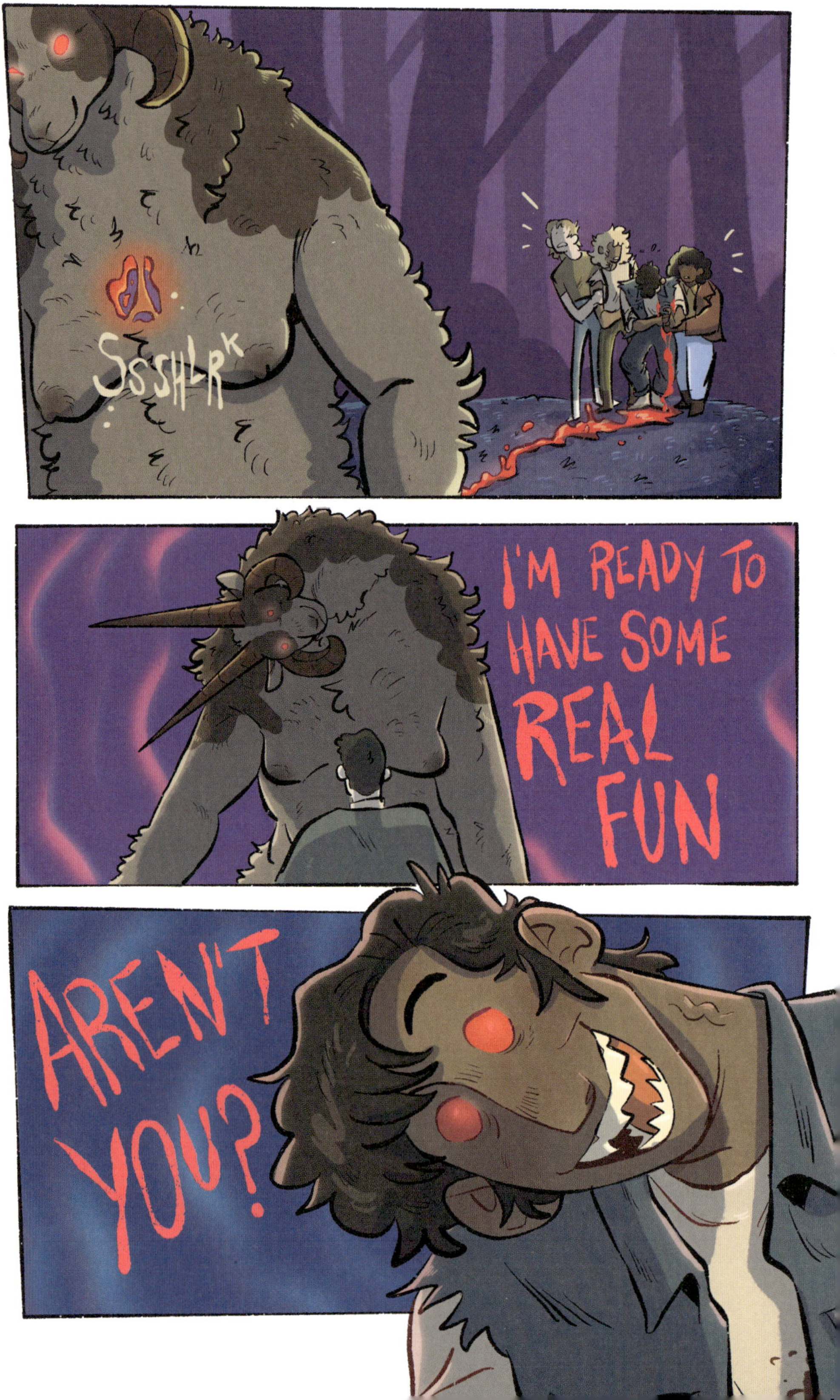
SSSHLRK
I'M READY TO HAVE SOME REAL FUN
AREN'T YOU?

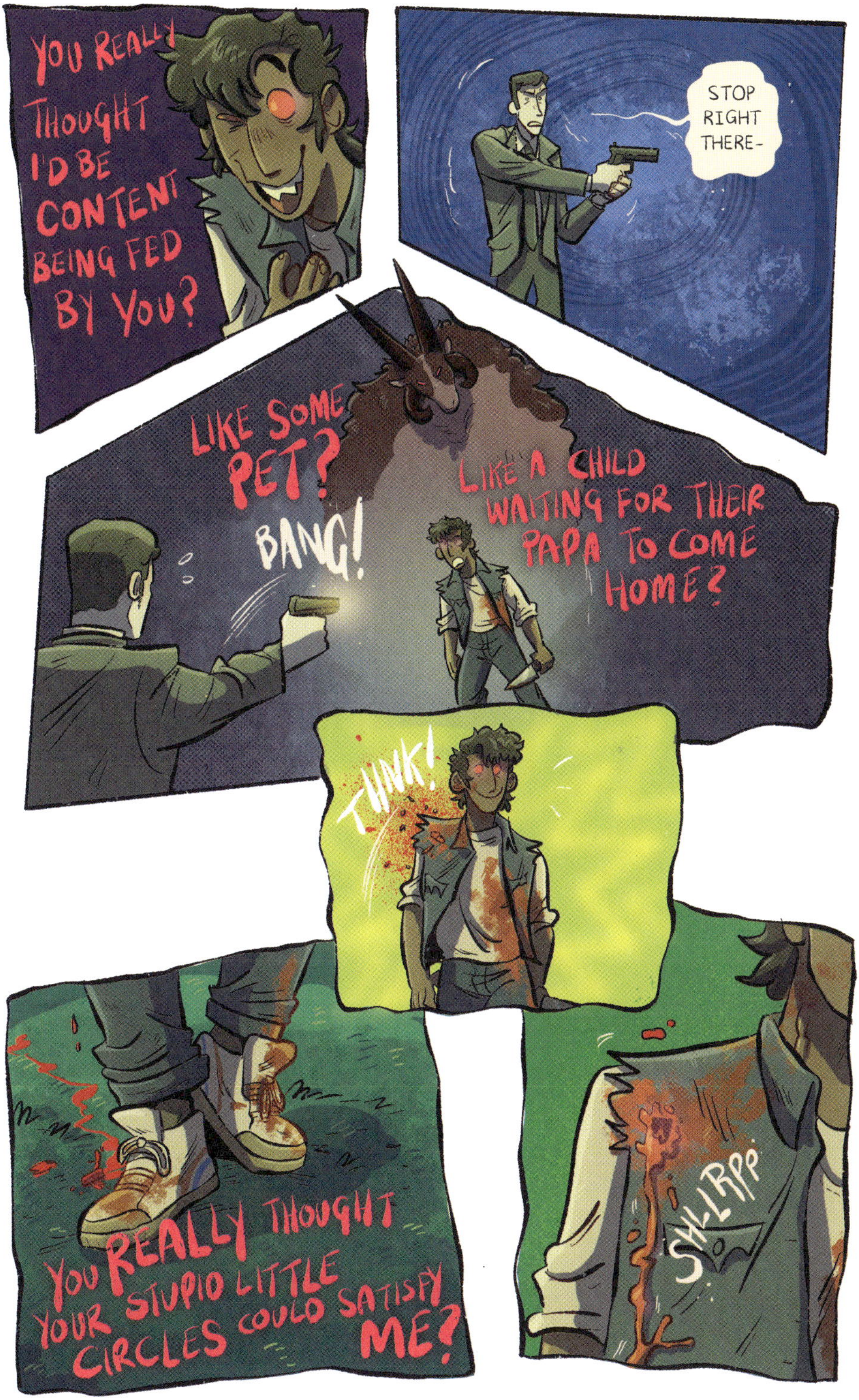
YOU REALLY THOUGHT I'D BE CONTENT BEING FED BY YOU?
STOP RIGHT THERE-
LIKE SOME PET?
BANG!
LIKE A CHILD WAITING FOR THEIR PAPA TO COME HOME?
THNK!
YOU REALLY THOUGHT YOUR STUPID LITTLE CIRCLES COULD SATISFY ME?
SHLRPP.

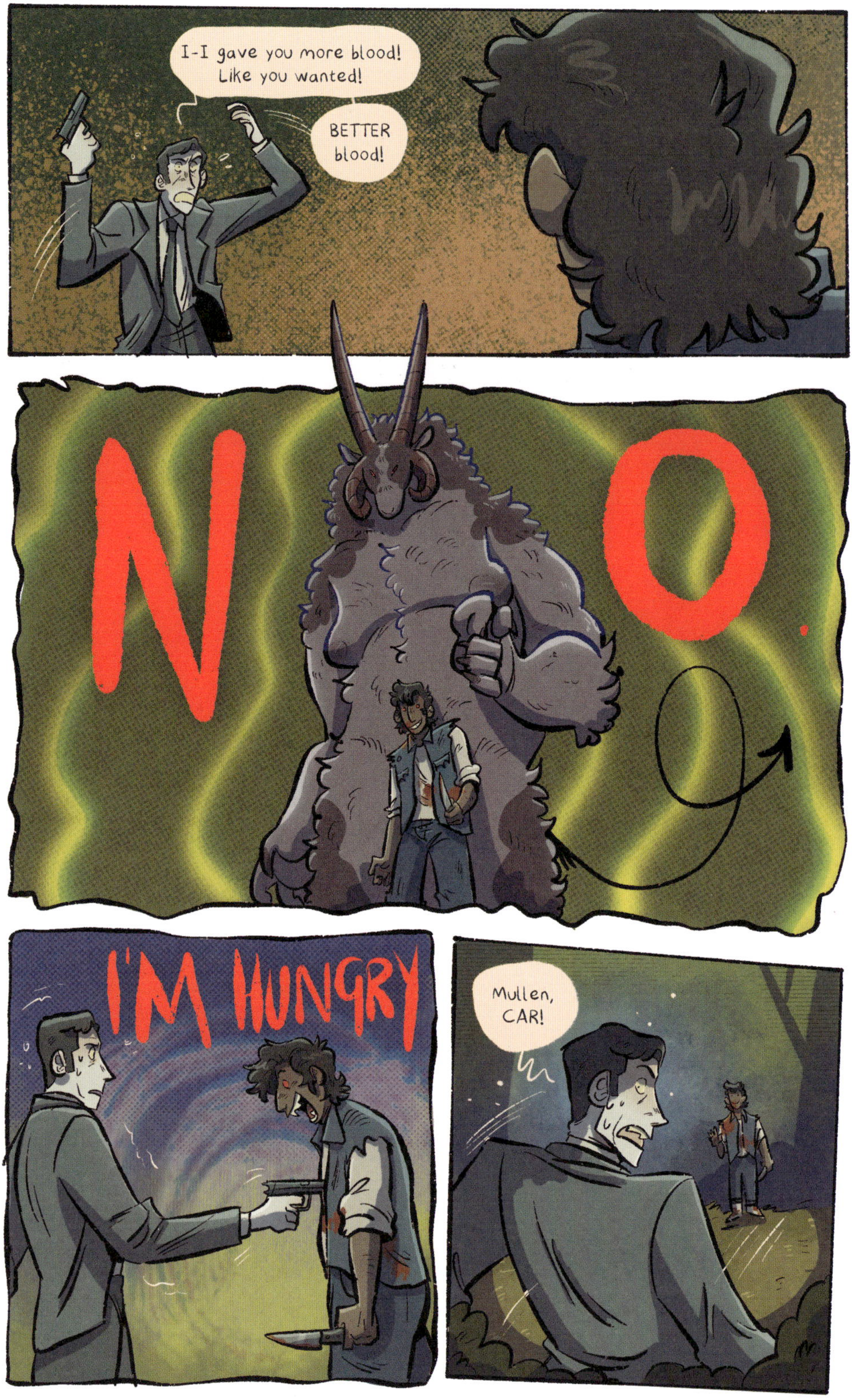
I-I gave you more blood! Like you wanted!
BETTER blood!
NO
I'M HUNGRY
Mullen, CAR!

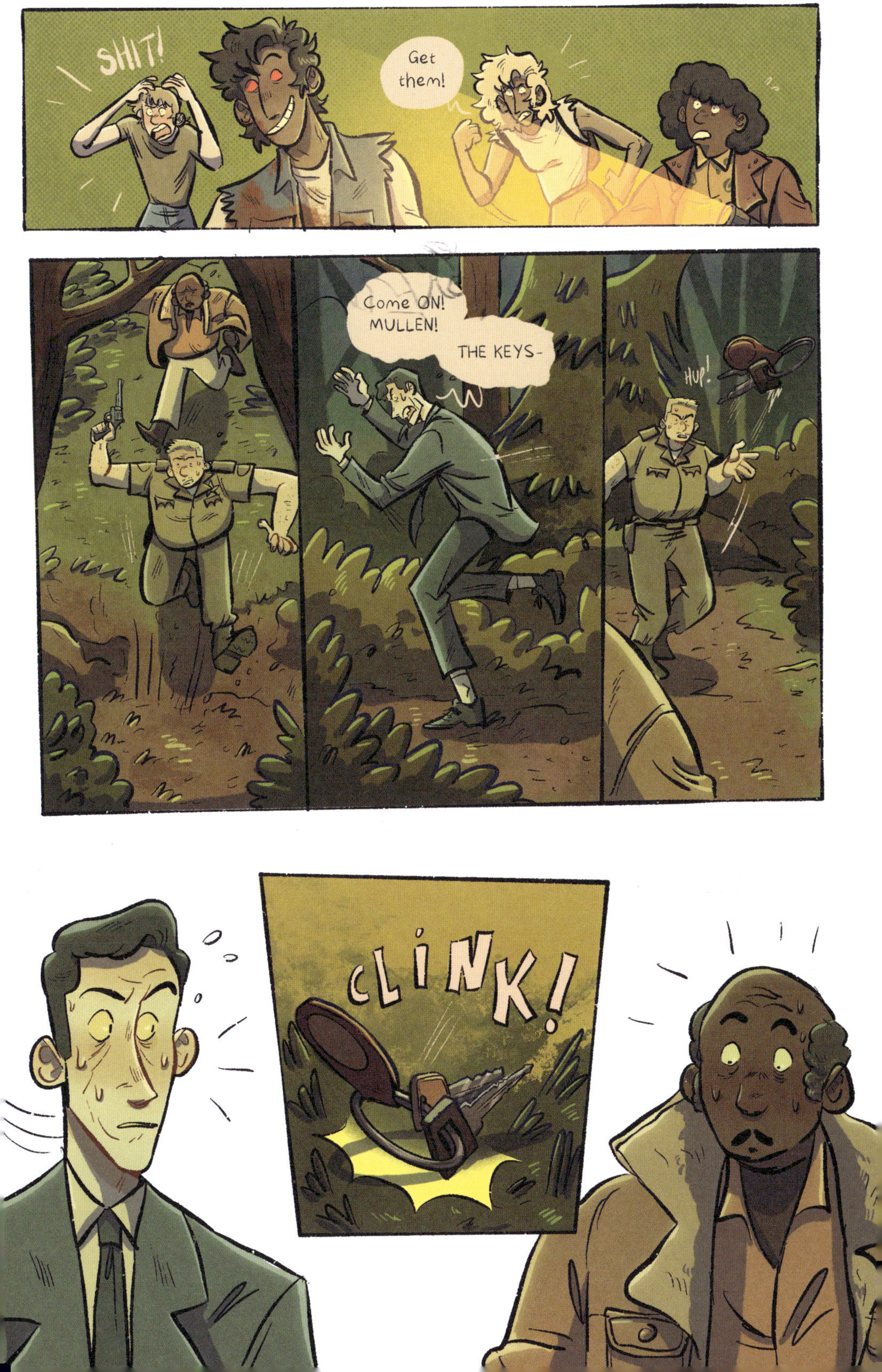
SHIT!
Get them!
Come ON! MULLEN!
THE KEYS-
HUP!
CLINK!

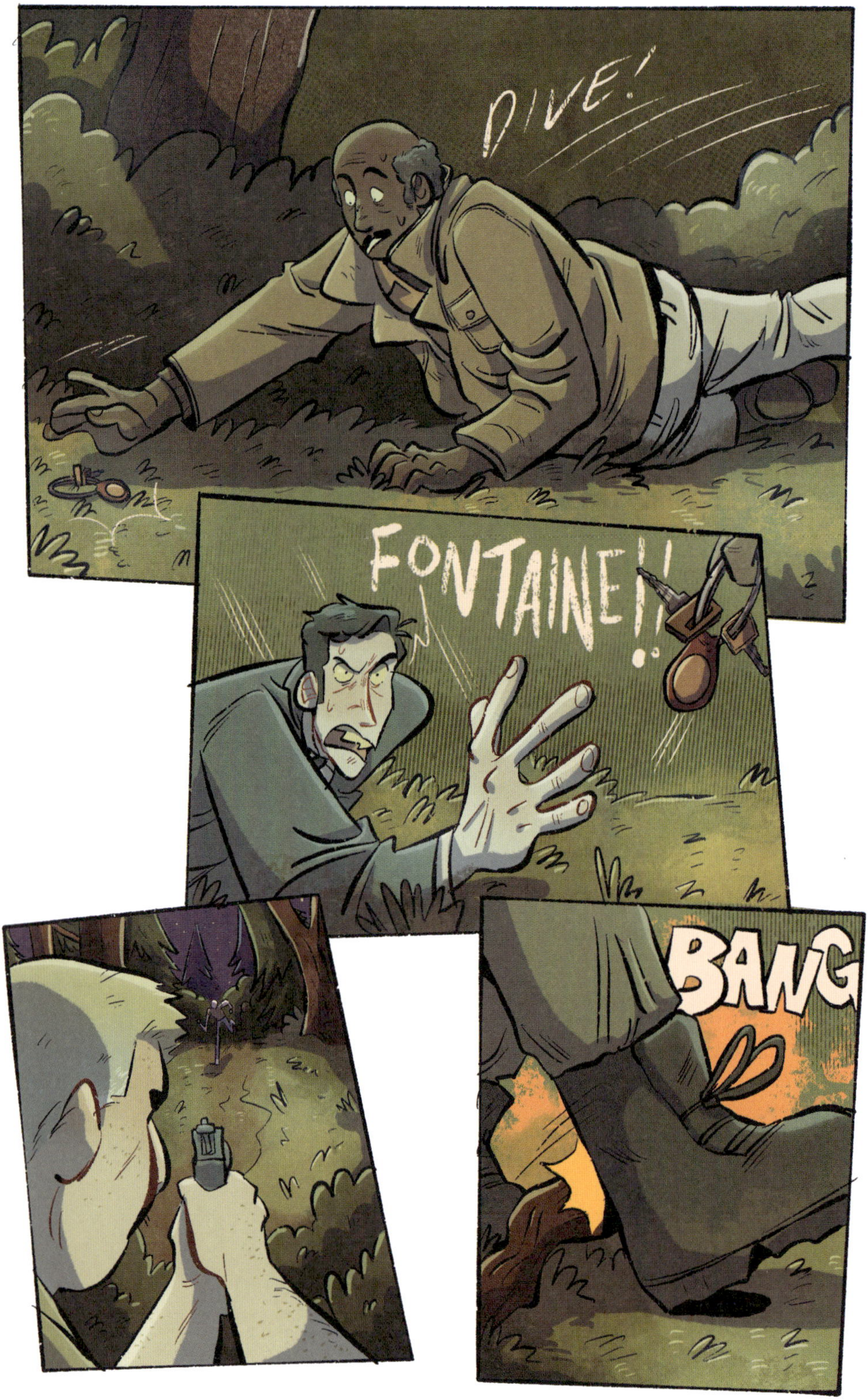
DIVE!
FONTAINE!!
BANG

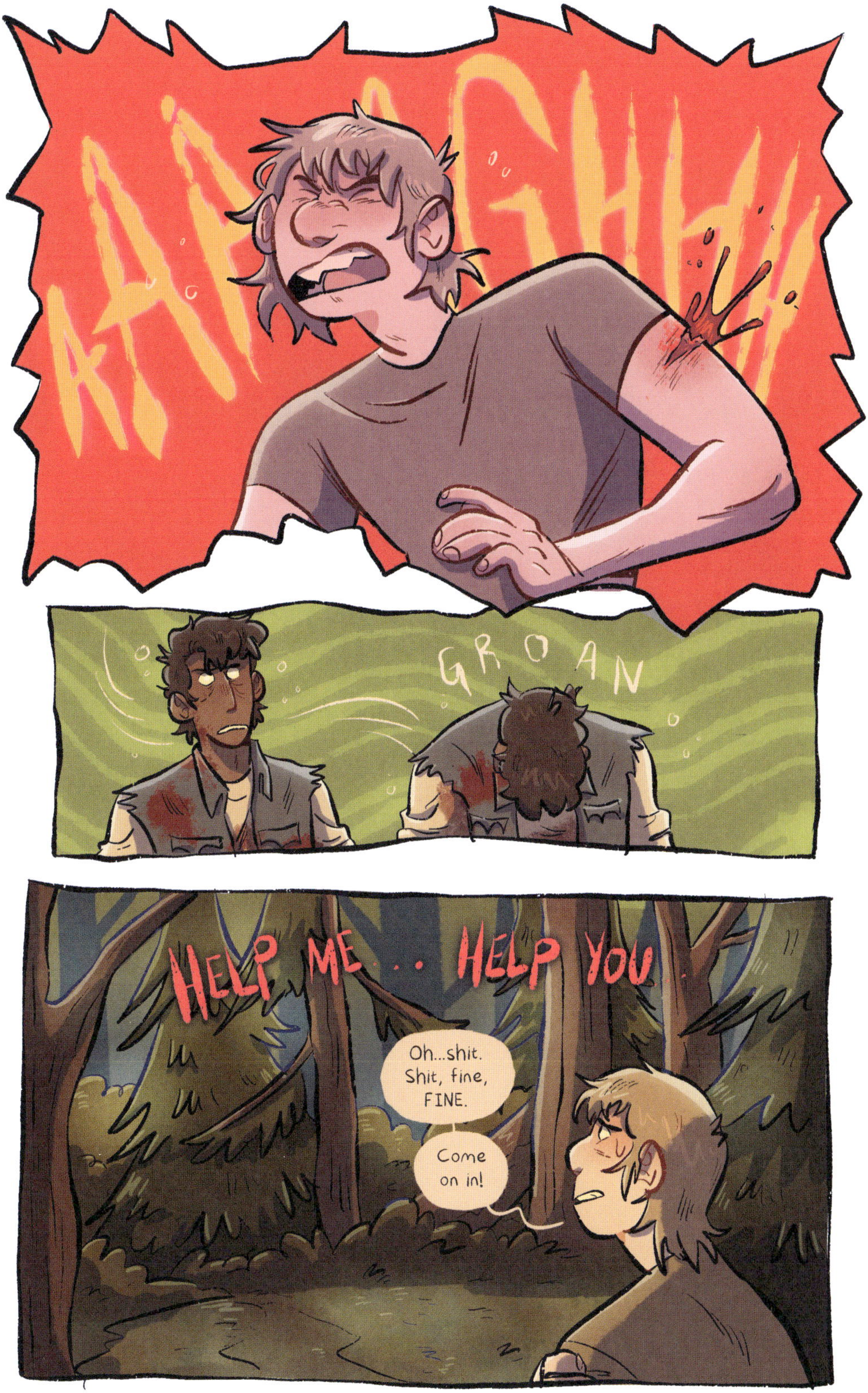
GROAN
HELP ME.. HELP YOU
Oh...shit. Shit, fine, FINE.
Come on in!

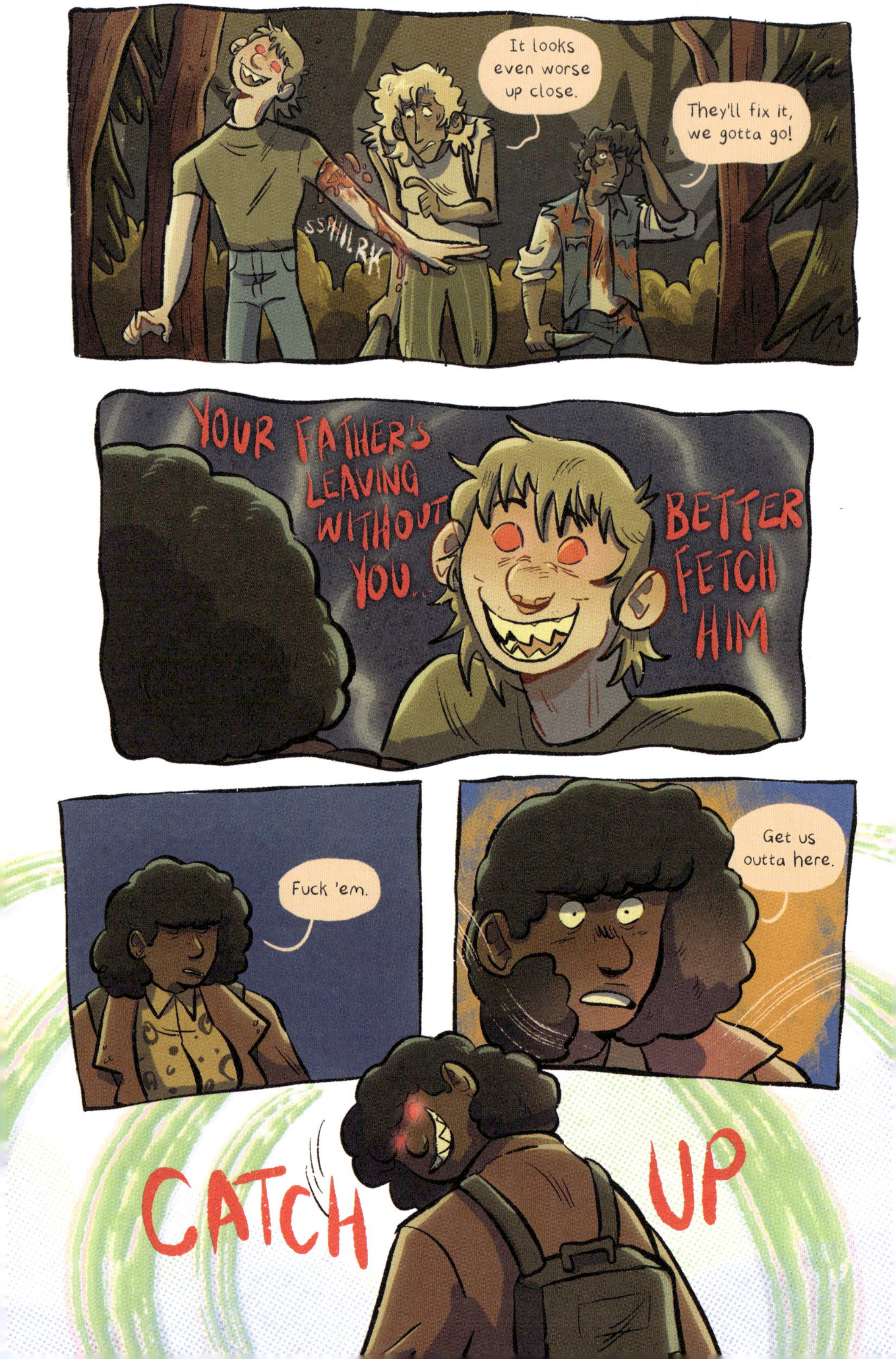

SSHHLRK
It looks even worse up close.
They'll fix it, we gotta go!
YOUR FATHER'S LEAVING WITHOUT YOU...
BETTER FETCH HIM
Fuck 'em.
Get us outta here.
CATCH UP

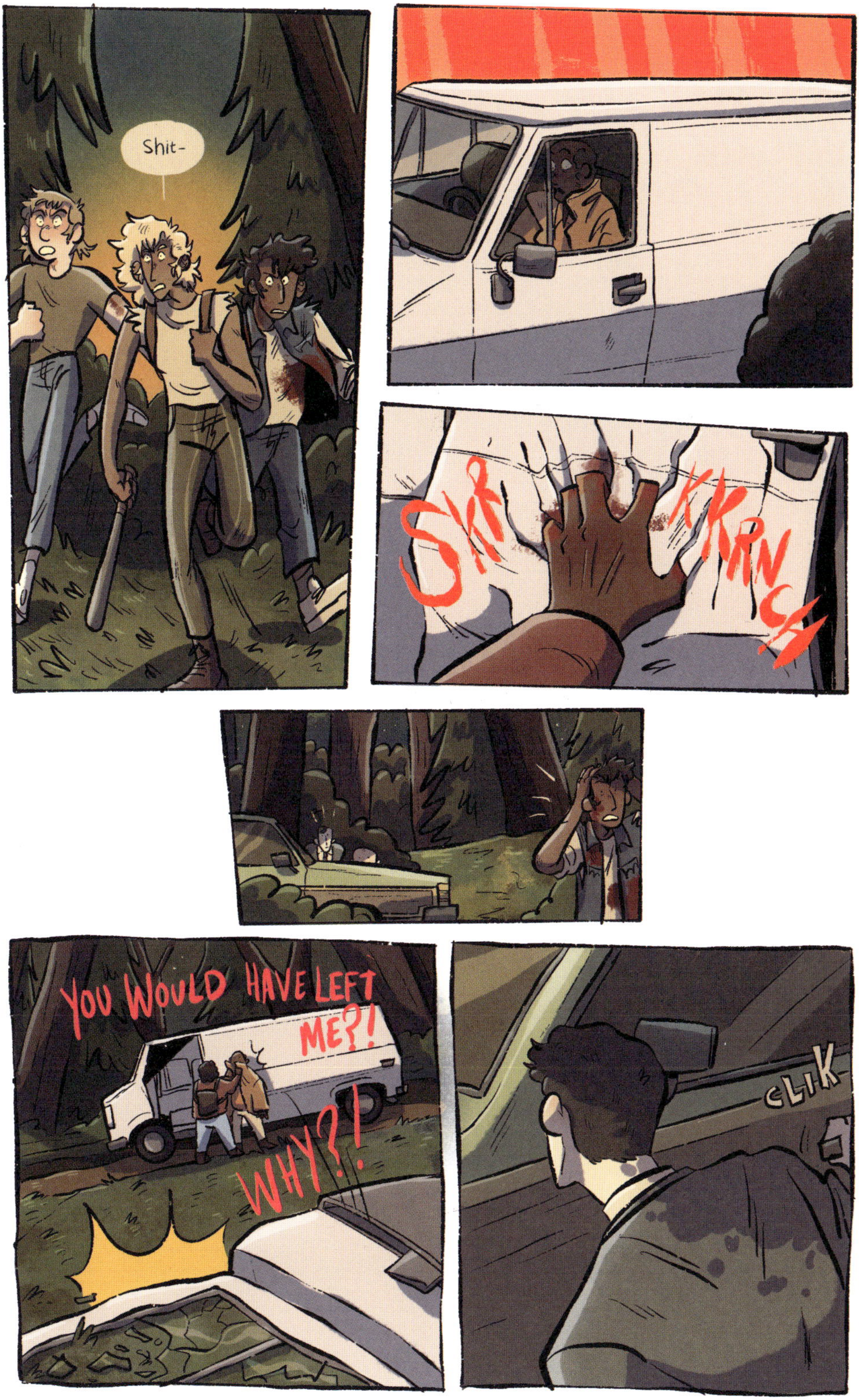

Shit-
SKR
KKRNCH
YOU WOULD HAVE LEFT ME?!
WHY?!
CLIK

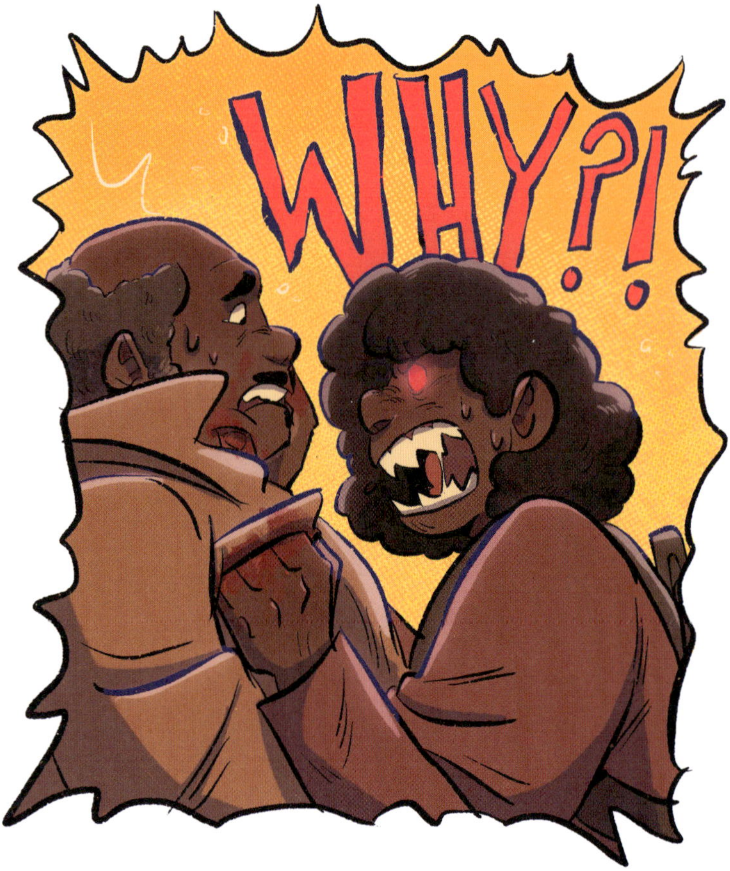
WHY?!

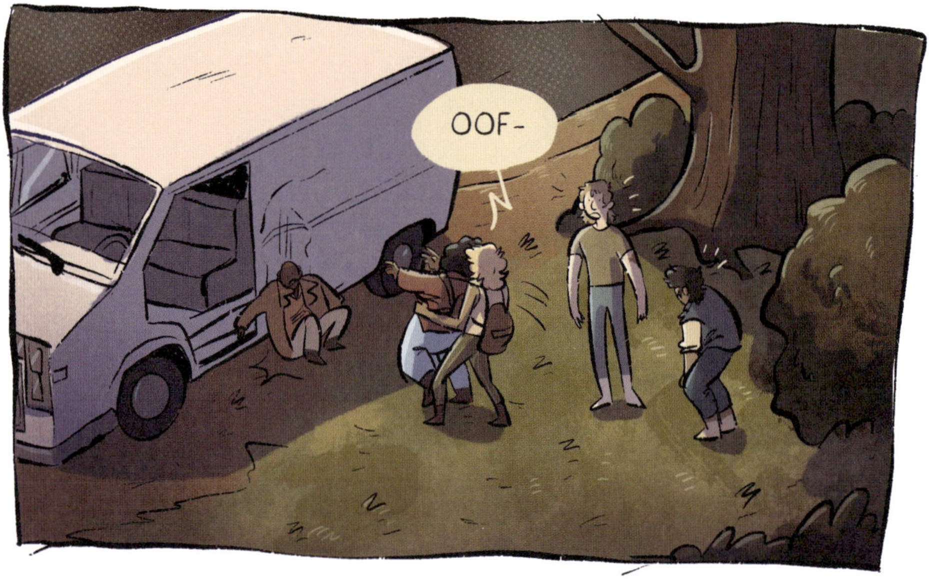
OOF-

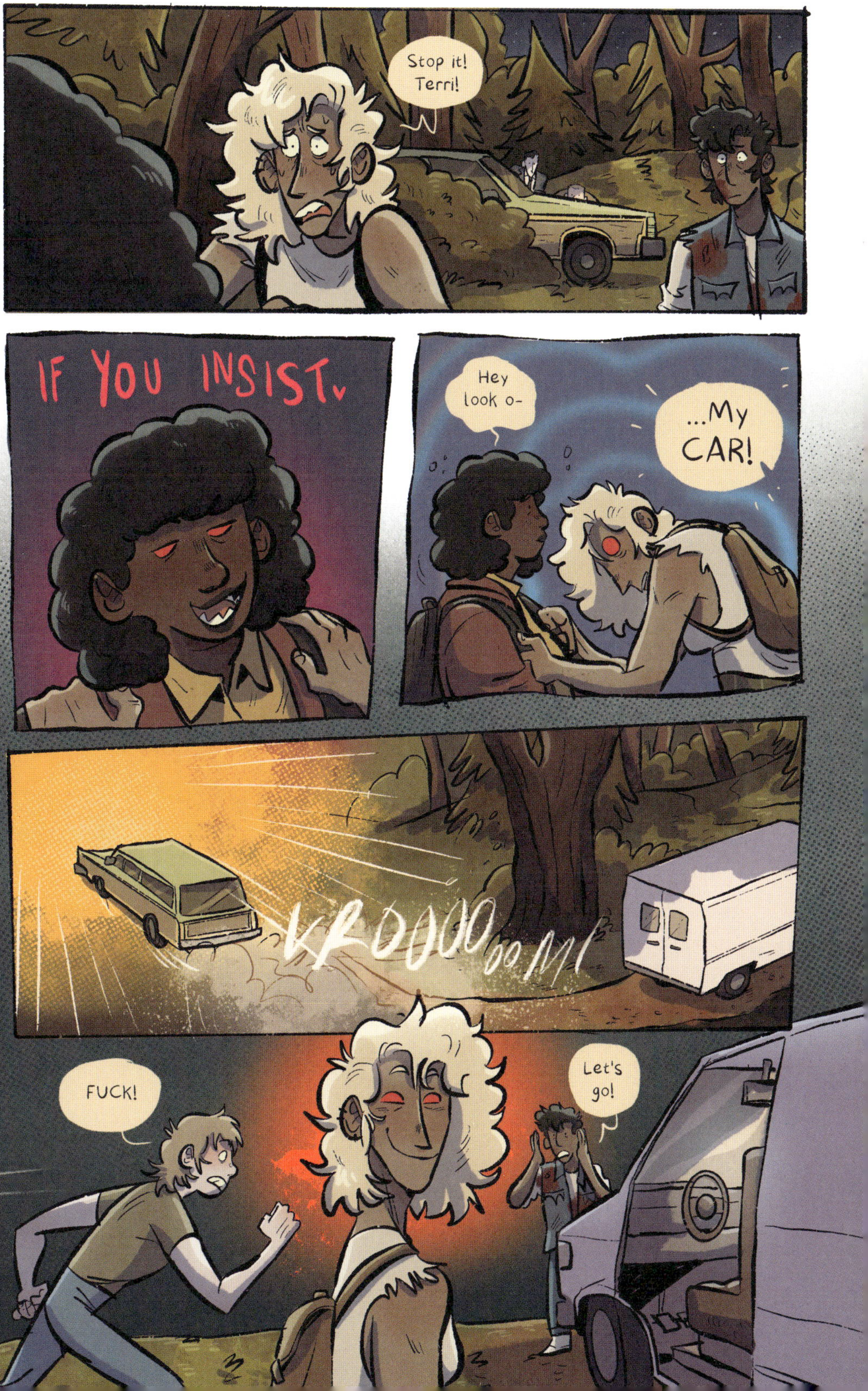

Stop it! Terri!
IF YOU INSIST.
Hey look o-
...My CAR!
VROOOOOOOM!
FUCK!
Let's go!

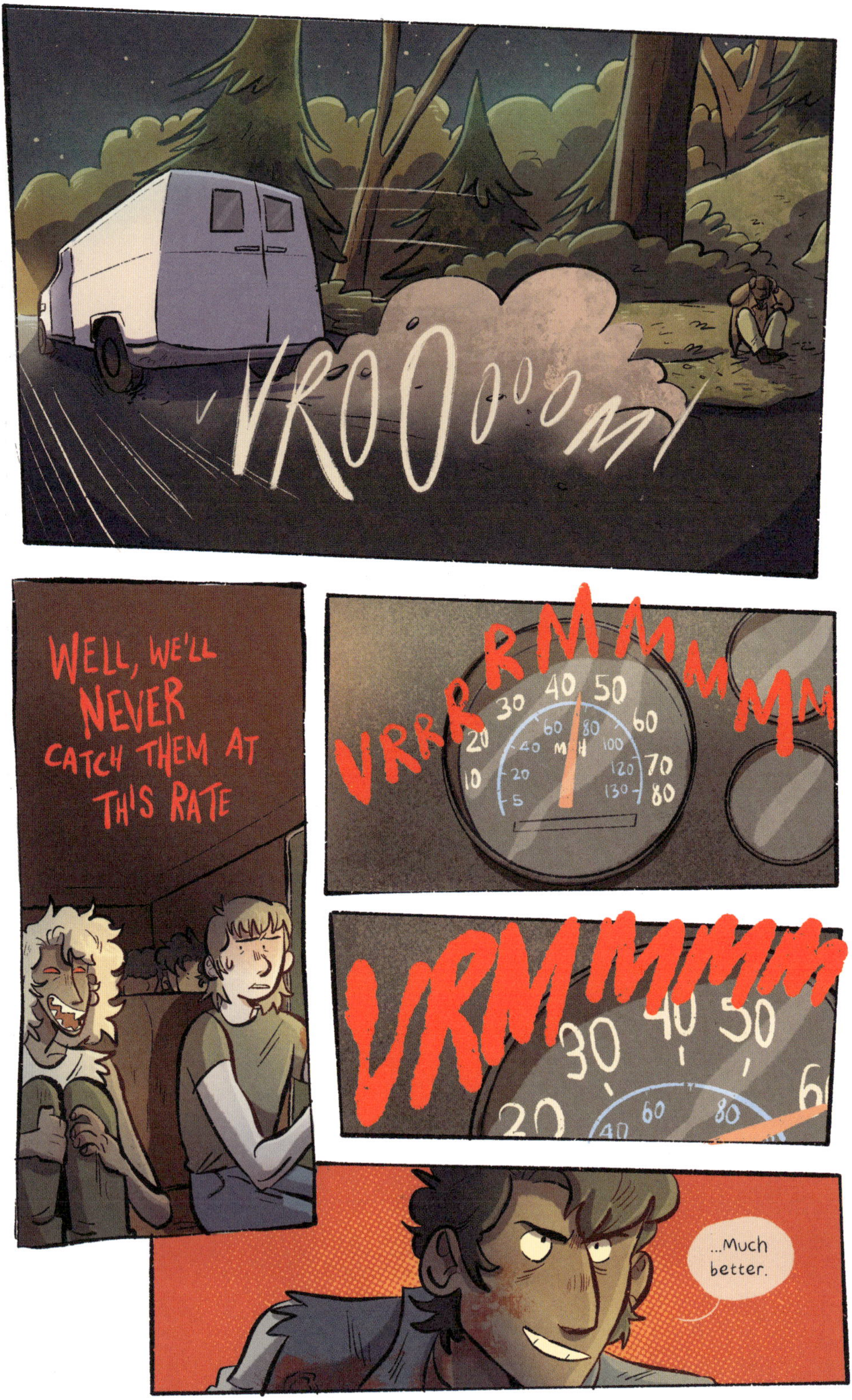
VROOooOM!
WELL, WE'LL NEVER CATCH THEM AT THIS RATE
VRRRRMMMMMM
VRMMMM
...Much better.

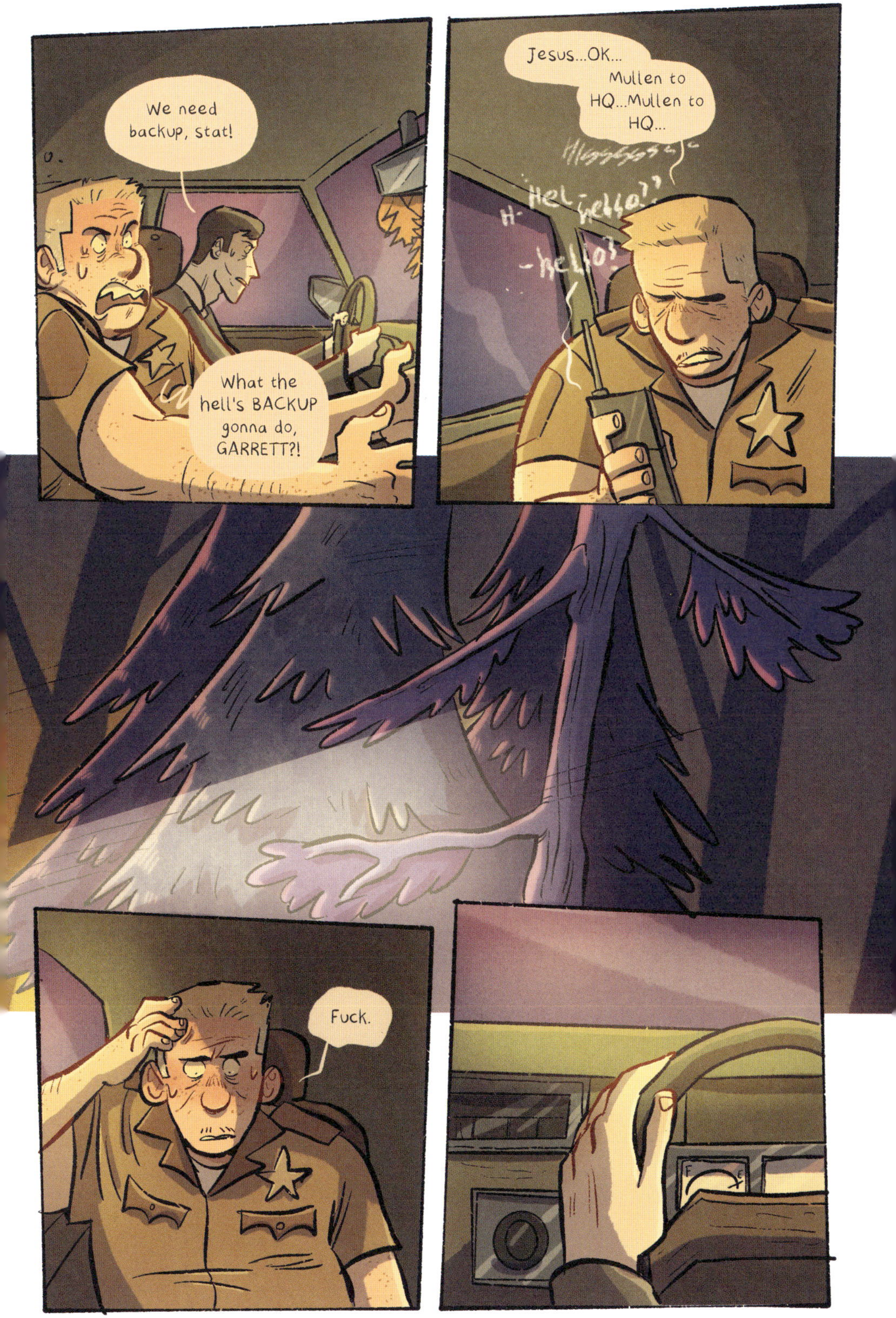
We need backup, stat!
What the hell's BACKUP gonna do, GARRETT?!
Jesus...OK... Mullen to HQ...Mullen to HQ...
hello?
-hello?
Fuck.

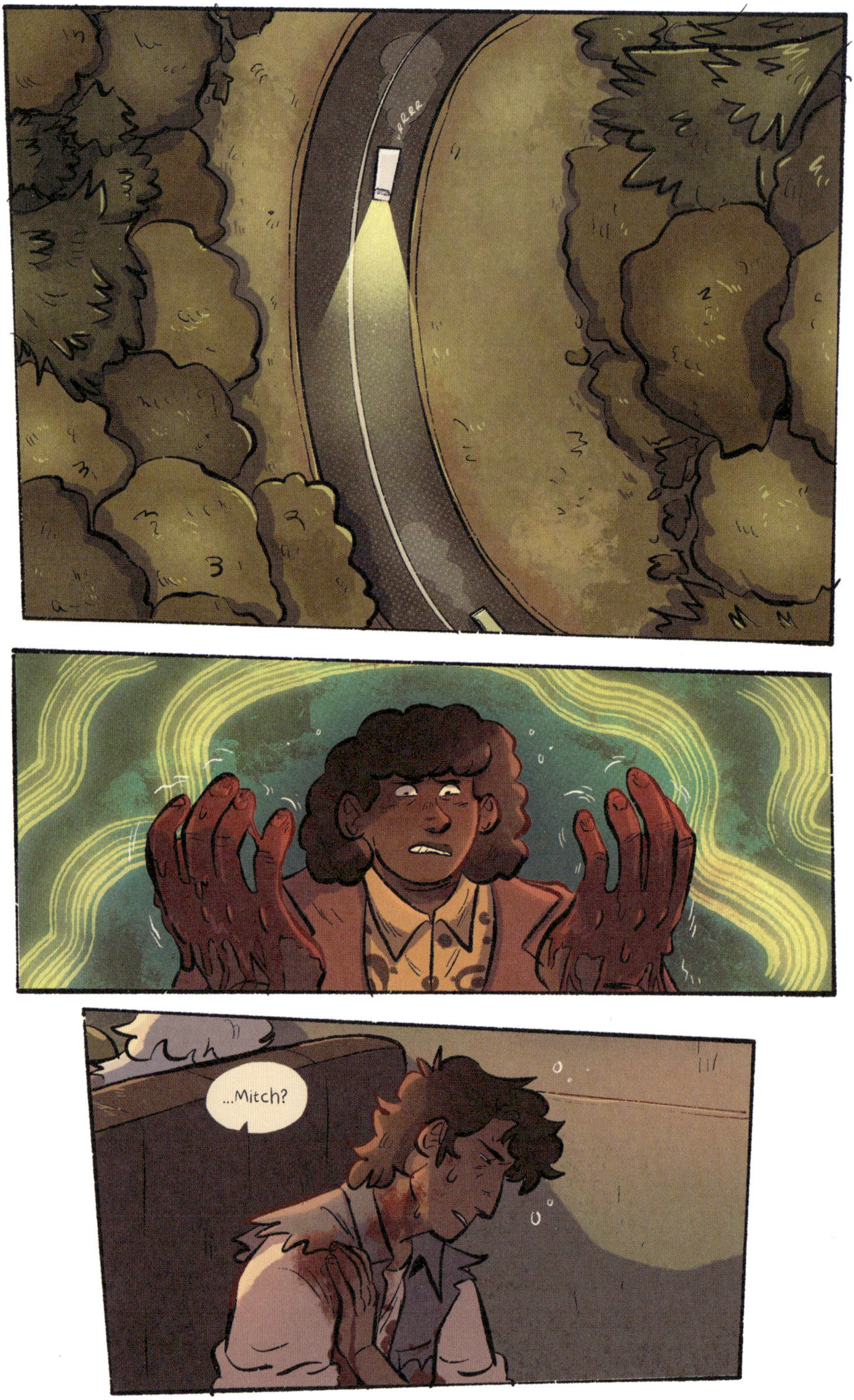
VRRR
...Mitch?

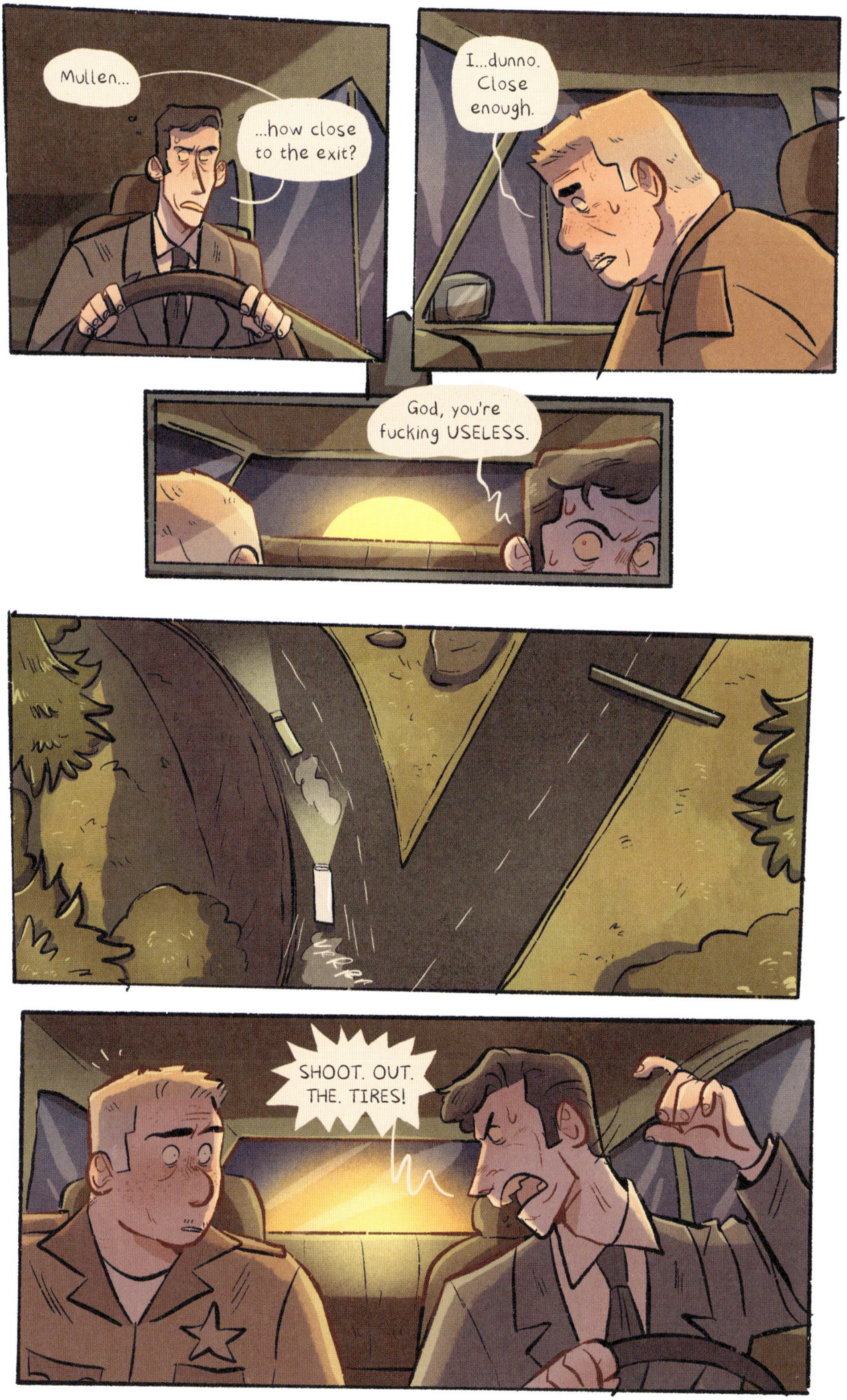

Mullen...
...how close to the exit?
I...dunno. Close enough.
God, you're fucking USELESS.
VRRRR
SHOOT. OUT. THE. TIRES!

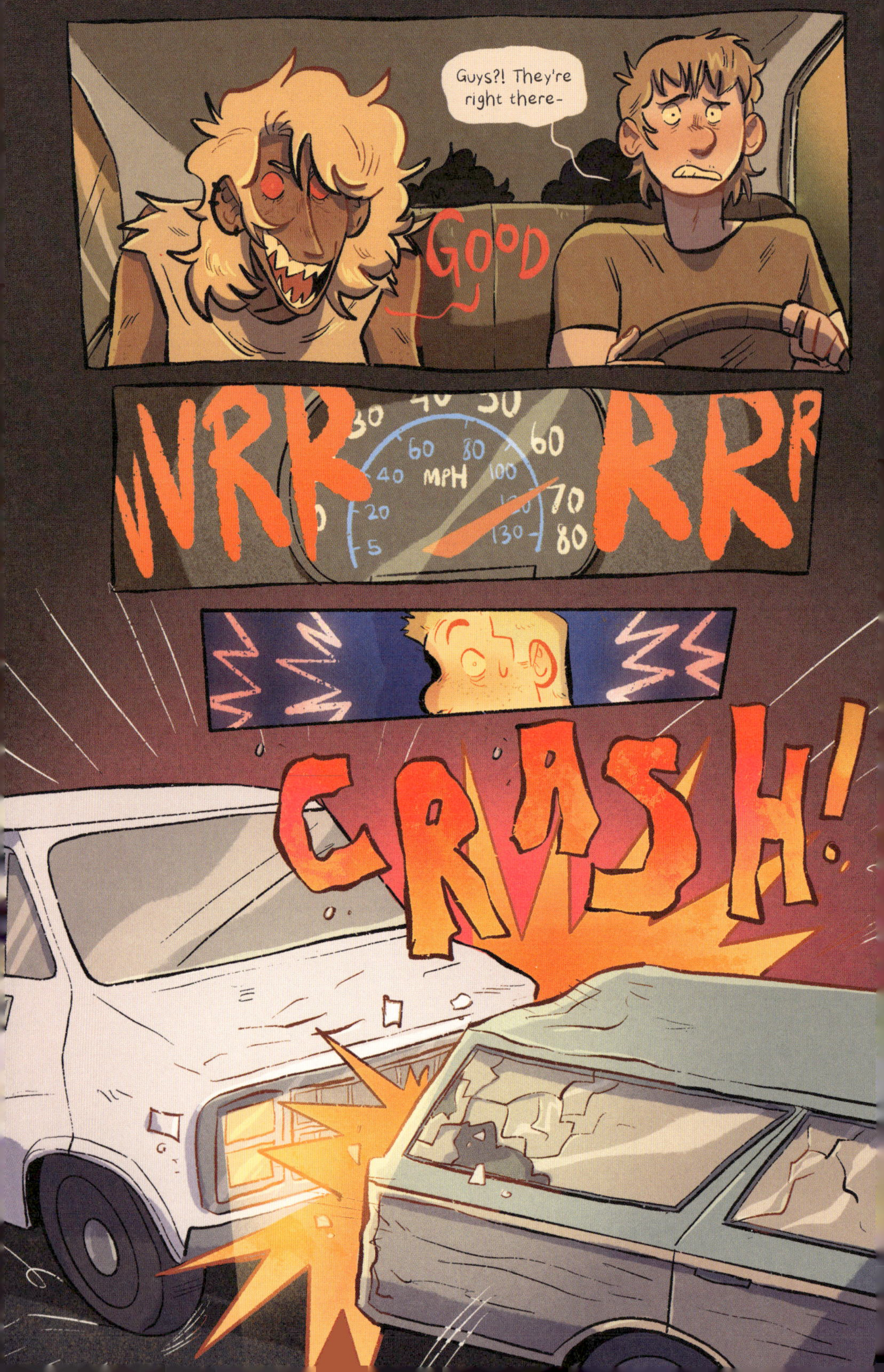
Guys?! They're right there-
GOOD
VVRRRRRr
CRASH!

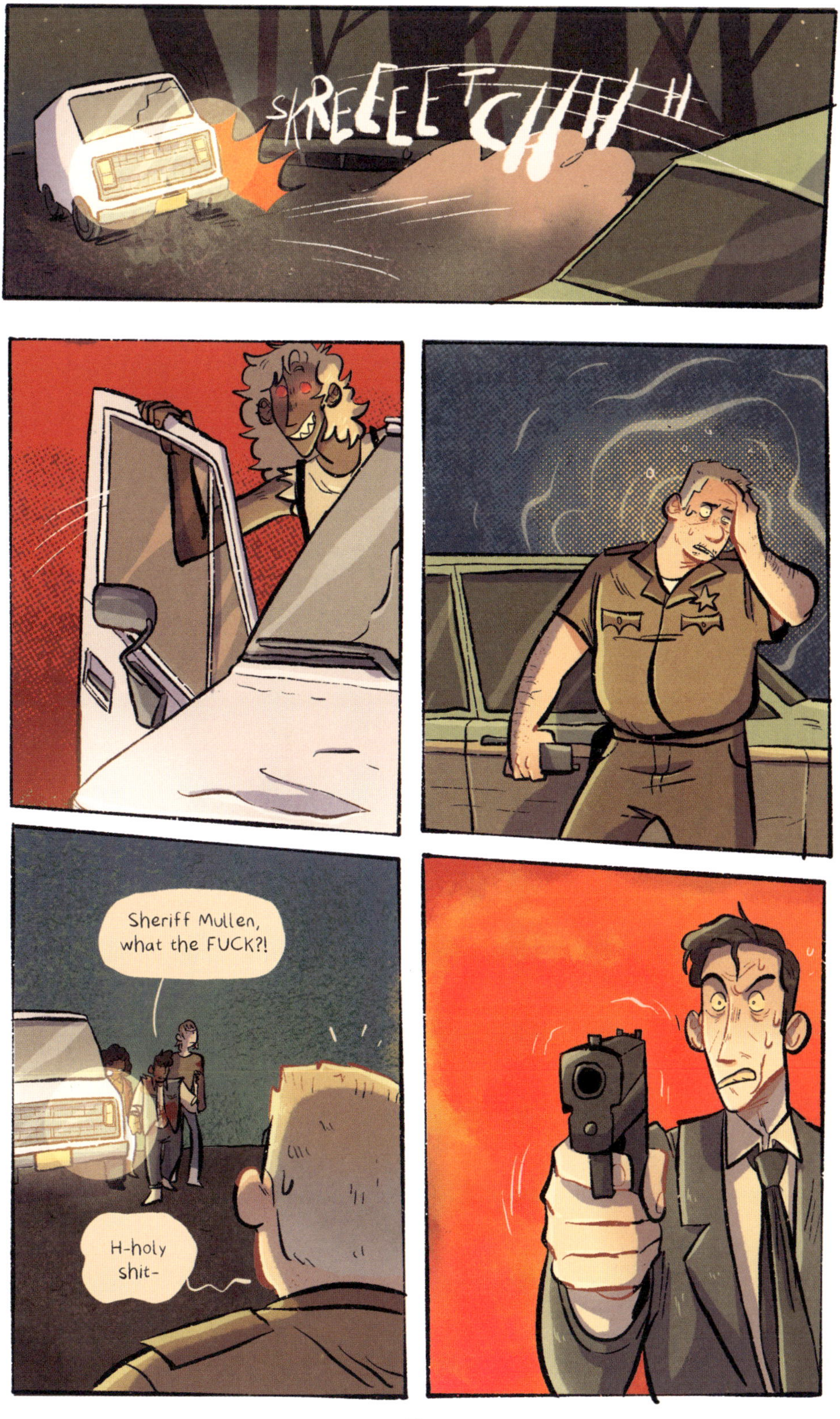
SKREEEETCHHH
Sheriff Mullen, what the FUCK?!
H-holy shit-

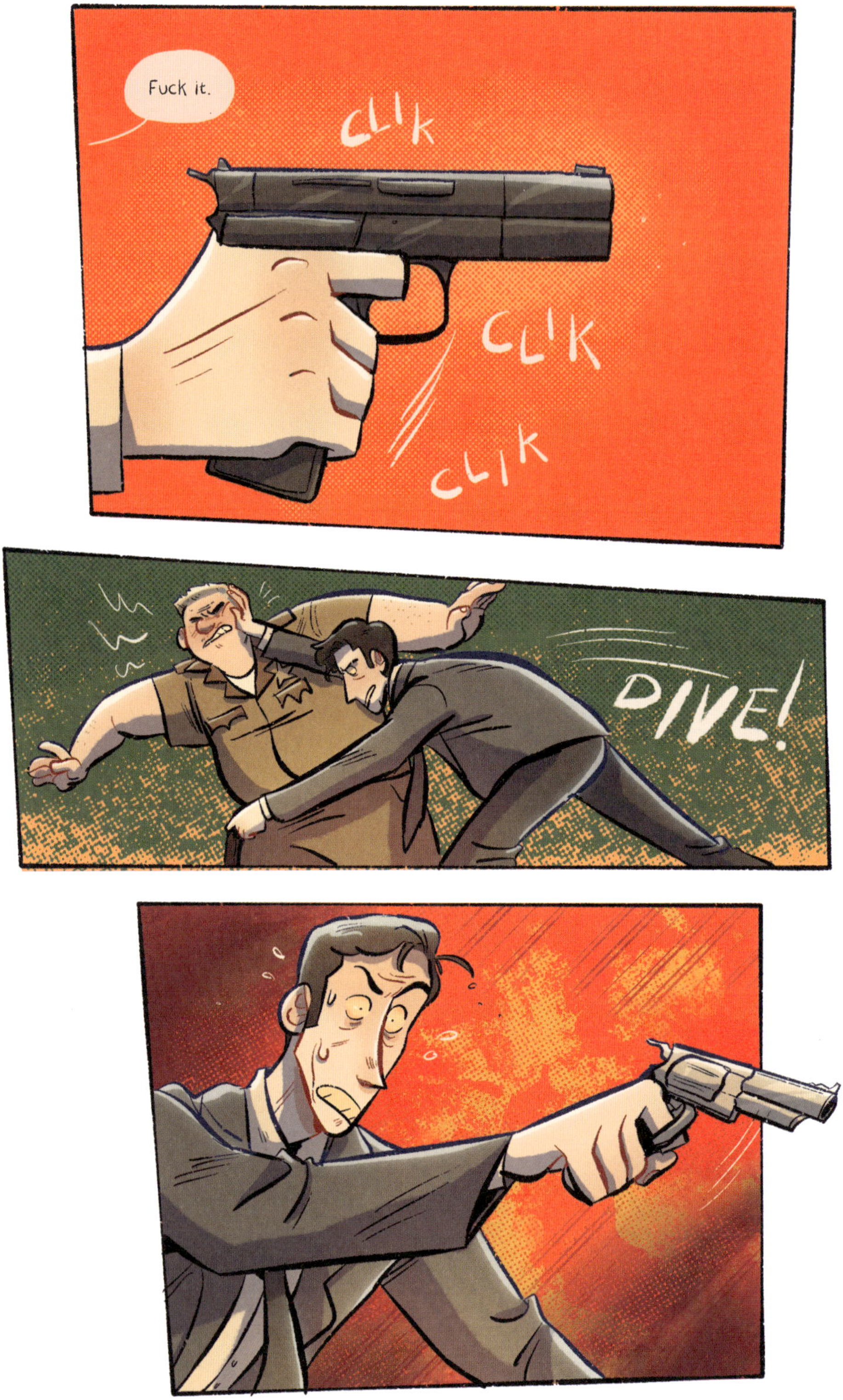
Fuck it.
CLIK
CLIK
CLIK
DIVE!

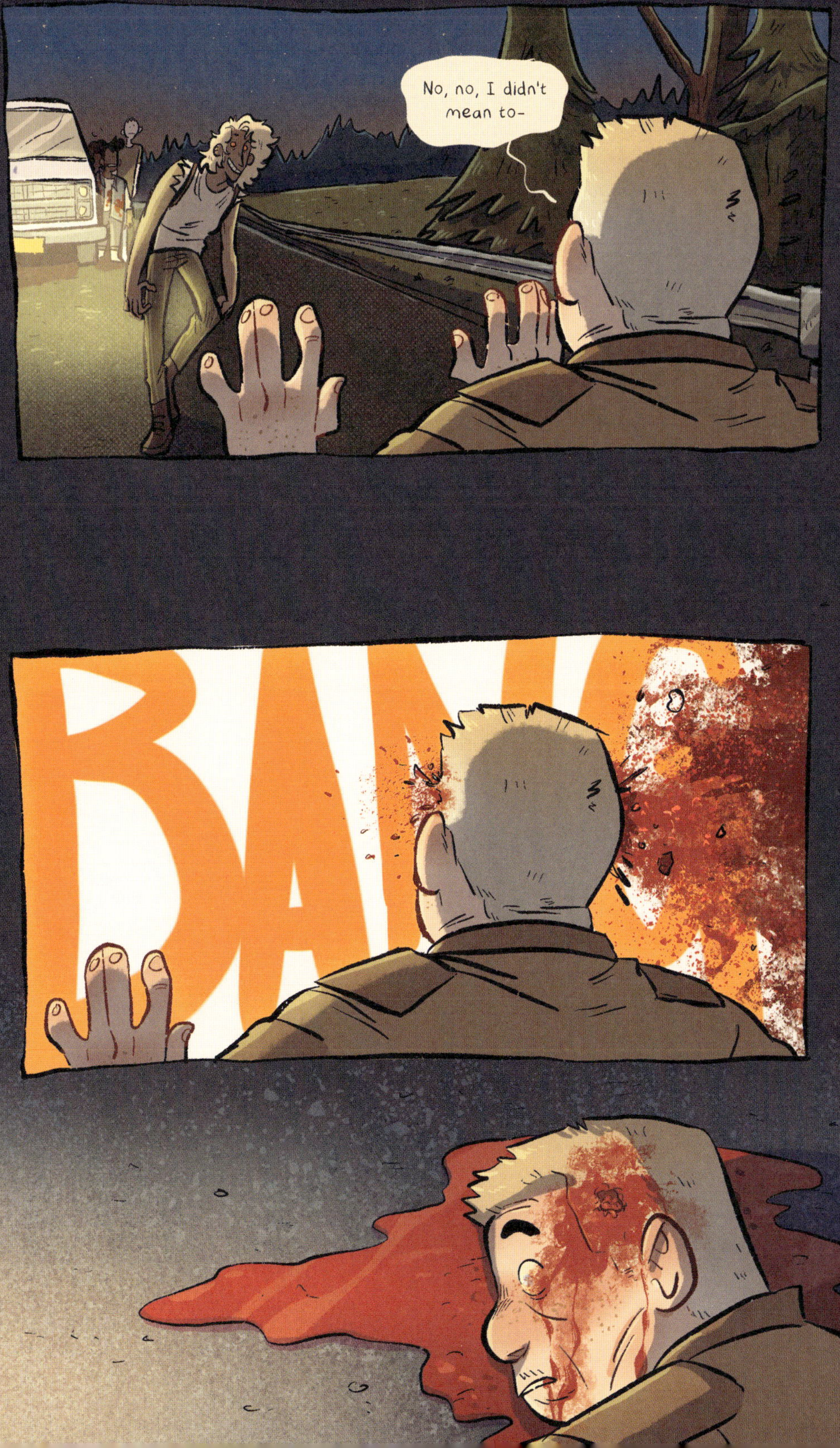
No, no, I didn't mean to-

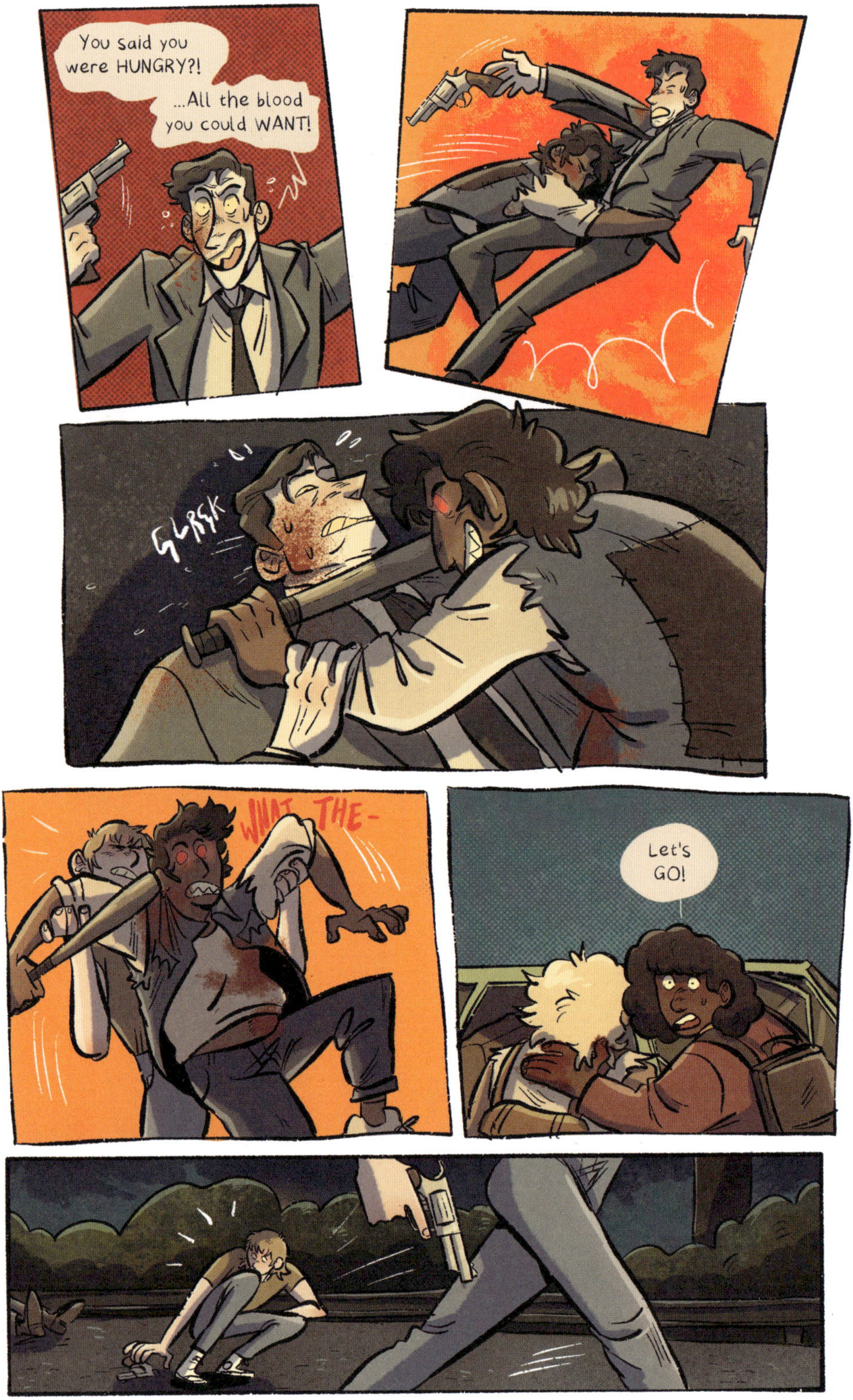
You said you were HUNGRY?!
...All the blood you could WANT!
GLRRK
WHAT THE-
Let's GO!

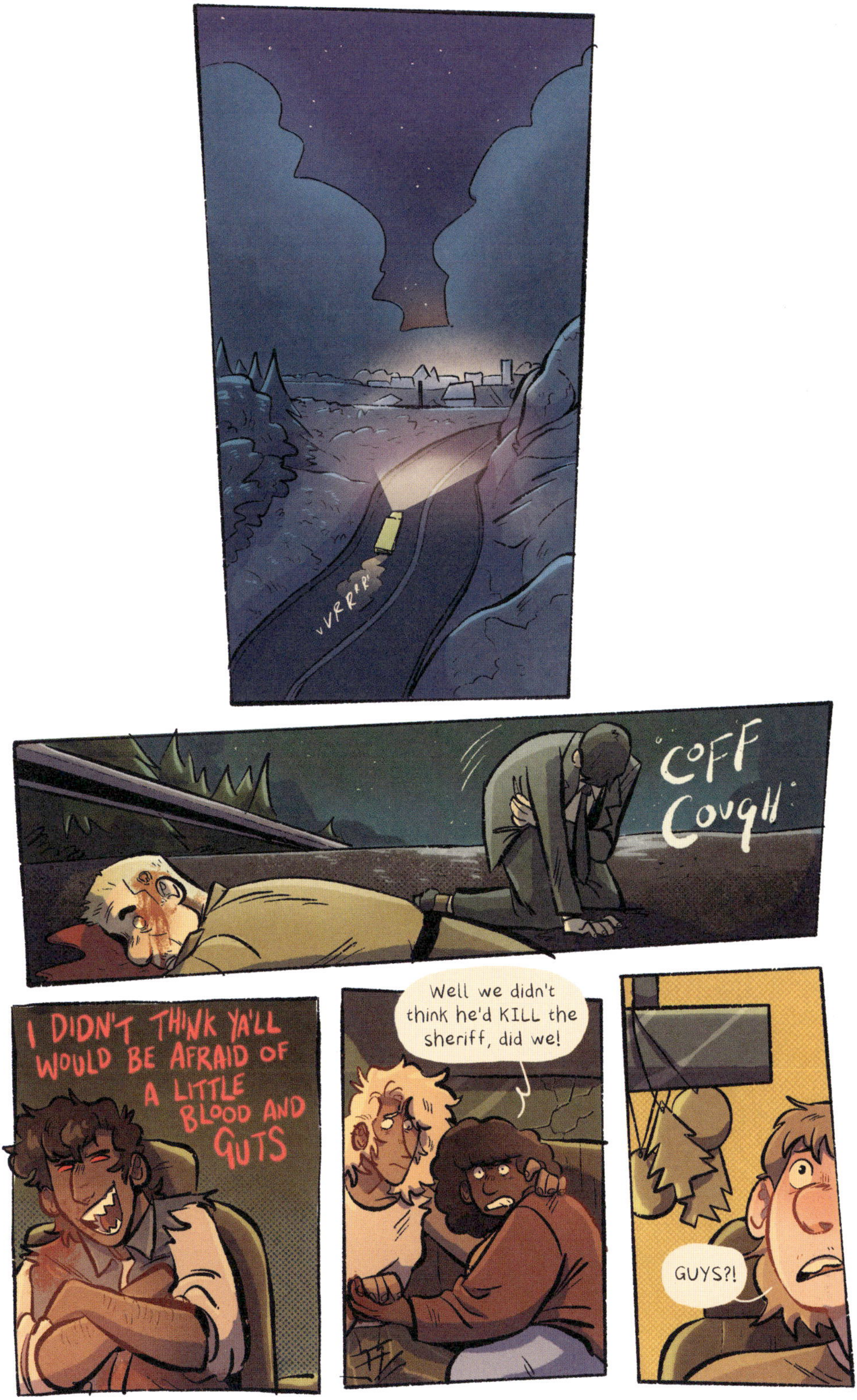
VVRRR
COFF
COUGH
I DIDN'T THINK YA'LL WOULD BE AFRAID OF A LITTLE BLOOD AND GUTS
Well we didn't think he'd KILL the sheriff, did we!
GUYS?!

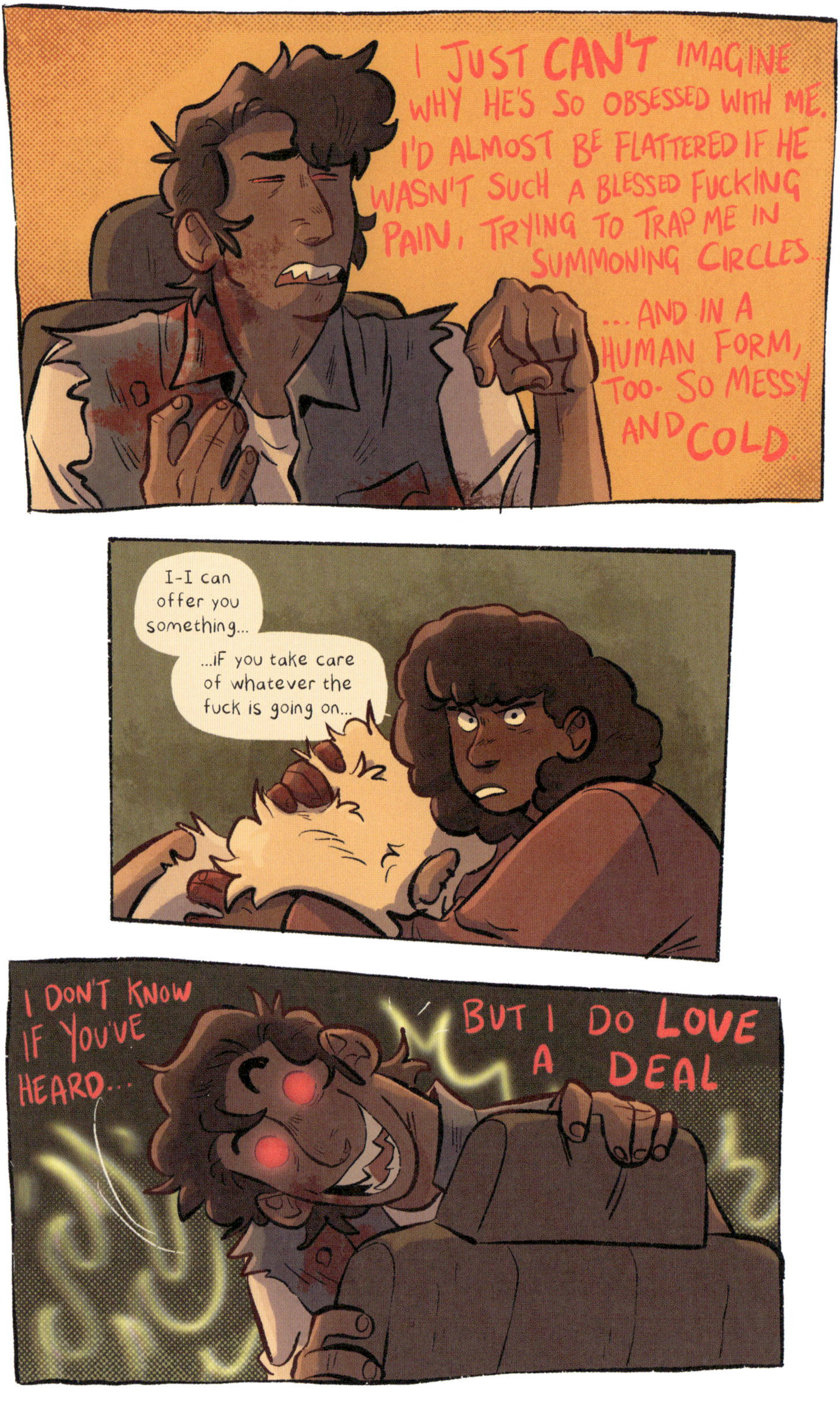
I JUST CAN'T IMAGINE WHY HE'S SO OBSESSED WITH ME. I'D ALMOST BE FLATTERED IF HE WASN'T SUCH A BLESSED FUCKING PAIN, TRYING TO TRAP ME IN SUMMONING CIRCLES...
...AND IN A HUMAN FORM, TOO. SO MESSY AND COLD.
I-I can offer you something...
...if you take care of whatever the fuck is going on...
I DON'T KNOW IF YOU'VE HEARD...
BUT I DO LOVE A DEAL

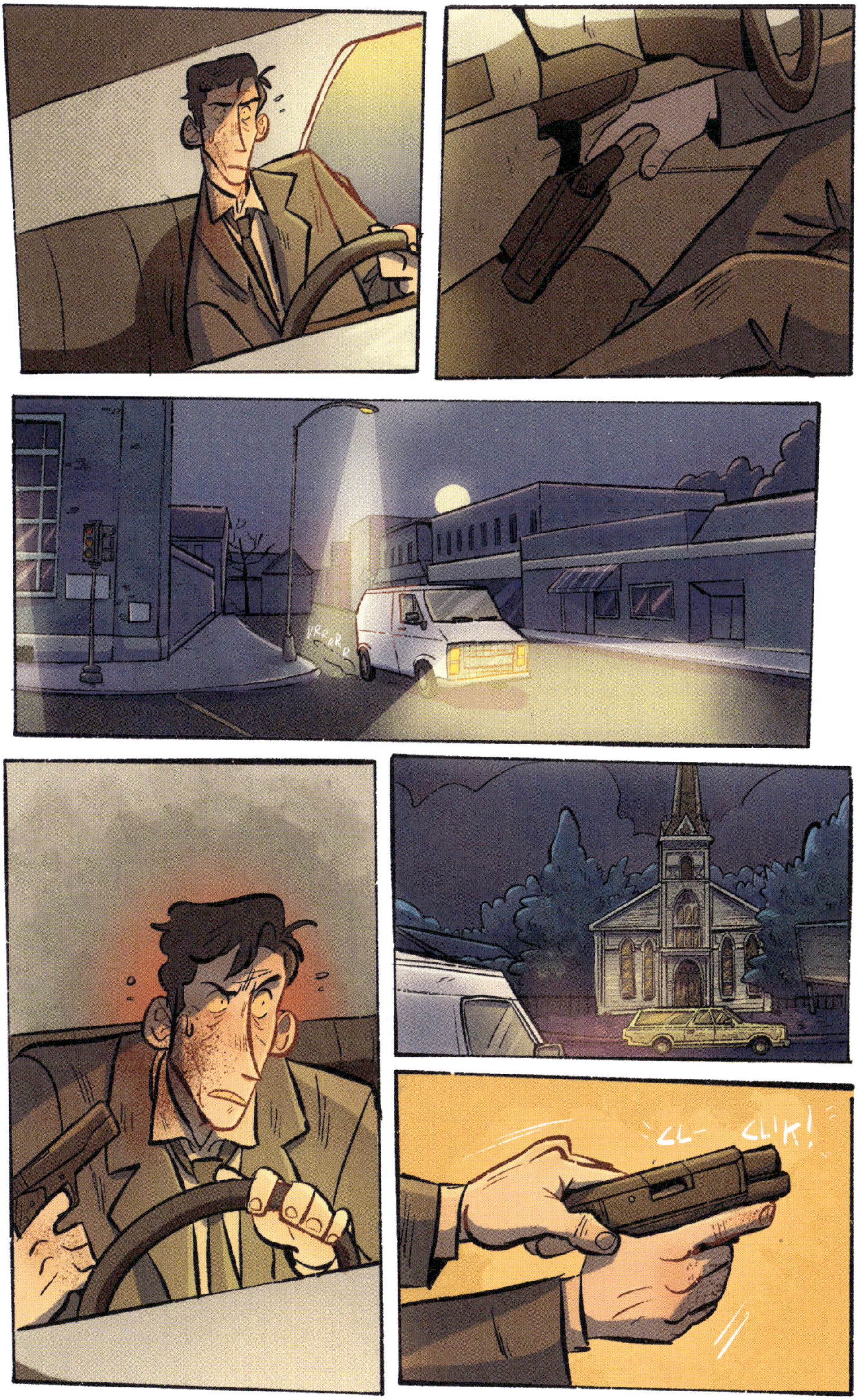
VRRRRR
CL- CLIK!

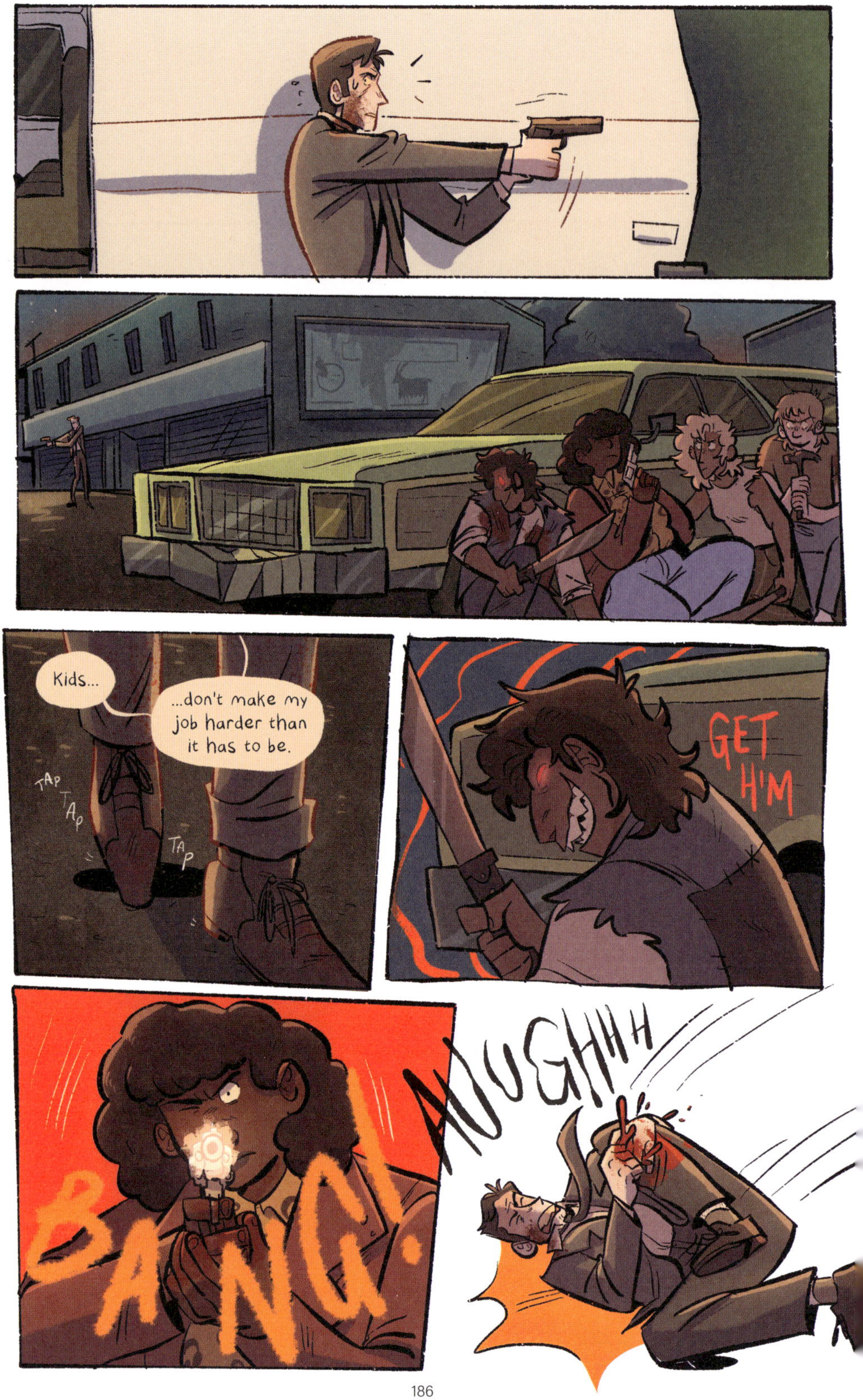
Kids...
...don't make my job harder than it has to be.
TAP
TAP
TAP
GET H'M
BANG!
AUGHHH

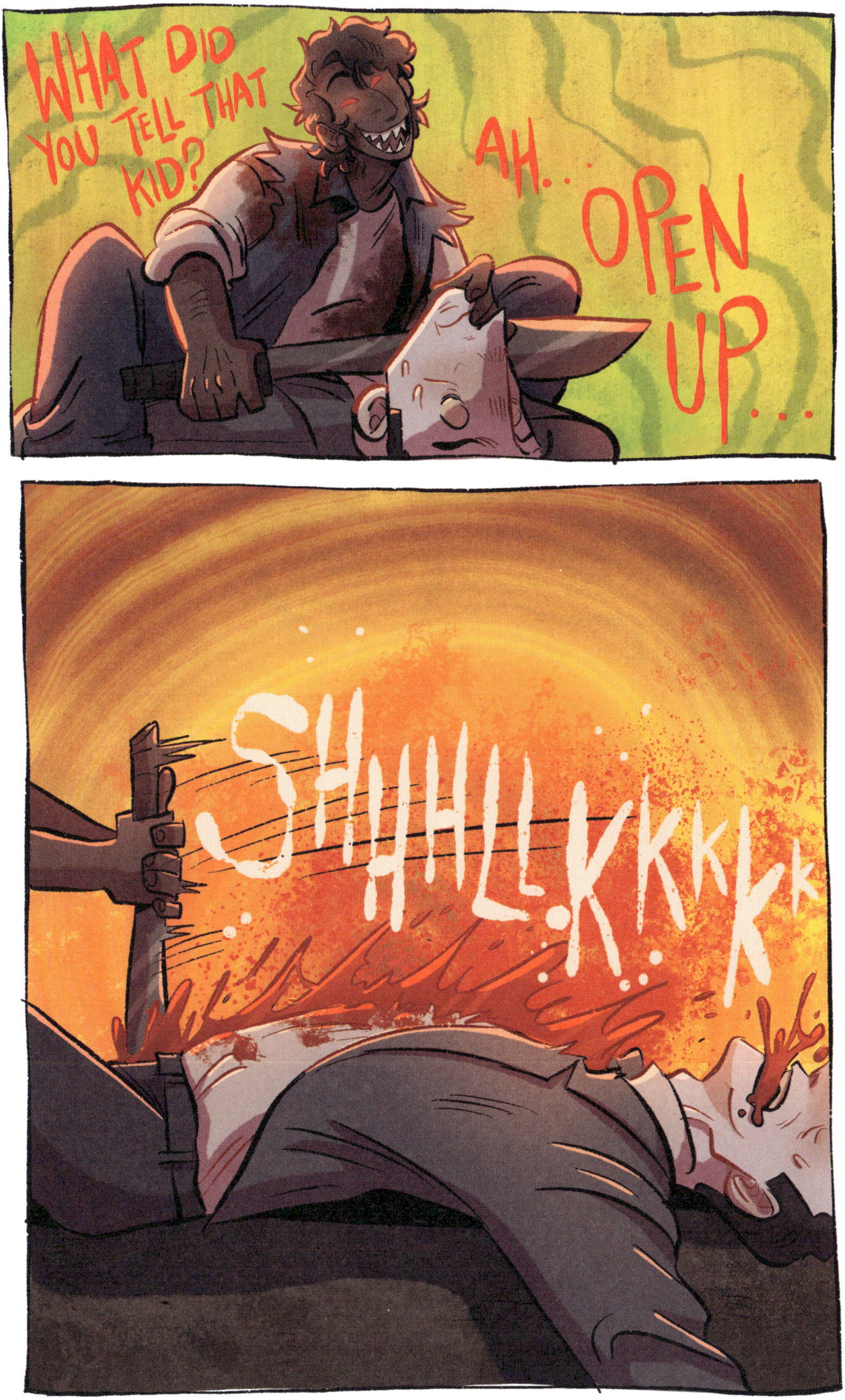
WHAT DID YOU TELL THAT KID?
AH... OPEN UP...
SHHHLLKKKKK

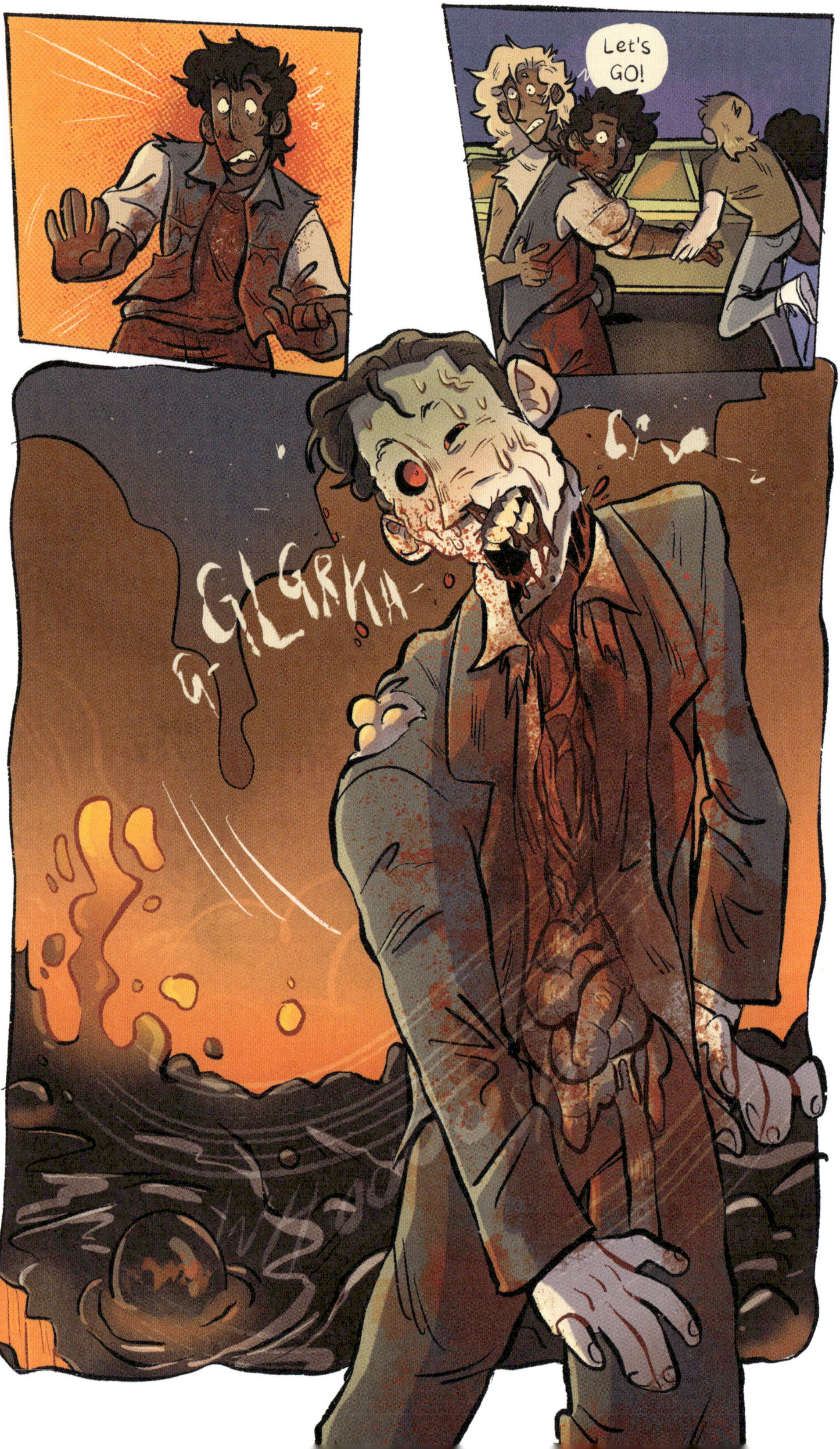
Let's GO!
GLGRKA

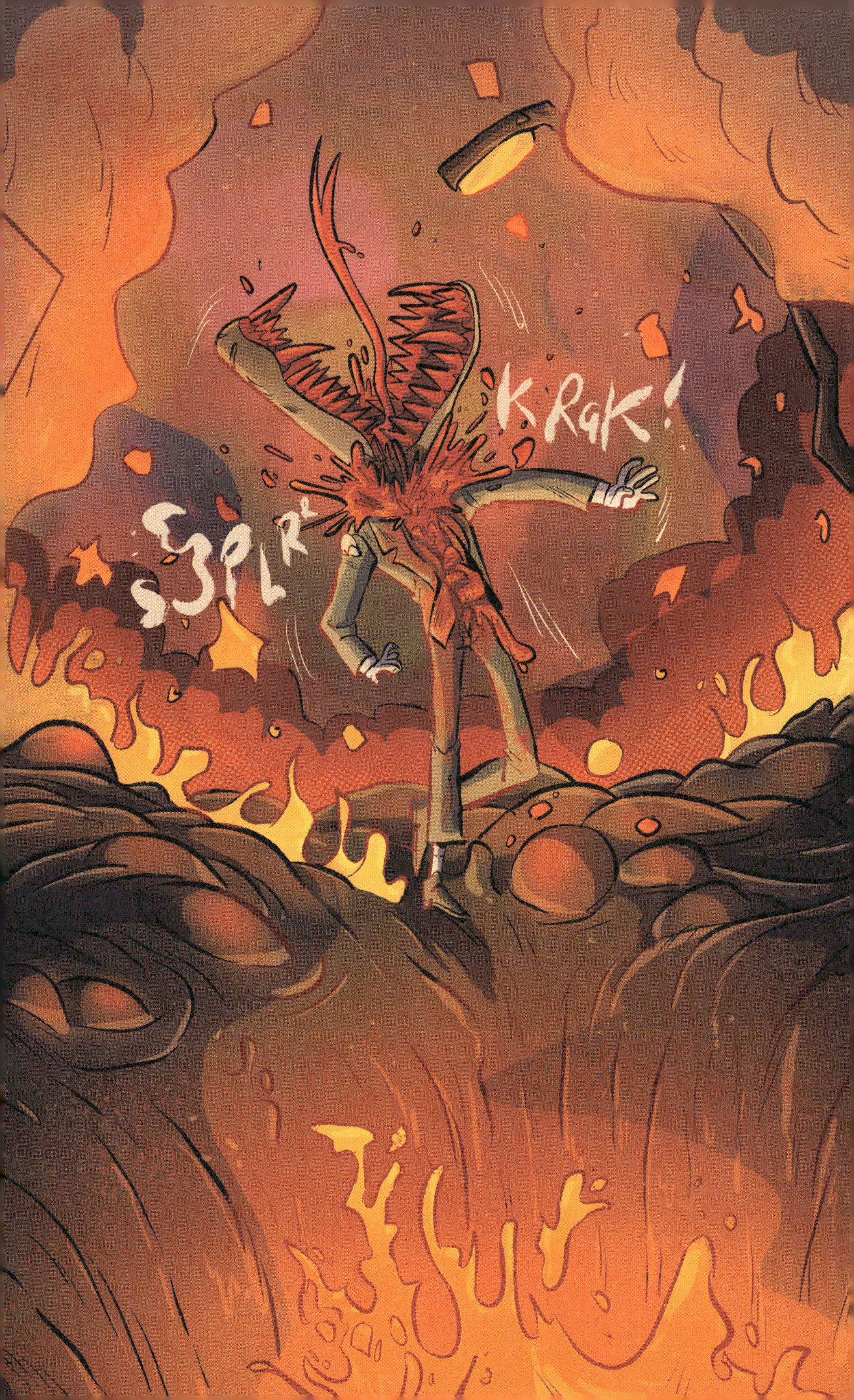

KRAK!
SSPLRR

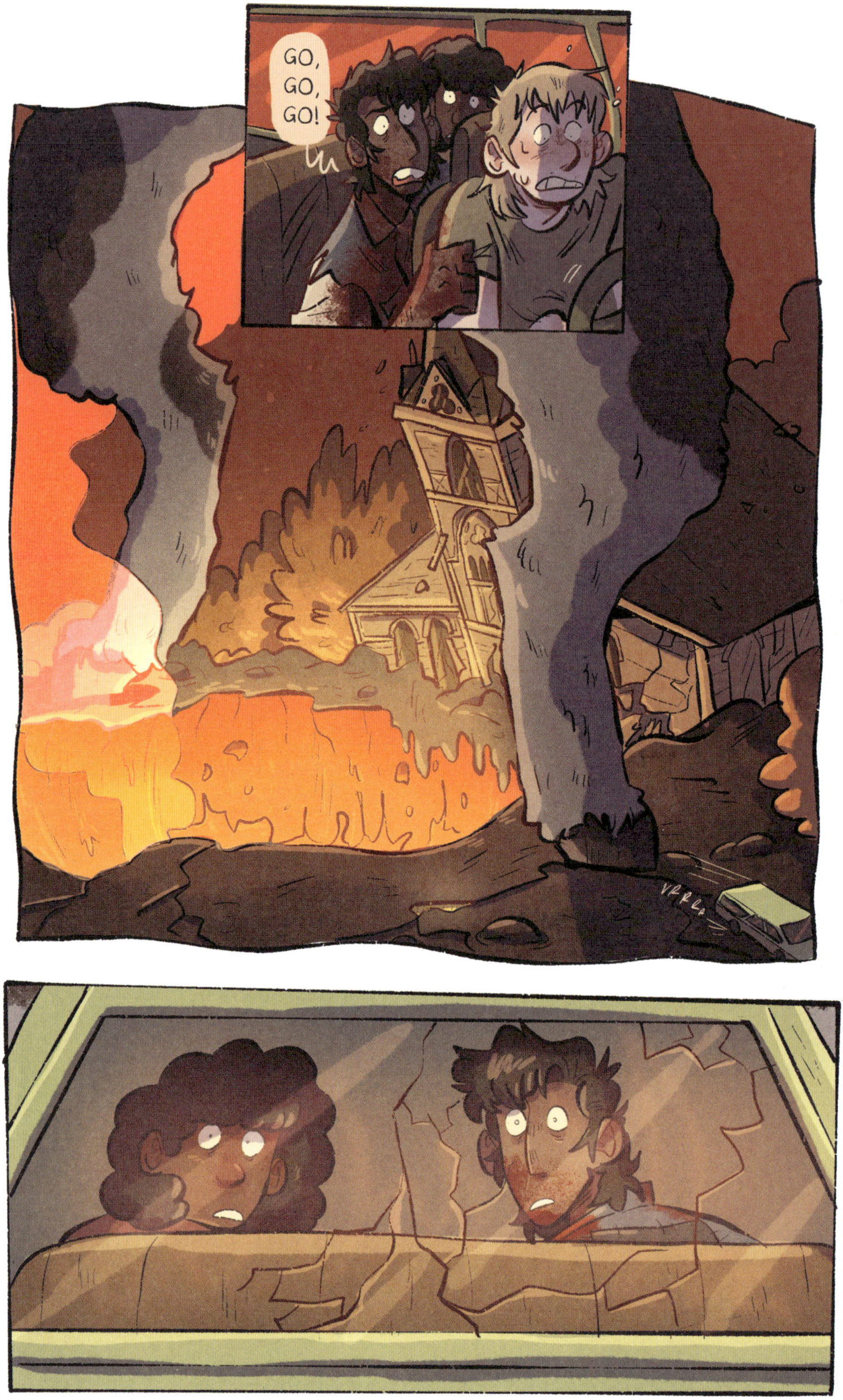
GO, GO, GO!

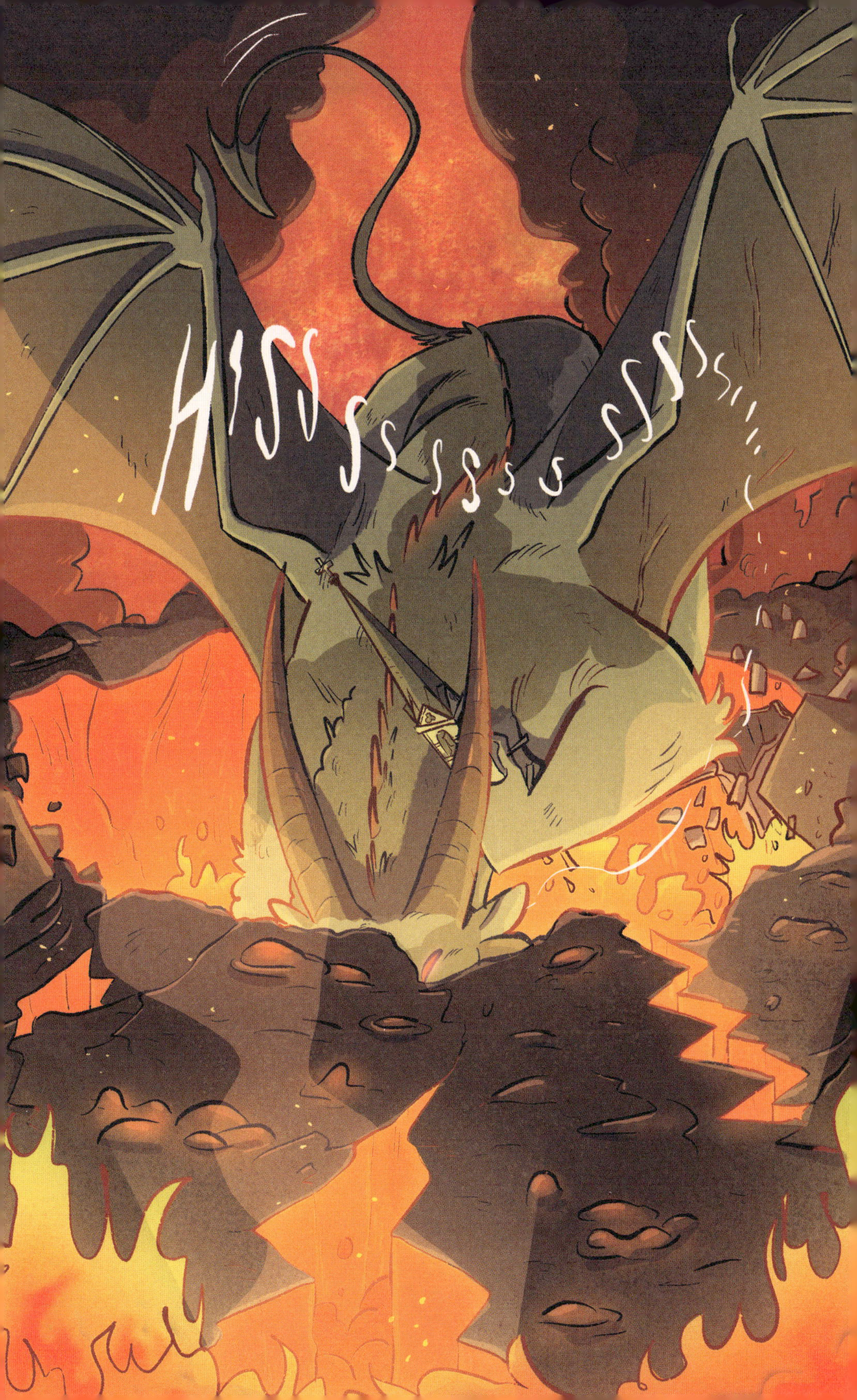
HISSSSSSSSSSSSSS...

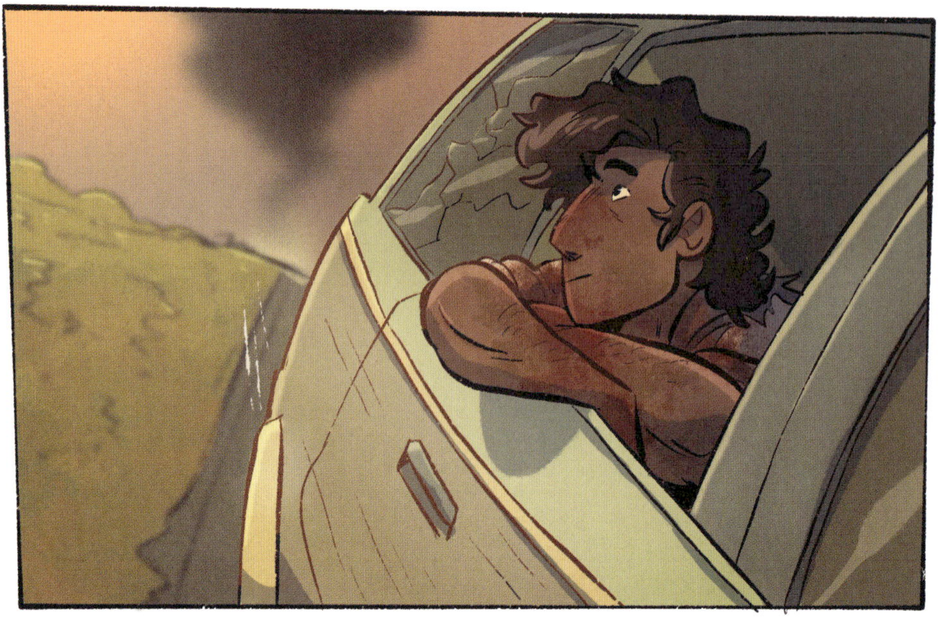

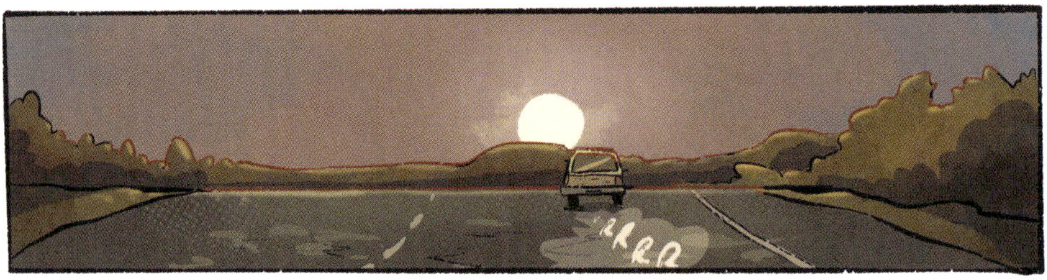

Let's get outta here...

...THE END?

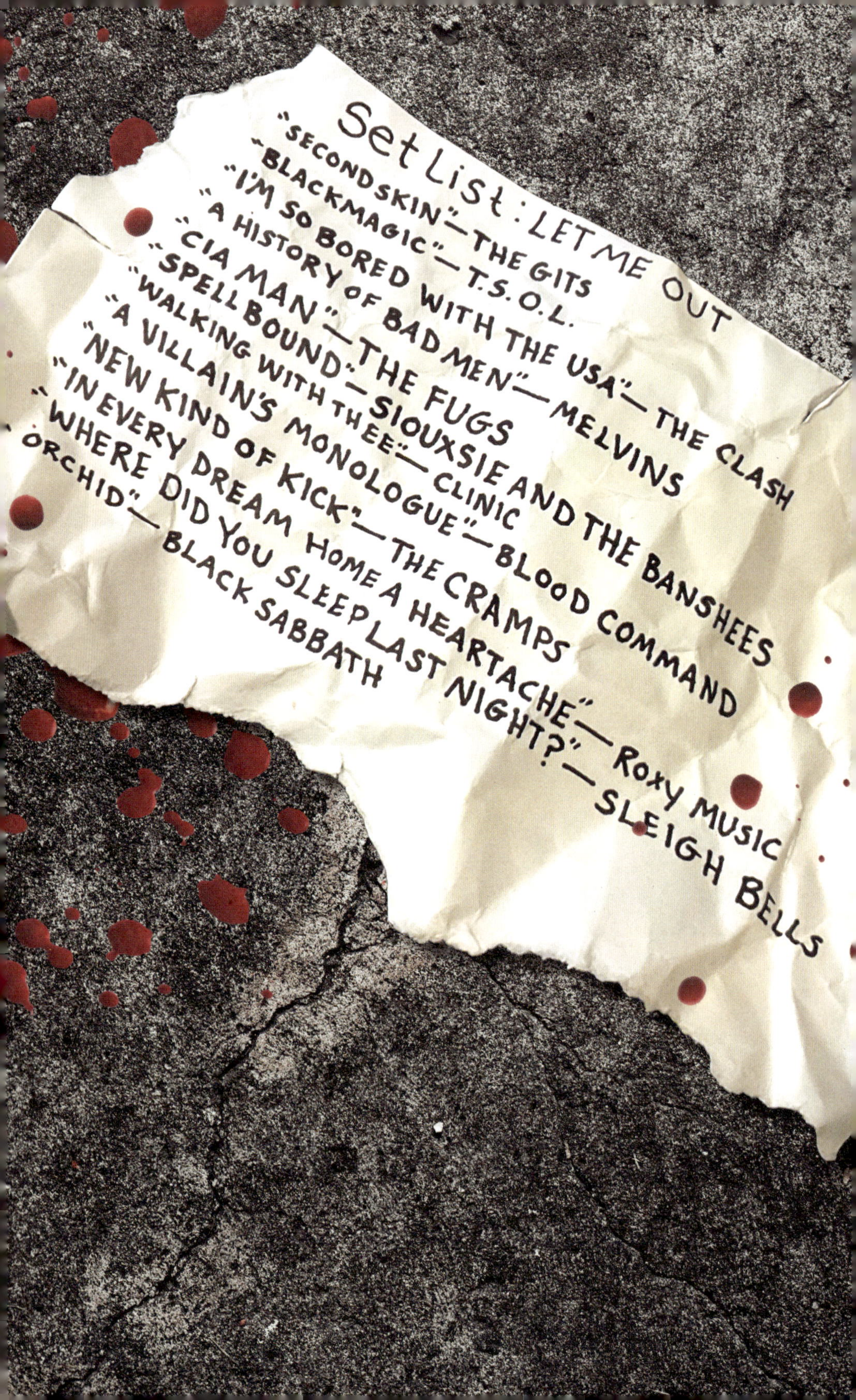
Set List: LET ME OUT
"SECOND SKIN"—THE GITS
"BLACKMAGIC"—T.S.O.L.
"I'M SO BORED WITH THE USA"—THE CLASH
"A HISTORY OF BAD MEN"—MELVINS
"CIA MAN"—THE FUGS
"SPELLBOUND"—SIOUXSIE AND THE BANSHEES
"WALKING WITH THEE"—CLINIC
"A VILLAIN'S MONOLOGUE"—BLOOD COMMAND
"NEW KIND OF KICK"—THE CRAMPS
"IN EVERY DREAM HOME A HEARTACHE"—ROXY MUSIC
"WHERE DID YOU SLEEP LAST NIGHT?"—SLEIGH BELLS
"ORCHID"—BLACK SABBATH

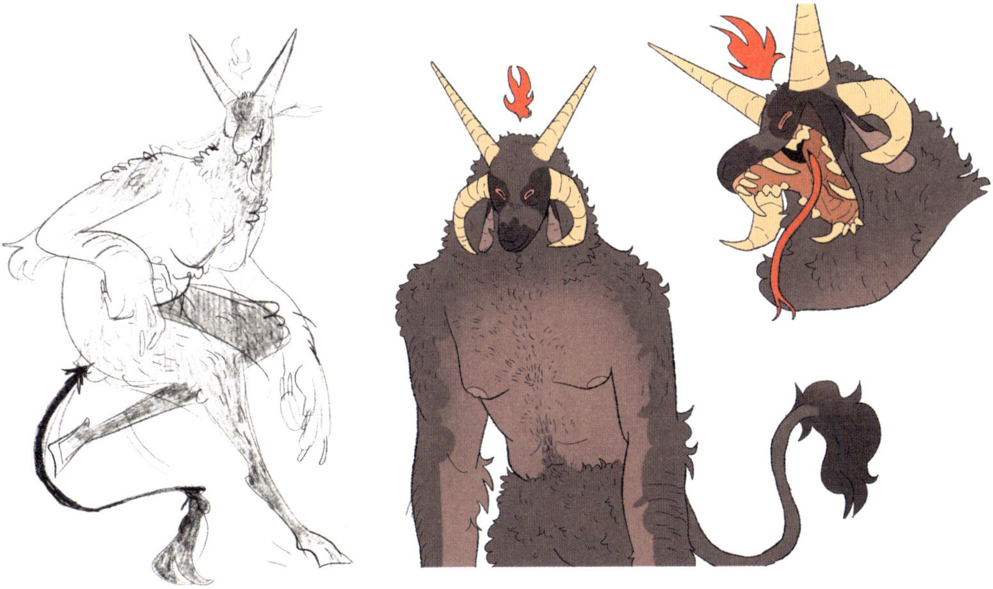

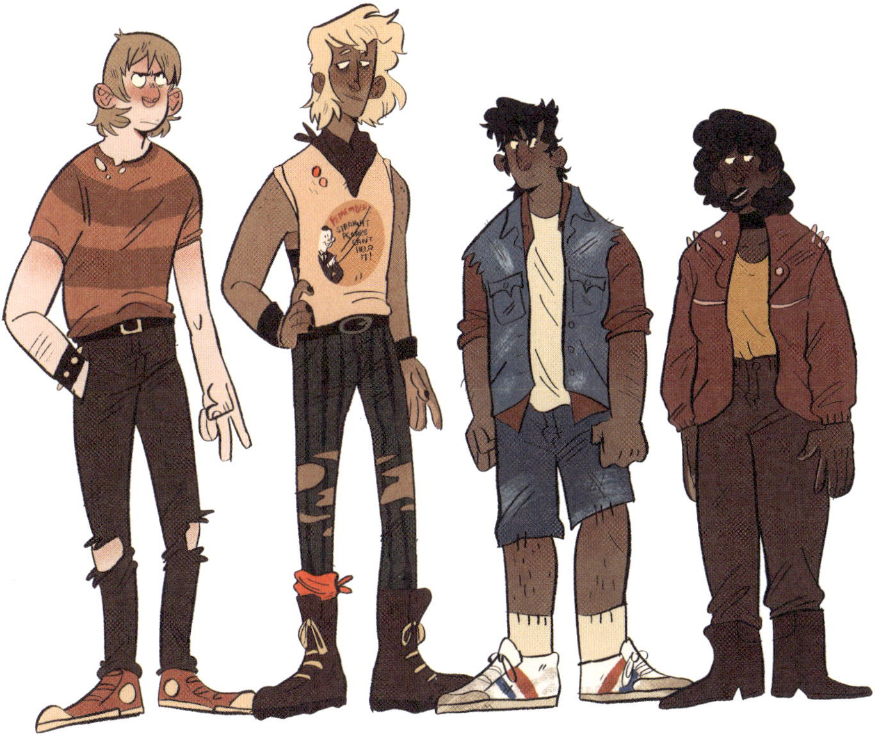

BY GEORGE WILLIAMS

SKETCHES & DESIGNS

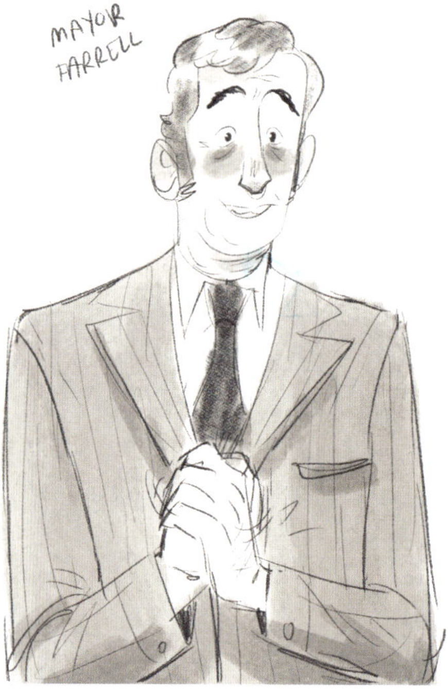
MAYOR FARRELL

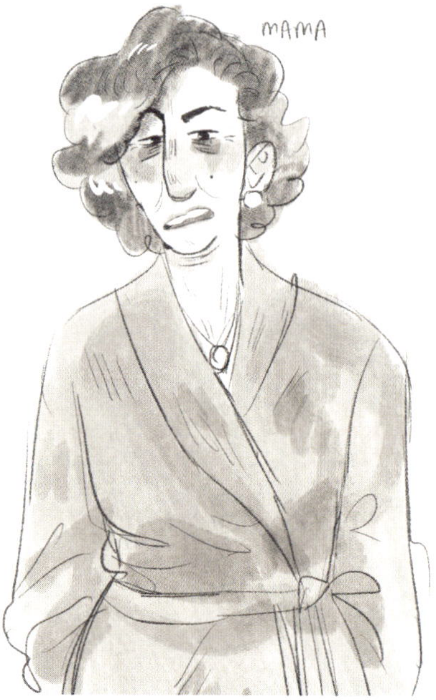
MAMA

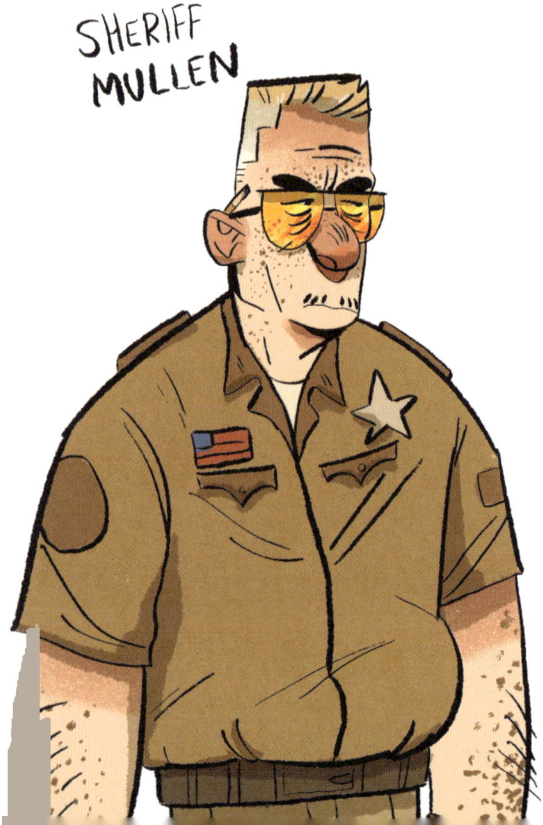
SHERIFF MULLEN

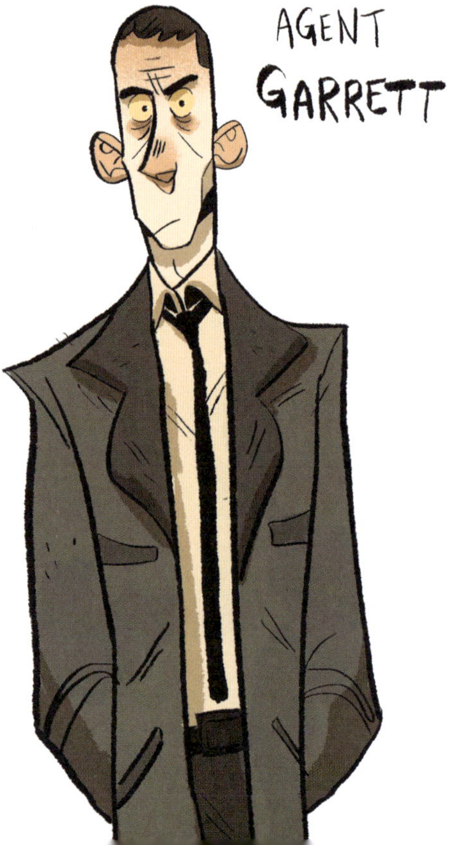
AGENT GARRETT

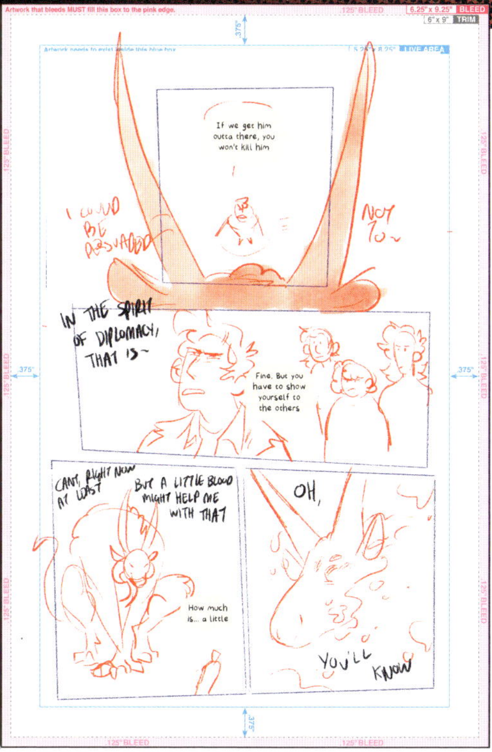
Artwork that bleeds MUST fill this box to the pink edge.
6.25" x 9.25" BLEED
6" x 9" TRIM
LIVE AREA
If we get him outta there, you won't kill him
I COULD BE PERSUADED
NOT TO~
IN THE SPIRIT OF DIPLOMACY, THAT IS~
Fine. But you have to show yourself to the others
CAN'T, RIGHT NOW AT LEAST
BUT A LITTLE BLOOD MIGHT HELP ME WITH THAT
How much is... a little
OH,
YOU'LL KNOW

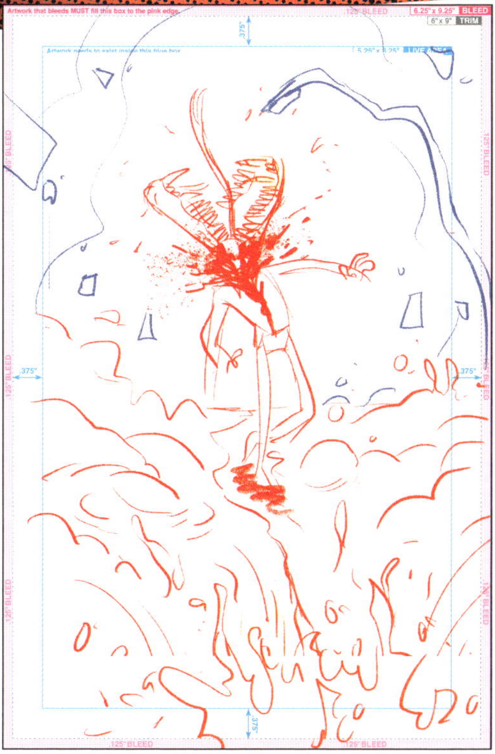
Artwork that bleeds MUST fill this box to the pink edge.
6.25" x 9.25" BLEED
6" x 9" TRIM

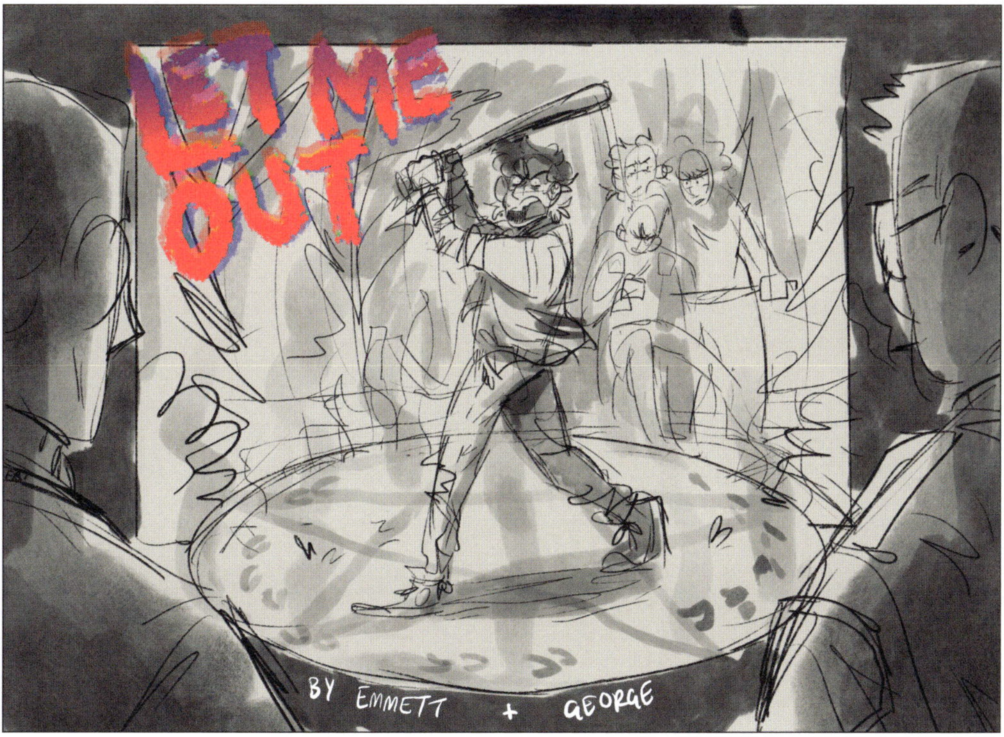
LET ME OUT
BY EMMETT + GEORGE

BY GEORGE WILLIAMS

COVER SKETCHES

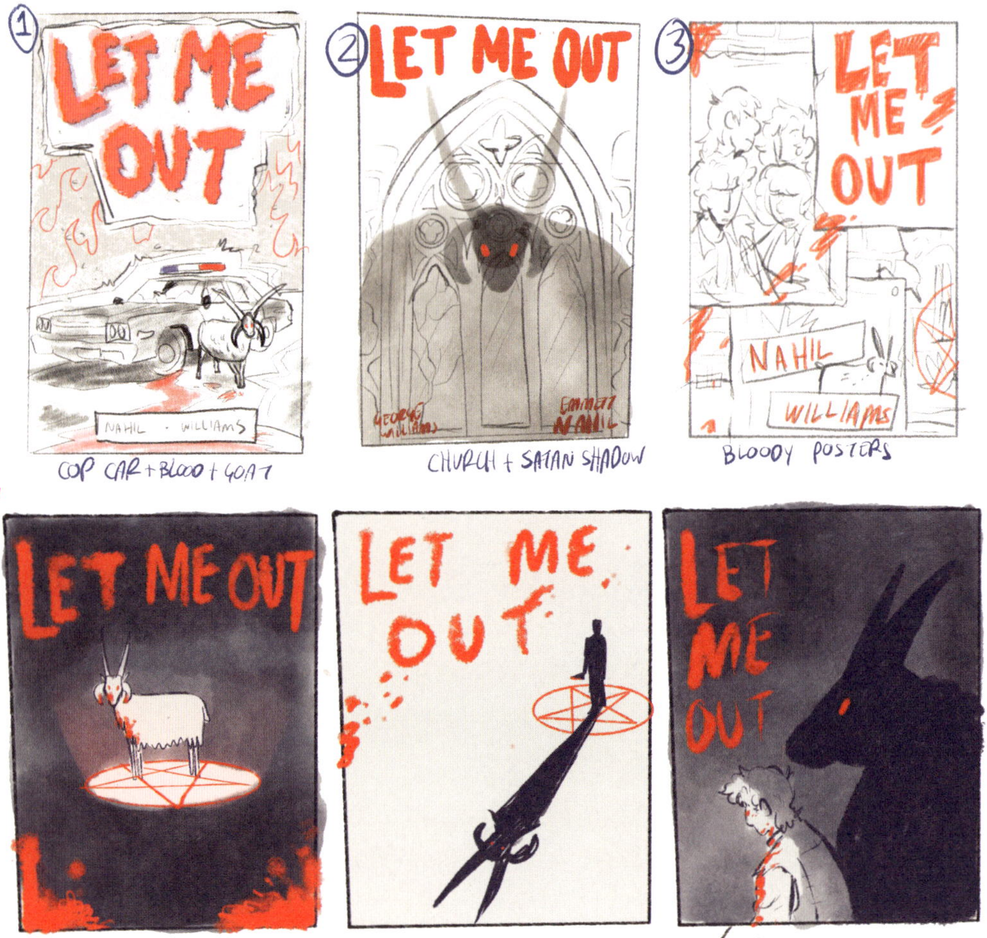
1
LET ME OUT
NAHIL · WILLIAMS
COP CAR + BLOOD + GOAT
2
LET ME OUT
GEORGE WILLIAMS
EMMETT NAHIL
CHURCH + SATAN SHADOW
3
LET ME OUT
NAHIL
WILLIAMS
BLOODY POSTERS
LET ME OUT
LET ME OUT
LET ME OUT

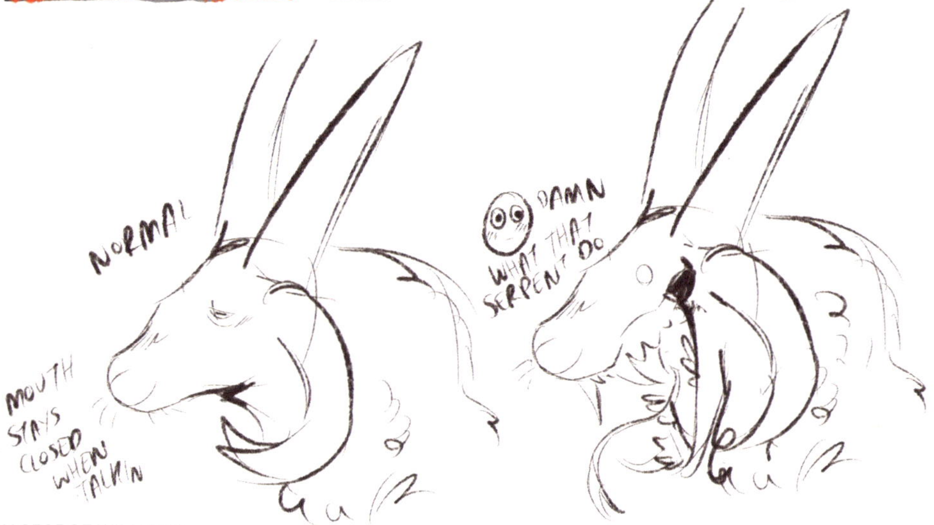
NORMAL
MOUTH STAYS CLOSED WHEN TALKIN
DAMN
WHAT THAT SERPENT DO

BY GEORGE WILLIAMS

ACKNOWLEDGEMENTS

As much as writing and illustrating a graphic novel can sometimes feel like the most grueling match of doubles tennis imaginable, the reality is that it takes a village to make a comic.

First and foremost, we would love to thank our agent, **TAMARA KAWAR**, for being a guiding light in the long and winding road to getting *Let Me Out* into the world. Your belief in the project and steadfast positivity has pushed us forward since the beginning, and we're eternally grateful for that.

We'd like to thank everyone at **ONI PRESS** for coming into the project with an open mind and a can-do attitude, specifically **DESIREE RODRIGUEZ** and **CHRIS CERASI**. The marketing and publicity team, the designers and proofreaders, and everyone involved have all helped to mold this graphic novel into tip-top shape for publication, and for that we'd like to say a big thank you!

We'd also like to thank our families and friends for being constant pillars of support from beginning to end—specifically to **CHRIS and JULIE NAHIL**, **KARYN WILLIAMS**, **MOMO**, and the Syndicate.

Last, but certainly not least, we'd like to send a huge, hearty thank you to our initial **KICKSTARTER BACKERS**, without whom we wouldn't be able to finish the comic at all! It means so much to watch a readership take shape in real time, and that support has helped us in more ways than we possibly can say.

To the reader who's gotten this far—queer horror is the future. Thank you for coming with us on this road to hell.

—**EMMETT NAHIL** & **GEORGE WILLIAMS**

BIOS

EMMETT NAHIL

is a writer, narrative designer, game developer, and literary jack-of-all-trades living in a haunted town north of Boston, Massachusetts. He's interested in intersectional analysis, diverse representation for other queer Middle Easterners, and bringing more nuanced work to genre fiction. He's been known to favor horror, along with sci-fi, fantasy, and really weird speculative literature. *Let Me Out* is his debut graphic novel.

GEORGE WILLIAMS

is a trans comic artist and colorist from the North West of England. He's been making comics since 2016, and spends a lot of time out on walks with his two dogs, Henry and Mabel, as well as taking care of the small army of birds that visit his garden.